WHERE THE BLACKTOP LEADS HOME

Summer Harbor, Maine ~ Book 2

Jenny Worster

To my Lord and Savior, Jesus Christ, whose love and
forgiveness know no bounds

To my husband, who encourages me through all the crazy ups
and downs of writing, no matter what

To my parents, who are my biggest supporters and most
devoted fans, even when the first drafts are awful

CONTENTS

THREE YEARS AGO

*T*he moment he knew his life was about to end, unfolded before him in achingly slow motion. The road below the Harley-Davidson's tires blurred as time slowed to a near standstill. His palms became slick with sweat and an icy bead of perspiration trickled down his spine. He resisted the urge to let go of the handlebars and swipe his hand on his jeans, but to be honest, it wouldn't have mattered if he'd tried. His arms had turned to lead. Muscles, old and unused, screamed as he tried to regain control of the motorcycle. Too fast. Even as his brain came to grips with the fact that this was the end, his body fought.

A futile fight.

The world stalled.

Hearing the ocean crashing against the shore, he was surprised that he could distinguish it over the rumble of the engine. Then again, maybe it was just the wind in his ears, not the familiar rush and clap of the tide as it beat an endless rhythm against the rocks. Or was the fading engine noise an illusion brought on by the slowing of the few remaining seconds that stretched out in front of him?

They say your life flashes before your eyes prior to death, but rather than a flash, he watched as a slow series of scenes, like the home movies of his youth, played out before his mind's eye. Some in mottled colors, others in black and white. Choppy and garbled, but clear enough to remember the moment. The first time he'd laid eyes on Jules. Their wedding day. Holding their son for the first time. The day he'd lost Jules, through no fault of his own. The day he'd lost his son, the fault his and his alone. He tried to go back to the first memory. Jules had been so beautiful on that bright fall day nearly three decades ago. That was the one he wanted to remember as he left this world. However, the dim impression flitted away, caught in a gust of wind, and with its departure, sound rushed back to deafen him.

His heartbeats, at first coming in a mad, painful rush as he realized he couldn't control the bike, had slowed in time with the sluggish tick of an invisible clock. He held his breath and tried to think, but his brain wouldn't cooperate. Instead, it raced with jumbled thoughts.

He should have gone to the police with what he knew.

What if he'd hidden things too well and they were never found?

What if he hadn't?

Who would get the house?

Who would take care—?

He shook his head to clear it and tried to focus. This was it. The blacktop that would have led him home would soon be out of reach.

"God, please."

He wasn't afraid to die. He knew for certain where he was going. He just hated to die with regrets.

So many regrets.

Some long-held and beyond his ability to correct. Some newer that he might have still had the chance to right, if only... But he couldn't think that way. He'd done what he could. What he thought was right. Now he had to trust that someone else would pick up where he left off.

The motorcycle's front wheel struck the dirt shoulder and twisted the handlebars from his grip. Bile rose in the back of his throat as he watched the wheel crumple, knowing he was next. Maybe he was a little afraid after all. Not of what was to come, but of the moments immediately before he left this world. As he watched the bike leave the blacktop he willed his eyes to close. He wanted to meet his Maker with a clean slate.

He felt the motorcycle tip to its side, gritting his teeth as his hip came down hard. Breaking. He screamed, the sound echoing in his ears. Gravel clawed at his leg as it dragged through the loose shoulder. The Harley-Davidson bounced against an obstacle, and then his body left the seat. Airborne. Everything went silent. Shouldn't there be some kind of noise? The stiff ocean wind? Or the sound of the bike's engine? At the very least, the impact of the bike with the cliff that loomed in front of him? And then he heard it. All of it. Every sound. Magnified.

Deafening.

"Please, God!" he called into the stillness. "Right the wrongs I never could!"

You know that for those who love Me, for those who are called according to My purpose, all things work together for good.

All things?

All things.

He felt peace settle into the marrow of his being. It coated him in warmth and soaked into all his cold, lonely places. The enemy had tried time and time again to convince him it was all for naught. That everything he'd done over the past six years was a waste. But now, with the end drawing nearer by the millisecond, he knew that no matter what, everything would work out for good. He smiled and left this mortal coil to step into the arms of his Savior knowing that God had it sorted.

CHAPTER ONE

The kitchen still held the faint smell of garlic and oil, burnt toast and overcooked eggs. Not much had changed in the ten years since he'd sat at the kitchen table and eaten a meal. Or in the two and a half since he'd come back to stand in the room. Alone. Would the smell ever go away? Or had it seeped into the very bones of the house? Harley couldn't decide if he wanted it gone or if he wanted it to stay. Forever. A reminder.

In a weary gesture that was becoming all too familiar, he ran a hand down his face and across his black beard. He moved to do it again, only this time his hand stopped at his eyes and he pressed his thumb and fore-finger deep into the sockets. So what if he worked sixteen-hour days and hadn't had one off in over three-and-a-half weeks? It was self-imposed overtime. Even as exhausted as he was, he wished he'd put himself into the schedule for the days' tours again. At least in a kayak on the water, he wouldn't have to be here, in this room, with his demons.

When his boss had asked, he'd said his plan for the day was to work on the house. After all, the list of needed repairs was as long as his brilliantly inked arm. The thing was, that had been the same plan for his days off since April two and a half years ago. He had yet to make good on those plans. Today he'd made it as far as inside the kitchen.

Progress.

With a tired, frustrated sigh, he pushed the door open and let the screen slam behind him as he jogged down the steps to the Norton Commando motorcycle he'd ridden for the last decade. Swinging his leg over the saddle, he kick-started it. The engine purred to life on the first try and he relished the loud burbling sound as he began to accelerate.

Some days, when he climbed on and hit the road, there was a temptation to never come back. He could ride west for days, and no one would miss him. He tightened his grip on the throttle, pushing the upper edge of the speed limit. Today the pull to just keep going felt like a taste in his mouth that wouldn't wash away. Bitter and metallic.

The bright white of the crushed shell driveways contrasted with the blacktop as it wound along the edge of the ocean in a lazy serpentine. The slow pace made him want to scream. A Lexus with out-of-state plates had slowed to a crawl in front of him and Harley ground his teeth as he resisted the urge to pull into the oncoming lane and open up the throttle. But the last thing he needed was a speeding ticket. Make that another speeding ticket. Or worse, to lose his license.

The motorcycle wasn't subtle. Harley let out a harsh, humorless laugh that no one could hear but himself. Who was he kidding? His bike wasn't subtle? Neither was he. The black wife-beater left his heavily tattooed arms bare to the hot, late-summer sun. Sturdy black work boots, black jeans, and mirrored aviators made him look like trouble on a regular day, but even more so with the growling bike between his knees and his dark mood all but dripping off him.

Taking a deep breath, he puffed out a sigh and eased off the bumper of the car. It wasn't their fault he needed to run, needed to clear his head, needed to be alone with his mistakes. Besides, it was people like those in the fancy car that paid the bills. Or at least some of the bills. Between back taxes and late mortgage payments he never quite got ahead. And he didn't even live in the house.

Couldn't.

Most of the time, on days like these, he would pick a road headed somewhere, anywhere, and just ride until the wanderlust was out of his system. Not today. Today he needed speed. He needed to be on the very ragged edge of control. To know he was one slip-up away from making a permanent payment for every failure in his past.

Coming down the hill into Gull's Cove, Harley held his breath and stared straight ahead. It didn't seem to matter how long he'd been back or how many times he'd driven off the island, he couldn't look at the faded white cross, now toppled, that perched on the side of the road. Maybe he never would be able to look at it. Regret burned in his chest and he pushed the bike a little harder.

It was still early enough in the morning that traffic hadn't clogged the road and an hour later Harley turned onto the highway headed north. With the road almost to himself, he opened up the throttle at last. With the bike going close to 80mph the air stung, razor-sharp, but he embraced it. Just another way to pay his dues. Another self-imposed penance. He wondered when he'd feel like he had paid his debt. Would he ever?

Probably not.

He rode for over an hour before he ran out of highway and had to opt for back-country roads. Stopping for gas in the middle of nowhere, he stood with his back to the sun letting it dissolve the chill from the wind. Taking a deep breath, he was surprised to find the dark mood from the morning had blown off along the way. The draw to keep going was trying to sink its teeth in, but he shrugged it off as he replaced the gas cap.

The bell above the door to the old mom-and-pop jangled as he pulled the screen open. An old man with a weathered face and gnarled hands pushed himself off of a stool behind the counter and flashed Harley a toothy grin as he stepped up to the register.

"Afternoon, sonny! Nice set of wheels you got there."

"Thanks."

The man peered over Harley's shoulder at the bike. "That a Norton?"

"Yes, sir. 1972 Commando." Harley liked the man

immediately. Most people looked at him with a wary glint in their eyes, but this man just grinned bigger and leaned farther over the counter to get a better look.

"She's a beaut. I had me a fine-looking bike after I got home from 'Nam. Can't ride her no more 'count of my hip." He patted the offending body part. "Man, I miss it."

"She is an exceptional ride." Harley pulled his wallet out to pay for the gas, but the old man waved him off.

"You're not from around here." It was a statement, not a question. Harley waited, wondering what the guy was getting at. "What do you say to trading that tank of gas for a chat with a bored old man?"

Harley slid his wallet back into his pocket. "I think I can do that."

"Clyde Irving," the man said, extending a leathery hand.

"Harley Beck."

Clyde nodded to a second stool pushed up against the end of the coolers before dragging his closer to the register and perching on it. Harley scooped the stool up one-handed and plunked it down near the counter. Leaning back on it, he hooked the heel of one boot on the bottom rung.

"Alrighty young man, what say you start by telling me about that sweet set of wheels you rode in here on?"

Harley couldn't help but smile. The old man had an infectious grin and the earnest interest in his eyes made Harley want to tell him everything. And not just about the bike. "The Norton?" Clyde bobbed his head, his smile widening. "It used to be my dad's. He picked it up when I was a kid and I helped him restore it. It handles like a dream and that rumble it makes when you first accelerate—"

"Sinks into your soul."

A chuckle bubbled out of Harley's chest and he was surprised by how unfamiliar the feeling was. How long had it been since he laughed? His shoulders relaxed and he leaned his arms on the high, glass-topped counter. "That it does."

"I'm gonna guess that when you're flying down the road, a

pretty lady's arms wrapped around your waist, and the wind singin' in your ears you don't want to be anywhere else."

"So, you're familiar with riding a classic motorcycle?" Harley laughed again when the other man's eyes twinkled with mischief. "It's been a long, long time since I could attest to the pretty lady's arms, but the rest... You're one hundred percent correct. I wouldn't want to be anywhere else."

"Only one place I ever remember wishing I was when I was on my bike. And that was home."

An image of the kitchen that morning flitted into Harley's mind and he felt the smile slipping from his face. No, he didn't want to be anywhere but on the back of his bike running away. Because that's what he was doing, had been doing. He'd run away ten years ago and he was still running away.

Clyde's eyes narrowed as he considered the change in Harley's demeanor before he slid off his stool. Hobbling over to the cooler along the back wall, he retrieved two long-necked brown bottles. Harley lifted one eyebrow in surprise. Chuckling, Clyde spun them around to show that they were only root beer before popping the tops off using an ancient Coca-Cola bottle opener attached to the end of the counter and handed one to Harley.

The bell above the door jangled and he shuffled to the register to ring up a cigarette sale. The young man, rough around the edges with a grimy gimme cap holding his hair down, looked askance at Harley before snatching his smokes off the counter and pushing back through the front door without a word. Harley didn't even realize he'd bristled until Clyde spoke again. "Don't you pay him no never-mind. That boy don't like nobody. Now, where were we? Oh, yeah, you were about to tell me where you're from and what brought you to this neck of the woods on a Wednesday afternoon."

"I was, was I?" Clyde just flashed an innocent smile and Harley felt the tension and unease of a moment before slipping away. "I just needed to ride, to get away from... things... on my day off. It was about time to turn the bike around and head home."

He froze as the thought registered. Home. He chewed on the word for a minute before swallowing it past a lump in his throat. How long had it been since he'd thought of Summer Harbor as home? Today it had slipped in unnoticed, and now, deep down, he knew he wouldn't turn westward again and ride until he hit the Pacific. No, he would follow the blacktop home, time after time, until he found a way to make things right. He looked back at Clyde and found the man studying him in a way that made Harley feel like the old tired eyes could see inside all his secret places. All the dark and needy spaces that he kept hidden away. Harley cleared his throat and sat a little taller on the stool. No. Those places were his to deal with. His alone.

"And where exactly is that?"

"I live down in Summer Harbor."

"Woowee, you *are* a long way from home."

"I am at that."

"You come up Route 1? Or'd you fly up 95?"

"I came up the interstate, but I'm thinking of taking Route 1 back. Slower. Easier to think." That's what he needed right now. To think.

Clyde gave him the I-don't-miss-a-thing look again. "Now what is it that's got you so tied up in knots you gotta escape on that beautiful machine and requires time to think when you're headed home?"

Nope, didn't miss anything.

"Am I that transparent?"

Clyde shrugged but met Harley's eyes with a steady, understanding look. "I wouldn't say 'transparent', but I do see a whole heck of a lot of myself in you."

Harley held the man's gaze for a beat before looking away. "I've got something I should be doing, but... Too many memories, too many hurts, and I just keep running away from it. I don't know how to overcome that."

A knowing look softened the creases in the old man's face. "Ah, yes. I know this one well." He leaned a little closer to

Harley. "My Arlene passed away nearly ten years ago, but you know what? Her reading chair and her Bible and her slippers still sit right where they always have in the corner of our bedroom. I know I should clean them out, but... Well, I come to the store every day instead."

The empathy swept over Harley. "So... there's no overcoming it?"

"Now I didn't say that. Used to be Arlene sat in that chair every morning and read her Bible and prayed. I couldn't move her chair, but I did find I could sit in it and read her Bible and pray. Not the same, but my own way of overcoming. You just need to find your way of overcoming. And it might not be what you picture it lookin' like."

"How'd you get to be so wise, Clyde?" Harley asked.

"Comes with age, sonny! And mistakes. And learning from them. Having a wise woman to love you doesn't hurt either," he added with a wink.

"Afraid I wouldn't know anything about that," Harley said, sliding from the stool and stretching his legs.

"Now that's a shame."

The old man had put Harley at ease, but now memories and guilt threatened to steal it away. "Thanks for the gas, Clyde, and... thanks for the visit."

"Don't mention it! Now, you come back here and see me, ya hear? It's always good to go home, but if you venture up this way again... well, I wouldn't say no to another chat."

"I'll do that." He stuck his hand out and Clyde grasped it in a firm handshake.

As Harley pointed the bike south, he lightened his touch on the gas. Somehow the afternoon spent making a new friend had brought some clarity to his situation. The disrepair of the house was a problem and it was time to face the fact that he wasn't going to be the one fixing it before winter. It was already fast approaching October and parts like the back porch wouldn't last through another snowstorm. He needed help, but... man he hated asking for it!

"Gorgeous!"

"Thanks." Erin felt her cheeks flush at the compliment and watched her friend Cori run a delicate hand along the edge of the birdseye maple box. From the small collection Erin had just delivered to her friend's art gallery, that one was her favorite as well.

"How do you make them so silky smooth to the touch? And the corners without any fasteners? They're... perfect."

"Would you accept 'a magician never reveals her tricks'?" Erin asked.

A giggle made her friend's nymph-like appearance even more fascinating. Today her waist-length, white-blonde hair was sectioned into small, messy braids that resembled dreads, and she tossed them over her shoulder as she laughed. "I'd say no, but, to be honest, I like the mystery." Cori paused and her smile dimmed. "I'm sorry I don't sell more of them."

"There's nothing that would make them stand out from all this," Erin said, waving her hand as she looked around the gallery packed with local art. Paintings of familiar seascapes, intricate wood carvings, handmade jewelry, pottery, and Cori's signature sea glass and driftwood sculptures filled the selves, covered the walls, and crowded the floor.

"Oh, pish-posh! I'm going to make a display of them in the window! That will move more. I'm also pushing them for Christmas presents. Early, I know, but I sold one yesterday as a gift box for a Christmas ornament the person bought."

"Thank you," Erin said. "Someday... Someday I'll have time to build more than a few boxes here and there. Someday I'll have a storefront of my own, full of *my* creations." She glanced at the work-of-art clock that hung on the wall above the register. "Until that day arrives, however, a nine-to-five is necessary to pay the bills."

Cori put down the box and pulled Erin close for a tight

hug. They were as different as night and day. Cori was tiny and delicate, a throwback to the flower-child days of the sixties. Erin wondered for the umpteenth time how her friend managed to look captivating in loose gauzy shirts, broomstick skirts, bare feet, and enough bangle bracelets to weigh down both her arms. She tried not to be jealous. Had she ever been able to make a skirt look good? She doubted it. In the grand scheme of things she wasn't tall, but she often felt like a clumsy giant next to her fairy-like friend.

Cori let go and wrinkled her nose. "I wish your beautiful boxes sold enough that you didn't have to work that awful job."

"It isn't awful. Honest." She might not be making art or building furniture, but she was still working with wood, and she loved that. "I'm enjoying working for Keaton."

Her friend's face said she didn't believe a word of it, but the frown only lasted a second. "Oh! I just remembered!" Cori exclaimed, bouncing on her toes with excitement. "I'm going over to Blueberry Island Saturday to look for sea glass. Want to join me?"

"I haven't been there since... well... high school field trip?"

Cori made a disgusted face. "That is simply too long," she scolded with her hands on her hips. "We have to rectify that."

"How do you plan on getting over there?" Erin asked. "The last time I was on a ferry it turned out to be a rather unpleasant trip that ended with me losing my lunch over the railing."

"Eww! Don't worry, no ferry. I usually ask one of the Williams to take me, but I had a great idea yesterday! This time I'm going to... Wait for it... Kayak over!" Cori's excitement was contagious and Erin could feel it growing as her friend clapped her hands together.

"Where on earth are you going to get a kayak?"

"From Noah who's got that kayak tour business, down there next to The Whale."

The idea was taking root and Erin grinned. "That... sounds like a lot of fun."

Cori bounced up and down on her bare toes again. "You're

grinning. Grinning is a good thing!"

"Yes, it absolutely is." She stole another peek at the clock. "Now, if I don't scoot I may have to work Saturday!"

"Eight o'clock at the kayak shop!" Cori called as Erin headed out the door. "And pack a picnic lunch!"

Walking away from The Whippoorwill Gallery, she pulled an elastic from her pocket and crammed her hair into it, thankful once again that her job didn't require her to look cute like Cori's did. She unlocked the door to the truck but paused in the hot sun, shedding the flannel shirt she'd needed over her tank top not an hour ago. Nope, she didn't do cute. No skirts, no bangle bracelets. Blue jeans, tank tops, steel-toed boots. She shrugged off the slight feeling of inadequacy that had settled on her and climbed onto the bench seat of the old beater.

Lord, I know I am not unlovable in Your eyes. Please keep reminding me that's what matters. Oh, and if You could make the truck start...

Turning the key, she listened to it whine before turning over. Someone was going to have to look at it. Maybe next paycheck.

She wasn't sure why she made a wide loop to drive past Coop's place. Again. She didn't need to take the detour and probably shouldn't have. It wasn't hers and would never be hers. It had a new owner now. Had for some time if she were to hazard a guess. She wondered what they'd done with the place. What they'd changed. Did the screen door still creak? Did the kitchen faucet still drip? The thoughts caused an ache around her heart. Since she'd gotten back into town, she'd driven by the house many times. Too many times.

The only sign she'd seen that anyone lived there was the handsome motorcycle occasionally parked along the street. Coop would have loved that. She grinned but shuddered. That was one love the man hadn't passed along. Stargazing, strong coffee, singing hymns, loving Jesus? Four for four. Motorcycles? That was a hard 'no!'

Today, the street was empty and Erin stopped to gaze at the

house. Whoever the new owner was, they weren't a fan of yard work. Not that there was much of a yard, but the shrubs up against the front of the house were looking pretty wild, and the wind had pushed piles of fall leaves against the steps. Not to mention the scraggly lawn. The last time she'd driven by she'd thought about stopping and knocking on the door, but what would she say? 'Hey, can I trim the shrubs and mow the grass?'

Shaking her head at the ridiculous thought, Erin looked away. It wouldn't take much to find out who owned it. While Summer Harbor, Maine boasted a summer population in the tens of thousands and catered to over three million visitors each tourist season, it was a small town at its heart. Most of the year-round residents knew everybody else's business. To be honest, though, a big part of her didn't want to know. She stepped on the gas, intending to watch the little house shrink in the rearview mirror, but the truck sputtered and stalled. "No, no, no! I don't have time today!" She tried starting it again, but it just whined and coughed. Popping the hood, she climbed out of the cab and onto the bumper. Not that she knew what she was doing. Nevertheless, she leaned under the hood, wiggled wires, thumped on things that looked like they could take it, and checked the oil. As she let out a frustrated sigh she heard someone behind her clear his throat.

"Y'all right there, sugar?"

She grinned and turned toward the familiar face. "Oh, man, Dox! Am I ever glad to see you!" She hopped down and hugged the man. "The old girl just died."

"Well, now, that won't do." His delicious southern accent matched his handsome face, and he flashed her a charming, deep-dimpled smile before leaning over the engine. She watched him push up his sleeves and reach into the bowels of the engine compartment.

"How long have you been fixing things in Summer Harbor?" she asked as he tinkered.

"Since long before you can remember, that's for sure," He

replied with a smile in his voice. "Give that a try, sugar."

She hopped back into the cab and turned the key. The truck didn't exactly purr, but it did start. "You seriously have a golden touch where mechanical things are concerned!" She climbed back out long enough to hug the older man in thanks.

"You get this junker into a mechanic as soon as possible, ya hear?"

"I promise."

The man waved her back into the cab and closed the door before continuing down the sidewalk, whistling a country song. He was a little older than she remembered, but if anything the gray hair made him look more distinguished. She smiled. He was right. As far back as she could remember he'd been calling every lady he came upon 'sugar' and fixing motorcycles, scooters, and the occasional lawnmower. And, apparently, hopeless old pickup trucks.

She gave the house a long look. It was time to move on. And not just today, although she did need to get to work. It was time to move on from the life where Coop had been there for her. His house wasn't a refuge anymore and the current occupant wasn't there to fill Coop's shoes.

The unintentional stop had cost Erin precious time and now she was running behind. With traffic, the drive down to the job in Gull's Cove took her close to an hour. The truck hadn't even come to a complete stop before she was leaping from the cab, hauling her tool belt out after her. She scanned the street and was glad to see Sawyer's truck was the only other non-tourist vehicle in the vicinity. She liked working with the older man, and not just because she knew he wouldn't rag on her about being late. Well, not as much as some of the guys anyway. She slammed the truck door and cringed as the hinges squealed. Then, pulling in a breath of clean ocean air, she headed inside where they'd been renovating an upstairs bedroom for the better part of a week.

The house, with its columned front portico and second-floor balcony, would best be described as Greek Revival, but Erin had serious doubts that it had started its life that way. She imagined that in its younger days, the huge residence overlooking the shore had been a simple Colonial. Somewhere along the way, a previous owner had gotten the idea into their head that adding two stories of columns to the front would make it look... What? She chuckled as she slipped through the front door. She knew what. Extravagant. And they had succeeded.

The front door clicked closed behind her with a whisper and a moment later she heard the whir of a saw on the second floor. After checking her boots to make sure she wasn't tracking anything into the opulent marble foyer, she took the stairs two at a time and stepped into the room just as Sawyer finished cutting a piece of solid oak flooring.

"Sorry I'm late," Erin rushed to explain. "Truck wouldn't start."

Sawyer looked up and grinned. "No worries, kid. I just got started."

Unlike a lot of the guys on Keaton's crews, Sawyer didn't seem to have anything to prove. At least ten years her senior, he worked at a steady pace and had an incredible work ethic. Get the job done, do it well. Period. She could learn a lot from him. And not just about carpentry. They attended the same church and conversations often turned to the pastor's latest sermon or something one of them had read in their Bible that week.

They worked in companionable silence for a while, Sawyer cutting flooring, Erin fitting it into place and securing it using a pneumatic stapler. To fill the lulls between the whir of the saw, the rumble of the air compressor, and the snap of the stapler, Erin started singing.

"I love that hymn," Sawyer commented as he handed her another board. "My grandmother used to play it on the piano in her living room. Good memories."

"I always wish I'd learned to play the piano."

"Yeah?" A bit of a blush colored the apples of the burly man's cheeks. "My grandmother taught me to play. I spent many an afternoon eating chocolate chip cookies in her kitchen after school, followed by piano lessons."

Erin grinned. "I cannot picture you playing the piano."

"No?" He gestured with a callused hand to his well-worn jeans, t-shirt, and work boots. It was clear he was having a hard time keeping a straight face. "You don't think I look like a pianist?"

Erin's lips twitched, but she tried to sound serious. "Oh, no, you totally look the part."

They both dissolved into laughter before he pointed his pencil in her direction. "I'm good. Darn good if I do say so myself. One of these days I'll prove it to you. "

"I'm going to hold you to that!"

The older man sauntered back to the saw, still chuckling, and pulled a pencil from behind his ear. "Singing, on the other hand? Nope. Not a chance. I'll leave that up to you." He snapped a tape on the next board and placed a mark for the cut. Erin took the board he'd handed her and fit it into place. The cadence of the stapler changed and she peered at it, realizing it had run out of staples. Reaching into her tool belt she came up dry, and the box by the compressor was empty, too.

"I need more staples," she said, getting to her feet and heading for the door.

"I think there's a box on the front seat of my truck," Sawyer called after her.

Erin was almost to the top of the stairs when the open door to the owner's bedroom caught her eye. The room they were working on overlooked the backyard and the bay beyond, but this one stretched across a good portion of the front of the house and opened onto the second-floor balcony. She knew she shouldn't be snooping, but the open French doors and billowing silky curtains beckoned and she slipped into the room.

The room was so peaceful. She understood why the owner would favor it over the others. Even facing the street, the balcony was quiet. Towering oaks and maples in the front yard shielded the house from most of the traffic noise and the sweet smell of the autumn clematis climbing the side of the portico wafted in on the salty breeze. It was the sort of lavish room her mother had insisted upon during the short time they lived in Summer Harbor. Peaceful and perfect.

Erin let her mind wander back to the days when expectation had ruled her life. Dress a certain way, speak a certain way, act a certain way. The house where her mother and stepfather had lived made this one pale in comparison. Her thoughts were turning toward the last few months before they'd moved away and guilt was settling in, when a sound at the door had her spinning.

"What the hell are you doing in my room?"

The tall wiry man outlined in the doorway vibrated with anger and Erin had to fight the urge to shrink away.

"I'm sorry, Mr. Jay. I was just admiring the view."

"Get. Out," he growled as he advanced into the room. "Get out of my room and get out of my house. Keaton Finnley will be hearing about this unprofessional behavior. Mark my words." His eyes darted around the room as if looking for anything out of place.

Erin's eyes followed his. She hadn't paid much attention to the room itself. Now, her fleeting glance took in the king-size four-poster bed, sitting area sporting leather furniture and a Persian rug, and what Cori would no doubt say were original works of art from lesser-known, but still very expensive, artists. One of the frames hung at an angle, revealing a wall safe. There was a door to a luxurious bath and another that Erin assumed led to a walk-in closet. The bed coverings, curtains, and throw pillows on the furniture were all made of silk, and every item was placed with meticulous care.

"I truly am sorry, Mr. Jay. I know I shouldn't have come

in." Erin hated that her voice hitched and she swallowed hard. How could she have been so foolish? She needed this job. Badly. Why on earth had she risked it for a peek at the balcony? She swallowed again. "Your view is so pretty, and the smell from the flowers... I just... Well, I wandered in without thinking."

Erin watched the man's expression change and it made her blood run cold. A sinister sneer curled the corners of his mouth and he took a step closer, crowding her personal space. She wanted to hold her own, stand up to him, but something about this man made Erin's skin crawl. Trying to shrink away only resulted in the backs of her legs pressed against a table.

"I remember you." His eyes narrowed. "You're that Wallace brat. Always too good for everybody else. Yeah, I remember you." His bloodshot eyes traveled down her body and gooseflesh rose on her arms. She took a step toward the door, but the man matched it, blocking the way. "I guess it isn't all bad, you being here in my bedroom and all."

"Everything alright, Erin?"

Erin squeezed her eyes shut in relief at the sound of Sawyer's voice. The insinuation in the homeowner's voice had turned Erin's stomach and she had to swallow back the bitter taste that rose in her throat. She cast a pleading look Sawyer's way.

"Ms. Wallace and I were just getting reacquainted," the man said, not taking his eyes off hers. It was hard to believe that this was the other half of Finch and Jay's Motorcycle Shop. There couldn't have been anyone further from the amiable Maddox Finch. How were they partners? She shot another look toward Sawyer, hoping he could read her expression. She didn't remember ever being acquainted with Lyle Jay, and she certainly had no desire to rectify that.

"Well, I'm afraid I need her to run to the shop for me. I wouldn't want a delay in your renovation. Erin?"

Hurrying past Sawyer and into the hall, she could feel Lyle's eyes following her every step. Reining in the urge to run, she held her head high and led the way to the front door.

Her coworker was silent as they walked. He opened the door

to her truck, stood back while she got in, closed it, and stood, waiting for her to roll down the window. She hesitated, sure she didn't want to hear what he had to say. She'd messed up good. Steeling herself for the well-deserved lecture, she rolled down the window and met his kind eyes straight on with far more gumption than she felt.

"There's a reason the boss put me on this job with you. That man has... a reputation. Keaton doesn't trust him and after what I just heard, I don't either. Head back to Finnley's, I'll be right behind you."

Erin spent the entire drive to the shop alternating between fuming and worrying. She was mad at herself for letting curiosity get the better of her, mad at Lyle for being such a jerk, and even mad at Sawyer for stepping in. Or maybe not that he'd stepped in, but that he'd needed to. That one faded pretty quickly though. The truth was, she was beyond relieved that he'd been there. Then the fuming turned to worry. The realization that she was now going to have to fess up to Keaton about going into the man's bedroom had guilt coloring her cheeks.

Their boss looked up from a set of blueprints when Erin and Sawyer entered the back of the hardware store. She'd never been able to nail down exactly how old the man was. Solid muscle, the guy could out-work anyone on his crews and not even look tired. The silver hair and salt and pepper beard suggested he was old enough to be her father. Not that it mattered. Keaton ran a tight ship, was well respected by both customers and employees, and had grown his father's small-town hardware store into a multimillion dollar construction and handyman business. Not too shabby whether he was thirty-four or fifty-four.

"You two done at Lyle's already?"

She hung her head. Before she could speak, though, Sawyer stepped up next to her.

"No, ran out of staples." He leaned forward and lowered his voice. "Listen, Erin was admiring the house and Lyle got a little more... familiar with her than I was comfortable with. I told him I needed her to run an errand. We're almost done with the flooring anyway. I think it'd be best if I finished it up and you assigned Erin to another job. One minus the lecherous old man."

Standing, Keaton frowned and crossed his arms. The thick muscles stretching the fabric of his plaid shirt made him appear far younger than his nearly white hair and salt and pepper beard. He looked over Sawyer's shoulder at Erin. "Probably a good idea. I shouldn't have put you on that job to begin with. My gut said not to. I should have listened. I'm afraid I don't have another job for you today, but you could work in the supply room. The space is in desperate need of help. It's a mess."

She nodded, not trusting her voice, and followed Sawyer into the cluttered room where he grabbed a fresh box of staples. "Thanks for not ratting me out to Keaton. I know I shouldn't have been snooping. Even if it was honestly just to peek at the balcony. I should have just gone to the truck and gotten the staples. Stupid."

"Don't be too hard on yourself, kid. Who on this crew hasn't looked at something that wasn't strictly part of the job? I remember one summer I was working on a house down past Butterfly Cove. The owner had an Aston Martin Vantage GT8. Only about a hundred-fifty of them were ever made. I snuck into the garage to take a look. It was a beautiful machine. I was some glad I didn't get caught. If Lyle complains I'll back you up, but something tells me he isn't going to bother," he said as he made a note on the inventory sheet on the wall by the door for the staples.

"Thanks all the same."

"I'm just glad I was there," he added with a wink and a smile as he headed out the door.

So was she.

Turning to face the storage room, she stood with her hands on her hips. Keaton was right, the place was a disaster, but she liked a challenge and this one would help keep her mind off other things. Like creepy old men. And houses she had no business driving past. And people she missed like the dry ground misses the rain.

Lyle Jay pushed a trembling hand through his unkempt hair and forced it to stop shaking by a sheer act of will. Anger and fear mingled in his chest before he tucked them away. Neither would do him any good. With a flick of his wrist, he slammed the hinged canvas closed to hide the safe door. What might do him some good would be to check in with his patrons. A sneer replaced the scowl on his face as he sank his weary frame into his chair and scooped the phone from his desk.

It rang for a long time before the man picked up. He always answered, so why wait? Did he think that avoiding the call would make it go away? He laughed and leaned back. If the man thought avoiding him would change anything... he was right.

The line crackled to life and he heard the sigh of a blown-out breath. "What?"

"Now is that any way to answer the phone? Especially when it's your benefactor calling?"

"My—!"

"Tsk, tsk. Temper! Now, I think you know 'what'."

The other man pulled in an audible breath through his nose. "I just paid you last month," he said through clenched teeth, his voice lowered as if someone might hear him.

"Well, that was last month. And since you seem to have gotten into the habit of avoiding me, let's tack on another grand for good measure."

"Another grand?! That's absurd! You son of a—"

Lyle emitted a shrill, maniacal laugh, letting the line go quiet before continuing in a menacing voice. "You know I don't care what you think of me. All I care about is that you understand that one call and the puny existence you've spent so much time, energy, and money building for yourself will crumble. Piece by piece. Until you have nothing."

Silence.

"You don't want that, do you?"

Silence. Again.

"That's what I thought."

"How much would I have to pay you to stop contacting me?"

Lyle laughed again. "I think you misunderstand how these things work. I know what you've done. What you are doing. What you plan to do. You don't want anyone else to know, so you pay to keep me quiet. Sometimes more, sometimes less. You can stop paying me whenever you want. Really. Just know that as soon as you do I will make that phone call and it all goes away. Your business and your house. Your reputation. The expensive whiskey you're so fond of. Do they serve whiskey in jail? No, I don't think they do. Just remember all of that whenever you think it isn't worth it. It is, after all, just some money now and then."

The man on the other end of the line was breathing hard. "Fine!"

"I'm glad we understand each other."

"Same place as last time?"

"Of course."

The line went dead with a loud crack. He smirked. Why weren't they more thankful that he was as unscrupulous as he was? An upstanding citizen would have gone to the police as soon as he'd learned about the... less-than-legal business practices the other man employed regularly. Yes, the man should be thankful indeed.

CHAPTER TWO

"That dry bag do something to you that I don't know about?"

Harley's hands stilled on the bright yellow satchel. He relaxed the death grip he had on it, thankful the thing hadn't ripped in two. "Sorry."

His boss, Noah, clapped him on the shoulder and took the bag, placing it on the shelf where it belonged. "I think that's the last of the stuff from this morning's tour. And if not, Gage can finish, since we only have one more tour today."

"Hard to believe we're already this late in the season," Gage chimed in from the other side of the shop. "Where'd the summer go, anyway?"

"I don't know, but your fellow guides deemed it over weeks ago," Noah replied with a chuckle.

Most of the summer help had moved on to warmer climates and winter jobs, so Harley and Noah took almost every tour themselves, with the help of Gage and Owen, the only guys who'd stuck around. It wasn't so bad. The serious influx of tourists had gone home and they were down to three tours a day, maybe less depending on the weather. Gage finished toweling off the stack of life vests he'd been wiping down, crammed them on the shelf, and disappeared through the open back door of the shop.

"Everything OK?" Noah asked once the younger man was out of earshot.

"Yeah." Harley dragged his hand down across his eyes and over his beard. Somewhere between doing seventy-five headed north the day before and creeping back into town long after the last rays of the sun had stopped warming the blacktop, the realization had come that he was never going to arrive at the house one day and think 'today is the day I stay and work'. He just couldn't. At first, he'd thought the knowledge would bring him peace. Maybe he could sell the house and be done with it. Instead, the guilt over one more failure had eaten at him all through the night making sleep impossible.

Not looking convinced, Noah jammed his hands in the pockets of his jeans, cocked a hip on the work table where they stood, and waited. When Harley didn't elaborate, he lowered his voice. "Dude, you're more than my employee. We're friends. You can talk to me."

Harley was tall at a little over six feet, but he didn't feel tall standing next to his boss. He stole a glance up but didn't meet his friend's gaze for the longest time. Finally, clearing his throat, he rested his hands on the table and hung his head. "No. Everything is not OK. I tried to work on the house again yesterday, but I couldn't."

It was a discussion they'd had before. At first, Noah had pushed him to sell the place. It would have been the logical thing to do. Or let the bank take it. Or the town. But over time his friend had come to understand that Harley couldn't do that.

"I know I have to do... something. I just..." Harley trailed off and kept his head down. It wasn't often he felt the flash of tears on the back of his eyes and he wasn't about to let Noah see them. Or hear them in his voice.

A firm hand on his shoulder told him the man didn't miss a thing. "You know I'd help if I had the time," Noah said, his voice gentle.

Harley nodded. He would, too. Had offered before. Numerous times. It had never felt right to pass off such a huge responsibility to someone else. Now all the man's free time, which wasn't much to begin with, was being spent at an inn overlooking Butterfly Cove. The new owner, Noah's girlfriend Lily, was updating the kitchen and Noah was doing most of the work.

"What's the most pressing problem?"

"The back porch. It's literally falling off."

"What about getting someone from Finnley's to take care of that and then trying again in the spring?"

"I can't afford—" Harley stopped. Frustration was lending an angry edge to his voice that he didn't like. It sounded ungrateful, but he wasn't. By a long shot.

"Just go talk to Keaton," Noah said calmly as if he hadn't heard. "Maybe he can cut you a deal."

"I doubt that."

"Hey, you've worked for him the past two winters. Can't hurt to ask. See what you can work out. Maybe an employee discount, or trade for work on another house."

Harley puffed out a breath and nodded his head, still avoiding eye contact. It wasn't a horrible idea.

"And… the afternoon tour doesn't leave for three hours, so go now," Noah continued, clapping Harley on the back as he walked toward the store at the front of the building.

Harley heard the door click closed behind his friend. For a second he let his eyes blur with painful tears of frustration and anger and guilt before swallowing them away. He didn't cry. Anger was his go-to emotion whenever he stopped long enough to feel anything. Busyness had some distinct advantages. Tears were new. And irritating. He hadn't cried in years and he wasn't going to start being a sissy now.

Pressing a hand across his eyes, his mind drifted back to the last time he'd let tears claw their way to the surface. It was the day he'd met Noah. Grief was weird. He'd been turned down for another job and it had all come apart at the seams. He'd found a quiet spot under the stairs behind Noah's shop and let the tears and anger come. But Noah had found him. Listened to him. Offered him a job and a place to live above the shop. As always, he was astonished that the man had taken a chance on him. He hadn't looked the part of a kayaking tour guide, that was for darn sure. And he'd made it hard at first. So hard. He knew it.

Why Noah hadn't fired him that first summer was a mystery.

Now, standing in the quiet storage room, he knew the job, and his friend, had saved him from leaving again. It would have been so easy to just get on the bike, ride away, and never ever look back. But a person needed funds for that, so angry-at-the-world Harley had taken the job. He hadn't realized at the time that he was looking for a reason to stay. Noah had given him that. Plus friendship, patience, trust. New concepts to a loud-mouth twenty-four-year-old kid.

Straightening and reorganizing the already-neat shelves of dry bags and life jackets took Harley half an hour. He wasted another twenty-three minutes cleaning up the schedule he kept on a giant whiteboard on the back wall. He knew he wasn't fooling anyone. He was avoiding taking his friend's advice. A good twenty minutes standing, rocked back on his heels with his arms crossed, in the open back doors of the shop brought him to a place where he simply couldn't avoid it any longer. With a snarl, he headed down the alley toward Carriage Street and then away from Main toward the hardware store a few blocks away. Noah wasn't wrong. It was just... he ran his hand over his weary face. It was just... Harley didn't want him to be right.

The day before, sitting and talking with Clyde had been a breath of fresh air. It wasn't that he couldn't talk to Noah. He could. About anything. But there was something about the old man that made Harley want to pour his heart out. His chest ached with the need to talk to someone. Someone who would listen, not try to fix it all, or tell him how much he'd messed up. He was well aware of that. No, he longed for someone who would just hear him.

Once upon a time, an entire lifetime ago, he had believed in a higher power. Someone he could talk to, turn to. It wasn't often that he longed for those childish days. He shook his head. There was no use going there. Even if his dad had been right all those years ago, the Big Guy wouldn't want anything to do with the failure that was Harley Beck. He deserved to be on his own. He deserved to pay the price, however high, for his mistakes.

Skirting the front of the massive hardware store that took up nearly a whole block of Carriage Street, he went to the employee's entrance at the back. If Keaton wasn't on a job, he would be in his office. Before stepping up to the door, Harley took a deep breath and urged himself to relax the hands that were balled into fists at his side.

Noah had worked for Finnley's every winter since he was a teenager and when Harley had needed work that first winter, his friend had put in a good word. Keaton was a decent boss, fair and skilled at what he did. He'd earned Harley's respect early on.

"I was hoping you'd be stopping by soon," the older man said when he caught sight of Harley. Rounding the thick planks of pine stretched across two old sawhorses that served as a makeshift desk, he offered a handshake. "You are planning on coming back on my crew for the winter, right?"

Harley attempted a half-smile and stepped just far enough into the room to take Keaton's outstretched hand. "Sure. If you need me. I've got a few more weeks at the shop, but then..."

"We've got more work already than I've got crews for, so whenever you can shake free."

Harley swallowed and his heart sank a little. He shouldn't have come. If they were that busy... Fixing the house was his responsibility alone. This had been a bad idea. Why had he let Noah convince him to ask for help? His feet itched with the need to leave and he shifted his weight back onto his heels.

"Since I doubt you came down here to tell me you weren't free to work yet, what's up?" Keaton leaned back on a wooden stool behind him and crossed his arms.

Harley's mouth started moving before his brain had a chance to stop it. "I... Well, I need to get the back porch of the house fixed before snow, or I'm going to lose it. The thing is..." Harley blew out a ragged breath, unable to find the words to continue.

"The thing is..." Keaton's eyes, hooded under nearly black brows, extended a kindness that said he understood in a way that few others did. "You can't work on it."

Was he that transparent? First Clyde, then Noah. Now Keaton. Inhaling his pride, he nodded and continued before he lost his nerve. "The other thing is, I can't afford to just hire someone to do the work." What with rent, taxes, back taxes, interest, mortgage payments, late mortgage payments, more interest, and the lawyer he'd hired to navigate probate court he just didn't have anything left over.

"Well, let's see what we can do," Keaton said as he pushed aside a set of blueprints and rifled through a pile of clipboards. The desk had a chaotic feel, but Harley was sure the man knew where every single item was. Pulling a clipboard out of the chaos, Keaton started flipping through the pages on it. Harley's eyes traveled around the room while he waited. It was very much like Keaton. Nothing fancy, everything tough and functional. He took a step toward a map of the town, quickly finding the house. Next to the map hung drafts of current projects, notes and photos from customers, and a framed picture of Keaton with country singer Phoebe Jennings.

"I don't think I have anyone I can spare right now."

Harley's shoulders slumped a little. He ground his teeth in frustration as he watched the older man continue thumbing through the papers on the clipboard. Now that he'd asked for help he wanted the job done.

Please let there be someone. Anyone. It was the closest Harley had come to saying a prayer in fifteen years and it felt odd to be pleading for help from some non-existent source.

"Oh, hold up. Erin *just* came off a job this morning. I think I can move a few things around on the schedule and get your porch taken care of. What do you say about giving me two weeks at the end of October in exchange? We're going to be up to our eyeballs in winterizing homes and I will need all hands on deck."

Relief rushed through Harley. "Yes. I can do that. Thanks."

Keaton smiled, but it was laced with both sadness and empathy. "When my brother-in-law, Jason, passed away a few years ago I couldn't go to my sister's house for months. The guy was my best friend and I just... couldn't. Vera needed help and I..." He trailed off, jaw clenched. "Anyway, I remember what it felt like to ask Sawyer to help Vera for me. Hard, but the relief... I'm glad you asked and happy I could help you out."

The comfort of a shared understanding settled around Harley, and he breathed out a breath he felt like he'd been holding for over two years. This could work. The back porch would get fixed before it caved in without him having to spend even a minute at the house. Hope surged through him.

"Eight tomorrow morning a good time to get started?" Keaton asked as he gathered up a pair of work gloves off the desk and stuffed them into his back pocket.

"Yeah, I mean whatever works for your guy."

Keaton was already heading for the door but paused to clap Harley on the shoulder. "Sounds good. See you around, Harley. And don't sweat it. We've got this."

The chill in the pre-dawn air had Harley's breath puffing out in hazy clouds as he jogged down the back stairs hours before anyone else was even stirring. Cold fog hung in strange layers over the street and the sun had yet to make an appearance above the horizon. They only had two tours scheduled, one mid-morning and one late in the afternoon. Sunrise tours were by far Harley's favorite, but the frigid mornings had driven their clientele indoors.

One of the things he liked most about the sunrise tours was the fact that his restlessness was easily masked by work. Nights were fitful at best, haunted by choices he wished he could change, faces of those he wished he hadn't failed, and regret that ate at his heart and robbed him of sleep. When he had to be at work by four-thirty though, it didn't seem to matter. Now that the schedule had changed he was restless and edgy.

The murky air smothered the glow from the few street lights still on. Opting to walk, over waking the whole neighborhood with the thunder of his bike's engine, Ignoring the eerie silence, Harley picked his way along the dark alley beside the shop and emerged onto the sidewalk. The sign on the restaurant next door creaked in the salty breeze and Harley almost laughed when he jumped at the sound.

Harley still couldn't believe Keaton had someone available so soon. What had he said the man's name was? Ian? Aaron? It didn't matter as long as the guy knew what he was doing. Pulling his heavy black chamois shirt tighter against the chill, he weighed his options. Since the last thing he wanted to do was arrive early and have to wait at the house, he turned away from Main Street and was soon walking past homes and inns instead of shops and restaurants. The red and orange leaves that would draw another wave of tourists to the island were still thick overhead and blocked any hint of light from the brightening sky.

Less than a mile down the road, Harrier Lake stretched out beneath the rugged mountains that cut across the island. The back road he'd taken wasn't very popular with the tourists, but Harley had always liked it better than the busier entrance south of town. Probably because it walked him past Finch and Jay's.

The motorcycle shop had been the one place he could remember agreeing with his dad on anything in the years after his mom died. They'd looked at the classic bikes for sale, discussed the pros and cons of chopping a bike, drooled over the occasional rare find, and picked up parts for the Norton. The first time anyone had called him Harley had been at Finch and Jay's. The place was dark this early in the morning. Still, he slowed and let the memories come.

He'd been nine years old the first time his dad let him drive his Harley-Davidson XL-1000. He could barely reach the handlebars and the footrests at the same time and he'd been so scared he was going to dump it that he almost threw up. But he hadn't. That short ride sparked a deep love of motorcycles that clung to this day. Despite… everything.

Leaving the shop and the memories behind, Harley picked up his pace. At the edge of the lake, he found a rock and sat, drawing his knees up, catching the heels of his boots on the rough surface. The gunmetal-gray sky overhead was giving way to a warm, creamy band of light along the eastern horizon.

His thoughts were a disagreeable companion this morning. They twisted and churned and he was glad he was alone. Sometimes finding a quiet spot to watch the night slip away was enough to quiet them. That was another reason why he liked the early tours. Other days, like today, it only soothed a little. He'd take what he could get.

This morning the fog would mute the sunrise, but Harley didn't care. He just needed quiet. He sat, arms draped around one knee until his legs started to go numb where they rested on the rock. He stretched out the kinks from the cold as he stood. There was no more avoiding it. He had to go meet Keaton's guy.

Early morning joggers had taken to the trails, school buses were moving around, and the streets were starting to bustle with activity as he picked up his pace and made his way back toward the center of town. He didn't want to wait around at the house, but he didn't want anyone waiting on him either.

As he turned down the street where the house sat nestled under the drooping arms of a weeping willow, he could see a ratty pickup parked on the street. No one was inside and as he neared the driveway he stopped to listen. It wasn't the country music or heavy stuff most of the guys listened to on job sites. No, this guy was listening to… a cappella hymns? Harley shook his head. He was positive that not a single construction worker he'd ever met had listened to hymns on the job.

A surge of long-buried memories flipped on like a switch. The hymn currently playing was one he'd heard many times growing up. A fading memory of his parents, standing at the kitchen sink washing dishes and singing, warmed his chest and tore into his heart at the same time. The song ended and another one began. Not as familiar, but one he'd heard before. Oh, how his mother had loved hymns. In the deep recesses of his mind, he saw himself seated next to her at the piano in their living room, learning to play *Jesus Loves Me*. She'd been smiling and he'd wanted to please her in the worst way. He could see his chubby childish fingers on the keys as he picked out the notes and her beautiful face as she told him how proud she was.

Cursing the lump in his throat, he pushed the memories aside along with the shrubs and cut between the garage and the back corner of the house. He needed to trim them before no one could even get into the backyard.

"Just add it to the list," he grumbled as he rounded the corner of the house and came to an abrupt stop.

Half an hour ago, when Keaton had handed her the address for her next job, Erin's hands had started shaking. Coop's. She tried not to wear her emotions on her sleeve, but she hadn't known whether to jump for joy or burst into tears.

"The porch needs to be replaced," Keaton had said.

Did it ever.

She now stood in the backyard, staring at the mess. She'd known, somehow, that the place wasn't being taken care of. The shrubs maybe, or the un-raked leaves. However, she had been completely unprepared for the ramshackle state of the porch. What was the owner thinking? Why would they buy a place in a town as expensive as Summer Harbor if they weren't going to keep it up? The little ranch had to have cost hundreds of thousands of dollars. For crying out loud, her foot had gone through the bottom step, and the roof had holes in it large enough to stick her head through. Maybe they'd just bought the place. That could account for the disrepair and neglect. She hoped that was the case.

And, alright, fine, so Coop hadn't kept up with repairs either. Too many more important things he'd always say. Priorities. Well, her priority was fixing the porch.

Keaton had assured her that the owner would be there at eight, but no one had answered her knock at the kitchen door. Sure, she'd been a little early, but still... To kill time until they showed up she'd hauled her tools into the backyard. She sang as she set up tarps to catch debris. Hymns. She always sang hymns while she worked and Coop's favorite seemed fitting this morning.

Poor and sinful though we be,
Thou hast mercy to relieve us
Grace to cleanse, and pow'r to free
Blessed Jesus, blessed Jesus,
Early let us turn to Thee

As the last notes drifted away, she glanced at her watch. It was now past eight, but she hesitated to start demolition. Staring at the rotted steps and peeling paint, memories flickered in her mind's eye and she swallowed back tears.

"I'm wicked proud of you, Erin," Coop had said the last time they'd sat on this very porch, in need of repair even then. They'd spent the evening chatting over sweet tea and sandwiches she'd made from leftovers he'd pulled from the fridge. Cold meatloaf, if she remembered correctly. The old metal chairs they'd sat on were still there. Rusted and worse for wear, tossed in a heap at the end of the porch, but still there. Didn't this guy have furniture of his own? Lacing her fingers across the back of her neck, she stared at the chairs as her eyes burned. She'd left for school on the mainland the next day and she'd never seen Coop again. A noise near the garage made her spin around, heart pounding.

"Sorry, I didn't mean to startle you," the man said, holding his hands up. The confused look on his face would have been comical if Erin didn't recognize it. It was the 'what's a girl doing here?' look she always got when she showed up at job sites. She understood, honest she did. Compared to the guys on most crews she was a shrimp, not to mention a woman. Most of the other construction workers didn't want her there and in the customers' eyes, she was too young to know what she was doing. Every day was a fight to prove she could do this job. Over time she'd perfected her reaction. A friendly smile, warm greeting, and firm handshake. Don't let them see that you're annoyed.

Her heart still hammered in her chest, but she didn't let it show. "Keaton Finnley sent me to work on the porch." His face was wary and there was something... familiar... Maybe around the eyes? She couldn't put her finger on it.

"Erin." He sounded as confused as he looked.

"Yes... Erin Wallace."

A sheepish smile curved his lips as stuck his hand out. "I guess I was expecting Aaron."

"I get that a lot," she said as she shook his hand.

"I bet you do."

"You're the owner?"

"Yes, Harley."

His grip was strong and wide with rough calluses on the palm, and she loathed that her heart rate skyrocketed at his touch. She didn't go for bad-boys. Not anymore. She snatched her hand back. "Keaton said you wanted the porch replaced?"

He looked at her for a beat before turning toward the back of the house. His eyes widened as if noticing the state of the porch for the first time. "Oh..." He swallowed and a strong emotion passed over his features. Familiarity teased again. She was sure she hadn't met him before, and yet...

"Yeah. I mean..." He crossed his arms over his wide chest. "Is it worth trying to save it?"

Now that was a question Erin didn't want to answer. Every fiber of her being screamed that the whole house, right down to the tacky, eighties linoleum in the kitchen, should be kept as is. It was all worth saving. But... A stranger couldn't possibly understand the connection she had to the house, or how much she longed for one more conversation with the previous owner. One more back-porch picnic, one more song, one more hug.

This job might just be her undoing.

Focus. Work. Porch.

"The floor's gone. So are the steps. I might be able to salvage the joists and some of the rafters, but it's going to need a new roof and about half the railing needs to be replaced." She stole a look at the man. He wasn't looking at the porch. Or at her. No, he was staring at the ground.

"Whatever you think needs to be done." He turned his back on the house and stuffed his hands in his pockets. "Listen, I've gotta get to work, so..." He turned away as if avoiding her.

Or was it the house he was avoiding?

At the edge of the yard, he stopped and looked back, catching her eye. "Thanks."

She nodded, but he'd already disappeared around the corner of the garage. Turning back to the porch, she blew out a long breath.

I'm going to need some help here, God. I don't think I can do this on my own. Please get me through this job.

Do not fear. I Am your strength.

A smile turned up the corner of her mouth as another one of Coop's favorite hymns came to mind. and she began singing again.

When peace like a river, attendeth my way
When sorrows like sea billows roll

She moved a ladder into position to reach the roof and, pulling a crowbar from the tools neatly lined up beside the makeshift workbench, went to work.

Whatever my lot, thou hast taught me to say
It is well, it is well, with my soul

This job was possible because whatever came along she could trust God that it would all be well with her soul. Maybe this was how she said goodbye. Maybe this was how she honored the man. By showing up. By doing her best.

Lord, the only way I can do this is with Your strength. Under my own power, I'd have cut my losses and run already. Thank You for sending someone my way a long time ago to teach me that when storms come I can trust You.

❧

Rolling to a stop, Lyle cut the engine on his pristine 1939 Knucklehead and listened to the throbbing roar of his most treasured possession fade. The person he was there to see looked up in surprise when he walked in.

"We need to talk."

The other man's face darkened, but he squared his shoulders and nodded toward a door in the back. They walked in silence, neither caring to utter a word until it clicked closed behind them.

"What do you want now?" the man asked as he picked at something on his sleeve. A nervous tell. Yeah, he should be nervous.

"I happen to require funds. Quickly."

"I can't help you."

A sly smile crossed his lips before he spoke. "Oh, I think you can find a way."

The man crossed his arms. "Like I told you before. I'm done."

"Well, here's the thing. I don't think you are. I happen to have some information that would be of some interest to... shall we say certain people in your current life? Information I am assuming you would rather I kept to myself."

If the man's face had lost color before, it went flat-out white at that. "And what would that be?"

And this was where the screws had to be tightened. "I happen to know exactly where a certain man's daughter liked to spend her time three years ago. The same daughter who OD'd on your watch. He might be forgiving of some of your past sins, but are you willing to bet your livelihood on him overlooking that one?"

Anger poured off the other man in waves. His face, white moments ago, was now a sickly red. His hands clenched and unclenched and fear settled in his eyes. "She survived."

"Oh, I'm well aware."

"I didn't have anything to do with it! I didn't even supply her with those drugs," he hissed.

"Do you think he'll see it that way?"

The man's anger drained away and his shoulders slumped. Lyle could see the moment he'd won. The moment defeat settled over the man's face.

"The thing is, I don't *want* to say anything. But it's going to cost you something to keep me quiet." He leaned forward and whispered a number into the man's ear and then rocked back to lean against the table, waiting.

"I don't hav—"

"Yes, you do. You think I wouldn't know exactly what you can provide before I came?"

The other man swallowed hard and nodded his head. "Fine. But this is the last time. You come at me again and I'll go to the police myself."

A smile tried to pull at his thin lips. It might be fun to call the man's bluff.

"One more thing. I need it soon." He raised his hand to silence the protest he knew was coming before it started, and pushed off the table. Striding to the door, he stopped and turned. "You have to know that deeds have consequences. This is simply the punishment fitting the crime."

"If that's the case then you should probably watch your back."

The sentence hung in the air between them and caused a chill to race down Lyle's backbone. He didn't like the feeling. Leaving quickly, he listened for the click of the door behind him. He knew he'd get what he asked for. In the meantime, it might behoove him to keep one eye looking over his shoulder.

CHAPTER THREE

It had been a month of Sundays since Harley had *wanted* to go to the house. As the afternoon crept on, however, the pull to see what Erin had accomplished over the day was at least as strong as the push away had been for the past ten years. The sensation made him edgy. Like too much caffeine, or the knowledge that someone was going to startle him at any moment.

"Hey, man!"

Harley nearly jumped out of his work boots at Noah's voice.

"Woah! Didn't mean to sneak up on you."

Harley glowered at his friend and turned back to the whiteboard. Friday meant it was time to lay out the schedule for the coming week. He knew he looked furious but felt helpless to change it. Why should *wanting* to go to the house cause so much angst? He redoubled his efforts scrubbing off the notes from the past week.

"Dude, you're going to scrub through the board." Noah's voice held a teasing note but also concern. "Or injure yourself."

Harley tossed the rag aside and picked up a dry-erase marker from the can on the cluttered work table that doubled as Noah's desk. As he filled in spaces for tours with all the needed information, his friend leaned back on the table and watched him. After a few minutes, Harley couldn't stand it anymore.

"What?" he growled.

"Not much. Just a little curious as to why you are scheduling five or six tours a day and putting yourself as lead on every single one."

Harley closed his eyes. Get it together! He sensed, more than heard, Noah push off from the table and step up next to him. He glanced sideways, but then busied himself searching for the discarded rag rather than addressing his friend's comment.

"We only have one more tour this afternoon. Why don't you knock off early? I can take Gage or Owen with me."

"No, I'm good." Harley scrubbed his name off some of the tours and eliminated others altogether.

"No, you're going to scare the customers." Again, Noah's tone was light but held enough of an edge to make it known that he was serious.

Trying to ignore his friend, Harley continued working on the whiteboard. It was no use. A long moment later, he puffed out a weary breath. "Someone from Finnley's started working on the house today."

"Ahh," Noah said. "That's... good. Right?"

Harley kept working on the schedule. Kept not looking at Noah. Kept trying to sort out the jumble in his head. He'd asked for help. Help had arrived. The man standing next to him was right. It was a good thing. So why did he feel like connecting his fist with the sturdy wooden frame of the shop door?

Why? Because it should have been him.

It should have been him for ten years and the fact that he still couldn't do what he was supposed to do ate at him. One of many failures on a long list. It was that failure that was gnawing on him today and making him a bear to be around.

Snapping the cap back on the pen, he tossed it in the general direction of the tin can on Noah's desk before he stalked out of the shop without another word. He knew Noah well enough to know his friend wouldn't take it personally.

Crossing the driveway that sat between the shop and the restaurant next door, he checked the lock on the building that housed the kayaks out of habit before picking his way down the alley that ran behind the Main Street shops.

He hadn't meant to turn toward the house when he reached the end of the alley. Didn't even realize he had until the beat-up truck came into focus. He slowed and considered turning around. But something stronger than his feelings of failure drew him forward.

Erin was busy sliding tools into the bed of her truck when he neared the house. That morning he'd been flustered, expecting a crusty old carpenter to be waiting for him. Someone like his buddy Sawyer. He hadn't processed more than the fact that she was young and beautiful before he beat a hasty retreat. Now, she looked up and smiled, and all the rancor from the past hours melted away.

Huh.

That was new.

"Hey," she said, lifting her hand in greeting.

"How'd it go today?"

"Want to see?"

No.

Yes.

When he nodded, Erin reached into the cab and turned the truck off. "Please start later," he heard her mutter as she closed the door. He let her lead the way back around the garage and into the backyard.

Glancing over her shoulder at him she grinned, a dimple appearing on one cheek. It made her look cute.

Everything about her was cute.

"I hope you don't mind. I trimmed a little off those shrubs. I was having a hard time moving things in and out of the backyard."

"No, that's fine."

She was shorter than he was, so he was looking at the top of her head where her hair was pulled back in two short braids, messed from the wind pulling wisps free. She was clad in a navy blue tank top and a pair of white painter's pants that hugged her curves in just the ri— He snapped his eyes back to the top of her head. *Not* going there.

"I didn't get quite as much done as I'd hoped for the first day," she said, oblivious to his train of thought. "There was a bit more that needed to be ripped out than I thought this morning. I managed to get all the rotten wood off and started working on the new floor joists, but I need more lumber." She stopped in front of where the back steps had been. It was now an empty space. "You'll need all new stairs, floor, roof, and railing. I did salvage part of the floor joists at the end and about half of the roof rafters."

Harley had stopped next to her and crossed his arms over his chest. With his feet planted wide, he was closer to eye-level with her. She was young. Early twenties maybe? A lot younger than most of the guys who worked for Finnley's. He wondered if she had to put up with as much harassment from them as he imagined. A sudden spurt of protectiveness hit him hard, but he tamped it down.

Focus. Porch.

He rocked back on his heels and looked at the scant bits she'd managed to save. It wasn't much. He could see out of the corner of his eye that she was waiting for some sort of a response, but he was having a hard time forming words.

"Looks good," he finally ground out in a terse tone.

"I'm sorry I couldn't salvage more. I tried, but the wood was so far gone—"

"You saved more than I thought you'd be able to."

Relief eased the worry lines from her forehead and she puffed out a sigh. "I should be able to get the rest of the floor joists in Monday morning and maybe start on the roof."

Harley stepped forward and ran his hand along the two-by-eight she'd replaced across the front edge of the structure. It was rough and had the delicious smell of hemlock. She did good work. But so could he. Would it have been that hard to replace the porch? Couldn't he have sucked it up for one day and accomplished what she had? His knuckles turned white where they gripped the top of the board in frustration.

Erin stepped up and leaned her forearms against the two-by-eight. "I hope everything's to your liking," she said as she peeled a splinter off the board and twisted it between her fingers. "Keaton said to replace it, so I assumed this is what you wanted. If something isn't right, just let me know."

He needed to reassure her it was fine. It wasn't her fault that he was fighting back emotions he'd rather keep buried. He tried to smile, but it must not have come across as very friendly because she took a step back and pushed her hands into her pockets.

"Well, I guess I'm done for today." She didn't look at him but instead took a last look at what she'd gotten done and backed away.

Harley ditched the smile. It wasn't working anyway. "Thanks for all your hard work."

"I'll be here bright and early Monday morning... as long as the truck starts." She laughed and turned another easy smile on him. Why did it look so effortless on other people? He wanted to return it but looked away instead. She mumbled something that might have been 'see ya' and beat a hasty retreat from the backyard.

Yup, he would have run from him, too.

He rested his arms on the board the same as she had and hung his head. It wasn't fair to have a Monday on a Friday and that's what it had felt like all day. Who was he kidding? It felt like he'd been living a Monday for two and a half years.

Erin took a tight grip on the wheel and set her jaw. She couldn't believe she'd all but run from the man's backyard. How embarrassing! But... self-preservation. She'd fled because what she'd wanted to do was reach out and smooth her hand over his wide, tight shoulders, easing the tension that radiated off of him. The thing was, she didn't go for bad-boys, and from the tattoos covering his arms and crawling up the side of his neck, his black clothes, his broody eyes, and the way his hands had gripped the edge of the board to the point of whitening his knuckles... that's exactly what he was. It was as if he could barely control his emotions, or barely control himself. He hadn't even looked up when she'd said she was leaving, strong emotion pulsed from him. Not anger but something hard. She knew trouble when she saw it.

Two right turns and a couple of minutes had her at the attic apartment she rented from her sweet friend Vera. Of course, 'apartment' was a funny term in Summer Harbor. It pretty much meant any space where a person could sleep and maybe cook a cup of noodles. In her case, it was the tiniest bedroom she'd ever seen with a microwave and sink at one end and a twin bed so small the box of odds and ends, which she'd easily kept under her bed through her teen years, didn't quite fit, its corners sticking out to catch her toes on. The bathroom was so small she could barely turn around in it and if she didn't close the curtain properly when she showered the whole room got drenched. She had no complaints though, because hands-down the most redeeming quality was the garage. As long as she didn't make too much noise she could have the entire thing to herself.

She pulled to a stop in front of the building and shut off the truck. With her forehead on the steering wheel, she took a deep, calming breath. Maybe it had looked like she was afraid of the tall, tattooed, bad-boy, but she hadn't been. After the run-in with Lyle Jay a few days before, she knew Keaton wouldn't have sent her to Harley's, alone, if he'd had even the slightest worry about the man. No, she hadn't been afraid of him. It was more she was afraid of herself. She hadn't liked how quickly her mind had gone to noticing how handsome he was. Or how troubled. Or how quickly she'd wanted to reach out and soothe the tension rolling off him.

No, best to call it a day.

Before climbing out of the truck she made a note on a sticky pad reminding herself to pick up more lumber in the morning for Coop's place. She flexed her hands. No. Not Coop's place.

That was going to take some getting used to.

Unlocking the door to the garage and stepping inside

always felt more like coming home than stepping into her apartment ever did. The sweet smell of wood and the pungent scent of the finishes she used met her before the warm light from the overhead fixtures illuminated the space. There was a familiarity with the tools and wood that centered her. She stopped in the doorway and pulled in a deep breath. Right now, she needed that more than usual.

This evening she wasn't going to worry about broody men, no matter how attractive they were. He'd either be there on Monday or he wouldn't, and she would do her job whether he was home or not. Her rational self hoped he wouldn't be there. It was hard to be at Coop's place and see someone else living there. Living there but not caring about the house. It was also hard to concentrate when Harley stood next to her and flexed his impossibly rugged muscl—.

Erin growled and stomped into the workshop. "Stop it," she chided herself. She pulled four thin boards from a stack on the far side of the garage. The boxes she'd delivered to Cori that morning had been simple, with mitered corners. They were quick to cut and easy to assemble. The time and effort came in the finishing. It took a lot of careful work sanding and re-sanding, finishing and refinishing, for them to feel like they were made of satin instead of wood.

A recent trip to Vermont and her entire, albeit minuscule, saving account had netted her a supply of mahogany, curly maple, walnut, cherry, and white ash. Ever since she'd gotten the shop squared away, she'd been itching to use the contrasting colors for dovetail joints. White ash and walnut were her favorites and she chose two boards with interesting grains running along the cool-toned wood.

As often happened when working, she prayed. It was her quiet time. Her time when her thoughts were hers alone and no one interrupted them. It was something she'd held tight to all through trade school. Those moments where the machinery was too loud for other people to interrupt. She wasn't a solitary person by nature. She liked busyness and noise and other people. Sometimes though, when her emotions were running wild, she needed to be alone so she could talk to God and collect herself. Tonight was one of those nights. She blew out a sigh and stilled her hands, her thoughts. Closed her eyes.

God, I am flustered and my mind is going in a million different directions. Please help me focus. Help me focus on You and what You want from me in this situation. Help me honor You. I want to do well on this job. For Coop. He loved You so much. Thank you for giving me the opportunity to do this for him.

She stood with her eyes closed for a few moments, listening to the sounds around her. Traffic from a street over, music drifting from a house nearby, the wind and seagulls.

Peace settled over her and the outside sounds faded away as she readied her workspace. Humming, she began to run the boards through the planer, and by the time she had them smooth and of equal thickness, she was singing. And smiling. And looking forward to Monday morning, whether tall-dark-and-broody was there or not.

Harley pushed himself off of the board where he'd been leaning since Erin left. In quite a hurry he might add. He didn't blame her. She was probably afraid of him. And why not?

He looked like trouble.

He knew it.

At work, he managed to mask it pretty well, or maybe the tourists didn't care what their guide looked like. He didn't usually care if people misread him, but for some reason, he cared that Erin had.

He ran his hand over his eyes and across his beard before turning his back to the porch and the house. His eyes settled on the backyard. It was small with a little stretch of lawn and a row of shrubs next to the garage. He hadn't set foot out there in ten years. Three summers' worth of unmowed lawn had left a tangle that stretched to the neighbor's fence.

It was smaller than he remembered.

Wasn't that always how it was, though? You remembered things from your childhood as immense, but when you saw them again as an adult they'd somehow shrunk. He had a passing thought that other things might be like that. What other monstrous things could he now look at and find weren't as big as he remembered?

Nope, they were still huge.

He heaved a sigh, wishing he'd brought his bike. He could use a ride, could use to get away for a few minutes or hours. Or days. But not tonight. For the first time in the two and a half years he'd been back in town, he wanted to work on the house. Not *in*, he wasn't ready for that. But he wanted to do... something.

The messy snarl of underbrush that had grown up needed to be dealt with. Dead and dried brown, it was ugly. He headed for the garage in search of some kind of mower or weed whacker, or some other tool that he could use to trim the jungle back to something resembling a lawn.

The light switch by the door brought one pitiful fluorescent shop light to life. Not much, even for the small space. He stood, waiting for his eyes to adjust. A large shape at the back of the single bay caught his eye. It was covered with a tarp but was unmistakable. His heart squeezed so hard it hurt, and his mouth went dry. He stood frozen in the doorway, finding it hard to breathe. Maybe it was the dust. Or maybe some invisible force had sucked the air from the room. Sure, 'cause that could happen. He knew better. When he could finally pull air into his lungs again, he ran a hand down his face. As much as it hurt, he followed his feet into the shadows and pulled the canvas off the bike.

The 1975 Harley Davidson XL-1000 lay on its side. The rear looked exactly like he remembered it. Shiny chrome exhaust, glossy black fender. The leather saddle was stepped so the passenger sat above the rear wheel, a little higher than the driver. He could remember his mom sitting there and laughing at something his father had said. It was a bittersweet memory.

The front, however, was obliterated.

What was left of the front wheel was leaning against the wreckage, along with a cardboard box of small pieces. The forks were ripped apart, the two sides hanging at weird angles. One of the handlebars was broken off and the other was twisted around on itself, the mirrors and gauges all gone. The fuel tank was smashed in and the entire side of the bike was scratched from where it had slid a long way across blacktop and gravel.

He snapped the door closed behind him with the heel of his boot, then crouched down, near the bike. With a shaking hand, he reached out and ran his palm along the saddle, stilling as he discovered a smudge of long-dried blood on it. It was too much. Tears scorched the back of his eyes and he knew what was coming. With his hand still on the leather, he sank to his knees. Putting his other hand across his eyes, he let the grief that had been clawing its way to the surface for days pour out in great wracking sobs.

"I'm so sorry, Dad."

It was long minutes before he was able to regain his composure. As the emotions passed and the room came into focus once again, Harley came to a realization. He might not be able to fix anything else, but he could fix the bike. This small part of the disarray and disrepair and discontent could be resurrected. He could do *this* for his dad. Maybe it would somehow atone for some of his wrongs. Maybe it wouldn't, but he could try. Rolling a tall metal toolbox over from where it was tucked under the workbench, he began searching the drawers for what he'd need.

The front-end would need to be completely rebuilt. He set the mutilated wheel aside and pushed the box containing the smashed remains of the instruments and mirrors, pieces of plastic, bits of metal, and other odds and ends next to it. As he wrestled the bike upright and planted the kickstand, he wondered if Finch and Jay's still had a boneyard out back that he could scavenge parts from.

With the motorcycle as stable as possible, he pushed the garage door up so sunlight could flood the space and went to work stripping what was left of the handlebars. A lump formed in his throat as his hand tightened around the throttle, but he forged ahead. The better part of a thousand days and this was the day he would start to say goodbye. Once the last part of the handlebars was disassembled he moved on to the forks and pulled them free.

An hour later he had a good portion of the bike in pieces and he stood surveying the chaos he'd created. It was going to need parts, but knowing his dad, there might be a decent supply on hand. As he worked he started a mental list of what he'd need, but soon the list was too long to remember. Scrounging in the top drawer of the workbench, he came up with a scrap of paper and an old carpenter's pencil. A few minutes later he had covered the paper with needed parts and notes. He hoped he hadn't decided to fix the bike only to find out that he couldn't afford to.

The first task was figuring out what he already had. The top drawer had netted him the paper and pencil but looked to contain mostly paperwork. The next drawer held an assortment of wire. He fingered a spool of black electrical wire. His dad always had been a stickler for authenticity. Good to know he could rewire the whole electrical system with what was on the spool.

The next three drawers held jumbles of tools. Everything from screwdrivers and pliers to wire strippers and a volt meter. Harley closed the next to the last drawer and puffed out a sigh before pulling the bottom drawer open with the toe of his boot.

Jackpot.

No need to buy an oil filter or a new speedometer or any of a dozen other small parts. He unloaded them onto the workbench and crossed things off his list as he went. By the time he was done his list had shortened to some larger, and therefore more expensive, parts.

He turned back to the bike. To make any headway on the rebuild he was going to need a front wheel, forks, and handlebars. He patted his pocket to make sure he had his keys, grabbed the busted handlebars, and yanked the garage door closed. If anyone local was going to have parts he could pull, it would be Finch and Jay's.

Several large bikes sat in the front parking area and all four garage doors were open, revealing bikes in each bay. The shop's team of mechanics and one of the owners himself were all busy. This was an environment that he knew. In the years he'd been back in town he hadn't needed anything done on his bike that he couldn't do himself. Now it felt strange going to the shop without his dad.

"That is one magnificent bike." Harley walked up to where Lyle Jay was tinkering on the underside of a tan motorcycle with a short metal saddle. He stopped, admiring the bike, as the older man stepped out from under it.

"Darn right." The man scowled at Harley over his shoulder as he pulled a rag from his back pocket and began wiping his hands.

Lyle had been the gruffer of the two owners as far back as Harley could remember. Ragging on the mechanics and snapping at his partner, Dox Finch. Harley'd even been on the receiving end of a few choice words as a kid. It didn't appear that much had changed in ten years. "I need handlebars for an XL-1000. Any chance you might have one out back I could pull them from?"

"That from your dad's bike?" At Harley's nod, Lyle's brows drew together and the corners of his mouth turned down. "You sure you're qualified to be taking on something like that?" he asked, disdain seeping into his words.

"I think I can handle it." Harley tried not to let the man's contempt gain a foothold. As a child, he'd held the older man in higher esteem than he deserved. A former motorcycle stunt driver, Lyle could do things on two wheels that ten-year-old

Harley could only dream of. Now, nearly two decades later, it didn't matter so much what the man thought. Harley knew himself to be more than capable. Lyle had been a friend of his dad's though. So, yeah, the guy probably didn't think he was good for much of anything at all.

"We'll see." Lyle reached for the handlebars. They were in bad shape. The older man looked them over, fingering the cables and turning to look at one grotesquely bent fork that was still attached. He opened his mouth to speak, but raised voices from the far bay caught his attention.

"Hey!" he yelled across the garage. "Not sure we can help you out. There's no XL-1000 in the back right now," he said as he handed the wreckage back to Harley and walked toward the disturbance.

Harley's shoulders slumped a little. He'd just started and was already hitting a wall. As he turned to leave, someone called his name from the office in the far corner. He turned to see Dox Finch striding toward him, a wide smile on his face.

"Mr. Finch," Harley smiled and shook the outstretched hand of his father's longtime friend. "It's good to see you again, sir."

"I heard through the grapevine that you were back in town, but I wouldn't believe it until I saw it with my own two eyes."

Harley felt twelve again, standing in the shop listening to this man and his father talk bikes. As a kid, he could have listened to that slow drawl all day long. Turns out nothing had changed in that regard either.

"I've been back a while, but—"

"Say no more! I understand. Now, what brings you by today?" Harley held up the remains of the handlebars and watched the older man's face cloud and his happy lilt turn serious. "Is that from your dad's bike?"

Harley nodded. "I'd like to fix it."

Dox took the assembly and ran his hand down the forks, letting one red brake cable slide through his fingers the same way Lyle had. "I think he would have liked that," he said, emotion thickening his voice.

A familiar pain sank into Harley's chest and he couldn't keep his thoughts to himself. "I doubt that, sir."

Dox wore a troubled expression when he looked up from the handlebars. "He missed you, Harley."

The knife twisted a little, but Harley ignored it. The man could believe what he wanted to believe, but he hadn't been there the day Harley had left. He hadn't heard the things he'd said to his father in anger. He hadn't seen the fury on Cooper Beck's face. No, he doubted very much that his father had missed him for even a minute. But what good would it do to argue?

"I was hoping you had a bike out back I could pull from to replace this," he said to change the subject. "But Lyle said you don't have an XL-1000 at the moment."

"Well, now, he's right about that. Let's see what we can find for you though." The older man set the ruined parts on the counter next to a computer monitor and started clicking through screens, stopping to type something now and then. Harley leaned his forearms on the back of a stool nearby and rested one work boot on the bottom rung, waiting.

After a few minutes, and several mouse clicks, Dox grinned. "Found one!"

Harley pushed off the stool and rounded the counter to look over Dox's shoulder. The older man stepped to the side and pointed out the like-new handlebars he'd located from one of his used parts suppliers. The only problem, it was going to cost him. A lot. His heart sank. "To be honest, Dox. I can't afford to buy even used parts right now. I'm sure it's worth every penny they're asking, but I already have to get pretty darn creative with my budget."

"Understood. No worries at all." The older man gave him a long, penetrating look before clapping him on the shoulder. "It was good to see you again."

"Good to see you, too, sir." He returned the older man's smile and gave the folk on the computer screen one last longing look. "I knew the shop having one I could pull had been a long shot."

By the time he was back at the house, however, Harley had worked out a tentative plan for fixing the rest of the bike. It might be a problem that he had no handlebars, front wheel, or forks, but he wasn't giving up. Excitement bubbled up in him as he pushed the garage door up, throwing light on the bike again. Of the many jobs he'd had, working as a grease monkey in a Missoula, Montana motorcycle shop had been the one he'd enjoyed the most. Thanks to hours upon hours in this very garage with his father, there hadn't been much he didn't already know how to do. Now it was time to put those skills to work.

As the minutes collected into hours, Harley organized the garage. The tour he'd missed would have gone out and returned by now. Noah had no doubt grabbed Gage or Owen to fill his place. He was very thankful for his boss. No, not boss. Friend. And he owed his friend an apology. Satisfied with the now-neat garage, he switched off the light and locked up. Walking toward the shop a tune came to mind and without thinking he began to whistle. It took him nearly to The Green before he realized he was whistling the hymn Erin had been singing that morning, *Savior, Like a Shepherd Lead Me.*

The slip of paper had been neatly folded and tucked into the frame of his front door when Lyle arrived home late that night. He'd plucked it out and shoved it into his pocket when he went for his keys, forgetting about it until moments ago. Now he sat at his desk, staring at the scrawled message and trying to quell the rising panic as he held the phone to his ear.

"Did you get my note?" rasped a quiet voice on the other end of the line.

He tried to answer, but fear was strangling him. He hated fear. It was so weak.

"I'll take your silence to mean you did. You of all people should know that there's always someone watching."

"What do you want?" he managed to ask.

"You seem to be under the misconception that you are untouchable. As someone who knows a little bit about that, let me just say... You are not."

The fear now tasted acrid. No one had ever figured it out. No one knew. He had played his cards carefully. The only way someone could know... "And you—" He hated how his voice didn't hold strong and swallowed before trying again. "And you are?"

"I think the last three years speak for themselves. Even you haven't figured out who I am. No one in this pitiful little town has a clue. You, on the other hand, are starting to get sloppy. Someone is going to notice and I don't want anything tracing back to me."

"Like you said, no one in this town has a clue. I can do anything I want."

"Your arrogance is going to be your downfall."

"And yours won't?"

"Just don't try anything stupid."

The line went dead and he stared at the note, reading and rereading it.

You've had three years, free and clear
No more
Your sins have found you out

The dilemma? Which sins were the note referring to? He let out a mirthless laugh. After all, there were so many. He thought he knew. What had possessed him to steal what amounted to millions of dollars from Rocco? A crime of opportunity. But mobsters have long memories and their successors don't play nice with thieves.

Why hadn't he run then and there?

But he knew why. He'd lied to himself for three years. Told himself he had plenty of time. Told himself he could pay the money back. Told himself that he was close to rectifying what he'd done. He'd even told himself that no one would ever figure it out. It seemed almost cruel to have his debts called in now.

Maybe he shouldn't have flaunted it quite so much, but what was the point of having it if he couldn't enjoy it. It wasn't like he advertised his wealth. Not really. The house had been an extravagance, yes, but he'd been sick and tired of living in the dumpy little cottage near the shop. He'd wanted luxury. He'd earned it. The rest... no one was the wiser. Because no one in this hick town had a clue.

Turning toward the wall safe his shoulders slumped. In reality, he was well short of the amount needed, time had run out, and someone definitely knew what he'd done. What was the price going to be? He'd exhausted his usual avenues for funds. If he was going to pay up, or even if he was going to disappear, he needed more cash. Fast.

A few weeks before, he'd come up with a simple solution. Sell back the extravagant purchase he'd made with money that didn't belong to him. Then he'd have what he needed when the time came. But the incompetent little wanna-be art dealer hadn't been any help at all. No, she'd smiled her naive little smile and told him she wasn't interested. If she only knew what he was capable of she might have at least offered him the respect of having someone more qualified look at the pieces. They were worth a fortune.

Swinging his chair back around he drummed his fingers on the glossy desk. The note was unsettling, but it was most likely Rocco's successor, whoever that may be, keeping him on his toes. After all, the status quo hadn't changed in three years. Why now?

However, as he sat in silence, other possible sins wormed their way to the surface making his skin crawl. Theft was only the beginning. Oh, the things he'd done! Some filthy, but necessary for his survival. Others done in the name of cleaning up other people's messes. Those shouldn't count. Not really.

Swallowing away the anxiety that skittered through his chest, Lyle placed the note next to the other items in his safe.

His heartbeat thundered in his ears and his palms itched to reach for something in the safe. Something to calm his nerves.

No. Not right now.

Not when he needed to stay alert and formulate a plan.

He took a deep breath, hoping that would suffice until he could settle the tension another way. After all, he wasn't addicted to the stuff like the weaklings at the end of the line. He just liked to let it wash away his worries now and then.

Reaching behind a stack of cash, he picked up one of the many bags of pills lining the inside of the safe and fingered the contents through the plastic. Yup, he still had options. He wasn't giving up. Not yet. However, until he figured out exactly what he was going to do, his best bet would be to continue as though nothing was out of the ordinary.

Keep the status quo.

With one eye over his shoulder.

CHAPTER FOUR

When Erin rounded the corner onto Carriage Street Saturday morning she chuckled. Today, Coriander Wren was an elf. Hopping from one foot to the other with excitement, the little sprite of a woman was wearing an elfin hat that was almost as long as she was tall. She'd traded her flouncy skirt for a pair of wildly patterned leggings and the huge bright orange wool sweater she wore hung well past her knees. And she looked adorable. Erin snorted out a laugh imagining herself in the same outfit. No, she'd stick to her jeans and flannel shirts, thank you very much. Although she had traded out her steel-toed boots for a pair of flip-flops and added a, much smaller than Cori's, wool sweater.

"Are you ready?" her friend called up the street.

"I am. Where do we get our kayaks?" Erin asked as she accepted Cori's hug.

"I called Noah the other day after you said yes to going with me. He's got it all set up! Ooooh! This is going to be so much fun!" Cori skipped ahead of her up the corner steps of the Acadian Adventures shop and pulled the door open with its wooden paddle handle. The outside of the shop was a mix of traditional and whimsy, with its weathered gray shingles, dark aqua trim, and yellow mullions in the windows. The inside was cozy and smelled of balsam fir. Knotty pine paneled walls were lined with racks of sweatshirts and shelves of hats, t-shirts, and water bottles.

"Gemma!" Cori squealed and ran around to hug the teenager working the register.

"Hi, Cori," Gemma said as she returned the hug, a wide smile revealing a mouth full of braces.

"I spoke to Noah about borrowing a couple of kayaks. Is he here?"

"Oh. I think so? Maybe. He was getting a tour ready to go out. Let me check." The girl's flame-red hair bounced off her shoulders as she spun toward the door behind the counter.

A few moments later a tall man loped into the shop with a grin on his handsome face. Despite the chill in the air, he wore only a t-shirt, a loose pair of jeans, and flip-flops. His blonde hair was in desperate need of either a trim or an elastic, and he pushed it out of his face as he approached.

"Cori!" He swept her off the floor in a bear hug.

"Noah!" Cori started laughing as he scooped her up and spun around before setting her back on solid ground. "How's Lily?"

A boyish grin and a slight blush spread across his face. "She's great."

Cori turned and gestured toward Erin. "This is my friend Erin. Erin, Noah Kingsley. And Lily is his totally-gorgeous and friendliest-ever girlfriend. You'll love her!"

"Nice to meet you." Erin stuck out her hand and Noah took it with a firm, friendly handshake and a smile.

He squinted his eyes at her for a second and then broke into a grin. "You sing in the choir at church, right?"

"Sure do."

"Nice to meet you, Erin. I've been trying to meet everyone at church, but gosh it's hard over the summer!"

"I hear you. There will be a smaller congregation over the winter, so we'll be able to tell tourists from locals."

"Ayuh! Listen, I've got a tour getting ready to go out, but let's head back and grab your life jackets and we'll get you all set."

Tipping her head back, Cori grinned up at him. "I'm so excited!"

The three of them headed through the door behind the register into a backroom that was larger than the storefront. Seven people milled around in various stages of fitting their life vests and filling dry bags with cameras and water bottles. A young man with wild blonde curls and a huge grin raised a hand in greeting as they came into the room, but quickly went back to helping one of the kids. Noah walked over to the wall of shelves and stood with his hands on his hips, looking over the vests.

"I think this one will fit you," he said as he took one off a shelf and handed it to Cori. He paused, looking at Cori's giant sweater, and shook his head. "You can't wear that sweater under the life vest, you'll never get it secured properly."

"No worries." Cori pulled the enormous sweater off over her head, taking the elf hat with it. Underneath was layer upon layer of thermal shirts.

"Better." Noah tried to hide his smile and went back to the shelves. "And maybe this one for you."

Erin took the one he handed her. She was glad she'd grabbed her windbreaker on the way out the door. There was a noticeable bite to the air. She was sure once they got out on the water it was going to be brisk, but the sun was brilliant and there was no fog today. It was going to be gorgeous. She pulled off the wool sweater and was fitting the life preserver over her own thermal shirt when Noah continued.

"I figured you'd need someone to drive you and the kayaks down to Eastern Harbor, so I asked one of my guys here to go with you today. He'll drive you down and paddle out to Blueberry Island with you."

"Harley!" Cori exclaimed.

Erin spun from where she was facing the wall trying to get the clasp on her life jacket untwisted. It was obvious Cori already knew the man standing beside Noah and she jumped up to give him a big hug. Erin was sure her friend knew everyone, or just about everyone, on the island. In Cori's dreamy, fairy-like existence everyone was a dear friend.

"Hey, Cori," he said, catching her and returning the hug. Then he met Erin's eyes. "Hey."

"Nice to see you again." Did her voice squeak? It sounded

like it squeaked. She swallowed and smiled. The next several hours had just gone from a fun girls' day to an exercise in concentration. Concentrating on *not* concentrating on Mr. Tall Dark and Handsome. She should just give up now.

"I've got to get this tour on the water," Noah continued. He flashed a lopsided smile their way before turning back to Harley. "You're all set?"

"Sure thing, boss," he replied with a salute.

Noah chuckled as he rejoined the group. The other young man had gotten everyone situated and they were headed out the door in less than a minute. Once the place was quiet, Harley grabbed dry bags off the shelf and handed them to Erin and Cori for their sweaters.

"I already grabbed three kayaks and put them in the back of the truck. We'll drive down to Eastern Harbor, put in there at the cove, and head out to Blueberry Island from there. Have either of you ever been in a sea kayak before?"

"Oh, my goodness, yes!" Cori answered immediately, her bubbly effervescent personality coming through in every word. "I love being out on the water in a kayak! I went twice two summers ago right after I took over the gallery. Noah was ever so nice and let me tag along on a couple of his tours, and, oh, my goodness, I just loved it! This is the first time I've kayaked to the island, though. I usually get one of the Williams to help me get there."

Harley was doing an admirable job keeping up with Cori's monologue. "The Williams? The guys who own the lobster pound down on the town pier?"

"Yes! One of them usually takes me over when they head out to pull traps, and then on their way back they swing by and pick me up. They're so sweet. But I thought this would be more fun today, especially since the weather is so... so... perfect!"

Harley flicked a glance Erin's way and she shrugged. "No, I've never been in a sea kayak before."

"Well, there are a few things you should know," he said and launched into an oft-repeated pre-trip safety talk, covering things like staying with the group and what to do if the boat capsized. Erin tried to listen, but the man was distracting. He stood, arms crossed over a wide chest, feet set wide apart, rocking back on his heels and then onto the balls of his feet. As he rocked, the muscles in his arms rippled and the tattoos danced.

No bad-boys, no bad-boys, no bad-boys, she repeated to herself.

This day was going to be so long. Once they got to the island Harley would go do something else while she and Cori searched for sea glass. Right? Because if he didn't, she doubted she could spend the entire day next to the man and keep her wits about her.

As they exited the back room into the brilliant morning sun, Cori looped her arm through Harley's and grinned up at him. Oh. Erin felt a twinge of something in her chest that just might be jealousy. Well, now she was being stupid! First of all, Cori treated everyone the same. Big grins, lots of hugs. There was no difference between how she was treating Harley and how she'd treated Erin the other day. Yep, it was stupid. Besides, she'd already decided 'no bad-boys'. Ever again. So there was that.

Erin squelched the feeling. She was going to enjoy today and she wasn't going to let being a third wheel dampen her spirits.

It was a perfect day on the island. Light breeze, not a cloud in the sky. Autumn in Maine painted the hills and mountains that dotted the area in vivid color. Maple and oak in brilliant shades of red and cranberry and mahogany, aspen and poplar and birch in shades of yellow, and the brilliant orange of sugar maple interspersed with the rich greens of pine, spruce, hemlock, fir, and cedar. They all added to the unique beauty that was Maine and lured tourists in long after the cold air had driven the beachcombers home.

When Harley took their life preservers and dry bags to put in the back of the truck, leaving the girls to climb into the cab, Erin stopped her friend from climbing onto the seat.

"Cori," she hissed. "That's the guy who owns Coop's place."

Cori's eyes were huge and strangely innocent. "Umm…" Her friend glanced over her shoulder to where he was slipping behind the wheel and turned back with an odd look on her face. "Yeah, I know."

Before Erin could question her further, Cori leaped into the cab of the truck and parked herself in the middle seat. She was already talking before Harley had a chance to start the truck, and the non-stop commentary continued most of the way to Eastern Harbor. At least it was varied, covering everything from people she thought they all knew to pieces of art she'd sold over the summer. She talked about places she'd been, the new developments that were coming in, and how she hated to see some things change and couldn't wait to see others change. Harley nodded and added comments that made Erin believe he was listening to Cori's chatter. He didn't smile, but at least the frown from earlier was gone.

In no time they were pulling into the parking lot opposite the beach and Harley started unloading the kayaks. Erin tried to help by grabbing hers but quickly gave up.

"The way he lifted them made me think they weighed almost nothing at all," she whispered to Cori. "But they're heavier than they look!"

"That's because of all those delicious muscles he has," Cori said with a hum of approval.

Yes. Yes, it was.

While Harley parked the truck, she and Cori managed to wrestle the kayaks down to the water. In no time they were skimming across the frigid green swells.

"Ladies. Up ahead you'll see Blueberry Island. A picturesque little chunk of land poking out of the Atlantic Ocean to the southeast of Summer Harbor." Harley's strong tour-guide voice carried across the water. "It's home to just over a hundred residents, a lighthouse, some hiking trails, and a mile of pebble beach."

"That's where I go hunting for sea glass!" Cori exclaimed before tipping to the side and screaming as she almost capsized.

Erin hung back a little as Harley paused his spiel to help Cori figure out paddling. The wind blew her hair free of its elastic and she pulled it loose, letting it blow around her face. It had been a long time since she had taken a day off. A very long time. She was determined to enjoy it.

Getting a feel for the boat beneath her pretty quickly, she pulled around the other two. She didn't get too far ahead. Just enough that she felt a bit like she was alone. Closing her eyes, she turned her face toward the sun and breathed in the salty sea air. This was a slice of Heaven.

"You might not have been on a kayak before, but you seem to have caught on fast," Harley said, making her jump.

She turned toward him and smiled. "It didn't seem that hard to pick up. Put the paddle in, pull the boat forward, keep my balance."

He chuckled. "Pretty much."

"Isn't this fantastic?" Cori squealed as she skimmed up on the other side of Erin's kayak.

Erin grinned at her friend. "It is indeed."

Never before had he been so glad that he'd grabbed his sunglasses on the way out the door. Not because of the glare off the water, although it was substantial as they paddled into the sun. No, he was relieved because try as he might, he could not keep his eyes from drifting to wherever Erin was. The contrasts between her and Cori were considerable and he had to stifle a chuckle. What was it his father would have called them? Mutt and Jeff. Cori was adorable in a little-sister-tagging-along way. She was bouncy and exuberant and could be a friend to anyone. Erin, on the other hand, met Cori's high spirits with quiet joy. She didn't giggle and talk non-stop. Instead, she offered honest smiles and thoughtful comments. There was a peace about her that he couldn't explain, but that drew him. He'd noticed it the day before and nothing had changed in the few hours since.

It was all he could do to concentrate on where they were going.

He pulled out ahead of her kayak hoping a little distance would get his head back where it ought to be. She seemed like a nice girl and he didn't deserve a nice girl. He needed to keep his thoughts on what he was, who he was, and not let them drift back to her.

"This is incredible," she sighed, startling him as she pulled up next to his boat and matched his paddling stroke for stroke. "I can see why you'd want this to be your office."

He tried to keep his eyes on the island ahead of them, but couldn't help stealing a glance sideways, murmuring a non-committal sound. She was lovely. He nearly swore as his mind drifted to what it would feel like to run his fingers through her amber hair. He swallowed the blue word that was on the tip of his tongue and made a mental note to repay Noah for torturing him today.

"You don't seem happy to be out here. I hope we didn't pull you away from something. When Cori invited me, she said we were just borrowing the kayaks. We didn't mean to—"

"No, it's fine," he cut her off. "There wasn't anything else." He tried again to put some distance between them, but she just matched him for speed and after a few strokes he stopped paddling, realizing that Cori was several kayak lengths behind them.

"Don't wait for me!" she yelled. "I just have to take twice as many strokes as you guys!" Her voice was charged with sarcasm and Erin and Harley both laughed. While they waited, Erin took her sunglasses off and looked at him, squinting a little bit. He shifted uncomfortably in his seat and looked away.

"Sorry," she said as she puffed out a breath and put her glasses back on. "That was weird. It's just..." she let her voice trail off and looked away. "Every once in a while I think we've met before. I just can't put my finger on it."

Before he could assure her that they had never met before yesterday, Cori paddled between them.

"Oh, my goodness! I am loving this, but my shoulders are going to kill tomorrow."

Harley winced. "Yes. Yes, they will."

"How much farther?" she panted.

Harley met Erin's gaze across the top of Cori's blonde hair. She was biting her lip trying not to laugh and he couldn't help chuckling, too. It was so easy to be happy around her. "Just a bit."

Erin hung back with Cori and didn't try to engage him in conversation the rest of their time on the water. Part of him was glad. He wouldn't have to avoid her if she was the one doing the avoiding. Another part, a teeny tiny part that was almost non-existent, yearned for someone to care enough to try harder.

Her smile made a pleasant feeling warm his chest and he almost let himself return it. Almost. *You don't get to have that,* he reminded himself. Pulling his kayak onto the rocky shore. He'd found a million ways to punish himself. Not getting to have the happily ever after was only one of them.

The two ladies pulled up onto the shore a few minutes later. Harley reached down and helped Cori out of her kayak, then hoisted it and carried it onto the beach. "I'll just wait here for you ladies," he said to Cori as he returned to fetch Erin's.

"I thought you were coming with us." Disappointment rang in Cori's voice. She pulled her dry bag out of the front of her kayak. "I brought extra lunch," she added, sweetening the invitation. The bag bulged with what Harley assumed was her sweater the size of a tent and a picnic lunch.

"Me too," Erin added more shyly, pulling her dry bag out as well.

He hadn't expected to be spending the day with them. Get them there and get them home, Noah had said. He searched for an excuse but came up empty. 'I don't want to' seemed rude. Plus, it wasn't true. "Sure. I mean, I guess I could... if you need me to. Yeah. Yeah, I can... I can go with you." *Well, that sounded intelligent. Not the brightest bulb on the tree, huh, Beck?* He knew his face had settled into a scowl. They wanted him to come with them? Fine. But they got what they got.

As they walked, he hung back watching them talking and laughing and pointing at different rocks and bits of this and that. Cori had a colorful cloth bag slung over her shoulder and every once in a while she would reach down and pick something out of the pebbles and stick it in the bag. The thing reminded him of the crazy-quilt his parents had kept on their bed, and he wondered momentarily if it was still there.

When morning turned to afternoon, they settled on a large flat rock overlooking the crashing waves of the returning tide and unpacked their lunch. Like the woman herself, Cori's was an eclectic mixture. Cheese and crackers, dried fruit, miniature Halloween candy, and homemade lime-fizz soda. Erin spread her contribution out as well. A thermos of hot coffee, slightly sweet with too much cream for his liking, some rolls, sharp cheese, and a container of roast turkey.

Harley had to admit that he was glad he came with them. He would have been bored out of his mind sitting on the shore for the entire day by the kayaks, waiting for them to return. Not to mention hungry.

"So this is what a day off feels like," Erin said with her face toward the sun.

Cori turned to Harley. "What she means is that she works all the time. All. The. Time. If I hadn't invited her today she would be at work. Sometimes a friend has to do what a friend has to do." She shot Erin a look that said she knew exactly what Erin would be doing if she wasn't on Blueberry Island. "I mean, she's been back on the island for weeks and has worked almost every one of those days."

Erin shrugged. "It pays the bills."

Harley nodded. He got that. "You haven't lived on the island long?"

"Just a month or so... this time," Erin said. "I've been away for a while."

He got that, too. He didn't remember her from… before. But that didn't mean much. She'd have been a kid when he left. He pieced together a sandwich with some of Erin's turkey and Cori's cheese, then turned toward the water to eat. The girls talked and laughed, obviously friends from when Erin had lived in Summer Harbor the first time. They grew quiet and he turned to find that Erin had finished her sandwich and gotten up, heading to where a small waterfall was cutting its way across some rocks before running into the ocean.

Keeping her eyes on Erin, Cori scooted closer to where Harley was sitting. "So…?"

"What?"

"So…," Cori said again with a hint of exasperation. "Isn't she great?"

If asked, Harley would have sworn he was incapable of blushing, and yet he was sure that his face was scarlet. He had to get this whole 'Harley's an open book' thing under control! "I don't know what you're talking about," he grumbled.

"Oh, pish-posh," Cori said, taking his arm and looping hers around his elbow. "You know exactly what I'm talking about. Listen. Here's the thing. I don't know most of your story Harley, but I do know this: We need someone to share our story. A story with only one character isn't very interesting and the problem never seems to get solved. The plot stagnates and there's no dialogue. But a story with even just two characters in it has spark and depth and passion. You need another character in your story."

He looked away but didn't shake her hands off his arm. "That's not in the cards for me." He didn't want to hurt her feelings, but she was right when she said she didn't know his story. If she did he doubted she would have been playing matchmaker between him and her friend.

"Aw, how come?"

"People get hurt." He glanced over his shoulder. "She seems nice. I don't want her getting hurt."

Cori sighed and then crawled onto her knees to kiss him on the cheek. "Just think about it, OK?"

When Erin got to the waterfall, she pushed her sleeves up to wash her hands, wiping them on her jeans to dry them. When she turned around, Cori was snuggled up to Harley and kissing him on the cheek. Erin sighed. Her friend was probably half in love with the man already. A pesky disappointment settled over her and instead of heading back to their picnic spot, she turned to look out across the water toward the picture-perfect harbor. Why did she even care? It wasn't like she was looking for romance anyway. And even if she was, she wouldn't consider the bad-boy covered in tattoos. No matter how friendly or good-looking he was, she didn't go for his type. Not anymore. Not for a long time. Not since...

Sinking to a nearby rock, Erin pulled her knees up to her chest. She'd thought briefly of not returning to the island after trade school. So much had changed. Everything important anyway. But in the end, this was the only place she'd ever called home and she needed home. Besides, where else would she go? For all her wishing, she still hadn't figured out how to patch things up with her mother. Maybe if she could find a way to rebuild that bridge she would have more options for where to start putting down roots.

For now, she lived here, and she was... mostly... happy. Busy but happy. Work had been taking up most of her days and any spare time had been spent first cleaning and organizing the workshop in the little garage and then building the wooden boxes that she sold at Cori's gallery. She worked seven to five Monday through Friday for Finnley's. Overtime was a given and most Saturdays she found herself back at a job site trying to finish something before the rest of the crew returned on Monday morning. Evenings and Sunday afternoons were spent in her workshop. It didn't leave much time alone with her thoughts, but then again, that just might be for the best.

She sat for a while, only heading back when Cori had started packing up. Her friend tossed the leftover bits of lunch to the seagulls who swooped in to gobble up anything they were allowed. Erin could hear her friend's delighted laugh and even their stoic guide had a bit of a smile as one of the gulls danced sideways across their path in hopes of more treats.

Harley side-stepped the bird. "I think I'll head back to the boats now, make sure they're ready to get on the water. We're not in a rush, but you should probably start heading back toward where we came ashore. I doubt you want to still be on the water when the sun goes down."

It felt like they had walked for miles, but Erin knew that the pace had been slow and they weren't all that far away from where they'd started. Harley took off, hands in his pockets, head down. Watching where he stepped? No, it was more than that. She wondered at the slump of his shoulders. You would think he'd be a little bit more chipper, what with Cori flirting with him. Maybe he'd turned her down.

She tossed the gulls the remnants of her lunch while her friend waited. As soon as she was packed up, Cori slipped her arm through Erin's and they set off back up the beach. After a few minutes, it became obvious that Cori was trying to slow their pace to let Harley get well ahead of them.

"So...?" Cori finally whispered.

Erin turned and looked down at her friend. "So..., what?"

"Oh, my goodness, the two of you are impossible! So... what do you think of Harley?"

"He's good at his job."

The exasperated sound her friend made was amusing. "No, I mean what do you *think* of him?"

She knew what her heart was saying. It was beating faster every time she looked at the man and she kept finding reasons to be just ever so slightly closer. However, if Cori was interested in him that would not be happening anymore. "He's alright I guess."

"Alright? You guess?" Cori hissed.

"Yeah, I mean if you like him he must be decent, right?"

"Me?" Cori looked confused. "Harley's like... well... like all the other guys in town. Big brother material more than anything." With a giant roll of her eyes and a long-suffering sigh, the impish girl continued. "There's not a single man in all of Summer Harbor that interests me. They're sweet and adorable and friendly and lovable and handsome." She nodded toward Harley's retreating form. "Even smoking hot. But none of them is my person. You, on the other hand? I can totally see you with a guy like Harley.

"You know I don't go for bad-boys," Erin said stiffly as Cori stopped to snatch another bit of sea glass out of the rocks. "You are unbelievable! I can't even see the bits of glass, but you catch every last one."

"It's a gift. Now, what I was saying..."

Erin rolled her eyes. So much for changing the subject. "Hmmm?"

"Here's the thing, I know some of your story, at least a few of the juicy parts, and I think you need somebody to share it."

"I'm not so sure about that," Erin replied dryly.

Cori sighed but dropped the discussion. Finally. She didn't stay quiet for long, though. Within a few steps, she'd launched into a running monologue on the town-wide festival that had just been announced for the following year. As they walked she gave Erin a rundown of the food, art, music, and fireworks from festivals in the past and how she thought the upcoming one would compare.

When they reached Harley he was sitting on a rock and had all three kayaks lined up on the shore waiting and ready. "All set?"

"Today was fantastic!" Cori said in a sing-song voice, a huge smile lighting up her face. She held up her bag of treasures. It was nearly full. Erin shook her head. She'd picked up maybe ten pieces along the way and, to be honest, that was all she'd seen. Good thing she worked with wood.

Harley stowed the bag safely in the front of his kayak leaving the compartments on theirs for the dry bags. Cori began nibbling on her nail and looking at the sky.

"Everything alright?" Harley asked.

"Do we have like maybe thirty more minutes?" she asked.

"I don't see why not."

"I could use some driftwood to go with the sea glass and I saw some back aways. Mind if I run and get it?"

"By all means," he said, waving a hand in the general direction of the beach. Cori clapped her hands together and scurried down the pebbles, skipping and twirling as she went.

Harley sat back down on the rock where he'd taken up residence while waiting and turned something over in his hand. "I found this on the way back. Guessing Cori would want it." He dropped a piece of dark lavender sea glass, polished smooth by the rocks and waves, into Erin's hand. Where his fingers brushed hers the skin felt momentarily singed.

What had Cori said? Smoking hot? Erin made a mental note to thank Cori later for putting *that* thought in her head. Not that it wasn't already there! Now that Cori had said the words aloud it was doubly hard not to think about it. She nodded before slipping the glass into her pocket. Perching on a rock ahead of him so that he wasn't even in her peripheral vision, she tried to ignore him.

Sitting and looking at the ocean, Erin realized how much she missed the tranquility of being near the water. She lived a stone's throw from the shore in Summer Harbor but hadn't set foot near it in the weeks she'd been back. Standing up, she kicked off her flip-flops near the kayaks and began picking her way down to the water. She was determined to get her toes wet. The gravel gave way to larger rocks covered in seaweed the closer she got to the sloshing waves and she had to choose each step carefully.

Erin wasn't sure what happened. One minute she was standing with the waves rushing in around her ankles and the next she was airborne. There was just enough time to realize that this was going to hurt, a lot, before she found herself held off the ground with Harley's strong arms around her. It was hard to tell if her breathlessness came from the near-fall or her proximity to his muscular chest.

"I've gotcha," Harley said, one large hand splayed across her back keeping her out of the frothy water as it rushed back out to sea over their feet.

She scrambled for a footing and slipped again, reaching out to fist her hand in the soft cotton of his t-shirt, afraid she'd fall. She needn't have worried. Harley's arms came around her, holding her. The hand on her back pressed her against his chest, the other hand, light and gentle, held her hip. She blinked, her mind racing for words. All the racing stopped, however, when his eyes moved to her lips. She tightened her grip, hope and doubt battling for the upper hand as she leaned in ever so slight—

"I'm back!" Cori called.

Harley jumped as if he'd been scalded by her touch, setting her upright as quickly as humanly possible before snatching his hands away and thrusting them into his pockets.

Erin stumbled for words and finally settled on, "Thank you. I'm not sure what just happened."

"Slippery rock, seaweed, tide coming in fast." He shrugged his shoulders and stepped away, but stood within arm's reach, as though fearful she might fall again.

He'd shed his flip-flops too and she noticed he wiggled his toes as the water rushed over them the same as she'd been doing. It was such a boyish thing to do for a grown man. She turned away to hide a smile, hoping he hadn't caught her watching him.

Harley turned toward where Cori was coming up the beach and started laughing. Erin turned, too, and snorted out a very undignified laugh that she quickly clamped her hand over. It was a good thing driftwood was lighter than its fresh equivalent. Cori's arms were loaded to the point Erin doubted the girl could see over it. Harley jogged to intercept and took the pile from her. "I probably got too much. Yeah, too much. I can see that now. I mean I overdid it. I shouldn't have been so greedy, but it was just... so pretty and I wanted it all and—"

Harley was still chuckling. "No worries. I got it." He rummaged around in the compartment of his kayak and came up with two large bungee cords. Using them, he secured the entire armload to his kayak.

Cori clapped her hands and threw her arms around him. "Thank you, Harley!" While he couldn't see her face she made eye contact with Erin and mouthed 'good guy, not bad-boy.' Erin rolled her eyes, but couldn't help the smile that tugged at her lips. Maybe he wasn't *all* bad.

Long, black shadows ate up any leftover light from the late evening sun. Street lights didn't reach far into the yard where he stood in the concealing shroud of a stand of fir trees. The man in front of him was little more than a shadow himself, having materialized moments before from God only knew where. He didn't like meeting in person. And outdoors at that. Too many eyes, too much chance of being caught. But three years of looking over his shoulder for the law, or the Angel of Death, or simply his past catching up with him had pushed him beyond reason. Beyond even caring anymore if someone found him out.

"Is it all here?"

The other man snapped the envelope into his hand. "Yes, it's all there." Disgust lined the man's voice. "You're vile. You know that, right? Your soul's as black as the shadows tonight."

"Save it. I sold my soul a long time ago."

"It would be a real shame if someone found out your secret the way you seem to find everyone else's."

A fission of fear snaked down his spine and he hardened his face to avoid giving anything away. This imbecile didn't know anything. Couldn't know.

Could he?

No. He glared at the envelope in his hand and looked back up at the unremarkable man before him. Unlike his other... he'd be honest, patsies... this one didn't appear to have the money to pay up, but he could get it. Lyle didn't know how, nor did he care. He opened the envelope and fingered the contents.

"Hey, I said it's there, it's there. What? You don't trust me?"

He let out a cheerless laugh. "No, actually, I don't trust you at all. But I don't need to trust you. As long as we have an understanding there's no need for trust."

The other man scoffed. "Some understanding. Remind me again what I get out of this deal?"

"What do you get? What do you get?!" His voice turned to a snarl. "What you get, *Arnie,* is to not have the cops show up at your door to arrest you. What you get, *Arnie,* is to keep living this make-believe life you've fabricated. You get to sleep at night not worrying that it will all flit away in the morning with one phone call from me."

Even in the dark, he could see the man's face contorting with anger, but he knew he had him right where he wanted him. Desperate. Desperate people would do just about anything to keep a hold of what they cherished most. His task was simple: figure out what that was and exploit it. So far it was working quite well.

He sank back into the shadows and waited for the other man to leave before slipping the envelope into this pocket and emerging from the darkness of the trees onto the sidewalk. He whistled while he walked and tucked his hands in his pockets, fingering the envelope that meant he was one step closer to living without constant fear.

CHAPTER FIVE

As usual, a restless night had Harley up before the sun. Standing by the window of his room above Noah's shop, he watched the meager activity beginning on the street below. He groaned. What had he been thinking? Erin was respectable. She was a good girl. A nice girl. Harley didn't get to have good or nice. What had come over him, flirting with her? Nearly kissing her, for goodness sake!

Before he could stop himself, he pulled his arm back and slammed his fist into the wooden frame of the window. The impact was hard enough to split two of his knuckles. Resting his forehead against the cold glass, he squeezed his eyes shut. When his knuckles began to throb he straightened and grabbed a bandana off the top of his dresser, holding it against the abraded skin. Beating himself up figuratively was one thing, doing it literally against a piece of wood was probably not his brightest idea.

The heavy punching bag suspended in the corner beckoned, and his gloves sat within reach on the dresser. He grabbed them and pulled them on. Tightening the cuffs centered him and he began to warm up. He was glad there were only two other guys still living there, both on the other side of the apartment. If the smack of bone against wood hadn't woken them up, the beating he was about to give the bag probably wouldn't either. He walked across his room, dancing from one foot to the other. He gave the bag a tentative jab with his left hand, followed by a solid punch. At first, he held off with his right knowing it was going to burn where his knuckles were already sore. Breathing hard and with sweat running down his neck to soak the back of his T-shirt, he eventually let his right hand connect.

He'd been right. It stung.

He welcomed it. Wanted it to hurt. Wanted every punch to hurt him more than it damaged the bag. He danced around, light on his feet, with one hand up as if protecting his face. Hit after hit slammed into the hard surface. Again and again and again.

The day before, he'd already been standing with his flip-flops kicked off next to hers when he'd seen the wave coming, higher and harder than the rest. He had no idea what he'd been thinking, whether he was going to go stand next to her or what. It seemed a little presumptuous to think that she would want him near her, but he'd headed in her general direction just the same and stepped behind her just in time to keep her from falling backward onto the rocks.

And then she'd been in his arms and the feeling that exploded through him when he held her had left him dazed and angry. Not at her, but angry at himself. Angry at putting himself in a position like that, a position to feel something.

On top of that, he'd had Cori's suggestion rattling around in his brain like a pinball. Did he like Erin? What wasn't to like? Both fists now pounded the bag harder, but the truth remained unchanged. She was everything he could want. Funny, strong, smart. Beautiful. If he was still the kind of man who let himself dream about happy endings, he could picture himself dreaming up one with Erin. He clenched his teeth to keep from swearing and hit the bag even harder.

By the time he slowed, he was so out of breath that he could barely stand. Sweat had soaked his T-shirt. His tattoos glistened with it, and his arms ached clear up past the shoulders. He was pulling a towel off the hook on the back of his door when there was a gentle knock. A growl hissed from his lips. He wasn't in the mood to talk to anybody.

"Yeah, I know! I was making too much noise," he said as he threw the door open, but jumped at finding Noah leaning against the jam. His friend just gave him a knowing look and stood, waiting for Harley to say something. Yeah, that wasn't happening. Pulling the towel over his face under the guise of drying it, he stood and waited. There was no way he was going to make eye contact with his friend. Feeling ashamed and dangerously close to tears, he turned away. What a pansy. Noah stayed leaning against the jam, hands in his pockets.

"What do you want?" Harley growled. Noah just stood, quiet. Finally, Harley pulled the towel down and turned toward his friend.

Upon seeing Harley's face, Noah finally spoke. "Aw, man. You OK?"

"I have the morning off and I'm beating my knuckles bloody on a punching bag. How do you think I am?" Noah held his hands up in defense. Harley clamped his jaw closed on a retort before turning to face his friend square on. "Sorry, you didn't deserve that."

Noah just shrugged. "I'm worried about you. It's been a rough two and a half years, but the last few days seem to have been especially brutal."

Harley looked away. If there was anybody he could talk to about what was going on inside his head it was Noah. Clyde's weathered face popped into his mind. He wouldn't mind a bit of the old man's wisdom, either.

When he'd arrived in town, roaring in on his bike that April, he'd needed a job. A lot of places wouldn't hire him because of the tats, or maybe it'd been his surly attitude. For years he'd sought out construction crews where the boss didn't ask a lot of questions. Ones that paid you under the table and didn't care if you decided to move on between Friday night and Monday morning. Not a lot of those in Summer Harbor.

Noah had taken a chance on him that first month and hadn't stopped taking chances on him since. He was a true friend and if you couldn't talk to your friends who could you talk to? A thought slipped through Harley's mind. *There is a friend that stays closer than a brother.* At least he thought that was how the verse went. Why were Bible verses popping into his mind?

He shook his head but looked back at Noah. "I feel completely out of control," he said at last. "I came back for one reason. I can't settle that and now it feels like there's no way to make things... anything right." Noah stood, not speaking, just waiting. Harley sighed and crossed his arms over his chest. "And I started to fix Dad's bike."

"Seriously? That's huge."

"Yeah." Harley pulled the towel down over his face again. "Then there's Erin," he said, finally pulling the towel away and tossing it with frustration into the hamper.

"Erin?"

"Cori's friend?"

Noah cocked his head to one side and raised an eyebrow in confusion. "What about her?"

"We had a good time yesterday."

It took a beat before Noah nodded his head. "You had a good time yesterday and now you're beating yourself up for it."

Harley blew out a breath. "I like her. My past though... I don't get a second chance like her. The things I did..." He hung his head and Noah reached out to squeeze his shoulder. Without looking up, he continued. "There's more. She's the 'guy' fixing the back porch."

"Whoa. For real?"

"I don't know what to do." He said when he finally brought his eyes up to meet his friend's

"Well," Noah said, keeping his voice calm and even. "I know exactly what *I'm* going to do." Harley raised an eyebrow in question. "I'm going to head upstairs and get on my knees and pray for you."

Harley was stunned. "You... you'd do that?"

"Of course," Noah said. "You're my friend. I pray for you anyway, but these are some pretty specific things to take to the Lord."

He knew that Noah had found faith over the past summer. Heck, everyone in the man's entire sphere knew. Harley hadn't processed what that meant beyond hearing the guy talking about God like they knew each other, which seemed weird. But now... Noah prayed for him? For Harley the screw-up with the bad attitude? He didn't deserve it.

If someone had asked if he believed in God, he would have scoffed. He hadn't believed in a higher power in years. Not since before his mom died. But somehow the knowledge that Noah was going to be talking to the Big Guy on his behalf made a peacefulness he couldn't explain settle into his soul. It spread out, washing over him like a cool breeze on a too-hot day. He wasn't used to feeling peace. It felt... good. A ghost of a smile touched the corner of his lips.

Noah snapped his fingers. "I almost forgot. The reason I stopped by. Tomorrow. Your birthday. Lily and I are taking you to The Hungry Whale for dinner, right?"

"You know you don't—-"

"You had better not say I don't have to. I know that. But we want to."

"Fine." Now he felt about an inch tall. He'd just been irritable and testy and had snapped at his friend. In typical Noah fashion, his friend just kept right on being his friend. Harley busied himself with taking off his gloves. When Noah didn't leave, he looked up again. The man still stood leaning against the door frame, ankles crossed and hands in his pockets, but appeared to be lost in thought.

After several seconds ticked by, Harley was the one to break the silence. "Something else on your mind?"

Noah took a long time to answer. Instead of saying anything he pulled his hand out of his pocket and handed over something small. Harley took it and opened his hand to find a delicate diamond ring. It was a simple gold band with a round stone that sparkled in the light. It looked to be an antique and sized for a very small finger.

"Aww, man! You know I love you, but... you're not my type."

Noah's laugh rumbled from his chest. "Good, 'cause you're not my type either."

Harley took a closer look at the ring. It was perfect for the person whose finger it would be going on. "I take it you're going to ask Lily to marry you?"

"That's the idea. I thought it would be easy. I mean, I love her and I know she loves me. But... man, it's a big step, ya know? I keep thinking that we've only known each other for... what? Four months? Is she going to say it's too soon? What if she doesn't want to get married?"

Harley handed the ring back. Noah and Lily were perfect for each other and it was obvious to anyone who spent more than about point seven seconds in their company that they were madly in love. It was a little sickening at times. The smile tugged at the corner of Harley's mouth again. Who was he kidding? It wasn't sickening, it was beautiful. "She'll say yes."

"You think so?"

"I know so." He was thrilled for his friend. He was. It was just... An ache that he thought he'd locked away long ago settled in his chest. He envied his friend. Plain and simple. "When are you planning to pop the question?" he asked, shaking off the longing that was trying to creep in.

Noah chuckled. "I bought the ring about a month ago at that antique store around the corner. It was just so... Lily. You know? I've been trying to come up with a way to ask her that isn't totally lame ever since."

"Sox game and have them put it on the Jumbotron?" Harley suggested, tongue-in-cheek.

"No," Noah laughed. "No Jumbotrons. No huge productions. I want to keep it simple, but I also want it to be memorable. And a complete surprise. I want to take her out for a nice dinner, but I think she'll be suspicious. We go out, but a fancy-get-all-dressed-up date? She'll know something's up. So..." Noah shuffled his feet and gave Harley a sheepish look. "I've got a huge favor to ask. Could I commandeer your birthday dinner?"

The dinner was Noah's idea anyway, of course he could hijack it. Harley hadn't celebrated his birthday in years before returning to Summer Harbor, but Noah insisted that they go out. Every year. He didn't mind skipping this year to help his friend out. "Absolutely. I can make myself scarce."

"No, no! I still want to do dinner."

Harley shot his friend a dubious look. "You want *me* along on the night you propose?"

"I just need to get Lily there unsuspecting. You'll see." Noah wiggled his eyebrows.

Harley shook his head, wondering what his friend had up his sleeve. Noah might say he wanted Harley to stick around now, but there was zero chance that he was going to stay for all the gooey, lovey-dovey that was sure to happen. No way. It would hurt too much. But he could play along. To a point.

Monday night, Noah wasn't sure he could eat anything. The ring in his pocket was the only thing he could think about and his stomach was tied in such tight knots he was afraid he might need medical attention. Somehow, when Parker returned to take their orders, Noah must have managed to sound coherent. No one gave him a strange look anyway. But he couldn't have told anyone what he'd ordered. As the conversation flowed he was so very thankful for his charming girlfriend-soon-to-be-fiancée and his friend. They were doing a wonderful job of carrying on as if he wasn't coming apart at the seams and about to start hyperventilating. Was it hot in here? It seemed hot. Very. Hot.

Noah pulled at the collar of his dress shirt and tried to focus on what Harley was saying. Something about taking Coriander and her friend to Blueberry Island. He scrubbed his palms across his pant legs and looked over Lily's shoulder just in time to see his parents slip into seats near the door. His mother grinned and waved and then nodded over her shoulder. Lily's sister Olivia smiled at him and waved before joining the Kingsleys at their table. He breathed a sigh of relief. Parker had seated them where Lily wouldn't catch sight of them. It took him a second to realize that everyone at the table had stopped talking and was looking at him. "Sorry. What was that?"

Lily smiled at him and slid her fingers into his. He wondered if his heart was out of his chest and on display the way hers appeared to be. Probably.

"I was just telling Harley that I haven't been to Blueberry Island yet. We should go before it gets too cold," she said. "It sounds lovely."

Noah nodded in agreement just as Parker passed their table to refill their water glasses. Lily turned her attention to his best friend, asking about business now that the summer rush was letting up. Noah leaned back in his chair, out of Lily's line of vision, and caught Harley's eye. He was so nervous he thought his heart might explode. Or stop. He swallowed hard and grimaced at his friend. Harley managed to hide a snort of laughter by coughing into his napkin. Go ahead bro, yuck it up.

"You going to make it?" Harley asked under his breath.

"Ayuh." At least he thought he was. Maybe. Harley's barely contained snicker wasn't helping. He couldn't explain why he was so nervous. At this point, he didn't think there was any chance at all that Lily would say no. However, there was something strange and wonderful and scary about making a move that would change the rest of his life as he knew it.

"If you'll excuse me, I need to powder my nose," Lily said as she slid her chair away from the table.

Noah cast a worried glance in the direction of his parents' table, but all of them had menus up, hiding their faces.

"Man, you look like you might pass out," Harley whispered once Lily was out of earshot. "Take a breath or something."

"Yesterday afternoon I pulled my dad aside and asked if he'd been nervous when he asked my mom to marry him. He said it was the scariest, most wonderful moment of his life. I figured I could handle scary. He should have said 'terrifying'.

Harley tried in vain not to laugh but sobered quickly when Lily slid back into her chair.

"Oh, yum. There's our food," she said as Parker swung the kitchen door open and headed their way.

It turned out he'd ordered one of his favorites. Pork cutlets in creamy mushroom sauce. So maybe he could eat a little something after all. Lily smiled her perfect smile at him and he returned it. Oh, man, she was perfection. From the cute little green sundress that she wore down to the heels that did things for her legs... Well, he *may* have dragged his feet a little as they walked into town, just so he could watch her walk.

Wait. Had she asked him something? "Hmmm?"

"Do you want to ask the blessing?"

"Oh." He blinked and tried to organize his thoughts. "Sure."

They all bowed their heads. *God, I need You! Please help me focus! And while you're at it, could you help Harley see Your hand in his life? That would be the best birthday present.* "Dear Heavenly Father, I thank You for... Well... Thank you for this time to share a special meal with friends— Our friend Harley on his... on his... on his birthday. Please bless our... ummm... time, conversation, and this... food. Amen."

He hoped his prayer had made sense. To his ears, it sounded like a mess. But God understood and that was what mattered.

Years from now their kids would ask them—

Kids.

A new wave of anxiety hit him square in the solar plexus. Was Lily going to want kids? Did he? They hadn't talked about it. What if he did and she didn't? What if she did and he didn't? No, that wouldn't be the case. He wanted kids. Someday. Visions of Lily pregnant and Lily with a little blonde-haired, silver-eyed toddler on her hip made his heart nearly burst. She'd be the best mom.

And those kids would ask about the night he proposed. He could picture it. Lily, face glowing and eyes alight with memories, would turn to him and he would stare at her, his mind blank. Crickets chirping in the silence. Great. He cast a nervous look toward his friend Parker who nodded at him.

Ready or not, it was go-time.

He sucked in a deep breath and, excusing himself, headed in Parker's direction. The man had been his best friend since kindergarten. They'd been close growing up, but ever since Noah came to Christ they were finding that the friendship was even deeper. Noah was so glad that his friend hadn't given up praying for him. It had taken years, but— The thought struck Noah that he needed to be that person for Harley. He needed to be the friend that never gave up praying. His chest tightened, resolve taking hold.

Parker was standing behind the bar-turned-lunch-counter filling soft-drink orders and talking with a young redhead who was sipping on a root-beer float and laughing at something his tall, dark, and handsome (or so the ladies said. Noah couldn't see it.) friend had said. The man could make women swoon and he didn't even notice. The eighty-hour workweeks he put in running the restaurant probably didn't help. Hard to think about meeting someone and getting involved when all you ever did was work and sleep.

"Brynlyn Sloane?" Noah asked as he stepped up beside her.

The redhead swiveled her stool around and reached her hand out. "You can call me Bryn. And you must be Noah Kingsley."

"Nice to meet you."

"Miss Sloane was just filling me in on her role in your plan," Parker chimed in, his voice quiet in the din. "Lily's going to love that you thought ahead to have a photographer capture *the* moment."

"That's the idea." Noah pulled at the collar of his shirt again. Was his tie cutting off circulation? It felt like it was. Maybe he was going to pass out. "I'm going to ask her to dance. Then as the song ends, as long as I don't pass out, I'll get down on one knee."

Bryn reached out and squeezed Noah's hand where it was gripping the edge of the bar. "You're going to do great. I've been watching you guys. She looks at you like you hung the moon." Bryn leaned in like she was sharing a big secret, before loudly whispering, "She's going to say 'yes'!"

Noah chuckled and looked back at the love of his life. She was in the midst of an animated story that involved much use of her hands and had Harley laughing. Yeah, Bryn was right. She was going to say yes. He appreciated the photographer's bubbly personality. It had done exactly as she'd intended and settled his racing nerves. It was time. He turned back to Parker. "Wish me luck."

His friend reached across the bar and stopped Noah, gripping his shoulder. "The Bible says finding an excellent wife is worth more than precious jewels. You don't need luck, because you've already found her. You are already blessed. This is just icing."

"Thanks, man." Noah clapped Parker on the shoulder before turning to Bryn. "Are you ready?"

"Sure am." She patted the camera in her lap and winked at Noah before swiveling back around so she would have a clear shot of the dance floor when the time was right.

The current song was winding down. Noah walked back to the table with determined steps and rested a hand on Lily's shoulder. She turned and smiled up at him, exactly how Bryn said she did. Oh, how he loved this woman. "Would you like to dance?"

If it was possible, her smile grew even bigger as she slid from her seat. He guided her with his hand on the small of her back and pulled her into his arms as soon as they reached the small dance floor, making sure her back was to the table where their family sat. The crazy-high heels that did magnificent things to her legs had the top of her head reaching almost to his chin. He breathed in the soft lilac scent that clung to her hair. How had he managed to find Lily? More importantly, how had he managed to live without her before they met? Holding her close, he closed his eyes and swayed to the music. As much as he feared he wouldn't, he wanted to remember this moment for the rest of his life.

All too soon the music slowed and the song drifted away.

Lily leaned back. "Thank you," she whispered. "That was splendid."

She started to step away, but Noah held on. As soon as she turned back toward him he took the ring from his pocket and dropped to one knee. Her hand flew to her mouth. It was fun to watch as each new emotion registered on her face. Confusion, surprise, shock, joy. Happy tears glistened in her eyes.

"Lilianna Hayes Emerson. I am so grateful that God saw fit to bring us together. We haven't known each other all that long, but it's been long enough for me to be certain that you're the love of my life. You're the one I want to build a future with and grow old with. Would you do me the honor of being my wife?"

Tears swam in Lily's silver-gray eyes as she nodded vigorously. Then, as though her hand wasn't strong enough to hold the joy in, she pulled it away. "Yes! A million times yes!"

The whole restaurant erupted in cheers as Noah slid the ring onto her finger and stood. A single tear escaped, running down her cheek. Reaching out, he swiped it away with the pad of his thumb. Then, cupping her damp cheek in his palm he lowered his lips to hers. Another wave of cheers washed over them and he felt her lips lift into a smile. He pulled back just far enough to rest his forehead against hers as the band began another slow tune.

"I love you," he whispered as they swayed to the music again. He held her hand close to his heart as they danced, exactly where he intended to hold it for the rest of their days.

Noah and Lily were headed back to the table, stopping every few feet for a congratulatory hug or handshake, when Lily caught sight of her sister and Noah's parents. Harley couldn't help but smile when she squealed and dropped Noah's hand, rushing to gather her sister up in a tight hug. Noah's mom was next while his dad clapped Noah on the shoulder, beaming from ear to ear.

This would be the point in the evening where Harley beat a hasty retreat. The lovebirds' return to the table was his cue to call it a night, regardless of what Noah had said the day before. He tossed his napkin on the table and started to slide his chair back when two heavy hands clamped down on his shoulders from behind.

"I hear there's cake!" Sawyer said when Harley looked up in surprise. "Happy birthday, man."

"Oh, my goodness," Lily exclaimed as she and Noah stepped up to the table. She sighed, looking down at the ring. "I don't know if I remember how to breathe! And you," she added, pointing an accusatory finger at Harley. "You knew, didn't you?"

No escaping now.

"Guilty as charged," he said with his hands up in surrender before standing to shake Noah's hand. It turned into a part handshake, part hug, part chest-bump sort of thing. "Congratulations you two."

"You're not leaving, are you?" Noah asked.

Busted. Before Harley could answer, however, Noah's parents joined the table.

"Happy birthday, young man." His mom stepped up and took Harley's face in her hands, beaming up at him and patting his cheek.

Lily's sister, Olivia, had followed them and was about to take a seat at the end of the table when Gage and Owen materialized next to her, falling over each other to be the one to pull her chair out. Harley couldn't blame the boys. Lily's sister was a knockout.

Sawyer pulled out the chair next to Harley but turned his attention to Noah's father as he sat. "Garvin, nice to see you again."

"Sawyer, my boy, how are you?" The older man reached out to shake hands across the table.

"Doing well, sir."

They all tucked into the table and Noah's father was just asking Sawyer about Finnley's when the band started to play *Happy Birthday.* The whole restaurant joined in as Parker came out of the kitchen carrying a huge birthday cake. Harley went slack-jawed for an instant.

"I think we're going to go," Lily said after the song was through. She turned adoring eyes on Noah. "This amazing man arranged for our engagement photos to be taken on the beach this evening and the photographer is waiting. We'll be back though! Save us some cake!"

"Is she seriously going to walk on the beach?" Olivia asked in a loud whisper as she watched them leave. Harley raised a brow in question. "In those heels, I mean. Is she going to go walk on the beach in those heels?"

"Nah, Noah will be carrying them before they even hit the public boat access," Parker replied with a chuckle as he stepped up to the table with a stack of dessert plates. "That man is a goner."

Olivia giggled and the sound was contagious. The cake was cut and served and the conversation around the table rose in volume. Parker pulled up a chair next to Noah's mom, a chef on the mainland, and they began a lively discussion of cake toppings and the merits of buttercream frosting. Gage and Owen continued to flirt shamelessly with the blonde-haired violet-eyed Olivia, each trying to one-up the other as they told her stories from their summer working for the kayaking shop. The girl was eating it up, flirting back just as shamelessly. Meanwhile, Garvin had pulled Sawyer into a discussion of the older man's tractor and its penchant for not starting.

Harley tipped his chair back on two legs and was wondering how best to make his getaway when he saw Erin come through the door. Dropping his chair back to the floor with a thump, he watched her weave through the crowd toward the bar.

He hadn't seen her since Saturday. Part of him had wanted to go to the house today, but he'd convinced himself he was needed at the shop. The entire day. After all, the life vests weren't going to inspect themselves.

Sawyer's chair scraped back and he sauntered across the room, stopping beside Erin with a grin. He propped an elbow on the counter and crossed his ankles as if settling in for a long visit. Harley wasn't privy to their conversation, but the way Sawyer kept nodding toward their table Harley guessed the man was inviting her to join their little party. Erin shot an uneasy look over her shoulder before sliding off her stool.

Maybe he could stay for a few more minutes after all.

When they reached the table, Sawyer made short work of the introductions. "Erin, this is Analise and Garvin, Noah's folks. That lovely young lady at the end is Olivia, Lily's sister. I think you might have met Parker before, he owns this place. The two boys there are Gage and Owen, and this here is Harley. Folks, this is my friend Erin."

There were a bunch of nice-to-meet-you's and handshakes before Erin turned her eyes on Harley.

"Hey," she said in a shy voice.

"Hey," he replied. Why couldn't he come up with something wittier? Sheesh!

Sawyer sat back down, nodding at the empty chair on the other side of Harley. "I haven't seen you since Lyle's. Keaton put you on another job?" he asked as Erin slid onto the chair.

"Yeah, he has me replacing the porch on..." She cast a questioning glance at Harley. "...a house here in town."

"My house," Harley added.

"Is that right?" There was a speculative tone to Sawyer's voice, but before Harley could analyze it the man continued. "You know, Harley here works for Keaton over the winter. What do you want to bet we all end up on a few jobs together in the coming months?" he said before returning to his conversation with Garvin about the tractor.

When Harley looked back at Erin she was giving him a peculiar look. "Yeah, I work for Finnley's, but I'm not fixing my own porch." Try as he might, he couldn't keep the edge out of his voice.

"Actually, I was thinking how much I like that Keaton makes sure his employees help each other out." She took a sip of water and then leaned in a little closer. "I feel like I'm intruding."

"No, not at all."

"What are we celebrating?"

"Noah and Lily just got engaged."

"And it's Harley's birthday," Sawyer added, looking over his shoulder with a grin.

Thanks, man. Harley tried not to glare at his friend.

"Oh, happy birthday!"

"Thanks. Have you eaten?" The second the words were out of his mouth Harley felt like an idiot. Of course, she hadn't eaten! She hadn't even had time to order.

"No, I was working on the porch and sort of lost track of time. Figured I grab something here rather than heating up a microwave lasagna at home."

Now he felt bad. "You've been at the house all day? I'm sorry I couldn't make it over..." The semi-lie died on his lips. He *could* have gone over. He didn't want to. No, that wasn't true either. He did want to, and that's what had kept him away. There had been a time many moons ago when he had simply snatched what he wanted and to heck with the consequences. Then one day the reality of taking things that weren't his to take had caught up with him. The shame of it still haunted him. No, he had to keep himself from wanting too much. so he'd avoided the house. Even the idea of working on the bike hadn't been enough to pull him today. He flexed his hand where the knuckles still smarted from his foolish outburst the morning before.

"No worries. I got a lot done. I didn't want to leave until I had all the floor joists in place and the new stairs installed. It looks great." Erin was reaching for a menu when Parker stood and announced that appetizers were on their way. She moved to set the menu back down and then hesitated. "I still feel like an interloper."

"I wish you wouldn't," Harley said softly, taking the menu

and sliding it back into its place. "I'm glad you're here."

It was adorable how her cheeks pinked. He was trying to decide the wisdom of telling her so when Parker arrived back at the table loaded with an assortment of appetizers. Everyone dug in and the conversation became chaotic. And loud.

"Quite the party," she said, trying to be heard over the din.

Harley leaned in to reply, but got a whiff of her lemon grass and pine chips scent and lost his train of thought for a beat. Man, she smelled good. "It was sort of a surprise. Dinner was a cover so Noah could propose, but then it turned into... this."

"Fun!" Erin grinned before popping a fried jalapeño in her mouth.

More appetizers arrived, and more cake was served. People started to push back from the table, full and content. Lily and Noah returned from the beach and the volume increased even more. Sawyer asked Erin a question about a job and they bantered back and forth. She was like sunshine and the longer Harley watched her delightful, expressive face, the harder it was to remind himself that happy endings didn't exist.

Not for him.

There had been a time in his life when he'd thought in terms of forever. Then he'd ruined it all. After that, one night was all he'd looked for. Regret burned in his chest as he watched Erin laughing at something Gage had said and he reminded himself that he didn't want her getting hurt. Even that reminder, however, wasn't enough to make him walk away. She was too bright, too happy, and his thirsty soul craved it.

Catching her yawning a while later, Harley smirked and leaned in to be heard. "Is it the company?"

She laughed mid-yawn, which was hilarious, and then giggled. "No, just exhausted. I think I'm going to bow out." She yawned again and it added another shot of guilt. She looked beat as she stood and squeezed his shoulder. "Happy birthday, Harley."

"I'll walk you out." He pushed his chair back and followed her to the door. When they stepped into the cool, quiet evening air, Harley took a deep breath. Yes, he wanted to walk Erin to her truck, but he also needed to extricate himself from the party without hurting anyone's feelings. This killed two birds with one stone. When they reached her beater he held the door, enjoying playing the gentleman for a few minutes.

"I'm glad you came," he said, his voice quiet.

"Me too. Maybe I'll see you tomorrow."

"Maybe," he said with a smile and closed her door, backing away, but waiting while she pulled away.

It had been an unexpectedly good birthday.

Shaking his head at the ridiculous spectacle on the dance floor, Lyle Jay finished the carrot cake he'd ordered. A long-time favorite that he'd indulged in after one last meal at his favorite restaurant. He wouldn't miss much about this town, but he would miss The Hungry Whale. Standing, he slid his arms into a butter-soft black leather motorcycle jacket before tossing some bills on the table and heading for the door. It was now or never.

His skin crawled with the idea that, even now, the man from the phone could be watching. It was time to either face the music, take the punishment for the crimes he'd committed, or run and never look back. No choice sounded appetizing, but one allowed him to keep both his life and his freedom... if he could pull it off.

To run he needed cold hard cash, and to get that he had to play every card he had left in his hand. The rich young brats who vacationed in this town were too easy and had already relieved him of most of the pills. That alone had netted him a hefty increase to his retirement fund. But he needed more and he needed it tonight. By this time tomorrow, Summer Harbor would be a distant memory and he would be on his way to starting over fresh somewhere else. Somewhere warm, with no ocean, no black flies, and no tourists.

Jogging down the sidewalk to where his bike was parked, he considered his last few options. He'd been holding one card close to his chest for over three years and it was time to cash in on it.

He ran a hand over the gas tank, happy that he'd be taking his prized possession with him when he left. It was sad that he'd have to change her color scheme. The countless hours he'd spent researching and applying the perfect combination of metallic royal blue and butter yellow were now a waste. But it couldn't be helped. Neither could swapping the VIN with one he'd swiped off a junker years ago. It was worth it though, to keep his baby when he ran.

Puttering along behind tourists was painful, but he didn't have far to go. The bike rolled slowly to a stop. He engaged the kickstand and sat for a moment collecting his thoughts, his feet planted on the ground. The place looked deserted. Just the way he wanted it. With quiet strides, he made his way to the front door and eased it open. Inside the air was still and he made a bee-line for the door at the back of the room. He wanted to turn on a light, but darkness was his friend tonight and he crept around to the safe he knew was hidden in an old filing cabinet.

The squeal of the drawer opening was too loud in the silence and he flinched, but it didn't matter. Who was going to stop him anyway?

A noise at the door made him spin around.

"What are you doing?"

A sneer was already forming on his lips. "Nothing you need to concern yourself with."

"You can't just—"

"I can. And I will. Who's going to stop me? You? You wouldn't dare." He turned back to the safe and popped it open, sliding a stack of cash from inside.

"No! That's—"

He spun again growing angry. "Just mind your own business."

"That *is* my business!"

"Not anymore." Lyle slid the cash into the inside breast pocket of his jacket and started to leave the room when a hand shot out to stop him. "Oh, you don't want to do that."

"Did you think I wouldn't figure it out?"

Lyle's blood ran cold for a second before it began to boil. "Whatever you think you know—"

"I don't *think* I know, I *know*."

Lyle laughed, loud and manic even to his own ears. It was time to go. Even if the cops were called now it wouldn't make a difference. He'd be gone and no one would be able to find him. He sidestepped the outstretched hand and headed toward the door. When he reached it he turned and met dark eyes looking back at him. "Besides, you won't do anything because you know I have proof of what happened three years ago. You wouldn't want that getting out, would you?" The eyes turned furious before he saw resignation settle in. With another sneer, he continued. "Proof is an odd thing. I mean, the fact that you aren't guilty at all doesn't mean I don't have 'proof' that you are."

The stunned expression was priceless. He snapped the door closed on his way out. Just a few more things to take care of and he was gone. A vapor. Here and then not. No one would find him. No one would know.

Within ten minutes he was swinging one thin leg over the bike and settling onto the saddle. Then, rolling the machine into the slow flow of traffic, he was headed out of town.

The exchange had shaken him more than he would admit, even to himself. If he'd been thinking straight for the past three years he'd have sold everything and slipped quietly into the night.

Why hadn't he?

He knew why. Because he was untouchable. The raspy voice might have thought otherwise, but he'd lived in this backwater town long enough to know exactly how much he could get away with. And he had. Besides, he'd always believed he could set it all straight before his debt was called in. Foolish. The greatest lie was there was always plenty of time. He knew better.

Hugging the yellow line, he leaned into the curves, relishing the feel of being one with the bike. He should probably slow down. Wouldn't want a cop interfering with his plans. Not tonight. Not when he was almost free. One more long, sweeping, downhill curve and then he'd ease up. His knee skimmed the asphalt as it followed the arc of the road. He righted himself as he entered the straight-away knowing he needed to slow down, but oh, how he loved the roar of the wind and the blur of everything except the ribbon of blacktop. The road was empty, he could afford a few more minutes of bliss. He rolled the throttle, picking up even more speed as the road dropped away toward the shore.

As his headlight illuminated the cliffs along the shore of Gulls Cove, he let up on the throttle, slowing slightly. It wasn't enough and he rolled the front brake forward as the cliffs loomed closer.

Nothing happened.

He pressed harder.

Still nothing.

Sweat beaded on his upper lip as the bike picked up speed on another sharp downhill slope. He had to slow down. Jamming the foot pedal down with far more force than was safe, he hoped he was wrong, but even as he depressed it, even as nothing happened, he knew.

He'd been one day too late.

One day.

CHAPTER SIX

"Oh my gosh! Did you hear!?" Gemma burst through the back door of the shop a good forty-five minutes before they opened, letting it swing closed behind her with a crash. Harley looked up from the pile of consent forms he was sorting to be filed. Her eyes were wide, making her round face and flaming red hair look almost comical.

"Hear what?" he asked, exchanging a quick look with Noah and trying to smother a laugh.

The tiny bundle of energy and smiles worked out front when she wasn't in school. An 'oh my gosh!' from Gemma was a daily, if not hourly, occurrence and could mean anything from a sale at her favorite store or a new ice cream flavor to the breaking up of Hollywood's 'it' couple or a release from the newest boy band. The girl was barely sixteen and still figuring out what really mattered.

"About Lyle Jay?"

That got Harley's attention. "What about Lyle?"

"Stacy heard from Robin whose dad got a call from Joe at the coffee shop who said when Chief Briggs came in for coffee this morning he said that Wade Smith got called out to an accident last night." Harley wanted to tell Gemma to take a breath *and* get to the point, but she was on a roll, her eyes getting bigger and bigger as she talked. "Lyle Jay crashed his motorcycle on the road going into Gull's Cove."

The news hit Harley like a roundhouse to the chest. "Any idea how he's doing?"

Gemma's eyes widened still more and her face drained of

color, making the freckles that were splattered across her nose stand out. "He *died.*"

Maybe it was because of how his dad had died, or maybe because he'd just spoken to the man a few days before, or maybe because lately whenever he'd taken his bike out he'd pushed the limits of what he could control, but whatever the reason, Harley's mouth turned to sand and bile burned the back of his throat. Too close to home. There was already a white cross on the side of the road heading into Gull's Cove. One he couldn't even look at.

"You knew him, right?" Gemma asked.

"Yeah, sort of. I mean... I know *of* him."

"I just figured since you both drove super cool motorcycles..."

"I was at his shop a few days ago. Do they know what happened?"

"Nobody's saying much. At least not that I've heard." And just like that, she dropped the subject. "I'll get the shop opened up before I go to school." She didn't wait for a response, just climbed the steps into the front room.

Neither of the men said anything for a long time. Noah broke the silence, placing a firm hand on Harley's shoulder. "You OK?"

"What? Oh, yeah, fine."

Noah considered him carefully but chose another train of thought over pushing. Another trait he liked about his friend. "Any idea if Gemma's got another job lined up for the winter?"

"Haven't heard," Harley answered.

"I wish Evangeline didn't work such long hours, but it's sure been fun having the pipsqueak around this summer."

"Can't imagine being a single mom."

"Right there with you." Noah shook his head. "I noticed that the half-hour before school and the half-hour after school two days a week that you schedule her for morphed into pretty much all her free time."

"I'm happy to keep an eye on her," Harley replied, knowing

he spoke for everyone who worked at Acadian Adventures. They all loved the kid and had gotten used to her overly enthusiastic personality. The place felt dull without it. But now his boss had him wondering...

Cramming the papers he'd been sorting back on top of the in-box on the desk, Harley followed Gemma into the shop. She already had the computer booted up and was organizing the shelves of sweatshirts and water bottles.

"Hey, Gemma, you figured out a job for the winter yet?"

The teen's face lost a lot of its sparkle and she looked down at the floor. "Nah. This town closes up and... well, there aren't enough jobs to go around as it is. Nobody's going to give a job to a kid." Her eyes glistened and Harley wanted to kick himself. Way to go, Beck, make the girl cry.

"I'll keep my ears open for something, alright?"

"Thanks, Harley." Her voice was dejected and her shoulders slumped.

Yup, he was a jerk. He walked over and gave her a one-armed side hug. "Hey, I didn't mean to make you sad. We'll figure something out. And even if we don't, you're still welcome to hang out around here whenever we're around, OK?"

Gemma's face brightened and her braces flashed when she smiled up at him. Then her eyes focused past him on the clock above the register. "Oh my gosh!" And there it was again. "I'm going to be late for school! Bye, Harley!" she called as she ran for the back door, snagging her backpack on the way.

"Bye, Squirt," Noah called as she zipped past him on her way out the door. He stepped into the shop, a smile on his face. "I love that kid."

Harley didn't say anything, instead turning to look out the window, arms crossed.

"You sure everything's OK?" When Harley didn't answer, Noah came to stand next to him. "Did you know him?"

Harley shrugged. "Not really. I mean I remember him from when I was a kid, but... It's more that I just spoke to him on Friday. Nothing earth-shattering. I stopped in at his shop looking for some parts for Dad's bike. Mostly talked to Dox, but... Crashing his bike in nearly the same place as Dad..."

Noah squeezed his shoulder. "I get it."

Harley scrubbed his hand across his face. Enough of that. He shook his head and turned toward his friend. "Last night was a success."

A slow smile spread across Noah's face and his neck turned a little red. "Ayuh."

"Congratulations. You are one lucky man."

"Thanks." Noah crammed his hands in his pockets and a grin took over his whole face, crinkling the laugh lines around his eyes. "And what about you? How was your evening?"

Harley narrowed his eyes at his friend a moment and then let a crooked smile work its way in. "It was great. Thanks for the party, by the way. You didn't have to do that."

"Of course I did! It was your birthday and I was ditching you. I had to make it up to you somehow." Noah stole a look at his watch. "Look, I've got a tour to get ready. I know you weren't close to Lyle, but if you need some time, just say so. Owen and Gage can cover for you."

Harley nodded. He didn't need any time off because of Lyle, he'd barely known the man. He was, however, tempted to take the day and go help Erin on the porch. His heart beat a little faster at the thought of seeing her again. Even exhausted, she'd been so pretty the night before. Yeah, a day off sounded like a perfect plan.

Sticking his head in the back room he caught Owen's attention. The man paused handing out life jackets and loped over to where Harley stood on the steps. "'S'up?"

"Can you cover the front for me?"

"Sure thing." Owen looked more beach-bum than an experienced kayak guide, but he was capable of standing in for any of them.

"Thanks, man." Harley hoped the guy would be back the following summer. Noah worked hard at creating a work environment that encouraged employees to return, and it would be a shame to lose Owen. Or Gage. Or any of the new guys from the past summer.

A few minutes later he was surprised that he couldn't hear Erin singing as he jogged up the driveway of his dad's house. Instead, she was hunched over a piece of underlayment lining up her hammer with the head of a nail. The yelp she let out as the hammer came down on her thumb made Harley grimace. Something was off. "You OK?"

She jumped and blushed. "Yes, fine." Then she squeezed her eyes closed."No. I'm having '*a day*'."

"I hear ya," Harley replied rubbing his hand across the back of his neck.

"You too?"

He met her eyes but was silent as he hooked his thumbs in the back pocket of his jeans. He looked away and stared at the porch, but he wasn't really looking at it. "I take it you heard about Lyle?" His eyes flicked back to hers and she gave a slight nod.

"Yeah." Erin laced her fingers together behind her neck but quickly dropped her hands, shaking out the one with the pounded thumb.

"That looked like it hurt," Harley said, reaching for her hand. Then he thought better of it and instead pushed his hands back into his pockets.

"At the rate I'm going, today's going to be a disaster. The crazy thing is, I didn't even like the man. He was arrogant and rude. But something isn't right and it's eating at me."

"How so?"

She took a deep breath as if trying to focus. "A few days ago I saw Lyle on his Knucklehead. You know what he did for a living before buying the shop, right?"

Recollection rushed at Harley full tilt. "He was a stunt driver."

"Exactly. I mean I watched him come up fast on a tourist who'd stopped their car in the middle of the road to look at their map. He didn't even slow down. Just leaned to the side and slipped around them. He avoided their bumper, then an oncoming car, then two kids jaywalking, and a tourist with a camera who stepped backward off the sidewalk without looking. The motorcycle might as well have been a part of him. How could he have gone from that to crashing his bike on a straight stretch of deserted road?"

Frustration made her movements jerky, but she reached for the hammer anyway. Before he could stop her, Erin took a swing. The nail bent in half and Erin growled, tossing the hammer down onto the porch floor.

"Hey, hey," Harley said, catching both her hands and turning her to face him. "Take a break."

It looked like she might cry and he rubbed his hands up her arms and with a gentle tug pulled her into his arms. He expected her to resist, and was prepared to let go. When she didn't, he tightened his hold and breathed in a lung full of fresh air.

"How well did you know him?" Harley asked after a few moments of silence.

"Oh. Wait, who? Lyle?"

"Yes, Lyle." Who else?

"Only in passing. I worked on his house last week. He was... unpleasant."

"He and Dox—"

"Dox!" Erin stepped back quickly, bringing her fingers to her lips. "I should go check on him."

Harley's eyes met hers and he hated how wrecked she looked. His gut told him it wasn't about Lyle. Not really. And he wondered about the strong emotions crossing her face. "I'll come with you."

She looked surprised but didn't argue. They took Erin's truck and rode in silence across town to the motorcycle shop. It was dark and the *closed* sign hung cockeyed in the window. No surprise there. Harley waited while Erin came around the truck, then led the way to the door, trying the handle. It opened but the interior was dark.

"Dox?" Harley called.

He saw movement on the far side of the room, behind the front desk. Dox stood up and heaved out a sigh. The man's usual tidy attire and jovial attitude had been replaced by grief that hung on him like a heavy, ill-kept coat. Erin must have seen him, too, because she pushed past Harley to walk behind the counter and wrap her arms around the man. He looked down at her with bloodshot eyes, blinking to focus.

"I'm so sorry, Dox. Is there anything we can do?" she asked.

The older man blew out of breath like he meant to answer, but then just shook his head. He took Harley's outstretched hand with a firm grip and a curt nod. Had it been a mere three days ago that they'd stood at this very spot and talked bikes? Dox looked ten years older this morning. As if the effort of standing was too much, he sank onto a stool and looked out the window, trying to pull himself together.

"I don't know what I'm going to do." He made a sound that might have been a laugh, but if it was, there was no humor in it. Erin wrapped an arm around the big man's shoulders as best she could. "I've been sitting here all morning just trying to figure out if I can keep the place going. Lyle kept the books, paid the bills, did the ordering... I just... Fixed bikes and talked to customers." Dox let out another laugh. "That last part wasn't Lyle's... strong suit." After a long pause, Dox sighed. "Maybe it's time to just be... done."

"Done? As in close the shop?" Harley asked in surprise.

"I—" Dismay made Dox's voice crack. "I just don't know what to do. It seemed like we were always on the ragged edge of going under. I mean with insurance and taxes and inventory and salaries... But... somehow Lyle kept us afloat." He pushed a hand through his thinning hair and sighed, his eyes glistening before he blinked the emotions away. "I don't know the first thing about that side of running the business. I know motorcycles. That's why we became partners years ago. He can— could fix a bike, but he didn't have an eye for detail."

"I thought he rebuilt that Knucklehead he drove?" Erin

asked.

"Oh, he did. Like I said he could do the work. But that bike took him years. It was just easier for me. He was better at running things..." Dox looked again at the pile of papers in front of him. "There's a real estate guy who's been looking to buy the place for months. Lyle wouldn't even entertain the idea, but the man seemed pretty desperate to get his hands on it. Probably give me a fair deal. Maybe I should just call him and be done."

"Hey man, don't do anything hasty. I mean, I could probably help you with some of this..." Harley rested his hand on the mess of papers. "I do a fair amount of that at the kayak shop and it can't be all that different."

Dox sighed and patted Harley's hand. "That's kind of you, young man. No, I should have paid better attention for the past twenty-five years." He shut his eyes and sighed. "I could use a drink."

"Dox..." Harley darted a glance in Erin's direction and found worry drawing her brows down.

The older man held his hand up. "I know, I know. Not the answer. You sound like..." He looked back and forth between the two but didn't finish his thought.

Harley felt his lips tighten into a grim line. He knew what the man had been about to say and the last thing he wanted was to sound like his father. How on earth could concern for the state of the man's mental well-being be likened to a fire and brimstone preacher railing against drunkenness from the pulpit? The thought grated on his nerves.

"Dox, promise me you won't do anything rash, like sell the shop or get drunk." Erin said. She patted him on the shoulder when he nodded. "If you need anything, you give me a call."

"Thanks, sugar."

"Same here, Dox. Anything you need."

The mechanic attempted a smile, but it fell flat.

If the drive over had been quiet, the drive back to the house was downright silent. Erin pulled up in front but didn't make a move to get out. Harley reached for the door but hesitated.

"Would you mind if I skipped out early today?" she asked, not meeting his eyes. "I don't think my thumbs can handle working on the porch."

"Yeah, sure. No worries." Still, he hesitated. "Erin, are you alright?"

She nodded, but he wasn't convinced. He couldn't claim to know her well, or at all, but the optimism he'd seen at their every meeting was missing. What he wanted was to pull her into his arms again. To give comfort and to be comforted. But those were dangerous waters where hearts could get hurt.

Hers.

His.

Besides, he had burned-out bridges to rebuild and that wasn't a two-person job. No, best to keep her at arm's length. He hopped down and closed the door, leaning his forearms on the open window. "See you tomorrow?"

She nodded and pulled away from the curb as soon as he stepped back.

Harley arrived at the house the following morning with his arms full. Unable to sleep, again, he'd climbed out of bed and settled himself at the huge island that separated the apartment's galley kitchen from the living room with a pad of paper. By the time the other guys were stirring and the smell of coffee hung in the air he had two lists. One was a continuation of the list he'd started in the garage a few days before. The other was of the things that he wanted to accomplish on the house. The second was a short list. No need to set himself up for failure right off the bat. It consisted of mowing the lawn, trimming the shrubs, and raking the leaves.

And cleaning the kitchen.

When Gage had stumbled through that morning to grab a cup of coffee, the idea came to Harley that if the kitchen at the house was clean Erin would have a place to make coffee, keep her lunch, etc. No more working overtime with nothing to eat on his watch.

Once he deposited his armload of cleaning supplies and trash bags on the kitchen table he stopped and could hear Erin singing in the backyard. The peacefulness the sound ignited was becoming something he looked forward to. He ran a hand down over his eyes and across his beard. Careful there, Beck.

He wanted to say hi but decided to let her be. She didn't need him poking his nose into her job. Instead, he looked around trying to decide where to start.

With a sigh, he reached for the spray cleaner and a rag. He could do this. He paused though. Would his efforts erase the smell? Just in case it did, he took a deep breath and tried to imprint it on his memory. He'd doubted the day would ever come when he could stand in that room and inhale the memories without running for his bike.

But it had.

And today was that day.

An hour later the smell of the cleaning products was getting to him and he opened the window above the sink to let in some fresh air. He could hear Erin, still singing. She stopped working and took a long drink of water before starting a new hymn. Did she know every song in the hymnal?

Memories flooded back, crushing him. He turned away from the window and allowed them to come. In his mind's eye, he was six or seven years old. It was before his mom passed away and he could see himself standing next to her in the front row at church. Her hand was resting on his shoulder while they sang. She had the beautiful voice of an angel. Or at least that's how he liked to remember her. Opening his eyes he found himself back in the kitchen, humming along. He ground his teeth. No, no, no, no, no, no. He wasn't going back there.

Moving to the other side of the kitchen where he wouldn't hear her, he cleaned out the pantry and the cupboards below the counter. Someone, most likely folks from the church or maybe neighbors, had had the forethought to winterize the place that first winter. He shuddered to think what the room would look like, smell like, if they hadn't. Visions of mold and rodent droppings turned his stomach. Not to mention busted pipes.

Finishing with the cupboards, he gave the refrigerator another once over and plugged it in before taking the garbage to the curb. By the time he stood back and surveyed his work, it was well into the afternoon and the kitchen was clean. Not bad. Not bad at all. He looked toward the back of the house. The closed curtains left the living room hidden in shadows, and the doors were closed on the two bedrooms. The kitchen was one thing but his childhood room? His father's bedroom? The living room where his mother's piano still sat? He couldn't face those parts of home yet.

There was that word again.

Home.

For ten years there had been no home, only a nomadic life and memories of a place he'd once lived. Then, in the span of just a few days... He shook off the thoughts and turned back to the freshly cleaned room just as a tap sounded on the back door. Pulling it open, he found Erin standing on a piece of underlayment. Open floor joists stretched in both directions away from her.

"Hey," she said with a shy smile that he found himself returning without even thinking. The way her eyes sparkled as they held his? Man, she was beautiful. "What do you think?" she asked, gesturing to the end of the porch where she'd finished part of the new floor. The plywood that had been giving her fits the day before had all been pulled up and she was methodically replacing it and adding flooring as she went.

It was good work. Or at least he assumed it was because that wasn't what he was looking at. Yes, the planks were neat and tight, but the flooring wasn't what had his heart slamming into his ribs. That was all Erin. He swallowed hard and tried not to cuss. She wouldn't realize it was meant for him, not her.

"Nice. Real nice. You've been busy!"

Her cheeks pinked at the compliment and he went completely tongue-tied.

"The reason I knocked... I wanted to ask you about the railing. I can probably get balusters to match the ones that are already here but it's going to cost... well, a lot, or..." A nervous blush pinked her cheeks again. Instead of speaking, she handed him a flat-sawn baluster that matched the general shape of the originals but exaggerated. "I could make these for almost nothing."

"You... made this?"

"Yes," she said with a shy smile. "I mean, I know a guy who can turn the ones to match so if that's what you want we can certainly go with those. I can call him tonight and—"

Harley put a hand up. "These would look great. I like them. They're simple. I like simple. And they sort of look like the old ones."

"I was thinking I could mix them with the ones I was able to salvage."

"Sounds great." She could have said she was planning to train cats to hold up the rail and he'd have agreed. Maybe that's why Noah seemed to go along with whatever idea Lily happened to come up with.

"I'll get on those tonight after work," Erin said as she propped the baluster against the back of the house.

His brows drew together. "You don't have to work on my house in your spare time."

"Oh, I don't mind." At his incredulous look, she hurried on. "I'm going to be in my shop anyway."

A silence settled and Harley searched for something to say.

Erin adjusted her tool belt. "I'll keep going until I finish up here in front of the door, just in case... I mean, I don't want you to come out through the back door and forget that there isn't a porch here." She shuddered a little.

"That would be rather spectacular," he said. "And painful." She giggled and turned to head down the steps for another board. "Do you want a hand?"

Erin looked back over her shoulder, her face brightening. "Well... sure. I mean, if you want to."

Harley stepped onto the piece of plywood and looked at the flooring she'd already put in. It *was* good work. After it was sanded and painted it was going to last a long time. "What color do you think it should be when it's done?"

"You can go with the same sea-green if you want, but I was thinking gray would be handsome."

"I like that. While I'm at it, I should probably paint the trim on the house to match, huh?"

"A gray that's darker than the shingles would make the house look very distinguished," she said as she headed toward the stack of tongue and groove flooring in the backyard.

"Let's do gray then." He hopped down the stairs behind her. "Oh, I almost forgot." He pulled his keys from his pocket, unsnapping one and dropping it into her hand. "Just in case you need to get into the house. You know, coffee and stuff."

She looked at the proffered key for a second before wrapping her fingers tightly around it. "Thanks."

The saw was set up to the side of the porch and he laid one of the boards across it, then watched as she measured twice and made a cut. While she continued cutting boards, he took them over and fitted them into place. The hum of the compressor and the squeal of the saw made conversation hard. Harley didn't mind. He was enjoying watching Erin work and, when the saw and the compressor were both silent, listening to her sing. After so long of not even being able to look at the place, it felt odd, but gratifying, to see a part of it looking nicer.

"Have you heard anything more about Lyle's crash?" Erin asked between cuts on the saw.

"No." He stopped what he was doing and handed her the water bottle she'd left in the shade of the steps to keep it cool.

"Thanks," she said after taking a long swallow.

"You can keep that in the fridge if you want. And help yourself to coffee whenever." She flashed him a dazzling smile and handed the water bottle back. "You still feel like something's a little... off? With the accident I mean."

"I do, but it's probably nothing. The police are looking into it, right? I mean, if it wasn't an accident they'll figure it out."

"I'm sure." But the idea had taken hold and was finding fertile soil.

They worked in companionable silence for a while, broken up only by a few instructions or questions about the project. Unbidden, the thought that he should ask her out slipped into his train of thought, but he tried to shove it away. No. Going out, even just for dinner, led to expectations and feelings getting hurt. He didn't want to hurt Erin. And he didn't want to be hurt, either. His brain wouldn't settle for that solid reasoning though, and frustration had him making silly mistakes. After having to bite back a blue word when he pinched his finger between two boards, he gave up and slipped into the garage without a word. Working on the bike was a better idea.

Working alone was a better idea.

A loud crash from the garage startled Erin as she finished fitting the last spruce board on the floor. Out of the corner of her eye, she'd seen Harley retreat to the outbuilding after he'd hurt his finger. Again. She didn't blame him. Now, with tentative steps, she moved to the door and cracked it open. Dust motes flitted through the sunlight streaming in the windows, swirling as if stirred by an invisible hand. Harley knelt in the shadows near the back of the space next to a motorcycle whose front-end had been demolished.

A motorcycle she recognized.

Erin's hand flew to her mouth. She never dreamed that Coop's bike would still be at the house. It made no sense. With every ounce of strength, she fought back the tears that stung her eyes and scalded her throat. There was no way she was going to cry in front of Harley.

Harley turned his head away from her and wiped the back of his forearm across his eyes. A heavy rolling toolbox lay on its side with its contents strewn around him, evidence of having tipped over. She wanted to close the door and walk away. No, run away. However, something held her there. Seeing the damage to the Harley-Davidson brought it all back. Opened all the wounds she'd meticulously kept bound up for the last three years.

She tried to tear her eyes away, but it was no use. Her heart clutched thinking of Coop on that motorcycle. Coop dying in the crash. There were good reasons that she hated the machines. "Is that...?" She drew a shuddering breath and tried again. "Is that Coop's bike?"

Harley recoiled as though someone had slapped him. "How do you..." He cleared his throat and tried again. "You knew Cooper Beck?"

Shaking her head, Erin backed away. She couldn't stand in the garage. Not with Coop's bike there. Not with this man messing with it. Things needed to make sense again! She stepped back out the door and bolted, but she only made it as far as the new back steps before her legs gave out. She collapsed on the bottom tread and dropped her face into her hands, trying to cover the meltdown that was coming. Some girls looked sweet and cute when they cried. Not Erin. Her pale skin went blotchy and her eyes turned red almost instantly. And there was always snot involved. Lots of snot. It wasn't pretty.

Memories of the moment Cori had called to tell her about Coop's accident flooded her mind in excruciating detail. Where she'd been standing, how she'd held the phone, how she'd tried so hard not to lose it in front of the guys in her basic woodworking class. How she hadn't succeeded.

With her face buried in her hands, she didn't hear Harley approach and jumped when his hand touched her knee. It took her a full minute to pull herself together enough to lift her head and meet his eyes.

"Erin?" He was crouched down in front of her, one hand on her knee and concern in his voice.

She used the back of her shirt sleeve to try and mop up her cheeks. "I knew him from before. From before I left for school," she replied. Understatement of the century.

Harley ran his other hand down his face but didn't get up or take his hand from her knee. The man looked as wrecked as she felt. They stared at each other for a long time, each trying to figure out who the other was. It had become obvious in the last few minutes that neither was exactly who they appeared to be. Not just the new owner of the house, not just the girl working on the porch, not just the guy from the kayaking shop, not just the girl who picked up hours at Finnley's to pay the bills.

Harley finally swallowed hard and looked just past Erin's shoulder to the back of the house. "Cooper Beck," he said, his voice turned rough with emotions he had to swallow away before continuing. "Was my dad."

The disbelief Erin felt had to be written all over her face. She'd never been good at hiding her emotions. Reaching out, she touched his hand where it still rested on her knee. "Wait," she said, studying him more closely. "Charleston?"

Harley almost chuckled, but it sounded like it tasted bitter. "Nobody calls me Charleston," he said. "Except my dad."

Her hand went to her lips as disbelief continued to wash over her. He looked away again, still trying to collect himself. It seldom happened, but Erin was speechless. It didn't help that his thumb was tracing slow circles on her knee which made it hard to think. When Harley didn't turn back to her, she reached a hand out again and touched his. The way he started, as if he'd forgotten she was there, made her think he'd been lost in thought, not there in the yard with her.

"Have you really been back for two and a half years?" she asked.

"Yeah." Harley's eyes glistened, but his voice was steady. "All that time I couldn't even set foot in the house."

Coop had often talked about 'his Charleston'. So often in fact that she felt she almost knew the seventeen-year-old version of the man in front of her. She wondered if Coop would recognize his Charleston now. It was too much to deal with all at once. Harley was Charleston, Coop's bike was still in the garage, and she was losing it in his backyard sitting on the porch she'd fixed. A hysterical laugh came from... where? Erin didn't know and she rubbed her hands over her face wishing she could go back to a few minutes before when her biggest hurts weren't front and center. Back to when they were carefully tucked away at Jesus' feet.

Oh, God, I don't want to hurt all over again!

Harley pushed to his feet and stepped away to stand at the edge of the fall-browned grass with his arms crossed, staring into the distance. The place where his hand had rested now felt cold and she rubbed her palm across it as she watched him. Now that she knew he was Coop's son, she could see it. Around his eyes and in the way he stood, even now, rocked back on his heels. His father had done the same thing.

"They said he was driving too fast along the road going into Gull's Cove." She waited for him to continue, but he was silent and she could tell he wasn't looking at anything, at least not anything here in this present world. After a few minutes, he rubbed his hand across his eyes. "I don't even know what I'm trying to do. It isn't like rebuilding the bike will bring him back." He sighed and glanced over his shoulder at her. "If I'm being honest, I'm not sure he'd even want me rebuilding it. My dad and I weren't close. He detested me, with good reason, and I avoided him. Also with good reason."

She wanted to argue, but her voice wouldn't cooperate. When he hadn't spoken again long moments later, Erin got up and stood next to him. He looked down at her and offered a half-hearted attempt at a smile. She tried to smile back, but it was a sham. She was standing in Coop's backyard next to Charleston. Charleston, who'd stolen his dad's bike. Charleston, who'd run away and never looked back. Charleston, who hadn't cared how much hurt he'd caused his father. Charleston, who wasn't around when his dad needed him. Heartache was quickly being replaced by an entirely different feeling, and it wasn't a pleasant one. It boiled in her core until she couldn't stand it anymore. She needed to leave. She needed to leave right now before she said something she'd regret. Rage made her chest burn and her hands shake.

"I gotta go." She didn't wait for his reply, just high-tailed it for her truck. Feelings she couldn't even identify burned through her until she could barely see the road through the haze of them. She slammed the truck into park and took the stairs to her apartment two at a time. By the time she threw herself on her bed, there was nothing to do but succumb to the ugly-cry.

CHAPTER SEVEN

The gathering twilight cast Erin's bedroom in a gray pallor. It seemed fitting. Clawing her way out of the exhausted sleep that had finally claimed her was painful. Grief was a strange companion. She'd been fine. Even working on Coop's house had felt... right. Of course she missed him, always would, but being there was beginning to give her the closure she craved.

Then... Harley.

She wasn't too proud to admit that she'd been attracted to the man. He was crazy handsome, with his black hair and beard, all those muscles, and dark brown eyes that could speak volumes without him uttering a word. He was also kind and funny and a little mysterious. Cori had sworn up and down that he wasn't a bad-boy and Erin had started to believe her. She'd even gone so far as to look forward to seeing him at the house, her heart thundering in her chest when she heard his deep voice.

Fine, yes, she'd started to like the guy. A little. Or a lot. And then...

Erin swung her legs over the side of the bed, barely managing to avoid both the box that didn't quite fit and the small wooden chair that doubled as her nightstand. Toe crushers, every last one of them. Hanging her head, she felt the burn of fresh tears start at the back of her throat. She swallowed them away and got up to find some aspirin.

Yes, grief was a strange thing indeed.

In the tiny bathroom, she looked in the mirror and cringed at her reflection. Red-rimmed eyes and blotchy skin, tangled hair that had come loose of its braids, and creases where the sheet had pressed into her skin. She was a mess.

Splashing cold water on her face helped. As did pulling her hair free of its elastics. Her favorite jeans were still draped over the back of the chair where she'd tossed them after their trip to Blueberry Island. She yanked them on along with a thick hoodie and left the apartment for the solace of her shop. At the bottom of the stairs, she veered toward the shore instead.

On the pebble beach that bordered the town, wind buffeted her, whipping hair across her face and stinging her still-damp cheeks. She didn't care. Wrapping her arms around herself, she headed away from the noise and lights, wandering past hotels whose windows flooded the beach with a warm glow and on toward the emptiness of the shore beyond the bustle of town.

Waves licked the sand and stones, pushed and pulled by wind and tide. Erin walked above the water line and tried to pull herself together. Tried to sort her thoughts and form a prayer. Her heart, however, betrayed her, filling with anger and sympathy and joy and irritation. And loss. And grief. And, oddly, hope. What was she supposed to feel?

"Why," she screamed toward the starry sky, her voice disappearing into the wind. "Why would You put me there? Him there? Why didn't You answer Coop's prayers? He wanted his son to come home for years and years, so he could make things right. Why would you not bring Charleston home until it was too late?" Her voice caught on a sob and in disgust she kicked a rock into the frothy water.

My thoughts are not your thoughts, and My ways are unfathomable. How unsearchable are My judgments because they are higher than yours?

I just wish it didn't hurt so much!

I am near to the brokenhearted. Your heart may fail, but I am the strength of your heart! In time I will wipe away every tear from your eyes.

Erin found a dry rock near the cliffs at the end of the beach and sat, pulling her knees up to her chest and wrapping her arms around them. Peace started to settle over her. Even though her heart felt like it would break all over again, God was faithful. She had clung to John 14:27 the past three years. There was no peace that the world could give her, but the peace that God gave surpassed human understanding. She had experienced it firsthand.

Closing her eyes, Erin breathed in deep gulps of the briny air. She let the cold settle around her and tried to quiet her mind. She could, with God's help, keep showing up. She could keep showing up at her job, at church, for her friends. She could finish the porch and say goodbye to Coop's place. She could study and learn and grow under Pastor James' teaching. She could be a friend to Cori and Sawyer. She could pray, and sing, and love others. Maybe she could even find a way to fix the mess she'd made with her mom. There was only one problem with her 'I can keep showing up' plan.

Harley.

God, how am I supposed to forgive him? I'm so angry at the way he hurt his father! I don't know how Coop could forgive him. He never said a bad word about his son, but I could tell how much his heart was broken. I watched him read and reread the notes Harley sent home. I saw him cry. I saw him on his knees praying for his son, day after day. How do I forgive like that?

New tears slid down her cheeks. Angry tears. She let them fall and listened for the Still Small Voice that so often whispered scripture to her when she needed it. However, at that moment all she heard was the wind and the rush of the waves on the beach.

"Don't You care?!"

Pastor James had preached the Sunday before on the calming of the storm. It occurred to her that she was no more trusting or understanding than Jesus' disciples who had woken Him from sleep to demand the same thing. Was God answering her the same way? Arising, rebuking, commanding 'Peace, be still'? The story wasn't about the storm, it was about the Master of the wind and waves. If she trusted Him,

WHERE THE BLACKTOP LEADS HOME

would the storm in her heart cease? She tried, but anger still simmered just below the surface. In frustration, she pushed off the rock and headed back toward town.

Each step seemed slower than the last until she stopped and squeezed her eyes shut. Standing on the moist sand as the wind whipped at her hair, a calm began to settle around her. Stillness. Erin breathed it in. Be still and know...

Relief washed over her.

Just like iron sharpens iron, friends sharpen one another because a friend loves at all times. Listen to advice and accept instruction, so you can gain wisdom.

Picking up her pace again, Erin headed back up the stone steps onto the pier and straight toward Cori's. Her friend might seem flighty, but she was also wise beyond her twenty-four years. Hard life lessons at a young age tended to mature a person. A snap of her knuckles on the door was the only warning she gave before pushing it open and throwing herself on the couch in the corner of her friend's studio.

A melodic giggle floated to where Erin lay with her arm over her eyes. "Well, come right on in. Make yourself at home."

Erin's lips twitched toward a smile at her friend's playful sarcasm. "Thanks, I think I will."

The room fit the pixie-like artist. Long workbenches ran the length of two walls and were covered with her signature sea glass and driftwood pieces in various stages of completion. The walls above the benches were lined with bins of supplies. Heaps of driftwood in the corner and huge spools of wire spilled out into the room. Floor-to-ceiling windows bathed the whole studio in extraordinary natural light during the day and gave a panoramic view of the twinkling lights of the town at night. What little furniture there was had come from antique shops and thrift stores and added to the eclectic mix. It even smelled like Cori, sea salt and caramel.

She heard the wheels of Cori's stool flying across the floor and sat up just as Cori stuck her bare foot out and planted it on the front of the sofa to stop herself.

"To what do I owe this unexpected, yet totally appreciated, visit? I hope it's you being all gooey-eyed from Saturday!" With Cori perched on top of the stool, they were eye-to-eye and Erin knew her friend had a front-row seat to the scarlet blush creeping up her neck and over her cheeks. "Ooooh! I knew it!"

"Oh, Cori, I'm so confused!" Erin groaned as she slid back onto the seat and covered her eyes again.

"About what?"

"Harley." She paused for a long beat before continuing. "You aren't going to believe this, but he's Coop's son." Silence settled over the space and Erin lifted her arm to look at her friend. Of course she knew. "Coriander Wren! You didn't think that was important information to pass on?"

Cori nibbled on her thumbnail as she avoided making eye contact. "Oh, Erin. I just didn't know how. And then... Well, Harley's a great guy. You're awesome. You like him. He likes you. I just didn't want to be the one to ruin it."

Erin laughed, but it sounded bitter. "He doesn't know anything about me. How could he like me? *Why* would he like me? What could I possibly have to offer a man like Harley?"

"Oh, pish-posh!"

Before Cori could elaborate, Erin barreled ahead. "Besides, he has no clue I know about him. How's that conversation going to go? 'Hey, Harley, your dad pretty much saved my life and I loved him like a father. Oh, and by the way, he told me all about you, and I've hated you for years and years, so... Surprise!'"

"I think you're selling Harley short if you think he can't handle you having known his dad."

Erin gave her friend an incredulous look. "I more than knew him. He raised me after I bailed on my parents."

"I know, sweetie. I know. But I've known Harley since he worked on the renovations at the gallery a couple years ago and let me tell you, that man is beating himself to death with guilt and anger. You don't have to punish him, too. He's doing a bang-up job of that all on his own. You, my friend, can be a light to him. Just..." Cori paused and fixed Erin with a hard stare. "Just give him a chance, OK?"

Erin chewed on her bottom lip. "I don't know."

"Listen. I know you have a 'no bad-boys' rule, but Harley isn't one. Not like you mean anyway. I know he looks tough, but on the inside, I think you'll find he's scared and unsure and trying to figure things out, just like the rest of us."

The icy fist that had been constricting Erin's chest all evening eased a little bit. She'd seen that side of Harley, especially today when he'd lost it while working on Coop's bike. Something tiny inside her yearned to be a balm to those abraded parts of him, but she knew she wasn't the balm he needed. "He needs God to heal the broken parts of his heart. Not me."

"Yes. But maybe, just maybe, you're who God's going to use to do that. Don't make God find someone else." Her friend patted her knee before returning to her work table.

Erin squeezed her eyes shut and tipped her head back with a groan.

"You know I'm right," Cori said.

She didn't want her friend to be right. She'd started to like Harley, but after she'd learned that he was Coop's son all those warm, fuzzy feelings had blown out to sea. She had to admit she'd created an unrealistic picture of the man in her mind. Based on what, she didn't know. Cooper had never had an unkind word to say about his son. Yet Erin had vilified the man. He was a prodigal and she had slipped into the parable, playing the role of the second son to perfection. Angry that the man had returned. Wanting desperately to hold on to what she had. How ridiculous was that? She wasn't even Coop's daughter. On top of that, her disdain had become comfortable. It would be so much easier to hold onto the feeling of superiority. So much easier to place blame. However, in her most honest moments wouldn't she have to admit she had done the same thing? What a hypocrite! Maybe the disdain wasn't entirely for Harley after all. Erin sat up and growled out a groan of frustration.

"See, I told you I was right."

"Sometimes I hate you." She shot her friend an annoyed look, but it had no ire in it.

"No, you don't. You love me and you love when I'm right."

Cori's smug face earned her an eye-roll before Erin pushed to her feet with a sigh. As usual, her wise friend was right. Needing a distraction, she wandered over to where Cori sat at a machine that resembled a drill press. "What are you doing?"

"Drilling holes in pieces of sea glass for the sculpture I'm working on." Cori nodded toward another table. A large piece of driftwood sat with what appeared to be a wire tree with sea glass leaves growing out of its center.

"It's beautiful!" Erin exclaimed. "Oh, that reminds me..." She dug into the pocket of her jeans. "Harley found this piece of sea glass on Blueberry Island the other day. I forgot to give it to you."

Cori took the large piece of frosted glass and turned it over in her hand a few times. "It's a gorgeous color. Makes me wonder where it came from." At Erin's blank look, Cori explained. "Most sea glass is from Coke, beer, or wine bottles. Teal, green, clear, and amber. Dark lavender like this isn't as common. Maybe an old medicine bottle?"

"Will you be able to use it?"

Cori tapped her lip for a moment before hopping off her seat and patting it. "I've got a better idea! Here, you sit.".

"Why—"

"I'm going to help you turn this into something."

"Cori, I don't think—"

"Pish-posh! Creating is good for the soul. You know that."

Her friend wasn't wrong.

Cori pulled a second chair over and handed the glass back to Erin. "Now, the first thing you're going to do is drill a hole in it. Put it here in this little pan of water, then you're going to use the Dremel. Just like the drill press in your shop."

"Isn't that going to break the glass?"

"No. The water keeps it cool. Now you're only going to drill halfway through on each side. And, make sure you have a good grip on it so it doesn't spin out of your fingers when the bit hits it!"

Following Cori's instructions, Erin bent over the small machine and lowered the tip of the bit into the water. Small clouds spun free into the water as she worked. Flipping the glass over once, she soon had a perfect hole drilled through one end.

"Cool."

"Right? This next step is super cool, too. You're going to gild a bit of one edge." The tiny woman already had a shimmering sheet of gold leaf out. "Wherever you paint on the adhesive size will be gold, so use it sparingly. I'd just do this little section right here where it's rougher than the rest. But you put it wherever you want."

"Now what?" Erin asked once she'd dabbed a tiny bit of the sticky substance onto the edge of the glass.

"Now we wait. The size has to dry before you put the leaf on. And while we wait, you can tell me what else is going on in that pretty head of yours, because I feel like there are a million things swimming around in there and driving you crazy."

"Only a million? It feels more like a zillion." She scrubbed her hands over her face before meeting her friend's concerned eyes. "There's all the Harley things, which is like half of the zillion. Then there's my mom—"

"How's that going?"

Erin shrugged. "No better, no worse. I called her last week, but she must have been out. I just wish I knew how to fix things. I mean, do I move there? I don't want to leave Summer Harbor, but maybe if I was close to her I could figure things out."

Cori's lip stuck out in an adorable pout. "I sure hope that's not the answer."

Looking away, Erin bit her lip. She didn't want it to be the answer either. "Then there's the whole thing with Lyle Jay crashing his motorcycle."

"What 'whole thing'?" Cori asked.

"I don't know. Just a feeling I have that something's fishy."

"Ooooo, intrigue!"

"I don't know about intrigue, but…" How could she put into words that there was just something… awry?

"The man was a creep." Cori wrinkled her nose in disgust. "He bought some very expensive art from me a few years ago. When he came in he was annoyed that my father wasn't running the gallery anymore."

"Seriously?"

"Right? I've got a degree in modern art with a minor in business for crying out loud. I think I can handle selling art. Anyway, what he bought was worth a small fortune. Paid cash for it. It was just weird. I mean most people buy a piece at a time, you know? Not that I'm complaining! I made bank on it."

"I think I saw some of the pieces he bought when I was working on his place a few weeks ago. Modern seascapes? Lots of texture?"

"Those are the ones. So he must not have found a buyer after all."

"A buyer?"

"Oh, he came in a while back wanting to sell the paintings back to the gallery. I didn't want them and I wasn't in a place to give him what he paid for them anyway." Cori shrugged and turned back to the work table. "Alright, I think the size is dry enough for you to gild this."

With careful instructions from her friend, Erin placed the gold leaf on the glass and used a small brush to dust off the excess and press the gold onto the textured edge.

"Gorgeous," Cori said when it was done. "Last but not least, you can slip it onto this ring and use it for a keychain, or onto this gold chain and wear it as a necklace."

"Keychain," Erin said without hesitation.

A melodic laugh bubbled from her friend. "I figured you'd choose that."

They slipped the piece of glass onto the ring and Erin admired it. Her friend had the best ideas. Maybe her idea that Erin should cut Harley some slack had merit, too. "Thank you."

"For the keychain?" Cori asked. "That was just fun."

"For the perspective," Erin said with a smile.

🐦

The following morning, Erin threw a disgusted look over her shoulder that could cut through metal.

And met Harley's surprised face.

He immediately raised both hands in defense. "Whatever I did, I'm incredibly sorry!"

Erin's eyes went huge and she let out an embarrassed laugh before clamping her hand over her mouth. "I am *so* sorry! That look was *not* meant for you!"

"If you say so," he said, the hint of a smile in his voice.

She'd been startled to see a man standing in the backyard when she'd arrived at the house a few minutes before. He'd been as tall as Harley but leaner, more polished. Impeccably dressed, his white shirt standing out against his Mediterranean coloring. There was no way he hadn't noticed her arrival, but instead of acknowledging her, he'd stood with his back to the house surveying the yard with his hands on his hips.

"No, I'm serious, that look was meant entirely for..." Erin fished a business card out of her pocket and glanced at it before handing it to him. "Edwin Hurst. He was here when I arrived and asked me to give you this. I swear, the look I inadvertently cast your way was meant for him. The guy is smarmy."

"So I've heard." Harley scratched his beard while turning the card over in his hand. "Noah's girlfriend had a bit of a run-in with the guy a few months ago. Thought he'd bumped off her uncle."

"That's awful."

Shrugging, Harley pocketed the card. "He say what he

wanted?"

"No, just to give that to you and that he needed to speak with you. When I told him I was just working on the house —" Erin ground her teeth. "He scoffed at me and then said 'whatever you say, sweetheart'." She did her best impression of his condescending tone.

"Idiot."

"Then he had the nerve to question my ability to work here." She threw her hand in the general direction of the porch and waved it around. "My boss and his girlfriend had a go-round with Hurst this past spring. Noah did not have much nice to say about the man, I can tell you that."

"I just pasted on my best I'm-too-much-of-a-professional-to-engage smile and he left." The man might be handsome on the outside, but Erin didn't think he was very handsome on the inside where it counted. "Listen, Harley, I'm sorry about bailing on you—"

"What?" he interrupted.

"Yesterday, when I left early. I'm sorry. That was very unprofessional of me."

"Are you kidding? You have nothing, and I mean nothing, to apologize for." His eyes were earnest and she wanted to believe him. Maybe—

"Knock, knock!" The shout was accompanied by a loud rap on the side of the garage.

Harley strode over to take the man's hand, and the two stood facing each other, arms crossed, feet planted firmly as they chatted. They mirrored each other in many ways. Tall, muscular, handsome. Harley's black hair and beard were the inverse of Sawyer's paler coloring. Sawyer was older by a few years, which probably accounted for why she always felt like his kid sister. Watching them laugh over something Sawyer had said, the realization hit Erin that, while she liked Sawyer, found him fun to be around, and easy to talk to, he was firmly in the friend zone.

However, that was *not* how she saw Harley. Even after

yesterday's revelations.

Oh, boy.

Her long-held anger seemed petty in the light of day, or, more accurately, in the light of getting to know Coop's son. Cori was right, Harley was doing a darn good job beating himself up. Heaping on more was unnecessary.

"Keaton asked me to check on you," Sawyer called over, interrupting her thoughts. "He wanted me to see if you needed any help since I'm not finishing that job at Lyle's."

She blinked, trying to free herself from her thoughts. "I hadn't thought about that. What does happen there?"

"Beats me," Sawyer replied, sauntering toward her with an easy smile. He stopped in front of the porch with his hands on his hips and surveyed her work. "That, as they say, is above my pay grade."

"Erin needs a hand getting the rafters into place," Harley said as he joined them. "That isn't a one-person job."

"Yeah, no problem." Sawyer crossed his brawny arms over his chest.

"I'd help, but I was really hoping to get the crater in the gas tank on dad's motorcycle hammered out today."

"Your dad's bike, huh?"

"Yeah, I figured it was time to fix it."

"Heck of a thing. First him and then Lyle." Sawyer shook his head, then looked between Erin and Harley, his face paling a bit. "I just meant... you know, accidents and all."

Harley's face tensed. "There wasn't any cause found in Lyle's crash either?"

Sawyer shook his head. "No. I ran into Chief Briggs this morning and he said the guy from the State Police finished looking at the bike yesterday. Couldn't find anything wrong with it and there wasn't any other evidence. I guess they're saying he might have swerved to miss an animal or something, but... it was more like he just drove straight into the cliffs near Gull's Cove."

Harley flinched and Erin wanted to reach out. Wanted to

take his hand or something. Wanted him to hold hers.

"Hey, man, sorry I even said anything. I... well, I can't even imagine what you must be going through."

Harley nodded and gave a half-hearted attempt at a smile before slapping his friend on the back and heading for the garage.

"And... now that I've completely ruined everyone's good mood," Sawyer said too brightly but with enough chagrin that Erin knew he felt bad. "Where are we at on this porch?"

After she pointed out what was already completed and what still needed to be done, they divided the next steps and got started. Before long, Erin was singing again.

"I know I say this a lot, but I love that hymn."

"You know, you still haven't proven to me that you know how to play the piano," Erin said as she handed him a board, already marked for the next cut.

"No, I haven't."

"So, I have an idea."

"Why do I feel like I should be afraid right now?"

"Probably because I'm going to ask you to play for me at church the week after next." Erin bit her lip, expecting a flat-out refusal.

"Whatcha singing?"

Or maybe not. "That's the tricky part, and it will test if you're as good as you brag that you are."

"It isn't bragging, I'm just that good." Sawyer's eyes twinkled at the teasing.

"Let's hope so."

"I'm heading over to see what that realtor wanted. Do you need anything before I go?" Harley asked as he pushed the back door open and smiled up at her through the roof rafters. "I can leave this door unlocked if you want to come in and wash up or..." Or what? Make herself at home? Now he felt foolish and wished he hadn't opened the door in the first place. Plus, he'd given her a key, so... Walking out the front door would have been oh, so much smarter.

A small smile spread across her face as she peered down. If she laughed, so help him—

"Well... I'm at a good stopping place if..." She trailed off and drew her bottom lip between her teeth. "I mean... if you wanted company, I could..."

"That would be great." Her smile widened and he wanted, more than anything, to see it grow even more. "I have to warn you, though, I'm planning to save myself some time and jump the fence into the neighbor's yard, cut across the street, and sneak through the shrubbery into Hurst's backyard."

He'd been right, the bigger the smile the more beautiful she was.

"If it's all the same to you, I think I'd rather take sidewalks like civilized people. Trespassing isn't my thing."

"Suit yourself. I'm just sayin' it would save us some time." The banter felt good. And the fact that she laughed at his lame attempt at a joke? Even better.

"So, what were you up to today?" she asked as they headed toward Main Street a few minutes later.

Now that was a complicated question. "Hiding."

Erin slowed and looked up at him with a solemn face. "You know Sawyer didn't mean anything, right? He felt so bad about bringing up Coop's accident this morning."

"I know. I guess my brain sort of latched on to it and held tight all day. I needed the quiet and you had help, so..."

"We got all the roof rafters up."

"That's great! I can give you a hand with the sheathing after the morning tour tomorrow. Don't try and wrestle it onto the roof alone, OK."

"Sounds like a date." Her sharp little intake of breath told him she hadn't exactly meant to say it that way. "I didn't mean — Oh, gosh. I'm going to stop talking now."

He chuckled as they walked up to the front of the realtor's

house. She was delightful.

"I was expecting... more," Erin said as Harley rapped on the door and waited. The one-story red clapboard cottage sat a few blocks from the hustle and bustle of Main Street, down a quiet lane lined with turn-of-the-century homes. It was impeccable, with a crushed stone walkway and pristine gardens. A shingle next to the black front door matched the business card Hurst had left. "I mean, it's lovely, just... I thought it would be more... extravagant."

Harley shrugged. She had a point. The man flashed his money all over town and drove a very pricey sports car. One would think he'd have a house to match.

A few moments later the door swung open. If Edwin was surprised to see them standing there, it didn't show on his face. His eyes drifted from one to the other, roaming over more of Erin than Harley thought proper before returning to meet Harley's.

"Harley Beck?"

"Edwin Hurst." Harley reluctantly took the proffered hand.

"I'm so glad you stopped by." The man's toothy smile didn't appear genuine, much like his slathered-on charm. All the man's charisma seemed fake and as he turned appraising eyes on Erin, Harley wondered how the realtor kept any business at all.

"Erin said you'd stopped by and wanted to speak to me."

Hurst looked back and forth between Harley and Erin before a smug sneer turned up the corners of his mouth. "She also said she was 'only fixing the porch'," the man said, his voice laden with innuendo. Stepping back, he held the door open for them and led the way down a short hall. As they stepped into his office at the back of the house it became obvious why the man's business wasn't in a million-dollar building. He had a million-dollar view. The huge back windows framed a perfectly manicured lawn lined with shrubs in varying shades of red, orange, yellow, and green that sloped toward the top of rugged cliffs and the azure sea beyond.

Edwin indicated that they should sit while he skirted the desk and perched himself on a huge leather chair. He steepled his fingers and waited for a few beats, probably for effect. Harley resisted the urge to squirm. He must not have succeeded because Erin's hand came to rest on his arm.

Finally, the realtor rubbed his hands together. "Harley, the reason I wanted to speak to you... Well, it's concerning your father's house. Am I correct that it's out of probate now?"

"What difference—?"

Hurst put his hand up. "Never mind. I know it is. The truth of the matter is that I had already struck a deal with Cooper to buy the house. Unfortunately, he passed away before I could get the paperwork from him."

"I don't believe you." It came out as a whisper, Harley's chest tightening around the words.

"No," Erin whispered.

He was surprised at the surge of emotion that rippled through him. His dad sell the house? No way. And yet... he hadn't been here. Hadn't been part of his father's life. Finances must have been tight because both the mortgage and taxes had been behind. By a lot. Had it been bad enough to force him to sell? His folks had loved that house, and this town. He flicked a glance Erin's direction, and her face said she felt the same.

"Please understand, this is strictly out of the goodness of my heart," Edwin continued as though Harley hadn't even spoken. "I can offer you a reasonable price for the house that will cover all that is still owed on it plus a little extra. On top of that, I'm willing to give you shares in a development project I have going. I have all the numbers if you want to see them, but folks right now are seeing huge returns on their investments."

The thought of selling out to the wheeling-dealing real estate agent left a dirty taste in Harley's mouth. The man's expensive clothes and slick hairstyle didn't sugarcoat anything as far as Harley was concerned. Lipstick on a pig his dad would have said. He'd met the likes of Edwin Hurst at job sites all over the country. Charm the big fish, step on those who couldn't offer anything. Well, Harley never had been any good at playing the part of a stair tread.

"No thanks," he said, surging to his feet. He knew if he ever did decide to sell, it wouldn't be to the likes of Edwin Hurst. "I'm not selling."

Edwin made a tsking sound, standing to block the exit. "Be reasonable, man. Selling the place would be your best bet. I'll offer you the same deal I offered your old man. It's good. Take it."

Harley couldn't believe that his father would have had anything to do with the likes of the realtor. No, Edwin Hurst was the kind of man his father would have preached about on Sunday morning. Banging his fist on the pulpit with his brows drawn down in disgust, he would have railed against the sin of greed, the sin of gluttony, and the sin of pride. It was hard to see Edwin as a businessman when his brain only wanted to see him as a sermon illustration. Wasn't it strange how something that he hadn't thought of for a third of his life would slip back into his mind as though it had never taken a hiatus? When was the last time he had thought about his dad's sermons? Not since leaving home and certainly not since returning. But now was not the time to be thinking about sermons or trying to fathom why his brain had picked that moment to reminisce.

"No. I'll figure something out. Refinance the mortgage. Something."

Edwin pushed out a cheerless chuckle. "No, Harley. No, you won't. I have it on... good authority... that the bank's going to be calling in its debts."

Harley narrowed his eyes. "Another extension on the taxes then."

The smile on Edwin's face went from cheerless to downright devious. "Oh, haven't you heard? The town council voted last night. No more extensions on taxes. You'll be getting a letter."

"I hadn't heard that."

"Like I told your father three years ago, if you sell it to

me now, before all the liens and nonsense, you'll make some money and lose the headache of the place." Edwin crossed his arms. "You won't get a better offer, especially if the town and bank get involved."

"I don't want to sell." He didn't mean for his voice to rise, but the man irritated him. He pressed his mouth into a thin line and looked away, searching for composure. "I want to keep my dad's place. I'll just have to figure out a way to do that."

"You might not have a choice, Harley." Edwin's voice had gentled, almost as if he cared. Almost.

Erin had stood when Harley did and now stepped past him. "Is that what you tell people when they won't sell?"

Both men turned toward Erin's sharp voice. She stood with her hands on her hips, staring Edwin down. To his credit, the man had the decency to look uneasy.

"Excuse me?"

"When you want someone to sell out to you and they don't agree. You tell them they're going to lose their property so they'll sell."

Edwin shifted from one foot to the other. "I have, on occasion, offered folks who might lose their home or business an out before the bank repossesses. That's not a crime. I think it's a rather neighborly thing to do."

"Were you just being 'neighborly' when you pushed Lyle and Dox to sell their place, too?"

"Not that it's any business of yours, but I simply made them an offer on the shop. They're both... Well, they were getting up there in years and I thought one or both might be interested in getting out from under the shop while there was still some time left to enjoy the profits." He winced as if realizing what he'd just said.

"And now?" Erin continued advancing on the man. She barely came up to his shoulder, but the fierce look on her face made the realtor take a step back. Harley had to squelch the smile that wanted to spread across his face. He loved her moxie. "Now that Lyle's gone, are you going to push and threaten Dox until he sells?"

"I'm not sure what you're hinting at, but I don't like your tone."

"I'm not 'hinting' at anything," Erin continued, making air quotes. "I'm saying that it seems mighty convenient that you only have Dox to convince now."

"Whoa! Hold up!" Edwin raised his hands and took another step back from Erin. "You think I'm *happy* that Lyle's out of the picture?"

Erin didn't flinch and didn't look away. She had grit in spades. Harley had no clue where the idea that Edwin had a hand in Lyle's death had sprung from, but it wasn't completely out there. Especially after the run-in Lily had with the guy just a few months ago. Dox had mentioned that Edwin had been desperate to buy the shop and that Lyle was the one holding up the deal.

"I'm going to have to go with Erin on this one. It does seem mighty convenient. Especially if Dox decides to sell."

Edwin looked back and forth between the two, his face growing dark with anger. He rubbed his hand through his hair, mussing it and leaving ends sticking up from the always-neat slicked-back style. "You two are insane. Yes, I wanted... want to buy the shop. But not so bad that I'd be happy Lyle had an accident." The man stressed the last word as if trying to cement it in their minds.

Or maybe in his own.

He continued to look between them and Harley touched Erin's shoulder, lending quiet support. She reached up and closed her fingers around his. It felt good, the solidarity, and he wanted to let the smile he'd been holding back tweak one side of his mouth. Instead, he drew his brows together in a frown

"Wait a minute! You don't think it was an accident, do you?" The man's face went from dark to pale. "You're crazy."

The realtor spun on his heel and strode back to the other side of his desk. Pressing the tips of his fingers against the shiny surface, he hung his head for a second. When he brought his eyes up, it was to give them a piercing look. "Of all the people in this town who had... issues... with Lyle, I didn't even make the list. If you honestly think someone had something to do with his..." The man waved his hand around. "...accident, there are plenty of other people around here you could be looking at."

Harley squeezed Erin's shoulder. "Want to share any of those names?"

Edwin looked away for a second before responding. "The day before Lyle died I overheard him fighting with Skylar Novak." At their blank looks, he continued. "The... I don't know what he calls himself. Cleric? At that... church over on New Sweden Ave. Anyway, it was getting heated and I heard the man say he'd 'kill' Lyle if he didn't keep quiet. I may want that property, but at least I never threatened to kill the man for it. Now, I think you two can show yourselves out."

Erin looked up at Harley and squeezed his hand where it rested on her shoulder. Then, stepping away, she headed for the door. He wanted to reach for her again, to feel the warmth of her under his palm.

Outside, Erin bit her lip and looked away. "Sorry. I don't know what came over me. He was just being so... arrogant and..."

"Are you kidding? That was awesome!" He let the smile that he'd been holding in check flow over his face as they began to walk back toward Main Street. "I wanted to give the man a piece of my mind, but everything I could think of sounded foolish."

"Thank you."

"For what?"

"For not thinking I'm crazy or paranoid."

"No, you were right. Lyle was too good a driver for the answer to be 'we think there might have been an animal'. Regardless of what the police say. I thought Noah was exaggerating about what a piece of work Edwin Hurst is, but I guess not."

"The guy's a creep." After a long pause, Erin turned toward Harley. "May I ask you something?"

"Sure."

"You've been back for... What? Two and a half years? Where were you before that?"

Harley stuffed his hands in his pockets as they walked and waited to feel the usual discomfort that, more often than not, accompanied personal questions. He didn't talk much about himself. If he was honest, Noah was the only person who knew much of anything about the seven years between the night that severed what was left of his relationship with his father and the afternoon he'd ridden back into town, cocky and mad and about to have his world disintegrate.

But the discomfort never came.

Huh.

"I was a lot of places but nowhere for very long," he said after a long pause. "I headed west at first, but it took me a while to get out to the Pacific. Oddest thing. It turns out you need this thing called money to keep moving around."

The corner of her mouth twitched at his attempted joke. "Where'd you stop first?"

"Just outside of Cincinnati. I ended up spending three months there. Worked construction. Good money, but... I could never stay in one place very long."

"What brought you back to Summer Harbor?" She was watching him very closely and he got the impression a lot was riding on his answer.

"I don't know." He drew in a long breath. She didn't need to know all the grisly details. "I guess... it was just time to come home." A smile turned up the corners of her mouth and her eyes shimmered in the afternoon sun. Oh, she was beautiful. He turned away. Time to squelch that train of thought. "What about you? What brought you back?" he asked.

"You know what? I can't say either," she said as they came up on her truck and she pulled the door open, pausing to look up at him with a bright smile in her eyes. "Maybe we came back for the same reason. It was just time to come home."

Tucked between a bed and breakfast and an antique shop several blocks up from Main Street, the Frank Lloyd Wright-esque building might have been a house except for an angular protrusion from the roof that Harley supposed was some sort of steeple. He crossed his arms, leaning a shoulder against the sturdy trunk of a maple tree in front of The Sanctuary of Harmony with the Sacred Spirit, and tried not to feel ridiculous. Edwin's mention the day before of the altercation between Lyle and the cleric had piqued Harley's curiosity. However, he'd had to ask Noah where the place was since he'd never heard of it. Harley chuckled remembering the repugnant look on Noah's face the night before.

"That place is just plain... weird," Noah had said, wrinkling up his nose.

Harley had laughed at his friend's expression. "You gotta give me more than that!"

"The men's Bible study I go to was talking about denominations the other day and I asked about that one. I mean, I'm new to this whole Christianity thing, right? So I don't have a clue about things like what different churches believe. Well, Pastor James got this strange look on his face and then said he didn't think they should be considered a sect of Christianity."

"That's pretty... drastic."

"That's what I thought! Turns out they have a few things they've borrowed from Anglican and Catholic churches, a priest-like person who oversees the church, daily services, confession, and lots of ceremony. *But,* and here's why he doesn't think they're Christians, unlike any Christian denomination, they don't believe in God. Or even a god."

It had taken Harley a few beats to process what Noah had said. "Say what now?"

"Yeah, that's pretty much the face I made when Pastor James was explaining it. I mean, I thought churches were for worshiping God, right?"

"That's what I would have said." Harley had replied. "What's the point if you aren't there for God?"

"This place though… They believe in a 'sacred spirit', not a god, comprised of nature and their own souls. I don't even know how that would work."

How indeed.

In the scant minutes between tours this morning, he'd called the place and asked to speak with Skylar Novak. The man had agreed to meet him. As if on cue, a tall, thin man emerged from the modern building as though stepping out of a sepia-tone photograph. His hair was neither blonde nor brown but a dull caramel. His tan skin, pale brown eyes, natural linen shirt, khaki pants, and white-socked feet tucked into leather sandals made him appear monochromatic.

"How may I help you, my son?" the man said in a tone of voice that was bland to match.

Harley pushed off the tree and intercepted him on the walkway. "Harley Beck. Thank you for meeting me."

"Yes, of course. Elder Novak." He reached out and Harley found that his handshake matched the rest of him. Dull and lifeless. Sudden recognition sprang to the man's face and he pulled his hand back with a snap. "Wait a minute. You're… You're Cooper Beck's boy, aren't you?"

Surprise knocked Harley back a step. It wasn't a stretch. Same last name and all. Still… "Yes, I am."

The older man tipped his head to the side. "You look like him."

"You knew my father?" Somehow Harley hadn't expected that.

"We were—" The man made a face as if tasting something sour. "We were acquainted."

Harley's chest tightened. He needed to get control of the conversation. He wasn't here to talk about his father, he was here to talk about Lyle. "I'm sure you heard about Lyle Jay?"

"I believe the whole town's heard."

"Well, I'm trying to piece together what happened."

The man's jaw tightened and his lips formed a thin line. "I thought they'd already ruled that an accident?"

"The police did, yes. And they're probably right. I'm just trying to satisfy some idle curiosity." Harley shrugged his shoulders trying for nonchalance. "The thing is, I'm not convinced it was an accident." He watched the man's face for a reaction. Only a slight tightening of his lips gave any indication of emotion.

"I see. So you're working with the police now?" When Harley didn't answer the man continued, his voice taking on a pious tone. "They agree that it might have been... something more?"

"Not... exactly."

"Mmmhmm." The man scrunched his face up in annoyance and lifted his nose into the air.

"Yesterday someone mentioned that they'd seen the two of you... talking... the day before he died."

"I see." Novak's eyes narrowed in displeasure and he met Harley's gaze with a defiant one of his own. "Well, your curiosity is going to have to go unsatisfied. I did speak to Lyle the day before he died, but what was said was between him and me. As his minister, I remain silent about things that were said in confidence."

"Lyle was a parishioner here?"

"He..." The cleric looked around as if searching the yard for the right words. "He attended confession when the mood struck him."

"Confession?"

"Yes, Mr. Beck, confession." Irritation had slipped into Novak's voice, but he took a breath and hid it away. "It's good for the soul to be cleansed of things that the mortal man finds upsetting."

"Without betraying any confidences," Harley began. He was

trying to play nice. Honest he was. Even though the other man's condescension grated on his nerves. "Did Lyle give you any indication that he was having... shall we say 'trouble' with someone?"

A look that was equal parts unease and annoyance settled over the other man's face. "I can assure you that nothing was said that had anything to do with the accident."

"If that's true, then what were you two arguing about?"

Anger settled into the lines on the minister's face. "I can't help you, Mr. Beck," he sputtered, turning and retreating back toward the mid-century modern building. He was moving far faster than necessary and his leather sandals made a slapping noise on the paving stones.

A smile twitched at the corner of Harley's mouth as he imagined his father going toe-to-toe with the man. Now that would have been a spectacle. They would have disagreed over everything from theology to footwear. Harley shook his head and turned in the opposite direction. He was already running late for their next tour and he needed that time on the water to think.

CHAPTER EIGHT

The man staring back at Harley from the mirror over the sink in his bathroom was glaring daggers at him. He combed his hair away from his face and ran the comb through his beard.

"What on earth am I even doing?"

Marching out the door and back into his bedroom, he cast a longing look at the punching bag. With a sigh, he snatched up his best chamois shirt, a black one that hadn't started to fade yet, and returned to the bathroom as he buttoned it.

They had been swamped all day Friday and Saturday. It had felt like the summer rush, and with only four guys working tours, they all worked non-stop. Exhausted, he'd come up from the shop after the sunset tour had returned to find a note pinned to the corkboard in the kitchen.

Join me for church? 10 AM Erin

Grabbing a water from the fridge, he'd stood and stared at the piece of paper before ripping it off the board, crumpling it up, and tossing it in the trash. Then he'd thought better of it and fished it back out. They'd had a nice Friday afternoon as they walked back from the realtor's office and the thought of spending a few hours with her on Sunday morning held a definite appeal. Now he wished, with all his heart, he'd left the darn thing in the trash.

He sighed and smoothed the black shirt over his chest, then fiddled with the collar trying to cover up the tattoo that crept up his neck. Maybe they'd just turn him away at the door. A man could hope, right? That way he'd be able to tell her, in all honesty, that he hadn't come because they wouldn't let him in.

A glance at his watch showed he needed to get a move on if he was going to get there before the service started.

"Now *there's* an idea!" He could show up late, and tell Erin he didn't want to disrupt the service. But something propelled him out of the apartment. Something like thirst that he didn't want to analyze.

He closed the door as quietly as he could, trying not to disturb Gage and Owen. He'd been hard on the new hires the past spring, but they'd proven themselves time and again. Noah would already be gone from his apartment in the attic. That man was never late for church, and he always went to Lily's beforehand so they could walk together.

The morning air had a crispness to it that hinted at the cold days ahead. The sun was sinking lower toward the southern horizon every day and it made the sunbeams angle through the trees and between the buildings. A few sparrows skittered around the dumpster behind Parker's restaurant, looking for crumbs, and seagulls squawked overhead looking for something more substantial.

All too soon he'd reached the small white church on the far side of The Green. His hope of being turned away at the door fizzled when instead he received a smile, a handshake, and a bulletin from the man stationed there.

Walking through the doors was like stepping back into his childhood. Many things were different, and yet achingly the same. The same wooden pews, but the deep red cushions were new. The same pulpit, but the sound system was new. The same simple stained-glass windows, but the bright white paint on the walls was new.

Taking a seat in the back row, he felt his neck slick with sweat. It gathered in the hollow of his throat and trickled down his chest. His palms were clammy and he rubbed them on his jeans. By outward appearances, he knew he looked... Well, at the least uncomfortable, and at the worst guilty. He shouldn't have come. Where was Erin anyway? She invites him to church and then doesn't show up?

Noah and Lily both smiled at him when they came in. For a terrifying moment he thought Noah would do the whole 'so glad you're here' handshake and spectacle, but something in the look Harley gave him must have warned him off and they slipped into a pew near the front without a word. He'd also gotten a nod from Parker before he joined Noah and Lily, and Sawyer Davis had raised his hand as he slipped into the other end of the same pew where Harley sat.

The day they'd gone to Blueberry Island, Erin had said she grew up here, but Harley had wracked his brain trying to remember her. Nothing. Granted, she'd have been in elementary school when he left, but he thought he ought to remember her from... something. Had her parents been parishioners? Were they still? The cold sweat that had started with entering the sanctuary now felt like ice. He stole a furtive look around, searching for an older version of Erin among the crowd. Let's face it, he wasn't what any mother wanted their daughter to bring home. He shook his head. She'd asked him to church, not home for Christmas dinner. This was not a date.

To Harley's relief, the pastor stepped up to the pulpit. The man was younger than he'd expected, probably only a few years older than Harley himself with a broad smile and a gentle voice. The barest hint of an Irish accent seeped in here and there. He invited the congregation to rise and they sang the doxology. Old familiar words. Every one.

However, instead of joining in, all Harley wanted to do was run. This had been a mistake. If he left now he could be on his bike and out of town before anybody, namely Erin, noticed. Especially since she wasn't even there. But the urge to run was tempered by the fact that everyone would see. If he slipped out quietly enough, though... Maybe while everyone was standing. He shuffled toward the aisle and two people in the next row turned to look. He stopped. Thrusting his hands in his pockets he stared straight ahead. Nope. Not leaving. Fine, he could endure this.

The pastor invited everyone to be seated and rattled off

a few announcements for the coming week. Harley was just eying the rear exit again when the man's words registered.

"I'd like to thank Erin Wallace for agreeing to do special music for us on short notice."

All thoughts of leaving faded away in the time it took for her to step up to the pulpit and carefully take the microphone from its place. She was still Erin, but she'd traded her carpenter jeans for a pair of black slacks and her tank top for a silky blue blouse. Her hair, which he'd only ever seen in pigtails, hung in loose waves that skimmed along her jawline. He held his breath as the music began to play.

Marvelous grace of our loving Lord
Grace that exceeds our sin and our guilt

He knew how beautiful her voice was alone, but accompanied by the piano it was exquisite. Clear and strong, in perfect harmony with the music.

Yonder on Calvary's mount outpoured
There where the blood of the Lamb was spilt

It was a song she'd sung a few days before, and just like it had then, Harley's mind drifted with the words. He looked around at the serene faces, the polite smiles. Of course, these people could sing about grace that exceeded their sin. It was easy to believe there was a God when all was right in your world, when you were well-behaved, when life was good. How much grace could it possibly take to cover their sins? Even as the thought crossed his mind though, the longing he'd been feeling off and on in recent days returned with a vengeance. What if it could be that easy? To just believe? He closed his eyes and let Erin's voice wipe out the hopelessness that had become his constant companion. At least for the length of the song.

After the last note drifted toward the rafters, Erin headed for him straight away. As she walked along the wall, the colored light from the windows washed over her, and Harley couldn't tear his eyes away. She was like something from a dream. Without a word, she slipped in next to him. Was that a blush on her cheeks?

He smiled and leaned over to whisper in her ear. "You were incredible."

"Thank you," she whispered back, her cheeks flushing a deeper red.

The pastor was easy to listen to, but at the same time, he didn't sugar-coat anything. He told it like it was but with the grace Erin had been singing about. Harley tried to focus on the sermon, but being back in the church was wreaking havoc with his concentration. A million thoughts vied for his attention and he kept losing his place. Until the end. Then the man's closing remarks slipped in past the noise.

"Grace means that Jesus is willing to meet you right where you are. Grace means He takes all the junk that you've stacked between you and Him and sweeps it out of the way to get to you. If you're sitting here this morning thinking you have to get yourself straightened out before Jesus will meet you, I'm here to tell you... You can't. But God's grace can."

When the sermon ended, Harley made a bee-line for the back of the church and freedom. Those final words were like a lump of hot coal searing his chest. He needed to escape. Now. His grand plan was to slip from the sanctuary unnoticed. He didn't even wait for Erin and was surprised to find her right beside him when he reached the doors.

"Charlie Beck?"

He slowed his rapid escape and turned to find two familiar faces. His heart squeezed in his chest for a second wondering at the welcome he would receive. "Mr. and Mrs. Puckett?" Feeling about sixteen again, Harley faced the barrel-chested man. His hair was grayer than Harley remembered, his face more weathered.

Mark Puckett thrust out his hand and took ahold of Harley's in a firm grip. Harley turned to offer the same hand to his wife, Frannie, but found her already closing in for a hug. She was taller than Erin but still had to go up on tiptoes to reach her arms around his neck. Like her husband, the hair was grayer and laugh lines crinkled around her eyes when she pulled back and held him at arm's length smiling up at his face.

"We heard you were back in town ages ago," she said. "I knew if it was true, we'd see you eventually."

"It's good to see you, son," Mr. Puckett added as he put an arm around his wife's shoulders.

Frannie turned toward Erin and pulled her in for a hug, too. "It's great to see you, too, Erin. Your hymn this morning was lovely. I'm so glad you were free and able to fill in. Maggie was going to sing, but little Hope woke up with a fever."

"Oh, it was no problem. Is Hope OK?"

"I'm sure she's fine. If you ask me? She's teething. I do not envy those two the next few nights!" Frannie turned a sympathetic smile toward the pastor as he tried to cover a huge yawn.

Mark looked back and forth between Harley and Erin, and then to his wife. Frannie gave him a subtle nod and he turned back to Harley. "Do you two have plans for lunch?"

Harley opened his mouth to answer, then thought better of it. Did they? Was Erin expecting them to get lunch? Was she expecting to go their separate ways? He sent a pleading look her direction and found her smiling at him. Not helpful.

"No," she answered, not taking her eyes off his. "No plans that I know of."

"Well, now you do!" Mark said, holding the door open for them.

"Something tells me we won't have many more days like this," Frannie said as she draped her coat, now unneeded, over her arm and took Mark's outstretched elbow.

Harley took Erin's Bible and tucked it into his arm before offering her his elbow just like Mark had done. Erin beamed at him as she took it and his heart gave a delighted thump in his chest. What would it be like to have this life? To walk home from church on Sunday mornings with Erin on his arm. It was tempting to dream.

They walked to Main Street under the scarlet leaves of oaks and maples. The Pucketts crossed over and started down a familiar side street.

"I don't remember you living this close to Dad."

"We moved here about seven years ago," Frannie said, sharing a meaningful look with her husband.

"At the time we felt we needed to be closer to the church," Mark added.

As they walked, Harley and Erin lagged behind the older couple. Once there was some distance between them Erin dropped her voice to a whisper and leaned close to Harley. "So..."

He looked down at her and raised an eyebrow. "What?"

She had the most adorable smirk on her face that pulled up one corner of her lips. He had to force his eyes up to hers and the teasing he saw there made him smile back before she'd said a word. "Charlie, huh?"

He grinned and hung his head. "Before... Before I left I was Charlie. Charleston, Charlie. Dad always called me Charleston. Everyone else called me Charlie. Well, except Dox. He was the one who started calling me Harley"

"Why's that?"

"I told him one day that I wanted to own a shop just like his and build bikes when I grew up. I think I was all of five."

"I can picture that."

"When I left... I introduced myself as Harley to the guys on my first job and... what with the motorcycle and all, it stuck." He puffed out his cheeks in a sigh.

"You needed to be who you were."

He nodded but didn't look at her. "For a long time after I left home, I imagined what people back here were thinking. That Beck kid, nothing but trouble, what a shame, what a disappointment. Never in all my imaginings did I picture smiles and a hug."

Erin pulled his elbow closer and rested her cheek against his arm.

Mark and Frannie slowed and Harley was surprised to find that they lived just a few houses past his dad's place. Mark

151

pulled keys from his pocket and unlocked the door, ushering his wife in, and then holding it open for Harley and Erin. It all felt so very... normal.

"Can I give you a hand?" Erin asked, following Frannie toward the kitchen.

Harley stood in the entryway and tugged the sleeve of his shirt down over his tattoos, feeling a bit self-conscience. Maybe he should have bowed out. Small talk wasn't his thing.

"Come on. I'm on table-setting duty." Mark led the way into the dining room. "You and Erin, huh?"

Harley could hear the women laughing behind the kitchen door and he smiled, but the smile faded as the other man's meaning registered. "No, sir. We're just... friends I guess. I mean, we just met, so..."

Mark handed Harley a stack of plates and napkins and then started pulling utensils from a drawer in the china cabinet. "I used to look at Frannie the same way you look at Erin. Probably still do." He winked before following Harley around the table placing knives and forks and spoons where they belonged.

"Erin's working on dad's house for me. Replacing the back porch."

"No kidding?" Mark opened his mouth as if he had more to say but then thought better of it. The table set, he nodded toward the living room. "Let's catch some of the game before lunch is ready."

In the modest living room, Mark dropped his large frame into one of two recliners while Harley perched on the edge of a plush loveseat. The TV on the far wall blinked on and the voices of the announcers filled the room, running down the stats of the two starting quarterbacks. Mark turned the volume down and snapped the footrest up.

"Not a bad way to spend a Sunday afternoon if I do say so myself."

"No, sir," Harley agreed, relaxing ever so slightly.

"I told Erin this is where we'd find you," Frannie teased as she came into the room, and perched on the arm of his chair.

"About thirty minutes until the quiche is ready."

Harley scooted over to make room on the couch when Erin walked over and slid in next to him. Just having her in the room eased the uncomfortable tension in his shoulders.

The TV cut to a commercial and Mark turned to Harley. "Been quite a week around here."

"Yes, sir."

"There was a time when nothing much ever happened in this town. A few speeding tickets, maybe a squabble here or there. But the last few years..." Mark trailed off, shaking his head.

"No, it sure hasn't been the same," Frannie added. "If you ask me, it all started when the drugs started coming into town."

Harley sat forward a little. "I don't remember it being bad when I was a teenager. At least not right here in Summer Harbor."

"It wasn't," Mark said.

"Then that Rocco Lowell started bringing his poison into town and everything started to change," Frannie added.

"The mobster?" Erin asked. "I thought they arrested him."

"That they did," Mark said, turning the volume on the tv up a bit for the kick-off.

"But too much damage had already been done by then," Frannie continued.

"You don't think Lyle's crash had anything to do with drugs, do you?" Erin asked.

"No—" Mark began, but Frannie cut him off.

"If you ask me, the man simply got what he deserved."

"Frannie!" Mark hissed.

She looked down at her hands clasped in her lap. "I know I shouldn't speak ill of the dead, but Lyle Jay was a scoundrel and he finally got his comeuppance."

"Dear, that's all in the past," Mark said, looping his arm around his wife's waist. "Come now. Let's have a nice Sunday afternoon without dwelling on all that."

She leaned into him and closed her eyes for a second. Harley stole a glance at Erin and found the confusion he was feeling mirrored on her face.

Frannie leaned over and kissed the top of Mark's head. "I know it's in the past, but that doesn't mean it stops the sting." She turned toward Erin and Harley and gave a nervous laugh. "Oh, that wasn't the nicest side of me."

Erin reached out and Frannie gripped her hand for a brief moment before letting go and dabbing at her eyes. "I guess I hold on to grudges far longer than I should." She looked between Harley and Erin. "The motorcycle shop hasn't always been Finch and Jay's. My daddy started working on bikes in our garage when I was a kid and by the time I was a teenager he'd turned it into a full-time business. When I was seventeen he hired this handsome mechanic—"

"That'd be me," Mark added, grinning and drawing a laugh from Erin.

Turning an adoring smile on the man, Frannie continued. "I was smitten, that's for sure. Anyway, after we were married we sort of thought that when my daddy retired he'd sell the place to Mark and me. But times got a little lean about forty years ago and Daddy decided to sell part of the business. We were young with kids and didn't have the money, so he let Lyle Jay buy half of it." Her face clouded and she took her husband's hand. "Daddy got sick right after and turned the running of the business over to Lyle. I think he believed he'd be back, but..."

The older woman's voice hitched and Mark drew the backs of her fingers to his lips again. Harley could see where the story was going, and it made him want to punch something. Erin reached out and laid a gentle hand on his arm. He looked down, startled by the gesture, and found his hands clenched tight into fists. He relaxed them and Erin patted his arm before folding her hands in her lap again.

"By the time Daddy passed away," Frannie continued. "Lyle had control of the whole thing. We tried to fight him, but it was all legal."

"It all turned out fine in the end," Mark added. "I was out of a job, but tourists were still in need of a mechanic, and finding another place to work wasn't all that hard. We were happy, weren't we? Saved up a nice little nest egg, retired, bought this place."

Frannie nodded. "That's why I said I'd held onto the grudge far longer than I should have. I didn't even realize I still felt that way about the man until I heard he'd crashed his bike. Then it all just... came back."

"I know what you mean," Harley said, his voice low and quiet.

"Oh, Charlie. I'm so sorry. Of course, this must be so hard for you." Frannie looked like she might start to cry. A timer chimed in the kitchen and she popped off the arm of Mark's recliner. "That would be the quiche! Give me five minutes and then head for the table."

After a delicious lunch and some, slightly, embarrassing stories from Harley's childhood, most featuring either the church balcony or the baptismal, Harley and Erin said their goodbyes and headed down the sidewalk. The sun had begun to sink, but the air was still warm and scented with the aroma of dried leaves.

"I can't believe you put a fish in the baptismal."

"What else was I supposed to do with it?" Harley stole a look out of the corner of his eye and found Erin smiling.

"I like that you do that a lot," he murmured. At her raised eyebrow he dipped his head, embarrassed that he said it aloud. "Your smile. It's real. Honest. So many people come through the shop and the tours with smiles that are there for a purpose. But when you smile... Well... it just seems like you have... I don't even know. Like joy inside you."

Erin's smile spread wider across her face and lit up her eyes. "That might be the nicest thing anyone's ever said to me." She slid her hand into the crook of his elbow again as they walked.

He liked the feel of her hand on his arm. It was warm and firm and just as genuine as her smile.

❧

"Are your folks still in Summer Harbor?" Harley asked as they strolled down the street where she lived.

"No. They aren't." She meant to just shake her head, but her mouth opened of its own accord and words poured out. "My father wasn't ever in the picture. When I was nine my mom remarried and I... I learned pretty quick I wasn't part of his world."

"That stinks."

"If I was good they ignored me, but if I got into mischief, I got their attention. I took getting into trouble to a whole new level."

She hadn't meant to share anything personal and she loathed that if she looked up now she'd find pity on his face. She'd made her choices, she'd come around, and she'd taken her sins to Jesus' feet. She didn't need anyone's pity.

When he spoke though, his voice didn't hold pity at all but empathy. "When I was eight my mom got sick. I don't think you understand what that means at eight. There were lots of visits to the doctor and she couldn't do as much as she had before. My dad took over most of the chores and she spent a lot of time in her chair in the living room reading her Bible. But I didn't know what it all meant. Not really. She got better for a while, but then it came back. She passed away when I was eleven."

"Gosh, that must have been hard." As rough as her relationship with her mother had been, as non-existent as it was now, she couldn't imagine losing her. Especially at such a young age. Who would she have had then? No one. She shivered at the thought. She needed to call her mom. Try again. One of these days she'd say the right words, do the right thing, and her mom would forgive her.

"I was so mad. So dark on the inside that bad was all I had left. So... I know what you mean when you say you took getting into trouble to a whole new level."

Encouraged by Harley's understanding, Erin puffed out a sigh and kept going. "I was working my way toward jail time when someone finally stepped in and said 'enough'. If that person hadn't stood between me and the sinkhole I was being sucked into... Well, I don't know where I'd be, but it sure wouldn't be here."

The side of Harley's mouth quirked up into a smile.

"What?" she asked.

"I'm just having trouble seeing you as a juvenile delinquent. Don't get me wrong! I believe you. I just... can't picture it."

Erin frowned. "I'm not proud of it. But it is part of my story. How about you? How did you break away from the darkness?"

Harley's smile vanished and a shadow crept over his face. "I never did," he replied, his voice quieting. "That's still who I am."

Erin stopped and used her hand in the crook of his arm to pull him around to face her. "You're selling yourself short if you believe that."

He looked away but didn't shake off her grip. "Erin, face it. No one looks at me and thinks 'hey, there's a good guy'."

"That's not true!" Harley made a sound deep in his throat that reeked of skepticism. "Harley. Seriously. People in this town like you. Keaton is bringing you onto his crew for the third winter in a row because he trusts you. Cori was so excited when she found out you were taking us on our kayaking trip that I thought she had a thing for you." Erin chuckled at Harley's startled expression. "I'm serious. I thought she was crushing on you big time. Anyway, yesterday you were so kind to Dox, I know he appreciated it. And your boss gives you a whole lot of responsibility for someone who doesn't think you're a good guy. I've only known you for what? A week? And I know you're a solid guy. Trust me. I've known some bad people and you aren't. You're protective and gentle. I like you."

I like you? What was she thinking? She'd let her big mouth run away with her again. The horror of what had just tumbled out must have been written all over her face because Harley raised an eyebrow and then snorted out a laugh.

"Is that the face you make when you like someone?"

"No. I mean… I mean…" She swallowed hard and snatched her hand back from where it was still holding onto his arm. "I didn't mean I *like you,* like you. Just that, you know, you're friendly and safe. I'm not afraid of you."

Erin felt the color rising on her cheeks and burning her ears. She needed to stop talking. She needed to stop talking right this minute and maybe even run away. *I like you.* It might be true, but she couldn't believe she'd blurted it out!

Wait.

It was true, wasn't it? She liked him. Genuinely liked him. Walking along with Coop's prodigal son and she had been completely honest. All those years of despising him, and then days of not being able to pinpoint her feelings for the man, but now she knew. She liked Charleston Beck. A lot. "I'm sorry. My mouth sometimes does its own thinking and I don't always get a chance to approve the words before they tumble out. I was just—"

"Erin, it's alright." He reached out and took her arms gently in his hands, stopping her mid-sentence. Then seemed to think better of touching her and let his fingers slide away. "The truth is… I don't think I'm worth liking."

"Harley—"

"No, let me finish. Until I came back to Summer Harbor, I didn't stay in one place long enough to get to know anyone, let alone give them time to decide if they liked me or not. I did it on purpose. I'd roll in, find a job, work, keep my head down, pay my penance, move on. My own father hated me, I didn't figure I could expect others to like me." Erin wanted to meet his eyes and argue, but he continued before she could form the right words. "But… well, I guess you've got a point. Keaton and Cori and Dox and Noah. And you. Well, you all don't treat me the way I see myself. I still don't think I'm worth it, but you're right that not everyone looks at me and sees trouble." He paused and when she looked up he smiled. Lopsided, but it made his eyes twinkle. Then he winked at her and a whole kaleidoscope of butterflies took off in her stomach. "Besides, I like you, too."

They'd come to the driveway leading up to her little garage workshop. "Come with me. I want to show you something," she said, reaching out and giving his arm a gentle tug

"Is this your workshop?" he asked as she unlocked the side door of the garage.

She licked her lips before answering, self-conscience about showing him this piece of herself. "Yeah. I mean it isn't much, but..." The dark cavern inside smelled of wood and she took a deep breath of it before flipping the switch. Fluorescent light bathed the shop in a warm yellow glow.

He stood in the doorway and looked around. "I like it. I mean I don't know much about this kind of thing. I'm more of a nail gun and two-by-fours guy." He stepped into the space and ran his hand over the workbench scattered with shavings.

Why was she so nervous? This was her domain. If she was going to feel comfortable anywhere it was going to be here. But for some reason, it mattered to her what Harley thought of this part of her.

"What do you make?" he asked, rubbing his fingers against his palm to knock the sawdust off.

"Right now I'm making wooden boxes. Boring, I know—"

"Wait, these?" he asked as he picked up a box off the table at the end of the room. It had a unique corner joint that was one of her favorites. The front of the box was dark walnut and the sides were pale ash. Where they joined each other at the corner, the pale wood was cut in a scallop with a hole in the center of each curve. The dark wood was cut in reverse and they fit together in perfect harmony. Made for each other.

"Yes, that's one style. I also make these." She picked up another box that not only had no visible joints at the corners but also appeared to be made of one continuous piece of wood, the grain seeming to turn ninety degrees and wrap around the corners.

"These are not boring."

"Thanks." She felt her cheeks heat. "Those aren't why I brought you in here though." She moved around him toward the other end of the shop as she talked. "These are what I wanted to show you. I finished them yesterday." She'd picked up a stack of identical flat balusters off another workbench and was laying them out side by side when he walked up beside her. He set the wooden box down before picking one of the balusters up and running his fingers along the satin-smooth edge.

"These are brilliant, Erin."

She placed her hand over one and caressed the curve with her thumb. "I think they're going to look marvelous mixed in with the ones I was able to salvage."

Harley set the baluster back down and reached out to slide his fingers along the back of her hand where it rested on the smooth wood. She stilled the instant he touched her. She should step away, but couldn't bring herself to move as he slid his fingers between hers. They stood for a moment with their hands laced together. Neither talking, neither moving. She suspected neither breathing. After a moment, he took her hand in a firmer grip and turned her to face him. She stared at the buttons on his shirt and wondered if he knew how fast her heart was beating. Probably not, because if he did, he'd be laughing.

"You got sawdust on your shirt," she murmured. When she reached out with her free hand to brush it away he caught her fingers and raised them to his lips. She swallowed hard but kept her eyes on his shirt. He placed her hand over his pounding heart and reached out a gentle finger to tip her chin up until her eyes met his.

If she wasn't careful, Erin was afraid her traitorous heart would jump right out of her chest and hand itself over, but try as she might she couldn't make herself look away. Harley's deep chocolate-brown eyes held hers with a look of uncertainty, as though he was searching for something. He closed his eyes and rested his forehead against hers. The hum of the overhead lights the only sound in the silence.

"I want to kiss you right now," he whispered long seconds later. He'd been looking for permission and now was giving her the opportunity to pull away or tell him no.

"I think I'd like that," she whispered back. His hand that had been holding hers slid up her arm to rest against one cheek. The other ran along her jaw to mirror it, cradling her face. His forehead still pressed against hers. Seconds ticked by in slow motion. Had he changed his mind? She was about to pull back, let him step away without it being too awkward, when he leaned in and brushed his lips, feather-light, against hers. His beard tickled and she felt herself smiling against his mouth. He smelled like the sea, and she let herself surrender to the kiss, enjoying the feel of his gentle, work-roughened palms against her skin.

He still cupped her cheek with one hand, the other sliding into the hair at the back of her head. He shifted his weight, pressing her back against the workbench as he tangled his fingers in the strands. She made some small sound of pleasure in the back of her throat and he groaned, deepening the kiss and pulling her against his chest. After a few seconds, he started to pull away and she made an embarrassing little chirp of dismay and threaded her fingers into the loose fabric of his shirt. He chuckled against her lips. Instead of pulling away, he hooked his hands under her legs and lifted her to sit on the workbench. Stepping between her knees, he ran his fingers along her arms and back up into her hair.

She melted against him relishing the feel of his strong arms and warm embrace. She was completely lost in the kiss when, with an abrupt jerk, he pulled away. She was glad she was sitting on the bench because if she'd been standing on her own two feet she feared she'd be a puddle on the floor.

Panting, she pressed her fingers to her lips and tried to squelch the giddy smile that was threatening to overtake her entire face. Harley had kissed her. Kissed *her*! And she'd kissed him back. An unfamiliar feeling had uncurled in her stomach and she'd thrown caution to the wind. Six years of carefully distancing herself from any man that looked like trouble and then in one sweet moment of desire she had kissed one with abandon. And if he hadn't pulled back, she'd still be kissing him.

She tried again to tone down her foolish grin and half-opened her eyes, planning on leaning in to continue the breath-stealing kiss. However, when she saw Harley's face the pleasure of the moment rushed away like water down a drain. His eyes had become dark and hooded, his black brows knit together in a scowl.

"I'm sorry," he muttered. "I shouldn't have done that."

"Harley..." She reached out to touch him, but he stepped beyond her reach.

"No, Erin. I need to go."

She opened her mouth to assure him that there was nothing to be sorry for, but his apology felt like a slap in the face. Old, long-hidden feelings of rejection floated to the surface. She wanted to go after him. She wanted to pull herself into his arms and feel them come around her again. But if he didn't want her... It was just as well that he was walking away.

She was still sitting on the workbench staring at the opposite wall when she heard the door to the shop slam closed. Stupid girl. Of course, he wouldn't want her. She wasn't what guys looked for. She wasn't beguiling like Cori, or glamorous like the tourists that swept into town in the summer, or poised like Lily. She was independent, headstrong, capable. Her hands were callused and she often had messy hair and dirt under her nails.

No, she was not what guys considered desirable.

"Yoohoo!"

Erin shrugged off the pity party she was beginning to wallow in and dredged up her friendliest smile before slipping her feet back to the floor and turning to greet her landlady. "Vera! How nice to see you."

The older woman pulled the door further open and looked around. She smiled at Erin, but it was tinged with sadness. "Jason would have loved seeing you use his shop."

"I hope so."

Running her hand across the surface of the workbench by the door the same way Harley had, Vera sighed. "I saw you had company and I didn't want to interrupt, but when he left in a hurry... well, I just wanted to make sure you were all set."

"I'm fine. Honest. That was... Wait, you might have known him from way back. Harley Beck? Coop's son?"

"Oh my goodness! *That* was Charlie?"

Charlie. The name somehow didn't fit the man at all. But 'Harley' fit like a glove. "Yes. I've been working on Coop's place and Harley stopped in to look at the balusters I made." She nodded at the pieces laid out on the table.

Vera eyed her with a knowing look that made Erin want to squirm ever so slightly before peering at the woodwork. "Lovely. I told Keaton he'd done the right thing taking you on. You have real talent."

Erin knew she was good at what she did, but she also wasn't above using her landlady's influence over her big brother when she'd needed a job. He'd listened to his little sister's advice and taken Erin on per diem. The more she got to know Keaton the more she saw similarities between the siblings. Some were obvious, like their prematurely gray hair. Others were more subtle, like their sense of fairness, and protective nature.

Vera hugged her arms around herself and stepped closer to Erin. "I wasn't sure I wanted to take a peek at this place again. It's been over three years since I've set foot through that door. Did you know I used to bring Jason coffee out here in the morning while he worked? I'd sit right there on that bench and he'd drink his coffee and we'd talk." Her tone had turned wistful and Erin's heart pinched. She was exceedingly grateful for the workspace, but she hated why it was available.

"Oh, look at me getting all teary." Vera blinked her eyes. "I miss him every day, but life has gone on, and... well, there are a lot of good days in between the not-so-good ones."

"I know I've said thank you a billion times, but... thank you for letting me use Jason's shop."

"Oh, sweetie, you're welcome. I couldn't bear to get rid of a single thing, but I was done letting it sit unused."

"I thought coming back here might be too hard, but you and Keaton and Sawyer and the folks at church..."

And Harley.

Oh boy. She needed to do a better job of guarding her heart. The guy was broken!

But so was she.

Wouldn't it work better if at least one of them was whole?

Oh, God, what am I doing?

"I remember feeling the same way about a certain Beck man many moons ago," Vera said, a knowing tone to her voice and a glint in her eye that told Erin the older woman hadn't missed a thing. "Charlie looks a lot like Cooper did when he was in high school. Not the beard of course, or the tattoos!" She laughed and it sounded beautiful to Erin's ears. "Oh, that man..."

"He was special, that's for sure."

"That he was." Vera got a far-away look in her eye. "After he and Jules got married, Jason got up the nerve to ask me out. I'd known him forever. I mean he and Keaton had been inseparable since grade school. But I think he knew I'd been half in love with Coop. Maybe a part of me still was, but Jason never cared. Just loved me for me."

Loved me for me. That's what Coop had given her. Not only had he, himself, loved her for her, but he'd introduced her to Someone who loved her for her and would never leave her. She hadn't had any experience with unconditional love before she met Coop, and the fact that he'd embodied, it made it so much easier to accept it from the Source.

Vera reached over and scooped up the box that Harley had set on the bench. "Are these the ones Jason taught you to make?"

"Sure are. Hanging around you and Coop and Jason, I was

either going to be a gardener, a mechanic, or a carpenter."

Vera laughed again. "Ain't that the truth."

"I've made some variations on the design he taught me to make," Erin said as she reached past Vera and picked up two more boxes. "These with traditional dovetailed corners, and my favorite pin and cove dovetails."

Vera took the second box and turned it over in her hands, admiring the unusual corners. It was a long time before she spoke and her voice sounded far away. "The police say it must have been a tourist. That's why they never arrested anyone."

"I'm so sorry, Vera."

The older woman handed her back the box and met her eyes. "I know they're wrong. I know it wasn't a tourist. I know —" her voice hitched and her eyes lowered to the box again. "Someday everyone will know the truth."

Erin stilled. "Vera, do you know who killed Jason?" The older woman lifted her eyes and Erin saw the truth written there. "Who was it? Why didn't you go to the police?"

Vera shook her head sadly and patted Erin's hand. "The police would have needed proof and sometimes there isn't any. Sometimes you just know."

"Vera, who...?"

She shook her head again. "I shouldn't have said anything. Just forget it. It doesn't matter anymore anyway."

"What do you mean it doesn't matt—"

Vera held up her hand, then patted Erin's cheek. "It just doesn't."

CHAPTER NINE

"**S**o, we're back to this, are we?" Harley muttered to himself as he stood straddling his bike at the end of the street and tried to fight the intense urge to run away. To hit the open road. To drive until he ran out of blacktop.

For the past week, he had looked forward to working at the house. Cleaning the kitchen, helping Erin with the back porch, and the rebuilding of his dad's bike may have looked like small steps, but to him they were huge. After last night though, all he wanted to do was run.

The day had been... amazing. Amazing and terrible all at once. Stepping back into the church had driven his anxiety level through the roof. Terrible. When Erin had joined him though, she'd shared her peacefulness simply by sitting beside him. That was unexpected. Lunch with the Pucketts had felt like a normal activity for normal people on a normal Sunday afternoon. Then Erin showed him her shop and let him see a tiny peek more of who she was. Which was amazing. She was talented and strong and independent.

And that kiss!

His lips twitched into a smile before he could stop himself. That kiss might have been the most incredible moment of his adult life. Then he had to go and ruin it. Marching himself out the door, he'd winced when it snapped close behind him. For all his good intentions he'd still messed up. He'd sworn all week he wasn't going to act on his attraction to Erin. Then, in the heat of the moment, some kind of yearning had taken over and he'd acted without thinking.

The amazing, terrible day had ended with his gloves, his bag, and about an hour and a half to bury the new regrets under screaming muscles and aching knuckles. If there was one thing he knew how to do, it was to punish himself.

And it had worked.

Almost.

He'd gone to bed wishing he'd never agreed to go to church with her in the first place.

He knew he couldn't look her in the eye this morning. She had to hate him. Kissing her as he had and then storming out? He'd hate him, if he were in her shoes. Why was it so easy to hurt people? If he hadn't had a tour that morning, he would already be gone. Long gone.

Turning back toward town he puttered slowly away from the house.

Coward.

Intending to cut through the police station's parking lot, he rolled past The Green toward the alley that led behind the Main Street businesses and ended at the rear of Parker's restaurant.

"Well, as I live and breathe! Charleston Beck!"

Harley's head snapped around at the sound of his name and he stopped. Jim Briggs, Summer Harbor's long-time Chief of Police, stood and pocketed the cloth he'd been using to polish the SHPD decal on the driver's side door of his cruiser.

The policeman thrust out his hand and Harley took it. "Chief. Good to see you."

"I heard you were back in town ages ago, but hadn't seen you." The barrel-chested man clapped him on the shoulder. "I guess that's not such a bad thing, though. It means you're staying out of trouble. Right?"

"Yes, sir." And just like that, he was fourteen years old again.

"I'm wicked sorry about your dad. He was a good man."

"Thanks." The chief's words stung in his chest for a moment, but with the sting, also came a desire to understand, to put the pieces together. Harley turned the bike off and set the kickstand. "I know I've been back in town a while now and it seems an odd time to be starting to ask questions, but I was wondering..." Harley swallowed hard and looked away. Man, it was hard, but he had to ask, now, before he lost his nerve. "Do you have a minute to talk about Dad's accident?"

"Oh, of course." The old man planted a hand firmly on Harley's shoulder. "Why don't we go into my office."

The police station, a tasteful brick building with huge planters of fall mums by the doors, was nestled along the west edge of The Green. Harley hadn't set foot in the building except once. Against his will, as a teenager. He could still taste the shame of his father arriving to collect him after being caught spray-painting a word on the back of the middle school gym that wouldn't have been tolerated at home.

Thirteen years later and Thelma, the chief's secretary, still sat at the same desk she had that day. However, her companion was new. A fluffy little black and white dog began beating its tail against the bottom of Thelma's chair when the two men stepped through the door.

"You look familiar," Harley said as he bent and ruffled the dog's ears. "You wouldn't happen to have come from Boston, would you?"

"Why, yes she did. Via that poor man who died this past spring. Such a shame, but I sure am glad I ended up with his Princess!" the older woman said as she scooped the little dog onto her lap.

"What is it that you wanted to know?" the police chief asked as he led Harley into his office and walked around to the other side of his desk.

What did he want to know? Harley ran his hand over his eyes and tried to order his thoughts. "I guess I just... want to know what happened. I mean I spoke with your deputy when I first got back to town and he gave me the basics, and I've gotten bits and pieces here and there, but... there must have been some kind of investigation."

Chief Briggs pushed his office chair back and it groaned under the abuse. He wheeled it over to the filing cabinet against the wall and opened a drawer, taking out a thin manila folder. Resting it on the desk calendar in front of him, he opened it with care.

"Of course we investigated, Charlie." The policeman picked up a pair of reading glasses off the desk and slipped them on the end of his nose before looking over them at Harley, his face serious. "Don't forget, he was my friend."

"I know. I'm sorry, sir. I didn't mean any disrespect. I just..." He trailed off.

"No, I get it. You're looking for closure." The man turned his attention back to the folder. "We took the bike into Finch and Jay's. Kept it under lock and key until the guy from the State Police came and did a vehicle autopsy."

"A what?"

"That's when we have an expert come in and go over the vehicle to figure out what happened."

"Is that what you did with Mr. Jay's Knucklehead? I mean, is that how it was ruled an accident?"

"Exactly. In the case of Lyle's bike, the guy was able to come the next day, but on your dad's it was done three or four days after the crash. It was inconclusive. There was a lot of front-end damage and some of the parts, well... You just couldn't tell exactly what happened."

Harley sighed. "I started working on repairing his bike last week. I know, I know." He put up his hand when the older man opened his mouth. "It's been two and a half years and I should have done it long before now."

"Actually, I was going to say, 'Good for you. That must be hard.'"

Harley pressed his lips together. The policeman's sympathy was unexpected. "Were there any contributing factors? I mean, it was the seventh of November. Was it icy? Did he swerve to miss an animal? Was he speeding?"

Chief Briggs thumbed through the few pages in the file, stopping now and then to read something. "To be honest with you Charlie, we just don't know. There wasn't any evidence of a cause. Nothing in the road he'd hit, no ice, no skid marks from trying to brake like you'd see if he'd tried to avoid an animal. His tox-screen was clean—"

"Tox-screen? Seriously? You ran a tox-screen on Reverend Cooper Beck?"

The other man's eyes softened. "Charlie, it's standard procedure. We didn't suspect anything. I'm just saying, we covered all our bases."

Harley ran his hand down his face again. "I'd hoped... I don't even know. That there was some reason for it. I'd hoped it wasn't just..."

"An accident?"

"Yeah."

Closing the file, Chief Briggs rested his elbows on the desk and steepled his hands. "As I said, we covered all our bases..."

Harley pushed himself up in his chair and leaned forward to rest his elbows on his knees. "But?"

The man took a long time to answer. "We didn't ignore anything. I promise. We looked at what there was, which wasn't much, and decided that we didn't have enough evidence to determine why he'd crashed. Maybe he fell asleep, maybe he had a medical incident. I don't know. But..." The man swiveled his chair so he was looking out the window. "But, that week was a madhouse around here. The FBI was in town. Big sting operation to catch Rocco Lowell. You heard of him?"

"Modern-day mobster, right?"

"That's the one. Turned out he'd been using Summer Harbor to funnel drugs and girls into the US. Makes me sick to think it was happening right under my nose. He'd come in on his fancy yacht, stay for a few days, and leave. This is a tourist town. No one thought anything of it. Until the FBI showed up."

"Didn't they finally get charges to stick?"

"I guess. The trial's set to start this winter or maybe next spring. At the time the FBI had an informant who was set to testify, but the way I hear it they lost track of the guy or some such nonsense. Anyway, that's beside the point. Except to say that my meager police force was stretched as thin as it gets. We didn't skimp on the investigation into your dad's accident, I swear, but we didn't dig very deep either."

"And now? Is there anything you can go back and look at now?"

The sigh that the cop puffed out was full of sympathy, but Harley knew what was coming before the man said a word.

No.

"I've got some cold cases that I pull out now and then." The chief patted a small stack of files on the corner of his desk. "A burglary at Maine Heritage Museum eight years ago, for example. The thief made off with a couple million dollars worth of art. Or the hiker who went missing six years ago. One minute he's with his buddies, the next, gone. Or Jason Whittley. Hit-and-run three years ago. No leads. If I'm going to put man-hours into a cold case, it's going to be something like that. Not an accident. I'm sorry, Charlie. I wish I had more for you. I really do. If I could give you closure, I would."

Disappointment weighed heavy on Harley's shoulders, but he understood. Pushing to his feet, he extended a hand to his father's old friend. "Thanks for taking a few minutes to talk about it."

Chief Briggs gave Harley's hand a firm shake but didn't let go immediately. "I hope you find what you're looking for Charlie."

After thanking the cop again, Harley headed out into the sunshine and climbed back on his Norton. He was barely moving by the time he walked the bike into the driveway of his dad's house and set the kickstand. He sat there for a long moment collecting his thoughts. It was time to man up and face the music.

Harley hadn't been at the house when Erin arrived that morning after stopping at Finnley's to grab the shingles she needed for the roof and paint for the floor. Thankful that he'd given her a key to the back door, Erin now stood at the familiar sink, looking into the familiar backyard, washing dark gray paint from her hands. She'd put down shingles on the roof until the sun was high enough to start searing her neck. Then she'd switched to painting the first coat on the floor. It wasn't anywhere near time to call it a day, but there wasn't much else she could do until the paint dried. She closed her eyes and breathed in the familiar smell of home. It had been diminished a little by the citrusy scent of the cleaner Harley had used, but it was still there.

God, please help me to not pick up any of the stuff I gave you last night. I mean, please help me not to pick it up again. You want me to cast my burdens on You. And if I do, You promise to sustain me. Please let sustaining include helping me where Harley is concerned.

After Vera left the evening before, Erin threw herself into building boxes. She'd worked late into the night trying hard not to think about Harley or their knee-weakening kiss. But when she dropped into bed, exhausted, in the wee hours of the morning, sleep had still eluded her. Finally, she did what she should have done in the first place and laid it all out before the Lord. All the hurts from her childhood that had resurfaced, the pain from losing people she loved, and the new hurt of being rejected by Harley. She'd held nothing back.

As the sky had lightened with the rising sun she'd been reminded with stunning clarity that God's mercies were new every morning. And hers should be, too. She didn't know what Harley was dealing with and she didn't want to hold onto hurt, so she'd asked God for help. Asked Him to guide her and give her wisdom. Asked Him to show her clearly what He wanted from her.

On her way to the house an hour later she'd remembered the box.

Coop had kept every single envelope that Harley had ever sent home in an old shoebox. She wasn't privy to what was inside the envelopes, but she'd seen Coop going through them again and again. He'd smile as he read the occasional slip of paper he'd pulled from one, sometimes wiping away a tear. He thought she hadn't noticed, but she had.

One Christmas, Erin had made Coop a wooden box to keep them in. Her first wooden box. She'd measured the shoebox to make sure the one she made was the right size. Jason Whittley had helped her build it, walking her through each step until she had a beautiful, silky-smooth maple box with a small brass latch. He'd cried when he lifted it from the wrapping paper.

On more than one occasion, Harley had made it clear that he believed Coop hadn't cared that his son had left, or even that he'd been happy about it. If she could find that box, maybe whatever was in it would help Harley see how much his father had loved him. Missed him. She didn't know for sure, but she had to try.

A glance out the kitchen window confirmed that Harley still wasn't there. Slipping down the darkened hallway to Coop's room, she eased the door open. The squeak of the old hinges sounded loud in the silence and she hesitated for a second.

The room was just as he'd left it. Slightly disheveled but clean. It still smelled like him. A little musty from being closed up, but she picked up hints of his aftershave and the cedar from his closet. It was her favorite scent, woodsy and masculine. The man had used one corner as a study area, with floor-to-ceiling bookcases crammed full of reference books and commentaries. She walked over to a small table buried in books beside his easy chair, his Bible on the top. She ran her fingers over the leather cover that was worn nearly through where it had rested in his hand, the edges of the pages tattered from use.

Within reach of his study area was the most logical place for the box and she started looking on the shelves closest to the chair, but they turned up nothing. Neither did his nightstand. Erin looked around the room, trying to think where he would tuck something that meant so much to him. The thing had to be here!

She was still standing in the middle of the room with her

hands on her hips when she heard the motorcycle. She took a peek under the bed before stepping back into the hall and pulling the door closed behind her. The last thing she wanted was to get caught! It was one thing to hand Harley the box and say 'I thought you might want this.' It was something completely different to be caught using the key he'd given her in good faith to snoop through the house.

Harley was setting his helmet on the seat when he caught sight of her. He sucked in a sharp breath and met her eyes. She knew she looked vulnerable but wasn't sure what to do about it. "I thought I heard you," she said shyly.

"I had a few hours between tours. Thought I'd work on the bike." It looked like he wanted to say more, but dropped his eyes to the ground, scrubbing his toe along a crack in the pavement. "Erin..."

And this was where the grace and mercy came in. She smiled and gestured with the two mismatched mugs from Coop's cupboard that she was holding. So what if she felt the tiniest bit of guilt for going into Coop's room without permission and was using the coffee as her silent peace offering?

"I hope you don't mind," she said. "But I took the liberty of making some coffee." His smile made her heart flutter and she swallowed away her misdeed. "Cream and sugar, or black?"

"Black, please."

"I was hoping you'd say that," she said as she handed him the larger mug. "Otherwise I was going to have to go fix that one up before I could drink it." She took a sip, watching him over the rim of her cup. "How's the motorcycle coming along, anyway?"

"Good." He gestured with the mug toward the side door of the garage and she followed him.

A series of busted pieces of motorcycle lay against the exterior wall and she shuddered. If she hadn't already been terrified of the things, seeing what could happen to one would have done the trick. No. Thank. You!

"I've got the front-end taken apart, and I'm working on the engine now." He shook his head. "I thought about replacing it, but I can't afford even a used one right now. So... I'm going to make this one purr."

They stood looking at the bike for a moment before Erin reached out and ran her hand against the saddle. It was softened from years of wear. She felt the tears coming and looked down at her coffee, blinking them away. She wasn't a crier, but being back at Coop's, and then Lyle's crash... it had just hit too close to home.

"Are you going to be able to salvage a lot?"

"Oh, sure. The saddle's fine, and it looks like this is brand new," Harley said, using the toe of his boot to nudge a section of exhaust pipe coming off of the engine and curling around behind the footrest. Gesturing with the mug he pointed out a stack of parts on the counter. Most of them appeared to be the same brand, neatly labeled on orange and gray boxes. His voice got quiet. "Dad always did all his own work on the bikes. It's where I learned..." He stopped talking and took another sip of coffee before setting his mug on the windowsill and moving to the workbench and rummaging around in the drawers. He cleared his throat and Erin suspected he was trying to pull himself together. She wanted to reach out, to tell him she understood, to offer comfort. Not for the first time, Erin was struck by how handsome he was. Wide shoulders honed from countless hours in a kayak, the dark intensity of his brooding face and black hair, his large hands that were so gentle whenever he touched her. She could feel her heart rate picking up speed

Now would be a good time to tell him how much Coop meant to you.

She opened her mouth, but the words curdled on her tongue. Cori was right, an omission got harder to correct the longer one waited.

"Huh," Harley said as he slipped a stack of papers from one of the small drawers in the workbench.

"What is it?" Erin asked, happy for any kind of distraction.

"It looks like invoices from Finch and Jay's for 'maintenance'."

"I thought you just said that your dad did all his own work?" She could attest to that being the case. Happy memories of sitting on the twirly stool in the corner and talking about life or school or Jesus while Coop tinkered, came back, making her smile.

Harley laid the bills out on the workbench and started arranging them in order by date. "Yeah, he did... At least he did when I was here." He picked up the last one and studied it. "Hold on..." He fished a piece of paper from his back pocket and unfolded it. "I've been carrying one around in my pocket all week. I thought it was just scrap paper." He held the list up for her to see, then flipped the paper over revealing another invoice. He smoothed it out next to the others. "This one is dated three days before he died." He methodically folded the bill into quarters and slipped it back into the pocket of his jeans. "I need to go talk to Dox."

Erin took a sip of her coffee before speaking. "Is this a visit you want to make alone?" She paused before continuing, unsure. "Or would you mind some company?"

"You want to tag along to the motorcycle shop?"

"I'd like to check on Dox. Give me a minute?" Taking his empty cup, she held it up in explanation and headed for the door.

Harley was waiting for her on the sidewalk when she emerged from the house. "Ready?" He'd grabbed his chamois shirt off the nail by the door and was shrugging into it when she joined him. They walked up to Main Street in silence, but as they turned onto the busier sidewalk, Harley cleared his throat. "You must have known my dad pretty well."

It was a statement, but held the expectation of response. She almost laughed, snapping her mouth closed just in time to keep it from escaping. She wasn't sure there was anyone out there who knew how close she'd been to Coop. Walking along a busy sidewalk, having to raise her voice to be heard, was not the time to have this conversation. Besides, saying something akin to 'he might as well have been my dad' didn't seem right for the casualness of the moment. Maybe there never would be a time to tell him the entire story.

Tell him.

She ignored the thought and opted for noncommittal. "Oh, sure. Didn't everybody? I mean... Reverend Cooper Beck. Am I right?" Yup, she sounded like an idiot. Better to move to safer ground. "What do you think is up with that invoice?"

Harley gave her a look that said he knew she was changing the subject, but didn't push. "I'm not sure. That's why I want to talk to Dox. At the very least, someone had eyes on the bike a few days before it crashed. Maybe they know of something wrong with it. Something that could explain what happened."

"Wouldn't the police have already checked that?"

"Maybe, maybe not. Chief Briggs said they were stretched pretty thin that week. Maybe somebody missed something?"

There was a melancholy atmosphere at Finch and Jay's that she could almost taste, but they were open and doing business. That had to be a good sign. Even Dox was working on the underside of a modern touring bike. When he spotted them, he wheeled the creeper he was laying on away from the motorcycle.

"Harley and Erin. What can I do for you today?" Dox asked as he hauled himself up from the floor, dusting off his jeans with a rag he'd pulled from his pocket. The man looked beaten. He'd lost weight and the smile lines that bracketed his mouth pulled it down in a frown.

"Hey, Dox," Erin said, hugging the older man.

"Mornin', sugar." The older man's voice sounded tired.

Once Erin stepped back, Harley slipped the piece of paper from his back pocket and handed it over. "I found this and was wondering if you knew what had been done on dad's bike?"

"Oh, your dad had it in here now and then for little things."

"Look at the date," Harley said.

Dox nodded toward his office at the back. Once inside, the older man heaved out a sigh. "What's this all about?"

Harley took a deep breath. "I don't even know what I'm looking for. Reason maybe? Or an explanation? An answer?" He could hear the frustration in his voice and felt Erin touch the back of his arm, calming him.

The older man nodded his head. "You're searching because answers help us make sense of things," he said as he scratched his head and looked at the bill again, running his finger down the sheets. He set it in front of Harley and tapped the last line. It read 'mechanic'. "Each of the guys has a number. Makes billing and payroll easier I guess. He'd be the one to talk to."

Harley picked the slip up and looked at it. "May I speak to him?"

Dox shrugged his shoulders. "He doesn't work for us anymore. Moved to a shop up the road. But I can give you the address."

Dox wrote out the information for the motorcycle mechanic and handed it to Harley. "Name's Alec Cohen."

Erin schooled her face to show nothing, but sweat slicked her hands and her stomach soured. Alec? Seriously? No, no, no! Memories flooded back. The smell of stale beer and unwashed...everything. The fear that she'd do or say the wrong thing and become an outcast, homeless and alone. The wretched hopelessness. The future shadowed by alcohol and drugs. He'd never physically hurt her, but she'd lived in constant fear that a drunk or high Alec might do something a sober Alec wouldn't have dared. She was trying to shake away the thoughts when she realized that Harley and Dox had continued talking, oblivious to the turmoil ricocheting through her brain. She swallowed hard and tried to pick up the conversation.

"—worked here for about three years before he... well, before he... left." Dox was saying.

"Left?"

"To be honest, Lyle was hard on the guy. Unreasonably hard.

I never understood it, but he rode the kid about every little thing. Couldn't do anything right in Lyle's eyes. I don't know how he lasted as long as he did. He just left a few weeks ago."

Harley cast a look in Erin's direction. "So this Alec guy had a beef with Lyle?"

"I guess," the older man answered. "So what?"

"Well, it's just that Erin and I keep wondering if… I mean Lyle was an awfully good driver to have simply driven his bike into a cliff. We're wondering if… he had help."

Shock widened the man's eyes and he sank into the chair behind the desk. "You mean… you think… someone…?"

"I don't know, Dox. It just seems like he ought to have been able to handle the bike and then we keep coming across people who had problems with him or reasons to want him out of the way."

"I just can't imagine…" Dox pressed his hand to his mouth. "People didn't like him much, but do you honestly think someone could have… You know…" Dox lowered his voice. "… Murdered him?"

Harley softened his tone. "Probably not. Just, if I'm going to ask this Alec guy about Dad's bike, I might ask about Lyle, too. You wouldn't happen to know anyone else we should talk to, would you?"

Dox shook his head, looking back and forth between Harley and Erin, his face still looking stunned. "No, just Alec. Like I said I can't imagine why the boy stayed on here. Three years is a long time to put up with being hammered into the ground by your employer. I tried to talk to Lyle about it on more than one occasion, but he told me to butt out."

Harley refolded the piece of paper and slid both it and the address into his pocket. "Thanks for the information," he said, extending his hand across the desk. Dox shook it, but Erin went around the desk to hug the older man before following Harley from the room, leaving Dox looking frayed and tired.

Emotions swam through Erin as they crossed the shop floor. She wanted to rip the slip of paper from Harley's pocket and tear it to shreds. The thought that Alec was still in town had never occurred to her. All this time she'd assumed he left, moved on. In her darkest moments, she even imagined that his life had caught up with him and he'd died the way he'd lived, drunk and high and not caring about anyone but himself. Rage boiled under her skin thinking that he'd been here in the shadows all this time. That he'd dragged others into the same life he'd drawn her into. Anger made the backs of her eyes sting, but she refused to shed one single tear over Alec Cohen.

They stepped out the door of the garage and into the radiant autumn sun. Birds chirped in a nearby bush covered in tiny fruit and the scent of the sea floated by. Erin closed her eyes for a second and filled her lungs with the warm, fragrant air.

God, I don't want to pick those old burdens back up! Please help me leave them where they belong. With you.

Be kind and tenderhearted. Forgive as I have forgiven you.

She opened her eyes to find Harley studying her.

She felt her cheeks heat and flashed him a smile she didn't quite feel.

CHAPTER TEN

J udging by Erin's reaction when Dox mentioned the name of his former employee, Harley suspected she wasn't going with him to question Alec Cohen. She'd stopped outside Finch and Jay's, turning her face toward the sun, and he just stood there like a fool watching her. She had to be the most appealing woman he'd ever met. Beautiful, yes, but it was more than that. There was just something...

When she opened her eyes and caught him looking at her, she flashed a smile that rivaled the sun itself and held his gaze. Even her hazel eyes smiled at him, making his mouth go dry. He didn't think anyone had ever looked at him quite the way she did. Like she saw him. Really saw him. And wasn't intimidated by what she saw. As if she didn't even see who he'd become, but instead, maybe, saw who he was meant to be. It wasn't the first time she'd looked at him that way and he had to admit he was growing rather fond of it.

They were well away from the motorcycle shop before Erin spoke. "I don't want to go with you to talk to Alec."

"I know." He'd been right. Too bad. He'd started liking their little Starsky and Hutch thing they had going. His lips twitched as he held the door open. He was most definitely Starsky, but she made a much prettier Hutch than David Soul. He snickered at the thought.

"What was that for?"

Busted. "I was just thinking that you are so much prettier than David Soul. And Owen Wilson for that matter."

"I don't know what that means."

"Starsky and Hutch?" He did his best to look appalled when

she stared at him blankly. "I am wounded that you don't know who I'm talking about. TV detectives from the '70s?"

"Sorry."

He thought for a minute and then snapped his fingers. "Frank Hardy and Nancy Drew?"

"That reference I get."

"What I was actually thinking, was that detective work isn't much fun alone." Something had her spooked. He wanted to press her about it, but at the same time, he didn't want the anxiety that had flooded her at the mention of Alec's name to return. He'd hated how her face had paled and the flicker of fear in her eyes.

They reached her truck, and Erin leaned against the rear bumper. "I need to tell you something," she said softly, not quite meeting his eyes. "When I was fourteen this guy moved into town. I knew he was trouble from the first moment I laid eyes on him. Big, lots of tattoos."

Harley tried not to chuckle because it was obvious she was serious, but he couldn't help it. "Trouble, huh?"

"Absolutely." The ghost of a smile tugged at her lips, but it faded as quick as it came. "Anyway, he was twenty and he paid attention to me. I was so infatuated with him that I couldn't... Or maybe wouldn't, see who he was." Erin shuddered as if the memories gave her chills. "One day I saw him selling something to a kid who'd been in my class. I'd known for a while that he was using, but not that he was selling. Or maybe I'd been purposely blind. I don't know. When I confronted him about it... he lost it. I was so scared."

"Erin—"

"That boy was Alec Cohen."

All sorts of protective feelings flooded Harley's system. His fists clenched and he had to deliberately uncurl his fingers. He wanted to punch something. Hard. Preferably Cohen.

Erin was quiet for a few moments. "I don't *want* to go with you to talk to Alec, but I will," she said, puffing out a sigh.

"No, Erin, you don't have to do that."

"I think I need to."

"Are you saying that because *you* need to go? Or are you saying that because you think I'll do something foolish if I go alone?"

"Yes."

Well, at least she was honest. He was at a loss for words. What do you even say to that kind of revelation? And going to confront what was certainly a painful memory? Crazy brave. Reaching for her door, he pulled it open and waited. "Alright, let's go."

A few minutes later, Erin pulled the truck to a stop in the parking area of a newer garage. It sat back from the road, tucked between a motor inn and a campground just outside of town. It wasn't busy. Only one bay was open, a burly mechanic standing in it with his back to the door. Harley had to fight the urge to snatch the man by the back of the neck and pummel him into the floor. Erin slipped her hand into his and held tight. Reassuring herself or restraining him, he wasn't sure.

"Excuse me," Harley said when the mechanic didn't turn around.

"I'll be with ya in just a second," he called over his shoulder. "I just have to get this oil filter back into place and... There we go! Now, what can I do for—" He stopped short as he turned to face them, shock blanching his face. "Erin?"

"Hello, Alec."

His eyes darted to Harley and his face lost what little color it had left. He took a small step back, pulling a rag from his back pocket, he wiped his hands, making the tattoos running up both forearms ripple. "What—?" He swallowed before trying again. "What can I do for you?"

According to Erin, Alec was close to Harley's age, but he looked far older. Worn around the edges. Harley scratched his beard, thinking about where exactly he wanted to start. Maybe with a question he already knew the answer to. "You know Lyle Jay?"

A vein ticked on the side of Alec's forehead. "Yeah, I knew

him. Why?"

"You hear about him crashing his bike?"

"Of course. The whole town's heard. I'm surprised nobody's put one of them little white crosses up on the side of the road yet. Although it beats me who would want to honor that man."

"I take it you weren't friends?"

The other man licked his lips and looked around the shop before nodding his head to the open garage door. They stepped into the fresh air and he lowered his voice. "The only reason I'm telling you this is 'cause you already figured it out..." he said, not taking his eyes off of Erin but keeping his distance from Harley. "Back then. Before. I wasn't *just* using. Lyle found out and held it over me."

"In what way?" Harley asked.

Alec finally looked his way. "Threatened to tell the police unless I worked for him. For no pay, I might add. I had to get a second job here just to eat. Then, a few weeks ago I'd finally had enough and left, but he just threatened to tell my boss unless I paid him off."

"He was blackmailing you?" Erin asked.

Alec nodded. "Part of me wanted to just run away. But... I'm tired of hiding and constantly worrying that today's the day that the cops show up to arrest me. When he came to me, week before last, demanding more money I swore it was going to be the last time. I told him if he came at me again I'd go to the cops myself."

"Must make you pretty happy that Lyle's no longer a threat."

"Hey now! Are you insinuating that I had something to do with Lyle's accident?"

"We're just... trying to piece things together," Erin said, tugging on Harley's hand to get him moving back toward the truck.

Harley nodded to the mechanic and hoped his expression conveyed his feelings for the man. Alec met his eyes but quickly looked away. Yup, message delivered.

In the truck, Erin sat staring at the steering wheel.

"You OK?" Harley asked.

"Yeah, I just... I needed to leave."

Throwing the truck in gear, she drove back to the house in silence, stopping at the curb. They sat in silence for a minute. What he usually wanted to do when he felt like this was get on his bike and ride west. For a long time. Maybe forever. But today, with Erin, laughing about hokey TV shows and playing detective... his need to run had evaporated. Replaced by a better idea. Harley cleared his throat. "I was thinking of heading out of town for a few hours. Want to... join me?"

A huge, shy smile spread across her face, but she dialed it back quickly. "Only if you want me to."

Aww, honey. What had he done? *Want* her to join him? Of course, he did! More than he should. And therein lay the problem. Wanting her had never been the issue. It was him. He was the problem. However, at the moment he didn't care. Right that second his only desire was to tuck Erin in close to his side, protect her, and try to absorb her calm. "I absolutely want you to join me."

Flashing the shy smile again, Erin turned the key to restart the truck. The old thing whined and coughed and fussed, but refused to turn over. She tried again and again, but Harley could hear the battery winding down. They weren't going anywhere in her old beater.

Hopping out of the cab, he grabbed her Carhart jacket from the middle of the seat and tossed it to her. "Come on, I've got this."

He was glad to see she had a decent jacket with her. It was hot in the sun, but it was going to be cold on his bike. Besides, risking his own skin was one thing, risking Erin's made him a little sick. Harley left Erin climbing out of the truck cab and went into the garage. Rummaging around on the shelves near the workbench he grabbed a second helmet.

"I think this used to be my mom's," he said as he emerged from the garage. Erin had a deer-in-the-headlights look on her face and he hoped it didn't mean she'd nix his idea. After helping her put the helmet on, he adjusted the straps so it fit properly. Man, she was adorable.

A memory flickered of his dad smiling at his mom like she hung the moon. He'd never understood that look. Until now. He swallowed hard. Stepping around her so she couldn't see the sudden emotion he knew was there on his face for all the world to see. Why the heck did he turn into a blubbering baby around her? He'd slung his leg over the seat and clipped his helmet into place before he realized Erin had yet to move from the sidewalk.

"Y'all set?" he asked. She was chewing on her bottom lip as she eyed the back of the bike.

"Yeah, sure. It's just that I've never ridden one of these before. I'm a little nervous." With great effort, she met his eyes. "Scratch that. I'm scared to death."

"Trust me?" He offered her his hand and held his breath. The words had slipped out before they could be stopped, and the sudden realization that she could decimate him with her answer had him feeling far more vulnerable than he was comfortable with. And it wasn't just this one answer that could hurt him. The woman had the ability to wound him in deep tender places that he didn't like to think about.

Erin didn't hesitate though, and that simple act spoke volumes to his ragged heart. She clutched his outstretched hand and climbed on the back of the bike, finding the rear footrests with her boots. He started the bike but didn't move, smiling as she tried to find a place for her hands.

"You're going to want to hold on," he shouted over the bike's engine.

"I'm trying to find a place to hold on."

He couldn't help the chuckle that rumbled from his chest. "Me, Erin! You hold onto me!"

He couldn't be quite sure, but he thought she was blushing. The instant she wrapped her arms around his waist he realized that every nerve in his body knew exactly where her hands were. Laughter bubbled from his chest. Again.

"What's so funny?" she asked near his ear.

"Clyde was right!"

"What?"

He worked his legs, walking the bike backward until they rolled out onto the road. "Nothin'. Just something a friend said."

At the end of the street, he turned them southwest and headed out of town. Instead of winding through the seaside towns close to Summer Harbor, Harley took a quieter, more direct road that cut through the center of the island. Within minutes they were turning south. The ribbon of blacktop took them past the sprawling fields of Wyldwinds, a farm that tried its best to look like something out of an old western. The rolling pastures were dotted with horses and the old farmhouse was tucked into the shadow of a weathered red barn and a worse-for-wear windmill. At a fork in the road, he stopped and turned in his seat to be heard over the noise. "Where to?"

Erin tightened her grip. "You pick. I trust you."

Harley felt his chest swell. Trust. He hadn't even known he wanted people to trust him. Craved it even. He liked the way she said it, too. As if she didn't even have to think about it. He turned away from the shore and took the long way around the island. He'd always liked the idea of getting on his bike and riding until there was no road left, but with Erin behind him and her arms wrapped around his waist, he never wanted to get off the bike again. Yup, Clyde had most definitely been right.

The road Harley had chosen meandered toward the less-populated side of the island. The loud growl of the motorcycle drowned out any chance of conversation while they rode, but Erin didn't mind. She wasn't sure she'd ever been as scared in all her life as she was the moment she realized what Harley had planned. At least she hadn't thrown up. That was a victory all by itself. Then he'd held out his hand and she just knew he wouldn't let anything happen to her.

Once she'd gotten over the wild adrenaline rush of the first few seconds she had started to see a bit of the appeal of the bike. The wind on her skin, the hard-muscled man under her hands, the delightful growl of the motor. Maybe not her favorite thing, but she could see the draw.

They dipped down through a section of the national park that was heavily wooded and passed several hiking trails, a ranger station, and a couple of parking lots before sliding into the first sleepy little village along the edge of the water. The harbor was dotted with boats and the tide was out just enough to reveal a pebbly beach. It smelled of salt and seaweed and Harley rolled to a stop in the same parking lot where he'd left the truck the day he'd taken them to Blueberry Island.

Balancing the bike with his feet planted on the ground, he waited for Erin to scoot off before engaging the kickstand and swinging his leg over the back of the bike.

"This spot is beautiful," she said as she unclipped her helmet and handed it to him. "Funny, I don't ever remember coming here before, and now I've been twice in just a few weeks."

Once he'd stowed their helmets in the panniers on the back of the bike they walked across the road and toward the edge of the water. Harley turned his face to the wind and looked out over the harbor. "My mom used to bring me. It was one of her favorite places. We used to walk along the shore and look for shells." There was a wistfulness in his voice and he took no time at all changing the subject. "You grew up here on the island?"

Erin shrugged and breathed in a deep breath of salt air. "Somewhat. My mom and I moved here from Connecticut when I was about six."

"Not a Mainer then?"

Erin looked at Harley out of the corner of her eye and found him trying to hide a grin. She laughed. "Nope. And never will be. What about you? Are you a Mainer?"

"Born and raised. Dad grew up here, too. He met Mom at seminary and they moved back here before I was born."

"You miss her," she said quietly when he didn't continue. She'd never met Jules Beck, but from the stories Cooper had told, she knew she would have, without a doubt, loved the woman.

"I do." There was a long pause while he collected his thoughts and Erin let him be. She was well acquainted with the complicated feelings that came with missing someone. If he'd turned the tables and asked if she missed Coop she'd have a hard time putting it into words, too. 'I do' wouldn't begin to cover it. He shrugged as if to say 'it is what it is' before looking at her. "It was a long time ago. What about your mom? You said she got remarried?"

"Yeah, they moved... gosh... eight years ago now."

He narrowed his eyes and she could tell he was doing the math. She looked away, out over the water. She didn't often think about that time in her life, but lately, the memories kept bombarding her. Even now, flashes of the last time she'd seen her mother, the decisions that had been made, the hurts that hadn't been mended. She wouldn't meet his eyes for fear that he would be able to read all the guilt and heartache from the past.

"I take it that by saying *they* moved instead of *we* moved that you didn't go with them?"

"I don't think..."

He waited, patient, rocked back on his heels with his thumbs caught in his pockets. When she didn't speak again, he slipped his hand into hers and turned her to face him, concern in his eyes. "Don't think what?"

She swallowed and tried to meet his eyes. She only managed to focus on the collar of his shirt. "By the time they left... I don't think they wanted me to go with them."

"Seriously?"

Finally able to bring her eyes up to his, she was surprised to find them full of compassion, not pity. Empathy, not disbelief. "It's a long story," she said and looked away. "Or maybe not long, maybe just unpleasant. I don't usually talk about it."

He hadn't let go of her hand and she tightened her hold as they started walking again. She could feel the roughness of his calluses against her palm and she figured he could feel the ones on hers as well. It didn't seem to bother him. They were nearing the middle of the beach, where an outcropping of red granite crept toward the water. Harley sat on it and, with a gentle tug, pulled Erin down to sit beside him.

"I don't mind long stories. Or unpleasant ones for that matter."

She thought for a long time, staring out at the little harbor but not seeing it. Harley's hand stayed clasped with hers, warm and solid and patient. "I already told you I was a troublemaker..." This was harder than she thought it would be.

He was quiet for a second and then a snort of laughter startled her.

"What's so funny?"

"I'm sorry. I'm just having a hard time picturing you being a little punk. Troublemaker? Really?"

She chuckled. "Right down to the black lipstick."

"That I absolutely cannot imagine."

It felt good to laugh. She avoided telling people who she used to be. It wasn't who she was anymore. It occurred to her that the next time she told her story she would have this moment to soften the hard edges of the memories. It also eased the tight feeling keeping her thoughts captive.

"When I was in middle school I started hanging out with the wrong people. Of course, sixth graders, how much trouble can you get into, right? By the time I reached high school though I was getting into trouble more than I wasn't. For some reason, I had made it my life goal to do the exact opposite of everything my parents wanted from me. They wanted good grades, I flunked out. They wanted me to stay out of trouble, I'd search for it. By the time I turned fourteen I was barely living at home anymore. On a rare night that I did come home, they told me they were moving to Cape Cod. I told them I wasn't going with them." She stole a glance at him not sure what she was expecting and was somewhat taken aback by the look of understanding.

"I can sort of relate."

When he didn't elaborate, she continued. "Anyway, they moved without me. In hindsight of course I wish it was different, but I don't know how to fix what I broke that night. I didn't even invite them to my graduation from trade school last spring. There was no point. They wouldn't have wanted to come."

Harley's hand tightened on hers. "They're the ones missing out."

It was her turn to shrug. "With help, I got my act together and I'm doing fine now. As much as I'd like to mend things, they aren't that bad, they're just... the way they are. I mean, if I can find a way to have a relationship with my mom again, I'll take it. I even thought about moving to Cape Cod. Maybe if I try to fit into their world..."

She leaned into Harley's arm and tipped her face up to smile at him. "What about you?"

And just like that, the lighthearted mood vanished. His face clouded. "I think that might be a conversation for another time." He puffed out a sigh and ran his hand over his face. "Suffice it to say, I was a troublemaker, too, but I didn't choose to stay. I chose to leave." After a long pause, he smiled and hopped to his feet, dragging her up next to him. "Come on. If memory serves, there's an ice cream stand at the end of the beach and I'm pretty sure today calls for mint chocolate chip cones."

As they walked up the slope of the shore and onto the road a few minutes later, Harley reached out and took Erin's elbow to steady her. When they reached the pavement, he let his fingers slide down her forearm and wove them with hers. A part of him screamed that he shouldn't. They'd been holding hands for the past half hour, but an old familiar voice had surfaced while they were ordering, telling him he didn't deserve her. Yet it almost felt like he was incapable of *not* taking her hand again. They walked back toward the parking lot along the edge of the road, holding hands and eating their ice cream.

"Can you believe this weather?" Erin asked.

Small talk. He could do small talk. "It might as well be the end of August instead of the end of September."

"I'm guessing when it turns cold it's going to turn fast." She licked her ice cream before continuing. "How much longer does Noah run tours?"

"Only until mid-October. By then he won't be going out every day, but we always get a rush of tourists wanting to see the fall colors. Good to end the season on a high note."

"And then Finnley's for the winter?"

He nodded his head and popped the last of his cone into his mouth. "Are you doing OK on the bike?"

She grinned at him over the top of her cone. "I'm good. I thought it would be scarier but... well, with you it isn't."

First, she'd shown that she trusted him by getting on the bike in the first place. Now she was saying she wasn't scared *because* she was with him? Couldn't she see him? He worked hard at not looking intimidating when he was working a tour. Had gotten good at blending into the background and appearing friendly when need be. But he knew he looked scary. Once upon a time that was how he'd held his own. How he'd survived. Some of that never went away. However, she looked at him like she didn't see it. Clearly, she didn't know him.

Which wasn't her fault.

She'd tried to wheedle her way in a few minutes ago and he'd barely been able to resist pouring it all out right then and there. Somehow he'd kept her at a distance. Arm's length was his MO. So no, she didn't know him.

Maybe he should keep it that way.

And yet... for the first time since his mom died, Harley wanted someone to know him. Really know him. Know the him that he didn't let other people see. The him that, ten years ago, he'd buried as deep as he possibly could under anger, and tattoos, and attitude, and choices he regretted to this day.

"How'd you get into kayaking?" Erin asked around a mouth full of ice cream.

"I needed a job."

"That's it?" She didn't sound convinced.

"That's it. How did you get into carpentry?" he asked.

She took another lick of ice cream before answering. "My landlady's husband. The shop was his. He was very kind to me once upon a time and I liked watching him make things. I used to go to his shop after school a lot. One day he asked if I wanted to build something. That's all it took."

"And working for Finnley's?"

She giggled. "I needed a job. Also, Keaton is my landlady's brother."

"No way." Sometimes, especially in the summer when millions upon millions of tourists descended on Summer Harbor, it was hard to remember that it was a small town. However, with just shy of five thousand year-round residents, that's what it was.

Erin nodded her head. "When I decided it was time to come home I got in touch with Vera and asked about the apartment and the shop and if she knew of any jobs in town." Her face turned sheepish. "I think she may have played the sister card to get me the job at Finnley's, but I'll take it."

"And your landlady's husband?"

"Jason?" She looked away and a little of the light dimmed from her face. "Killed in a hit-and-run three years ago."

"Oh, Erin, I'm so sorry."

"I miss him, but he gave me some remarkable things before he passed away. Like a listening ear, a love for wood, and the ability to whip anyone at cribbage." Her grin still held a tinge of sadness, but it wasn't consuming her.

He wanted peace like she had. He wanted his past mistakes and regrets to fade away the same as hers had. The small bit she'd shared about her teenage years had been heartbreaking. He'd wanted to somehow make it go away. Then losing a friend in such a tragic way... Despite her past though, she had a beautiful light that shone from within her. That's what he wanted. That light.

"How do you do it?"

"Do what?"

"Go on with life and have this... this... I don't even know what to call it. Brightness?"

"Are you sure you want to know?" she asked as they neared the motorcycle. Her thumb was running gently up and down the side of his and he tightened his grip. How could something as innocent as holding hands make his heart soar? It was crazy.

"I do."

"Jesus." His face must have registered the skepticism he felt because she laughed softly and squeezed his hand. "I'm not just saying that."

She had to be kidding. "It's a nice thought, but Jesus doesn't take *everyone's* bad stuff and turn it into something that shines out of them." He should know.

"Have you asked Him to?" He looked away, but with a gentle tug, she pulled him around to face her. The sweet smile on her lips made his heart beat faster and his spirit lighter. "Harley, He wants everyone to give Him all their junk and leave it at His feet. But He lets them come to Him. He isn't going to wrestle it out of your arms against your will."

He sighed. "There was a time I might have thought it was that easy, but I'm not a child anymore and life has taught me that's a lot harder than it looks. Impossible even."

"The hard part is letting go. Of the anger, the grief, the sin that we're comfortable with. Taking it to Jesus isn't hard. *Leaving* it with Him is. I even pick it all back up sometimes. I'll get to thinking about ditching my parents, or the places I've been, the things I've done, or the people I've lost… Shame, and sorrow, and hurts… I have to choose not to pick them back up. But as long as I leave them at Jesus' feet, He takes care of them for me. The anger and hurt of making my parents leave without me? He turns that into an understanding that while *I* might have abandoned them, *He* used that to save me. The sorrow of losing Jason and —" Her voice hiccuped and she pressed the back of her hand to her mouth, looking away from him toward the boats bobbing in the inlet.

"Aw, honey. I didn't mean to make you cry."

"You didn't. It's one of those times I have to choose not to pick it up, that's all. Jesus' sacrifice and the fact that Jason loved Him dearly means that I'll get to see him again someday. I'm sad for me and how much I miss him, and for Vera, but I'm not sad for Jason. He gets to be with Jesus. How could I be sad about that?"

He smiled at the joy on her face and leaned down to press his lips to the top of her head. She smelled of something citrusy and the paint she'd put on the porch floor earlier and he wished he was tasting the sweet tang of the ice cream on her lips instead. He nearly leaned in but thought better of it. He'd had a glimpse of her and he liked her all the more for it. However, once she got a glimpse of who he was, would she still want to hold his hand? Would she let him kiss her hair? He wasn't convinced she would.

They were on the bike and cruising back toward Summer Harbor when the idea struck Harley that it was time.

Time to let someone in behind the wall that he'd built.

And if she decided she didn't like what she saw, well, his heart would probably heal…

Someday.

He used the next few miles to mull over exactly what parts to share. He didn't want to share too much, but he also didn't want her thinking better of him than she should either. Or maybe he did. At least a little bit. He had to admit the way she looked at him felt pretty darn good. He hoped that didn't change.

He could at least tell her about leaving. She might look down on him for running away, but in the end, was it all that different from her choices? There was a pretty good chance she could overlook it. The more shameful bits he might just keep hidden forever. Somehow, the idea of seeing condemnation, disgust, or loathing on her face wasn't anything he could stomach right then. The man looking back at him from the mirror every morning did enough of that. He didn't want it from her, too.

But it was a chance he was going to take.

Pulling into a parking area on the side of the road, he sat, fighting the anxiety in his chest. To ease it ever so slightly he focused on where Erin had her arms wrapped around him. Heat spread across his chest, calming his racing heart. If there was just some guarantee that she'd still want her arms there when he'd said what he needed to say—

"Everything OK?" she yelled.

He cut the engine and pulled his helmet off, resting it on the gas tank. Sucking in a breath, he closed his eyes. "The last words I ever said to my father were that I hated him."

Erin knew that in Coop's mind those hadn't been Harley's last words to him. How many times had he held the note with the scrawled 'I love you, Dad' on it? How many times had he rubbed it between his fingers, smoothed it out in front of him, prayed over it? But convincing Harley of that was another story for another time. If she could have just found that box! She should try harder. It had to be there. Somewhere. For now, she rested her hands on his shoulders and let him talk.

"I was seventeen and..." It sounded like his words were being forced out. She wanted to assure him that he could tell her anything, but she was afraid if she spoke he'd stop talking.

"Like I already said I made some bad choices about who I was hanging out with. Trouble. I guess you can relate. Anyway... I let one of the guys, he was older than me, probably nineteen, talk me into getting a tattoo." He pushed the sleeve of his t-shirt up to reveal a turquoise and orange dragon's head on his bicep.

"We'd been up to Bangor for the day and decided to stay at his friend's house overnight." He swallowed hard. "Without letting my dad know where I was. Sometime around 2:00 AM, it sounded like a good idea to go to the tattoo parlor the next morning. My friend had dark hair like mine and let me use his driver's license. Guess the guy at the tattoo place didn't look too closely at my ID or didn't care." He let out a chuckle. "It hurt like a son of a... gun. When we got back to Summer Harbor that night, Dad was livid."

Erin sucked in a slow breath. From here on she knew a lot of the story, but she bit her tongue. Waited.

Lord, I want to fix his hurts, but I know only You can do that. Please show me what You want from me!

Be quick to listen but slow to speak.

Erin unsnapped her helmet and rested it on her knee. Pressing her cheek to his back, she traced the dragon with her fingertip and waited, hoping he would continue. They were quiet for a long time. She was thankful that he'd shared a tiny piece of himself with her. Even if that was all he shared, it was enough for now.

A slight tremor rippled through his back and she knew he was wrecked.

"The more he yelled, the angrier I got until we were screaming at each other, neither listening. I just walked out the door and got on his bike. He came out the front door of the house yelling at me as I pulled away and the last words I ever said to him—" His voice caught on a sob that he swallowed down.

Erin slid her arms around him and held him close, her tears dampening the back of his shirt.

"I wish those hadn't been the last words I ever said to him. I always thought I'd have time. That someday maybe I'd have a chance to make it right. And then I'd remember that fight and I'd ride farther away."

"What made you finally decide to come back?"

"I don't even know. Something… pulled me in this direction. Like it was just time." Harley ran his hand over his eyes, wiping the moisture on the leg of his jeans.

"I'm sorry you were too late." She said it so quietly that she wasn't sure he heard her. He said nothing for a long time.

When he did speak again his voice was roughened by emotion. "Yeah, well, I doubt he would have forgiven me anyway."

"Oh, Harley—"

"No. It's true. And it's fine. I don't deserve to be forgiven. I was rebellious. I went against everything he preached. I was defiant. Heck, I stole his favorite motorcycle. And that's just what he knew about. After I left…" Guilt and regret broke his voice. And her heart.

Pushing herself off the back of the bike, she came to a stop in front of him and took his face in her hands, making sure he was looking at her before she spoke. "There would have been forgiveness."

He took her hands in his, pressed his lips to the palm of one, and looked away to where the eastern horizon was starting to darken to indigo. "Not from my father. You didn't know him. He hated sinners. And that's what I became. I became the exact thing he hated most in the world."

She opened her mouth to protest. To tell him how wrong he was. About all of it.

Be quick to listen but slow to speak.

Then Cori's words echoed in her mind. *Maybe you're what God's going to use to help him heal.* She pressed her lips together and waited.

"The thing is, I don't want you getting the wrong idea about me. I'm not a good man. The things I've done…" He swung his leg over the bike and leaned back on it, arms and ankles crossed, head hanging. He toed a rock around and she watched it tumble away from his boot. "I always thought I'd be a certain kind of man when I grew up. But after I left... being a teenager, even a big one who could hold his own, was hard and scary and it wasn't long before I'd done things I wasn't proud of just to survive. After a while, you sort of go numb to the shame of doing things you never thought you'd do."

The man standing beside her may have thought he'd gone numb, but if that was true he wouldn't still be punishing himself. No, he still carried that guilt, allowing it to color every facet of his life. Oh, Harley. If only he could see the grace that was so freely offered. There for the taking. She waited quietly, but when he didn't elaborate, she stepped away from the bike and reached out her hand. "Come on."

Harley uncrossed his arms and legs slowly, stowing the helmets before taking her hand. She tugged him along behind her as she walked to a trailhead a few hundred yards ahead of them. The setting sun slanted orange light through the trees, casting the woods in strips of shadow and light. They wound their way along the side of a hill, cresting it just as the trees gave way to jutting cliffs. The ocean below, crashing against the rock face, and the sky above, cloudless and stretching to the sea, were breathtaking. Even though the sky was beginning to lose its light, no stars had twinkled to life yet.

She'd found this spot as a teenager and loved how alone she felt when she was there. Farther along the crag was Lookout Point, a popular place to watch the stars come out. She preferred this deserted spot with the same stunning view.

She continued to lead him along the tops of the rugged outcroppings of granite until they reached a spot where the trail ended on a huge, flat rock. Erin walked to the middle of the rock and dropped down, sitting criss-cross. The surface still held the heat of the day, but she could feel it cooling under her fingers. Harley sank onto the rock beside her and stretched his legs out, hands behind him. Erin rested her head on his shoulder and ran her hand up the long column of his arm and back to where his palm rested on the stone.

A quiet had settled over them as they walked up the trail and now they sat in silence. The whole expanse of the Atlantic Ocean stretched out before them into the dwindling twilight. The sky above them was still a brilliant royal blue, but along the eastern horizon, it was fading from indigo to black velvet.

On her fingertips' third trip down his forearm, Harley captured them and sat up, weaving their hands together. "I feel like I didn't scare you off the way I thought I would. Feared I would."

"Harley, we're all sinners. We all have things in our past we're ashamed of. Is that man you just described to me, the man you are now? Is that who you want to be?"

He shook his head and looked down at their linked hands, running his thumb across her knuckles. "I haven't been that man in a long time. But… I don't know how to shake off the shame."

She turned to face him and reached out her other hand, ran it along his cheek, and tipped his chin up to look at her. "I think you do."

He didn't answer, but after a long moment, he nodded. She let her hand slide away from his cheek and turned back to the view just as the first twinkling light appeared overhead.

"Would you believe me if I told you that isn't a star?" she asked.

"Of course it isn't a star. That's Ma—"

"—rs," She giggled and leaned on his shoulder again.

"You can tell it's not a star if—"

"It's brighter than the stars—"

"Doesn't twinkle—"

"And isn't part of a constell—"

"—ation." He chuckled and the sound vibrated through her, warming her heart. "Plus, Mars is orange. Somebody remembers astronomy class."

"No." She paused. "I used to watch the stars with…

someone"

"Oh yeah? My dad and I used to watch the stars on the back porch when I was a kid." He blew out a sigh. "I think that's why I wanted to save the porch so bad. He and my mom and I would sit out there and he'd tell us the names of the stars and planets and constellations."

Memories hung in the air. She well remembered sitting on that back porch with Coop watching the stars and listening to him tell tales of kings and queens and princesses and heroes and hunters. She was searching the sky for more stars when her eyes came to rest on his. Even in the dwindling light, she could see the intensity in them.

Harley let go of her fingers and took her face gently in his hands. He didn't move for the longest time and she tried to remember to breathe. At last, still searching her eyes, he leaned in and brushed his lips against hers. He pulled back and searched her eyes again. She leaned forward, bringing her lips to his with much more passion than the chaste brush of his lips had been. He groaned as he pulled her closer, looping one arm behind her neck. His other hand slid down her arm and circled her back. Then, with tantalizing slowness he lowered her to the rock, his arms cradling her from the hard surface.

His lips were warm and tasted ever so slightly of mint and salt. She brought her arms around his neck, enjoying the brush of his beard against her soft skin. He slanted his mouth across hers, drawing her lower lip gently between his teeth before delving back in, deepening the kiss. The fingers she'd tangled in his hair dragged along the back of his neck and then trailed a slow path across his shoulder. When she reached the edge of the sleeve of his t-shirt her fingertips encountered icy cold skin. She stilled. Then pulled away just far enough to meet his eyes.

"You're frozen."

Laughter bubbled up, rumbling through his chest and he rested his forehead on hers, breathing hard. "Trust me, Erin, I am anything but cold right now." He laughed again and was still smiling when his lips pressed against hers, slow and light, as he eased her back up. He pulled away and drew her to sit between his knees with her back against his chest. He held her there, circled in his arms, as the last of the sun's rays slipped from the horizon.

If she'd thought it possible to lose her heart to this man before, she now feared she'd already handed it over.

Lord, please don't let him break my heart, she prayed silently as they watched the stars blink on and fill the moonless sky. *And please don't let me break his.*

CHAPTER ELEVEN

Harley's heart hammered in his chest until he was afraid it would burst free. Drawing in a deep breath he caught the subtle scent of her shampoo mixed with the briny tang of the ocean and wondered if there was anything better in this world than the moment they'd just shared. He could still taste her on his lips and he gave in to the urge to brush a kiss along her neck where it curved into her shoulder. She shuddered and he grinned. He'd sit here and kiss her forever if she'd let him.

They'd watched the stars come out one by one and now the sky was splashed with light. Even the Milky Way was visible in the pitch dark of a moonless Maine night. It was magnificent, but he almost didn't care. He'd sit in the fog and be just as happy as long as Erin was in his arms.

He tightened his hold on her and she sighed, leaning her head back on his shoulder and snuggling into his arms. They sat in silence for a long time. With the sun long gone and the wind picking up, Harley began to rethink being warm enough. Gooseflesh broke out along his arms and he resisted the urge to shiver. Maybe he should have grabbed his chamois shirt after all. Suggesting they head back to the bike was on the tip of his tongue when Erin spoke.

"You don't think Alec had anything to do with Coop's accident, do you?"

Shock rippled through him and all thought of the cold vanished. "Dad's? I was thinking Lyle's." His mind raced. Could the man have had a hand in his father's crash? He'd worked on the bike a few days before, so at the very least he would have known if there was something mechanically wrong with it. But... even that was a stretch. Now he wished they'd asked Cohen about the invoice! Maybe— He shook his head. This was not the time to start grasping at crazy ideas. He was feeling a modicum of peace. He was... happy. That thought galvanized him. He *was* happy. Or happ*ier* anyway. He didn't want to rock the boat. And yet... "Why would you think he might?"

"I guess I don't. I just..." She took a deep breath and sat forward, hugging her knees to her chest.

He didn't want her to move out of his arms, but he let go, his arms now colder than ever. Leaning back on his hands he felt the sharp edges of a mussel shell bite into his palm. He scooped it off the granite and fiddled with it, running his fingers along the edge.

"Doesn't it seem odd that Alec worked on Coop's bike right before the accident? I mean wouldn't he have seen if there was something wrong with it? On top of that, he had a problem with Lyle who then had a *very* similar accident."

His gut didn't like where her thoughts were headed. "Coincidence?"

"Maybe. Oh, I don't know." She sighed and slumped back against his chest. He slipped the shell into his pocket and wrapped his arms around her again. "I guess I just *want* there to be an explanation. Not just happenstance or a mistake."

Both Lyle and his father could handle a bike. Lay it down? Sure. Sometimes that couldn't be helped. Harley'd even laid the Commander down a time or two. Scary. For some guys, scary enough to never ride again. But to crash it on a straight stretch of open road? One of them, unlikely. Both of them? In the same place? He was beginning to see why Erin had voiced the question. "What are you thinking?"

"I don't know. I didn't have a clue that Alec was still in town then, but..." Erin let out a bitter laugh.

"What?"

"Well... I don't get why he would have been working on Coop's bike. He hated Coop."

"Hated?"

"It's a long story," Erin said as she pushed herself up and dusted off her jeans.

Harley got to his feet. "You can't just leave it at that." Oh, how he wished he could see her face. Questions bombarded his brain. Without another word, she began to inch her way along the granite outcropping toward the trail. He pulled his keys from his pocket and tried to keep their path lit with the tiny penlight he used for a keychain. "Erin!"

She didn't say anything as they navigated the top of the cliff, but when they reached the trees she stopped and looked at him. "Suffice it to say there was no love-loss between Alec Cohen and your father. I heard him threaten Coop." Erin stepped away, but Harley caught her hand and stopped her. "I shouldn't have said anything. I'm sorry, Harley. I just—"

Pulling her hand free, she led the way back to the almost deserted parking area and made a bee-line to the bike. She waited while Harley opened the panniers and retrieved their helmets. When he handed hers over, Erin scrubbed her cheek with the back of her hand before reaching for it. And now he felt like a heel. His questions could wait.

"Hey." Harley pulled Erin into his arms and rested his chin on her silky hair. "Let's not ruin a nice afternoon, OK? We'll sort it all out tomorrow. Or the day after. Or whatever." She nodded against his chest and he pressed his lips to the top of her head.

"Evening, Charlie. Erin."

They both jumped at the sound of the friendly voice. Erin stepped away quickly and wiped her eyes.

"Mr. and Mrs. Puckett?" Harley squinted into the dim pool of light cast from the lone lamp post at the end of the parking area.

"Sorry we startled you," Frannie said, elbowing Mark. "I told you we should have made more noise. You scared the livin' daylights out of poor Erin."

"Been down to Lookout Point watching the stars?" the older

man asked, looking adequately chagrined.

"Yes, sort of," Erin answered. "You?"

"Figured it wouldn't be long and it'll be too cold or the moon will be out. Not too many perfect nights like this," Mark said.

"It was lovely," Erin added.

"Dear, we should let these two get going, and I could use a cup of cocoa."

Mark slung his arm around his wife's shoulders and started steering her toward one of the few cars left in the lot. "You two have a lovely evening," he called over his shoulder.

Erin waved and then reached for her helmet. Harley donned his, and his chamois shirt, before swinging his leg over the seat and starting the bike. They were only a mile or so outside of Summer Harbor, but when Erin slid on behind him and tightened her arms across his chest, Harley wished they were hours away. He disengaged the kickstand and rolled the bike toward the edge of the parking area. They were the only ones on the road as he accelerated along the ribbon of blacktop that led home, leaning into the curves as they climbed away from the shore. Heat still radiated off of the pavement, but the wind bit and he was glad he'd taken a minute to shrug on the long-sleeved shirt.

The sound registered before anything else. The ragged popping made every muscle in Harley's body tense and his stomach clench. He tried to steady the front of the bike, but the blown front tire was pulling him in a wild arch across the oncoming lane. Erin's arms had tightened around his chest a millisecond after the rubber gave way and, as he fought to control the motorcycle, her terrified screams joined the chaos.

He didn't want to lay the bike down. That one thought blared in his ears, blocking out everything else. He'd only laid the bike down twice before and both times the road rash had been agonizing. Imagining the pavement marring Erin's perfect skin made bile rise in his throat.

His arms and legs were screaming with the exertion of holding the machine upright. His biceps cramped, and his fingers and forearms ached to let go of the handlebars. Seconds stretched, the scene playing out in slow motion.

They'd crossed the full width of the road and the gravel shoulder loomed in the swath of light from the bike's headlight. He watched as the sand and rocks, tufts of sod, and broken bits of pavement came up to meet the front wheel. It couldn't be avoided. They were going down.

And it was going to hurt.

He let go of the handlebars with his right hand and placed it over Erin's slender arms, holding them in a vice grip. If he could keep her from reaching out for the ground she might avoid a broken wrist. Logic told him to hold onto the handlebars, and guide the bike down as best he could, but instinct told him Erin would try to catch herself as they hit the ground. He tightened his grip.

"Hold on to me!" he screamed, hoping his voice carried above the noise of the bike. Above the sound of her screams. She was terrified and his heart hurt at the thought. Just another second and it would all be over. He closed his eyes at the last instant.

God, if You're out there, don't let Erin get hurt. Please!

He felt the pavement dig into his hip, ripping his jeans as they caught on a loose chunk of asphalt. He hoped not the flesh underneath, but from the flash of pain, it was a distinct possibility. Next to come into contact with the ground was his shoulder and the jarring of it smashed his helmet off the ground, ringing his ears. His chamois shirt offered some protection for his arm, but he felt the fabric tear and then gravel claws dug into his flesh. He roared in pain.

They came to a stop a few yards off the road in a cloud of dust and flying bits of turf and gravel. Harley sucked in his first breath since hearing the tire let go. While in reality only a few seconds, it had felt like ages, and the air he pulled in was cool and welcoming.

Adrenaline surged through his system, making his hands shake. The urge to do nothing but lay there and breathe for a few seconds, to allow his heart to slow, was all but forgotten as Erin began to sob behind him, trying to wrench her wrists from his grasp. Letting go, he managed to extricate himself from the bike and spun on his knees to where Erin lay, one leg still pinned under the motorcycle.

Oh, God, don't let the exhaust be touching her leg!

"Are you hurt?" He hated the desperate edge to his voice, but in the near dark, he couldn't tell if her screams were fueled by terror or pain. Her sobs were growing hysterical as she clawed at the ground. He reached for the bike and tried to find a handhold to lift it off her leg, but from his kneeling position, he couldn't get any purchase. Her panic was drawing his nerves so taut that he thought he might freak out as well. Placing a heavy hand on her shoulder, he lowered his voice. "Erin, shhhhh. honey, I'll get the bike up, but I need you to calm down."

She was trapped. Under a motorcycle. In her worst nightmares, this was how she died. Why, oh why, had she agreed to get on the back of Harley's deathtrap? She knew better. Fear was a healthy thing! Fear kept you from doing crazy, stupid things. Most of the time. Erin's fingertips dug into the gravel on the side of the road until they stung. She had to get out. Now. She bit her lip in an attempt to stop the hysterical outburst that had overtaken her when they stopped moving, laying on the side of the road in the dark.

Harley was speaking to her. She could hear him, but her brain wasn't engaging. All she could think about was getting out. Getting away. Getting safe. She threw an arm out, scrabbling again for anything she could latch onto, and instead hit something solid. Harley let out a groan at the force of her blow and grabbed her wrist, stilling her. She was panting and her brain still screamed for her to get free, but Harley's warm, strong hand stilled her world just enough for his words to register.

"Erin, honey. I can't get ahold of the bike with you thrashing around. Please, be still for a second and I'll lift it."

She was still biting her lip and couldn't help the whimper that escaped past her teeth. Try as she might though, she couldn't get it together. Terror drove her. She tried to drag her wrist from his grip, to find some way out, but he held her fast and began to hum, of all things. The sound quenched a little of the panic coursing through her as she strained to hear him. Something familiar, but—

"There you are," Harley said.

Her breath still came in fast pants, her heart still raced, tears still wet her cheeks, but the hysteria was ebbing. She gritted her teeth and pulled in a deep breath through her nose.

"I'm going to let go of your wrists and lift the bike so you can slide out, alright?"

She could only nod, her teeth clenched too tight to speak. He stood and moaned, from the exertion or an injury, she wasn't sure, and lifted the motorcycle's seat far enough for her to pull free. In her haste to put distance between herself and the bike, Erin half crawled, half rolled onto the grass, and tumbled down the small embankment into the ditch, landing in a heap where the headlight illuminated the grass.

Harley was beside her in a flash, crouching down. He'd shed his helmet somewhere along the way and she clawed at hers until he reached out and undid the strap. With it tossed aside, she launched herself into his arms, sobbing in relief. Her momentum carried them both over into the grass. Harley took the brunt of the fall, landing on his back and grunting when she came down hard on his chest and shoulder. He used that momentum to roll them back into a sitting position, her body carefully cradled in his arms.

"Are you hurt?" he asked, his free hand exploring her arm.

She shook her head, not trusting her voice yet.

"No broken bones? Road rash? Did you hit your head?"

She shook her head again and closed her eyes. She was safe. In Harley's arms, she was safe. "What—?"

"The front tire blew. I tried to keep it up, but the dark and the hill and the curve..." He trailed off. "Are you sure you're not hurt?"

"Yes. Scared, but... at the moment nothing appears to be broken."

"I think the pannier protected your leg." He lifted her hands into the light.

Bloody knuckles on her left hand had Erin pulling it closer, looking at it. "That's weird. It doesn't hurt."

"I don't think it's yours."

"What? You're hurt?" she asked as she pushed herself up on her knees, looking him over. He rolled his shoulder around to catch the light. The shirt was torn and the abrasion underneath was wet with blood. "Oh, Harley."

"Hey, no worries." He shrugged and brought his hand up to her face. "It's just a scratch. I'm fine. I'm so sorry I laid the bike down. I tried to keep it upright."

With a shudder, she closed her eyes and leaning into his hand, tried to steady herself. She felt his lips brush her forehead and his arms go around her, holding her. She melted into him and clung to his uninjured arm.

"I heard the popping sound, but it didn't register that anything was wrong until I felt you tense up." Her hands started the shake. His reaction and the wobbling front of the bike had thrown her into a full-blown panic attack. Mortified, she buried her face in the crook of his neck. "When I was freaking out, were you humming something?"

Harley brushed his hand over her hair. "It's an old hymn my mom used to sing when I was upset. Bedtimes, temper fits, bad days." He cleared his throat and then, in a clear baritone, "Be still, my soul: The Lord is on thy side."

Holy smokes! The man could sing!

"Did Charleston Beck just sing a line from a hymn?"

His chuckle warmed her heart. "I also prayed." He said it so quietly she almost missed it.

"You..."

"Yeah. I mean I don't know if Anyone heard it or anything, but... Well, I asked for you to not get hurt, and... you aren't."

Taking his face in her hands, Erin leaned in close. "Harley, He hears you. I promise He does. And He misses you so much," she said in a whisper.

"We should..." His voice was thick with emotion and he stopped, swallowed, and tried again. "We should get the bike up. Do you think you can help me stand it up?"

"I'm not getting back on." Ever. She wanted to say that out loud but didn't want the man to feel worse than he already did about dumping them. It wasn't his fault. If anything, her inexperience on the back had contributed to him not being able to keep the motorcycle upright.

"Neither of us is tonight. I'm going to push it into town. It's only about three-quarters of a mile and flat. But I can't lift it by myself." He turned his shoulder into the beam of light and she looked away, not wanting to see the damage the blacktop had caused. She stood and reached a hand out to help him up. They dusted themselves off and she stood over the bike while Harley used his penlight to inspect the damage.

"Looks like just the tire. And my shoulder." He motioned toward the forks. "If you stand with your back to the bike and lift here, I'll lift under the seat near the rear tire."

They stood the bike up, which was harder than she expected, and got it back on the shoulder.

"I'm really beginning to wish the town council would vote to allow a cell tower."

"Right? Listen, it's less than a mile to Sawyer's. I could go get him to come help." Erin offered.

"I've got it. Besides, I'd rather walk a mile with you, pushing a motorcycle, than sit on the side of the road while you go for help."

She reached out and pressed her hand to his where it gripped the handlebar. Memories of their kisses flooded her mind and she was glad for the cover of darkness to hide the heat rising on her cheeks.

Half an hour later, Erin felt relief flood her as they pushed the bike into the garage at Coop's house. Walking a mile pushing a four-hundred-pound motorcycle would have been exhausting. Doing it with limbs that had started to stiffen up from the tumble they'd taken made her want to weep with exhaustion as the door closed. "I don't know what I want more right now, food, a shower, or bed." Or another kiss. Without question another kiss. Her face heated. Yup, she was glad for the darkness.

"Yes," he said with a chuckle.

It felt good to laugh. "All of the above it is! But, if it will start, we're taking my truck. I don't want to walk another step."

"Deal." Harley slung his uninjured arm over Erin's shoulders and guided her toward her truck. "How about we grab a bite at the Lobster Tail?"

A sigh of pleasure was all Erin could muster and she snuggled in closer to Harley's warmth. All the heat from the day had evaporated and she felt chilled despite her jacket. Or maybe that was the fatigue.

"I would like to stop at the shop and change," Harley added with a wave at his ripped jeans and mangled shirt.

She grimaced at the blood-encrusted fabric, but he wasn't even limping. "Does it hurt a lot?"

"It will. But, no, right now it doesn't hurt."

"I'm not sure I believe you. I didn't even hit the ground and I'm starting to ache."

He took her hand and ran his thumb over where his blood had dried on her knuckles. "You need to wash up, too." He held her door for her and she started the truck with only a mild protest from the engine.

Erin glanced over at him while they drove, catching his profile in the glow of a streetlight. She wondered if Harley knew how much he looked like his dad. Not the black hair. That must have come from Jules, but the high cheekbones, the straight nose, the tall forehead. Now that she knew he was Coop's son, she wondered how she ever could have missed it.

Pulling into the small lot behind the kayak shop, she followed Harley up the stairs to the apartment and waited while he rummaged around in a cabinet in the kitchen and came away with a brown bottle and some gauze.

"You can wash up in there," he said, motioning toward a door on the other side of the room as he headed down the hall.

Standing at the sink, scrubbing Harley's blood off her hand, Erin rested her forehead against the mirror and closed her eyes.

This is long overdue, but thank You for protecting us today. I was so scared, but You were there. Thank You for answering Harley's prayer. Please show him that You hear him, and love him, and miss him.

She jerked upright when Harley tapped on the door. Had she fallen asleep leaning against the mirror? She dried her hands and opened the door, but the motion made her wince and she ran her hand along her shoulder where the muscles cramped.

"Are you OK?" he asked in a voice deep with concern. "We can skip dinner."

"No! I'm starving.

A smile spread across his face and he took her hand, leading her back to her truck.

The Lobster Tail Alehouse was an old-fashioned Irish pub in the basement of a Main Street shop. The sounds of laughter and a rambunctious game of darts, and the tangy smell of hops drifted up from the open door as they made their way down the stairs. It wasn't packed on a Monday night at the end of September, and Harley caught her hand again as they walked to an empty table. A young waitress in a too-short skirt appeared with menus and rattled off a lengthy list of locally brewed and imported stouts, porters, and reds on tap.

Erin met Harley's eyes. "I don't drink, but I don't care if…" She flicked her wrist toward the waitress, feeling ridiculous.

Of course, he could drink if he wanted to. Sheesh. She felt her cheeks burn and slid the menu up to cover her face before mumbling, "Water, please." Good heavens, she blushed a lot around this man!

"Root beer," Harley added.

After the waitress left to fill their drink orders, Erin looked over the top of her menu at Harley and found him studying her. Self-conscience, she reached up to straighten her hair, but he caught her hand and held it, running his thumb over her knuckles.

"I enjoy a beer now and then, but ever since I've been back in town I can't bring myself to order one. It's like The Good Reverend Beck is still looking over my shoulder. I guess it keeps me on the strait and narrow."

The Good Reverend Beck kept a lot of people on the strait and narrow.

Tell him.

Erin opened her mouth, but... Would he understand? Could she make him understand? She closed it again and went back to looking at the menu. "I haven't been here in ages. Do they still have the beer-battered cod and chips?"

"We sure do," the waitress answered as she scooted their drinks onto the table.

"I'll have that," Erin said. "And malt vinegar for the fries, please."

"Of course. And for you?" the young woman asked, turning to Harley.

"Irish stew and soda bread."

"I'll get those orders right in." She winked at Harley as she gathered their menus.

Erin had to resist the urge to roll her eyes. She didn't want to look across the table and find Harley drooling over the cute girl in her low-cut shirt. A gentle squeeze from his fingers, though, brought her eyes up and she blushed, realizing he was focused on her. It caused a lovely warm feeling to creep through her.

"I always forget how small this place is," Erin said after the waitress had left.

"I hear the owner's been trying to get Parker to sell him The Hungry Whale for ages."

"Parker? Sell The Whale?"

Harley chuckled. "Yeah, I can't see it happening either."

A loud cheer went up from the group playing darts and Erin was quiet for a minute, watching them. What. A. Day! She was taking a sip of water when Harley snapped his fingers.

"I completely forgot to tell you. On Friday morning, I stopped and spoke to that guy that Edwin Hurst said he saw fighting with Lyle."

"Skylar Novak? What did he have to say?"

"Not much. He wouldn't tell me what the fight was about. Claimed Lyle was a 'parishioner'." Harley added air quotes and rolled his eyes. "Then he clammed up, said Lyle was there for some sort of confession, and wouldn't say anything more."

"Strange. I didn't picture Lyle as religious," Erin said

"I agree. Plus, he got real squirrelly when I pressed him about it. I think he's hiding something. I just don't know what."

The only warning they had before someone spun a chair around and dropped it at their table, was the scraping of chair legs on the scarred wood floor. Edwin Hurst sat down on it backward and plunked his empty tumbler on the table.

"Speak of the—" Harley mumbled.

"Har-r-r-ly Beck!" Edwin looked over his shoulder and started snapping his fingers at their waitress. When he caught her attention, he pointed at his empty glass. "J. J. Corry on the rocks!"

The man's slurred words made Erin cringe and she looked across the table at Harley. He caught her eye and raised a brow.

"What can we do for you?" Harley asked, his jaw tight.

"What indeed? What indeed?" Edwin's eyes turned to Erin and she suspected he was having trouble bringing her face into focus. He blinked and then broke into a Cheshire cat grin as he swirled the ice around in his empty glass and knocked back whatever dregs were still in the bottom. "Er-r-r-in Wallace. I didn't put two and two together the other day. But I should have."

Erin began to squirm. She had a pretty good idea where Hurst was going with his comment and she didn't like it. No. No. No! This was not how she wanted Harley to find out that — She licked her lips nervously, but was saved from having to respond by their food arriving.

"As much as I'd like to try and convince you to sell me your house, that's not why I dropped by." He laughed as though he'd cracked a hilarious joke, but sobered when the waitress set his whiskey on the table. Why couldn't the man just leave them to their meal? All she wanted was to eat, go home, shower, and try to sleep. Although she wasn't sure how well she'd be able to keep the nightmares of crashing on a motorcycle at bay. She stole a glance at Harley and found annoyance in his expression. "After you left the other day, I couldn't stop thinking about your..." he swiveled his eyes to Erin, "accusation. Thanks for that by the way." He paused and took another pull of whiskey, sucking air through his teeth before setting the glass on the table. With his forearms resting on the back of the chair, he spun the glass in the condensation it left on the glossy surface.

Harley nudged Erin's toe under the table and she met his eyes. *Eat,* he mouthed and nodded toward her plate. Gladly! The cod smelled divine and her stomach growled in response. Breaking off a succulent chunk of batter-dipped white fish, she let it melt in her mouth. It might be the fact that all she'd eaten that day was a mint chocolate chip ice cream cone, but she'd have sworn under oath the fish was the most delicious thing she'd ever tasted.

"Seriously, Hurst, did you have a reason for interrupting our dinner? Because it has been 'a day' and I'm not in the mood." Harley stirred his stew and broke off a chunk of bread.

"Sheesh, Beck. Don't get your shorts in a twist! What I wanted to *say* was that you got me to thinking about who might want Lyle... out of the way so to speak." Edwin took another pull off his glass and licked his lips before leaning toward Erin and lowering his voice. "I have it on good authority that your landlady has a reason to be happy the man is gone."

"Vera?" Erin couldn't keep the surprise out of her voice.

Edwin shook his head and looked around, lowering his voice. "The way I heard it, she thought he knew who killed Jason, but the man wouldn't tell the police."

Shock rippled through Erin. That must have been what Vera meant! All this time Lyle knew and he hadn't said anything? She could understand how that knowledge could have driven Vera to the edge of sanity, but to the point of murder? No. No way! She looked across at Harley and met his eyes, but she couldn't tell what he was thinking.

"And she isn't the only one," Hurst continued. "There's this kid who used to work for Lyle. Cohen, I think his name was. Anyway, I was over to the shop to talk to Lyle a month or so ago about selling— Trying to sweeten the deal, you know? And this Cohen kid was telling Lyle off when I got there. Stuff like 'You can't do this to me!' and 'You'll be sorry!' I'm sure there was more, but I don't remember all of it."

It didn't surprise her to hear that Alec was mouthing off.

As the realtor finished off his drink and spun the ice cubes around in the glass, Harley nudged Erin's foot again. When she looked up he raised an eyebrow in question.

Tell him.

The thought made her dinner congeal in her stomach. No. Not tonight. She took a drink of water, hoping she could enjoy the rest of her meal.

Edwin turned and waved his empty glass at the waitress. "Another!"

"Hurst, don't you think—"

"Don't tell me you're turning into your old man, Beck? He thought I had a pr-r-roblem, too." The man pushed away from his chair and slapped the empty glass onto the tray a passing waitress was carrying. Turning back to the table, he narrowed his eyes. "I still think you two are nuts for thinking there was anything more to Lyle's crash than a... tr-r-agic... accident. But if you're going to go around sticking your nose in other people's business, it had better be people other than me. People who had real reasons to despise the man."

After Edwin made a show of spinning the chair back around and snapping it under the edge of their table, he strode off and retrieved his fresh drink from the waitress, slapping some bills down in its place. Harley took Erin's hand from where she was worrying the edge of her napkin and held it until she looked up. He smiled and winked at her. "Don't let a jerk ruin your dinner."

She blew out a breath and relaxed her shoulders as best she could. "You're right," she said, trying to smile. He *was* right. The day had been a rollercoaster of emotions and experiences, but they were ending it with a hearty meal, good company, and maybe... just *maybe,* a goodnight kiss. She felt her cheeks warm. Yes, he was right, she wasn't going to let Edwin ruin it. Squeezing his hand before letting go, she dug into her fish again. They ate in silence for a few minutes, both lost in thought.

"Odd," Harley said as he pushed his empty bowl away and wiped his mouth. "That both Edwin and Dox mentioned Cohen's issues with Lyle."

Tell him!

Instead, Erin gave a non-committal shrug and pushed her plate to meet Harley's in the middle of the table. A weariness had settled over her and now that her stomach was full, all she wanted was to go home and go to sleep. It must have shown because Harley took her hand in one of his and signaled to the waitress for the bill with the other.

"Let's get you home, shall we?"

She tried to smile, but it felt false and she had to stifle a yawn. Harley chuckled and pulled a few bills from his wallet. Erin pulled cash from her pocket as well, but Harley stopped her when she reached to add it to his.

"I got it."

"It's extra for the waitress. Judging by the look she gave him, I don't think Edwin tipped her."

"Are you serious? What a jack—" He snapped his mouth closed and met her eyes with a sheepish half-smile. "Sorry. I mean, what a jerk. How does he stay in business?"

"I don't know." She slipped the money under the bill and took his hand as they headed for the door. "Maybe he's nice and we've just caught him on off days?"

"Maybe. If every day is an off day."

"Good point." Erin fished her keys out of her pocket. "Do you want me to drop you off?"

"I'd like to see that you get home safe. I can walk back."

His concern gave Erin warm fuzzy feelings. It had been a long time since anyone had made sure she got home safe. Once upon a time, her mother might have. Before Erin ruined everything.

CHAPTER TWELVE

The night had been a restless mix of waking up thinking she was trapped under the bike, replaying their conversations from the day before, and dozing off while sinking into the sweet memory of Harley's kisses. By five, Erin couldn't stand the rollercoaster anymore and got up.

One conversation kept coming back to her mind. At dinner, Harley said that when he talked to Skylar Novak the man had gotten... What was the word he'd used? Squirrelly? Erin didn't know the man personally, but something kept nagging at the back of her mind. A conversation with Coop maybe, or something she'd overheard. She had a distinct feeling that Novak was living a lie. What that lie was, she had no idea, but as soon as she got dressed and her hair braided into pigtails she was going to find out.

Ten minutes later Erin burst out her door and came to an abrupt halt. It was cold. Not just early morning chill but downright cold. Thick frost lay on the grass and the wind held the bite of the coming winter. She ran back inside for a sweatshirt and pulled a tuque down over her ears. The wool cap would probably be too hot later, but before six with the wind blowing the icy fog against her face? It felt marvelous.

Even though the library wasn't open yet, Erin hoped the librarian would already be there. The sky had lightened to a dull blue-gray, but the towering maples and firs that surrounded the east side of the old brick building cast it in deep shadow. She smiled when she saw the welcoming orange glow of lights through a downstairs window. She sprinted up the steps and tapped on the front door. A moment later, Lucille

Wolcott's smiling face appeared.

"Oh, Erin-dear, what are you doing out and about so early?" she asked as she pushed the heavy door open and stepped aside, gesturing Erin in.

"I needed to do a little research and I was hoping you wouldn't mind me using one of your computers before work."

"Of course not! You go right ahead." The older woman's dark blue eyes glowed and her riot of salt-and-pepper curls danced as she led the way into the main part of the building, turning on lights as she went.

"Do you ever go home?" Erin asked, humor making her voice light.

Lucille laughed. "Sometimes." She winked at Erin before turning on one of the computers and pulling out a chair. "There you go. Just let me know if you need anything."

"Thank you."

"Of course, sweetie. You know you're always welcome here."

The search engine loaded and the cursor blinked at her, waiting. What exactly was she looking for? Her first attempt, *Skylar Novak*, returned thousands of hits. Most were for a professional female wrestler. There were a bunch of white page listings, a few obits, and several offers for her to 'search her Serbo-Croatian heritage'. She bit her lip. That wasn't getting her anywhere. Adding *Summer Harbor Maine* netted her better results, but nothing they didn't already have. The website for the church, various articles and blog posts about their charitable work, more white page listings, and birth record searches. She tried everything she could think of but came up empty. An hour later she let out a frustrated sigh and pushed back from the desk, stretching her back and rubbing her eyes.

"Couldn't find what you were looking for?" Lucille asked from behind a cart full of books.

"I would have more luck if I knew what I was looking for," Erin said with a frown.

The older woman set down the books she was holding and

came to stand behind Erin's chair. She leaned over, looking at the search results. "Is that the man from that place over on New Sweden Avenue?" When Erin nodded, Lucille leaned over and added *Arnie* to Erin's search. The results blinked onto the screen. "That first one's a news article."

"Arnie?" Erin asked as the page loaded.

"Well, I didn't know if it would help, but I heard that man who died last week call Mr. Novak that once." At Erin's raised brow, the older woman continued. "They were out back of the library and I don't think they knew I was still here. I mean, it was late and you know... I'm always here." She laughed and then seemed to remember what she was saying. "Any-hoo, I heard arguing and went and peeked out the window."

"And you saw Skylar Novak and Lyle Jay arguing?"

"Oh, were they ever!"

"When was this?" Erin asked, more interested in what Lucille had to say than the news article that had finished loading on the computer screen.

"Oh, gosh, it had to have been... three years ago anyway. I just remember it because my granddaddy's name was Arnie and after I heard Mr. Jay call him that... Well, every time I see that Mr. Novak around town I call him Arnie in my head." She laughed and headed back to the pile of books. "If you need any more help, just holler."

Erin turned her attention back to the computer. Her heart beat faster and faster as she read down through the article. Hitting print, she jumped up from her chair and grabbed the pages, calling goodbye over her shoulder as she ran for the door.

The house was empty, but it was obvious that Harley had been there. The lights in the kitchen glowed through the window, the back door was unlocked, and the coffee pot was still hot. He must have had a tour. She shivered imagining being out on the water in this cold. Crazy tourists!

She poured herself a cup of coffee and leaned against the counter. The kitchen felt like home and she spent a moment breathing in the memories. If only Harley could have that same feeling when he was here. But she suspected he felt quite the opposite when standing in the small room. A restless feeling settled over her. There had to be some way she could prove to him that all had been forgiven.

Coop's box flashed in her mind again. It might not be enough, but if she could find it she might be able to use it to convince Harley that his dad had loved him. She would also have to explain how she knew about the box, but she'd deal with that hurdle when it came. A glance at the clock confirmed it was just after seven-thirty. Even if the tour was an early one, she had a good forty-five minutes before he'd be back, if not more.

She left her too-hot coffee next to the pot and made her way down the hall to Coop's room. The last time she'd looked for the box she'd been sure it would be near his chair. She could almost see him sitting there opening it, pulling an envelope or two out, running his hands over them, eyes closed in prayer. Tears burned the back of her eyes and she shook her head. Focus!

It had to be here somewhere.

Maybe in the closet. She pulled the door open and found the upper shelf stacked to the ceiling and at least two boxes deep. Looking around she found a straight-backed chair in the corner and dragged it over. At first, she tried opening the boxes where they were, but it was impossible to see what was in each one. She lifted a stack off the shelf and set them on the floor near the chair.

The first one contained blankets. She ran her hand over the small blue one on top and tried to imagine baby Harley. She set that box aside and moved on to the next. Summer clothes. Another held throw pillows, probably sewn by Jules and stored by the ever-practical Coop who wouldn't have wanted them on his bed.

The second stack of boxes was more of the same. This was getting her nowhere. The last stack at least held more than bedding, but the tax returns and old bills weren't what she was looking for either. She went back to the beginning and opened all the boxes again, pressing her hands down inside each, hoping she'd missed the box at the bottom of one.

The air had a bite to it that he hadn't felt since last spring. Harley didn't care. Welcome to Maine! A high of eighty the day before, but they'd be lucky to top fifty today. He'd woken early with an aching shoulder, but the lightness of his heart made it almost unnoticeable. His step had a bounce to it and he whistled as he walked back toward the house from Finch and Jay's. He'd picked up a new tire and had just about enough time to put it on the bike before the first tour of the day. Gage was scheduled to go with Noah, but Harley thought maybe he'd tag along, too. It was going to be gorgeous. The cold air that morning would give way to a brilliant blue sky and the ocean was smooth and clear.

Maybe he'd even ask Erin to come along.

It would be a lie if he said he wasn't looking for her truck when he turned the corner. He even acknowledged the twinge of disappointment when it wasn't parked on the street yet. The kitchen light still glowed where he'd left it on. He smiled thinking how much Erin would appreciate the coffee already brewed when she got there. He imagined her smiling at him. Despite the fact that she'd been exhausted and disheveled from their adventure the night before, she'd been beautiful. A grin tipped up the corners of his mouth remembering kissing her goodnight. She'd tasted like... redemption.

The electric heater was still running in the garage where he'd left it pointed at the old tire and rim. He grabbed the now-hot wheel, and left the new tire in its place. After collecting his tools, he knelt with the rim on the floor. It only took a few minutes of prying with a couple of tire irons and a set of rim protectors to pop the ruined rubber off the rim.

With the shredded tire off and resting against the wall,

Harley grabbed the new one and wrestled it onto the rim. He'd done it so many times in the motorcycle shop he'd worked at, it felt like he could do it in his sleep. As he kneeled on the tire, working the irons around to get the last bit to snap into place he let his mind wander. He wasn't naive. He knew he couldn't be in love with Erin. Not yet anyway. But he let his brain play 'what-if'. What if they did fall in love? What if she could see past who he'd been and still want to be with him? What if he could have 'that' life? Erin was full of a brightness he longed for deep in his soul. She was real and honest, and, while she didn't pull her punches, she was kind and gentle with the truth.

The day before she'd said she trusted him. Him! And it went both ways. He was beginning to think he was going to end up trusting her with his heart. The offending organ kicked it up a notch, hammering in his chest at the thought. But why not? Why shouldn't he be willing to give his heart to someone he trusted? Someone patient? And, OK, yes, she came with some baggage, but he did, too. So. Much. Baggage. But it was like she didn't see it. She just saw him. And he liked that. Very much.

Grinning like the fool he knew he was, Harley flipped the little air compressor in the corner on and filled the tire, waiting for the popping sounds when the beads seated. He checked the pressure and then mounted the rim on a pin his dad had in the wall. It spun and settled and he marked it for balancing. While he worked he kept an ear out for Erin's truck. She needed a new one, or she needed someone to fix the clunker properly. Maybe he'd offer to work on it. Like Noah had for Lily and her kitchen. The idea of doing something nice for Erin made him smile.

It didn't take long to balance and remount the wheel on the bike. Harley wiped his hands on a rag he'd hung by the door and headed for the house. It had to be at least eight, where was she? He sprinted up the back steps two at a time and let himself in the back door. The smell of coffee greeted him and he reached for a mug but came up short when he saw a cup already sitting on the counter, not quite warm to the touch and with far too much cream and sugar.

Confused, he looked around and opened his mouth, ready to call her name, when a sound from the back of the house caught his ear. He followed it, pushing open the door to his father's bedroom. Erin's head snapped around and the look on her face told him everything he needed to know. Guilt. Pure, unadulterated, guilt.

"What are you...?" The words died on his lips as he took in the scene before him. Erin sat on the floor, the contents of his father's closet strewn about her. She appeared to be looking for something. Boxes were open and their contents spilled out on the floor. She opened her mouth like she was going to speak, but only one word came out.

"Harley..." Her cheeks flamed and she looked around in dismay.

He waited for more, but when she just began putting things back in the closest open box his patience wore thin. "What the hell are you doing?"

"I'm... sorry," she whispered.

"Sorry? For what? That you're somewhere you don't belong? That I caught you?" He knew his temper was rising and he tried to swallow it back. "Sorry you made me trust you?" Tried. Unsuccessfully. Could there be a logical explanation? Something that didn't make it look like she was searching his dad's room for... for... "What are you even looking for?"

His growled question didn't seem to go over very well. Erin straightened her back and squared her shoulders. When she turned back to him, her eyes shimmered with tears and she swallowed. Enough. He needed to breathe, and he couldn't get enough oxygen standing here in his father's room. He hadn't even opened the door since he'd been back, let alone stepped inside. No, what he needed was to run.

"Get. Out."

"Har—"

"Just..." His voice was weary, even to his own ears, and he ran his hand over his eyes. "Just get out." He waited for her to walk past him. She paused as if she wanted to say something, but he glared at her and the look must have done the trick because she sucked in a breath and disappeared toward the front of the house. He waited until he heard the screen door squeal before stepping back into the hall and slamming the door closed behind him.

He needed his bike. He needed speed. He needed to leave. Now.

Erin was nowhere in sight when he left the house. Good. His bike rumbled to life and he took off, headed straight out of town. The desperate feeling in his chest was nothing new, but it had been days, even weeks since he'd felt it. If he was honest, he hadn't felt it since he'd met Erin. And now she was the cause of it. Maybe he'd just keep going this time. The season was almost done. Two more weeks. Three tops. Noah could finish it out with just Gage and Owen. He didn't even need his stuff. It was just stuff. Then the bank and the town and Edwin could fight over who got the house. He didn't want to analyze why the thought of leaving for good made his stomach clench

He couldn't remember getting off the island, which didn't bode well. He attempted to shake off the weight of betrayal and focus on the road. Attempted and failed. When he got to the highway he stopped, a war raging inside him. He itched to turn south and disappear. But something held him back.

Maybe his friendship with Noah.

Maybe his promise to Keaton.

Maybe the need he still felt to make things right. Somehow.

Maybe Someone steering him north.

Maybe even Erin.

Whatever it was, he turned the bike toward the thick woods of northern Maine and opened up the throttle.

Erin heard the rumble of Harley's bike fade into the distance as she rounded the corner onto her street. The tears that she

had held in check by sheer will when he found her in his dad's room overflowed somewhere along the way home and blurred her vision. Why hadn't she answered him? She'd tried, but nothing had come out. She felt like she'd been caught with her hand in the cookie jar and her mind had raced for an explanation, and excuse.

How about the truth?

Yeah, she could have led with that. Could have told him exactly what she'd been looking for. Explained. Huh, what a concept. A fresh batch of tears sprang up and she swiped at them, angry.

Angry at herself.

She ran up the steps to her apartment and slammed the door. It was a Tuesday morning and she should be working. Should be working at Harley's. Did he want her to finish the porch though? All she had left was the rest of the roofing, installing the railing, and painting the second coat on the floor. Three days tops. But he'd told her to leave and it held the note of finality.

She called Finnley's and got Sawyer. Willing her voice not to betray her emotions, she asked if he knew whether Keaton had any other jobs she could work on.

"Sorry, kid. I think he's all set today. You done at Harley's place?"

"Nearly. I just need something... different today."

"I'll call if Keaton needs someone, but the crews are already out for the day. I'm just back picking up sheetrock."

"Thanks, Sawyer," she said as she hung up.

Great. No work meant no pay. She could head down to her shop and build more boxes, but in her current state of mind, running a table saw might not be the best idea. Besides, she had about a billion that she'd made on Sunday evening. She flopped back on the bed and covered her eyes with her arm. Tears leaked down into her hair, but she didn't care enough to move.

She must have dozed off because a loud ringing pulled her from a deep, dreamless sleep. Disoriented, she fumbled for the phone, picking it up just in time to stop the answering machine. She tried to make herself sound chipper and wide awake in case it was Keaton calling with work, but she knew she'd failed the second she said 'hello', slurred and stuttered. She pressed her fingers to her forehead where it pounded.

"Erin Elizabeth, are you alright?" Her mother's sharp voice was enough to bring Erin fully awake.

"I'm fine, Mom."

"It's 'Mother'."

"Sorry. Mother. What can I do for you?"

"I was just returning your call. Why aren't you at work?"

"Just popped home for a bit."

"In the middle of the day? Are you sick?"

If her mother thought she'd be at work, why did she—? Oh. Because if she called in the middle of the day she could just leave a message. Erin tried to keep a sigh from slipping out. "I'm fine. Busy. How are you and… Father?"

"We're wonderful." Her mother launched into a long monologue about her charitable work and volunteering, then segued into Erin's stepfather's business dealings. Erin half-listened as she pawed through her medicine cabinet looking for something to soothe her headache. And almost missed what her mother was saying.

"…come home."

Erin's hands stilled and she stood up straight. "Excuse me?"

"I said, the ladies at the club were all talking about their children coming to visit and I told them all that you planned to come home, too."

Erin wasn't sure if her head was spinning from the conversation or reeling from the headache. Whether it was the crying jag, being awakened from a deep sleep, or trying to process her mother's words, Erin feared her skull might explode.

Oblivious to Erin's silence, the older woman continued. "You'll need to be here no later than Sunday night so that you can join me for the country club luncheon on Monday."

"Mom, I have work—"

"It's Mother. And don't be ridiculous."

"I'm not being ridiculous. I can't..." Can't? Or won't? Wasn't this what she'd wanted for years? An opportunity to set things right? It was the closest thing to an olive branch her mother had ever offered. Was she even considering turning it down? Erin was silent for a long time. Long enough that her mother decided to try another tactic. There was a quiet sniffle and then a hint of a hitch in her mom's voice when she continued. "Erin Elizabeth, you know I tried, and tried, and tried, but you made it so hard. I feel like no matter what I do, you don't even want to be a part of this family." Another sniffle.

"No, I do." Erin leaned forward and pressed her aching head against the mirror. "I'll try, Mom— Mother?"

The older woman sighed. "If that's the best you can do."

"I lov—" The line went dead. She sighed and slumped back down on the bed. Twenty-four hours ago her answer would have been a resounding 'no'. Remembering how Harley had cradled her while they'd kissed under the stars, his gentle, strong arms keeping her off the hard stone, brought on a fresh batch of tears. She flicked them away. That was yesterday. Today? Today she felt like she had no answers. To anything.

Cry to Me when your heart is overwhelmed and I will lead you.

Lord, I don't know how I managed to mess things up so much in such a short amount of time. I'm used to making mistakes, but this might be a new record even for me. I'm sorry I haven't included You in all my decisions and actions. I got carried away thinking I knew what was best, that I could fix things, but clearly I was wrong. Besides. that's not my job. That's Yours. But if You want to use me, I'm here. Available. Hoping for another chance.

She got up to find the medicine she had been looking for in the bathroom and tripped over the stupid boxes under her bed. Again. In frustration, she kicked at them, smashing them enough that they, mostly, fit under the frame. She gave the worst of the bunch another solid kick and then trudged off to the bathroom. She downed the aspirin quickly with a glass of tepid water from the sink and pulled on her flannel shirt. She'd heard Harley's bike earlier and it sounded like he was heading away from town, but maybe he was home by now. She could fix this. Well, not her, per se, but she trusted that God could use her to fix this. And she was going to start with something she should have started with a long time ago.

The truth.

The garage was dark and locked when she got to the house. So was the kitchen. No sign of Harley anywhere. She went into the backyard and found one of the old metal chairs she'd set aside when she fixed the floor and set it back on the newly painted porch. She curled herself into it, but a minute later she hopped up and grabbed the other chair, setting it next to hers. Just like they'd been years ago.

Even before she became a Christian, Erin didn't believe in ghosts or talking to the dead. Even more so now. However, it was comforting having Coop's chair sitting where it always had. She almost felt like she could tell him things if she sat there like that. Oh, how she wished she could tell him things.

If he were there she'd tell him about Harley, and about her mom calling, and about how she'd messed up. Again. Shocking. She'd ask him what to do, and he'd give her Bible verses and they'd figure it out. Best of all, he'd love her no matter what.

God, I know I can't talk stuff through with Coop or ask his advice or listen to his stories anymore, but I can talk to You and ask Your advice. I thought that I was in Harley's life to point him to You. To fix this thing between him and Coop. But I tried and all it did was make a mess. I don't even know if he'll speak to me again. But if he will, Lord, please give me wisdom and the words to say. Would You please fix the mess I've made?

What do I require of you? Speak the truth. Speak it in love and rejoice in it.

Well, there was one answer. Erin ran her fingers under her eyes and pulled her knees up to her chest, wrapping her arms around them. She should have told Harley the truth from the beginning. If he let her, she'd tell him now.

All of it.

Please give me another chance, Lord. With Harley and with my mom.

As the sun sank low the temperature dropped. The metal chair was cold, but she didn't care. She and Coop had once sat in these chairs on New Year's Eve and listened to the party-goers ringing in the new year on The Green in the center of town.

Coop had chuckled. "What a lot of nonsense to celebrate the earth going around the sun one more time."

Erin had hugged her hot chocolate with her mittened hands and giggled. Coop was so practical. But even in all his practicality, he'd known she would want to celebrate. He'd whipped up a batch of special homemade hot chocolate and gotten gingerbread cookies from Vera. They'd welcomed the new year by watching the stars and talking about how there is a time for everything.

A time to keep silent, and a time to speak.

A time to speak.

CHAPTER THIRTEEN

It wasn't until he was well on his way to the end of the highway that Harley remembered Clyde's store. The hope of a kind smile and wisdom drew him off the highway and onto the back country roads. The last time he'd been there the man had made Harley feel... hopeful. Right now, he craved hope.

Pulling into the parking lot, he saw the old man watching him from the doorway. Arms crossed over his chest, one shoulder propped against the door frame, his old jeans sitting low on hips thinned by age. A grin creased his wrinkled face.

"I thought I heard you comin' down the road, sonny."

Harley turned his lips up, but he doubted it looked like a true smile. "Wasn't sure you'd remember me."

"Nah, but I remember the bike," Clyde said with a wink. "I'm just pullin' your leg. 'Course I remember you. Come on inside. Looks to me like you need to have a sit and a talk."

Harley followed the old man into the store and sat down on the same scarred wooden stool that he'd pulled up to the counter the last time he was there.

"Now, what's been keeping you busy these days?" Clyde asked as he pulled two root beers from the cooler and handed one to Harley.

What had been keeping him busy? Erin, his dad's bike, work, Erin, Lyle's crash, the house, Erin. Where did he even begin? Probably someplace safe. "I've been rebuilding my dad's Harley Davidson XL-1000."

The old man's eyes twinkled and he leaned forward. "How's that going?"

"Good," Harley replied. "I'm going to need forks and handlebars for it eventually. And a front wheel. Couldn't find any to pull and ordering them isn't in the budget right now. I did get the gouge in the gas tank hammered out and waiting for a coat of paint. Straightened the front fender, too, and the motor purrs like a kitten."

"Kitten, huh?"

"Or maybe a grumpy old tiger. But at least it's running."

Clyde looked contemplative. "You mind me askin' why it needs to be rebuilt?"

Maybe the bike hadn't been the safest subject after all. Harley swallowed and looked down at the glass bottle in his hands, picking at the label while he tried to get a grip on his emotions. "He wrecked it. Three years ago now."

Clyde reached out a gnarled hand and took Harley's shoulder in a strong grip. "I'm sorry to hear that, son."

"It is what it is," he said with a shrug and picked up his root beer, downing a long swig.

"When do you think you'll be able to get it back on the road?"

"I'd like to ride it before winter, but I'm not counting on it." Harley rolled his shoulder. It was still sore from the night before. He pulled the sleeve of his t-shirt up revealing the road rash just above his dragon tattoo. "Laid the Norton down last night."

Clyde's eyes grew wide. "You alright there, sonny?"

"I'm fine. Just a scratch. Sore."

"Just a scratch, huh?" The old man studied him for a few seconds with the same pensive look as last time. The one Harley feared saw too much. "Dumpin' the bike isn't what's got you down, though, is it?"

The laugh Harley let out fell flat. "No, it's not. How did you know that?"

"You rode in here on her. If you'd wrecked it, well, then I could see ya bein' down in the dumps. Nope, has to be somethin' else."

Clyde waited, content to sit and sip his soda pop and let Harley speak when he was ready. It was one of the reasons he'd come back. That quiet patience. His throat tightened and he tried to swallow the lump. What did he even want to say? It wasn't like he was going to drop it all on Clyde. Erin. The fact that he was very much afraid he'd already fallen in love with her. Her betrayal. He ran his hands over his eyes. "There's this girl..."

"Ahhh, that explains a lot."

A chuckle escaped, but it was half-hearted. "I thought she was special. But this morning she showed her true colors. She was after something, it just wasn't me."

"That's rough."

"I don't know why I thought..." What had he thought? "... that she liked me despite..." He gestured toward himself with the bottle.

"What happened?" Clyde asked. His voice was low and mellow like he genuinely wanted to know and had all the time in the world to listen.

"I told myself over and over not to fall for her. I told myself she was too good to be true. But she got under my skin, you know?"

"The fairer sex tends to do that."

"I started to believe that she might be able to find a way to overlook my past. Then, this morning, I came back to my dad's house and she was searching it."

Clyde was silent for a beat, his eyes pensive. "Do you know what she was looking for?"

"I asked her, but she wouldn't say. I can't shake the feeling that she got close to me so she could look for something in the house."

Clyde ran his thumb over the condensation on the side of his bottle. "What'd you do?"

"I told her to get out, that's what." He tried not to think of the stricken look on her face or the way her eyes had filled with tears before she left. "I don't have any room in my life for a liar.

She didn't even tell me she knew my dad!"

Alright, that wasn't entirely true. She'd said she'd known him. What had she said exactly? 'Didn't everybody?' What she hadn't said was that she'd known him well enough that she had a reason to go searching for something in his house. He wished he knew what— No. No, he didn't. It wouldn't matter. The fact was, she'd misled him. Anger boiled in his gut, and he set the bottle down on the counter with a bang, the sweet soda going sour in his mouth.

"I'm gonna take a wild guess that you weren't too subtle when you told her to leave?"

Harley snorted. "No."

"Oh, my boy. If there's one thing I learned from being married for years and years... and years," he said with a wink and grin. "It's that a surefire way to get a lady to clam up is to come at her all angry and loud. Nothin' got my sweet wife's ire up like me bein' bull-headed and yellin'. Her lips would press into a line so thin you couldn't even see them. That's when I knew I'd done messed up. Now, are you certain, absolutely certain, she was up to no good?"

Harley frowned. "Doesn't matter. The fact is she conned me."

"Did she now?" Clyde asked. He scratched the stubble on his wizened cheek and studied Harley. "Sounds to me like you were gettin' scared and took the opportunity to high-tail it out of there."

"No—!"

Clyde held up his hand. "Let me give you some advice, my boy. Go home. Make things right. I'm not sayin' you have to let her back in, but if you hold on to hurt, it will eat you alive. You need to forgive."

A lump formed in Harley's throat and the words he pushed out came as a whisper. "I don't know how."

"Aww, sonny. You've got to be forgiven, then you can forgive others proper-like."

He was shaking his head before Clyde had finished speaking.

"Not gonna happen. The forgiveness I need is from my dad, and he's gone. I'm never going to get that."

"If it's true that your father never forgave you, that was his burden to carry, not yours. I'm talking about accepting forgiveness from The Almighty. And then turning right around and forgiving your father. And yourself. I think you know, in here..." Clyde reached out and gave Harley a hard thump on the chest, "...that it's high time to stop being angry. At him. At yourself. At this girl."

Harley took Clyde's words like a punch. "How do you know I'm angry at anyone?"

"Young man, you walked in here a few weeks ago wearing condemnation like a badge of honor."

The truth of the man's words made Harley's shoulders slump and he dropped his head into his hands. The old man was right. He'd been angry most of his life. Angry at his mom for leaving, angry at God for taking her, angry at his dad for not loving him the way he needed to be loved. Angry at himself for the mess he'd made of his life. Now angry at Erin... for what? What had she even done? Was Clyde right? Had he run because he was scared? Being angry was easier than being scared. But he was so tired of being angry. No, not just tired. Weary. Weary to the marrow of his bones. Tears pricked his eyes, but he refused to let them gain a footing.

"I'm gonna give you a little more advice. Do what you know in your heart is right. Be humble. Don't insist on your way. Be gentle, kind, and patient. As much as it depends on you, make peace with your dad, with God, with yourself. With this girl. Don't let the sun set while you're still angry."

Harley wasn't sure he was capable of doing all that, or even most of it, but one part he knew he could accomplish. He could go talk to Erin before the sun went down. If he hurried.

"Thanks, Clyde," he said, holding out his hand.

The older man grinned and took it in a solid grasp. "You come back now, you hear? I want to see that hog when you're finished."

"I will, sir."

"I'm gonna be prayin' for you, sonny."

All Harley could manage was a curt nod before bounding to his bike. He needed to hit the blacktop and follow it all the way home.

It was many hours before Erin heard the distinctive rumble of Harley's bike coming down the street. She was chilled to the bone and it hurt to unfold herself from the chair, but she had things that needed to be said, and she didn't want to wait even the few seconds it would take to work the kinks from her limbs.

She was waiting by the garage door when he turned into the driveway. The clothes she'd been wearing all day were rumpled and she wrung her hands as nerves tried to get the best of her. Her heart hammered against her ribs. *Please help me, Lord.*

You know the truth, and the truth will set you both free.

Alright. She'd say what she had to say and the rest was out of her hands. Knowing what she needed to do didn't make the nerves settle, though, and she wrapped her arms around her churning stomach. What ifs tried their best to drag her under, make her run. What if he was still angry? What if he wouldn't hear her out? What if— No, that game wasn't getting her anywhere. She tried to square her shoulders and waited to face him. She would lay it all out and the rest was up to him and God.

Parking the bike, Harley swung off and shucked his helmet, dropping it as he strode toward her, not slowing until he was directly in front of her, his hands cupping her face. Her breath lodged in her throat and she couldn't form the words she wanted to say. One thumb ran along her cheekbone. She imagined it probably came away wet.

Closing her eyes she summoned every ounce of courage she possessed. "I'm so sorr—"

Harley's mouth came down on hers, swallowing her apology. There was a glimmer of desperation in the kiss and she clutched the front of his shirt, not wanting him to pull away. He tasted faintly of root beer and she leaned into him, pressing her lips to his until he pulled back enough to look her in the eye.

"Please forgive me," he asked, his voice raspy and low. "I'm so, so sorry."

She shook her head. "No—"

"No, you won't forgive me?" It was said with a hint of humor, but she could also hear the vulnerability in it. He was worried she wouldn't.

"Of course I forgive you!" She smiled up at him and brushed the back of her fingers along his beard before looping her hands behind his neck. "I was going to say, no, you don't need to apologize. If anyone does it's m—"

Harley pressed a finger to her lips. "Please let me go first. If you still feel the need to apologize when I'm done, I won't stop you." She nodded. He took her hand in his and led her toward the house. "You're half frozen. How long have you been waiting for me." When she didn't answer, he turned and looked at her. "Oh, honey. All day?"

"Not *all* day."

He pulled his house keys from his pocket and unlocked the kitchen door. "Do you want coffee?"

"If for no other reason than to hold the hot cup, yes." She leaned against the kitchen table and rubbed her arms.

Harley busied himself with dumping out the coffee from that morning, still hot, but bitter from sitting all day, and starting a fresh pot. When he was done he stilled, leaning on the counter with his back still toward her. He hung his head. "I've been angry for a very, very... very long time. Being angry is easier than being hurt, or scared. Being angry is easier than dealing with mistakes, or righting wrongs, or hearing people out. I've been angry for so long... I'm sick of it. I don't want to be angry anymore."

He turned to face her, leaning back against the counter and crossing his ankles. "Last night was... maybe the best night of my life. Minus the blown tire, of course. And the road rash. But it was also scary. I'm scared I'll mess this up. I'm scared you'll come to your senses. I'm scared I'll hurt you. When I came to the house this morning..." He rubbed his hands over his eyes and Erin couldn't take it anymore. He must have heard her because he didn't so much as flinch when she touched his arm. Reaching out a long arm, he hooked it around the back of her neck, gently pulling her forward. As she stepped up to him he enveloped her in his hard muscles, warm and safe. Stepping fully into his embrace she wrapped her arms around his waist.

Gracious words are like honey from a honeycomb, sweet to the soul, and healing to the body. Let your words always be said with grace, as if seasoned with salt.

"Harley, I need to tell you something," she whispered into his shirt. He smelled like autumn, with a touch of motor oil. She breathed in the scent before she began just in case this didn't go well. He pressed his lips to her hair and she closed her eyes, trying to pick where she wanted to begin. She swallowed hard and tried to think. Harley's chest was warm and strong under her cheek. "Remember when I told you about being fourteen and Alec moving into town?" She felt Harley tense under her arms, but she had to get it all out. No more half-truths, no more hiding things. "There's a lot more to the story than that. I told you yesterday that my parents moved. When they left they gave me an ultimatum: Leave the guy and go with them, or stay and they would wash their hands of me."

Harley sucked in a ragged breath. "Aww, honey."

She took a moment to enjoy the security of his arms, drawing strength from the smell of the wind on his skin and the way his lips felt brushing against her hair. "I chose him and stayed. No home, no job, no car, no... anything. I'd painted a picture in my mind of this happily ever after we were going to have. Silly teenage-girl fantasies. At first, he thought it was cool that I'd chosen him over my parents."

Erin shuddered as the memories came. "What I hadn't been able to see before was how controlling he was. It got worse and worse until I was scared of him. He never hit me, but he made me believe he would. I couldn't leave the house, couldn't talk to my friends. I was a kid and I was scared and I didn't know what to do. The day I saw him selling something..." Tears stung her eyes at the memory and it felt like she was forcing the words out. "I was so scared."

Harley went perfectly still. The muscles in his chest tightened under her cheek, and his breathing quickened. She leaned back and met his eyes. "It's in the past. Over. Done. Promise me you won't do anything... foolish."

Fury simmered in them and a little piece of her loved him for it.

Wait. Loved? No. She couldn't.

Could she?

No.

And yet... something about the way he tucked a strand of hair behind her ear and watched her, waiting. The way his palm cupped her cheek and his thumb rubbed out a tear that had escaped her lashes. Yes, there was a very real chance that she could love this man.

It was a few beats before he nodded and she saw the anger begin to fade from his eyes. "I promise."

It had been years since anyone had wanted to stand by her side and fight her battles with her. Three years to be exact. She puffed out a sigh. There were still things, important things, that needed to be said. She slipped out of his arms on the pretense of pouring the coffee. She expected him to ask questions or say something, but he stayed quiet and waited for her to continue. "While Alec was screaming at me, this man showed up. Just walked up to the door and knocked. Alec opened it and the man didn't even look at him. Looked right past him to me. He offered me a safe place to go. I knew who he was. Knew he helped kids who were in trouble. So I went with him."

She wanted to go on, finish the story, but emotions clogged her throat and stole her voice. The coffee pot gurgled, and the faucet dripped. Somewhere outside the house, a branch slid against the siding. Finally, her throat allowed her to force out the most important part of the whole story.

"Harley, that man was your father."

CHAPTER FOURTEEN

ll the air in the room vanished. Harley tried to make his lungs work, but Erin's words had wrapped themselves around his windpipe and squeezed it shut. With a Herculean effort, he managed to drag in enough air to speak, but thinking was a different story. "What?"

Erin had stepped away and perched on the edge of the table, holding her cup of coffee like a shield. He jammed his hands in his pockets to keep them from shaking. Or fisting at his side. He wasn't angry, and that alone shocked him, but his brain felt like the gears were slipping. His father had rescued Erin? *His* father?

"Please..." She trailed off and looked down at her coffee. "Please don't be angry. I wanted to tell you, but... I couldn't figure out how. At first, I didn't know you were Coop's son. I thought you'd just bought this place. Then, that day you started working on his bike, I almost told you, but the words... I didn't know what to say. Then the longer I waited, the harder it got..."

Harley watched her bite her lip and look up at him through wet lashes. He wanted to go to her, reassure her, hold her. But he needed to know the truth more. "How well did you know my dad? Really?"

Placing her feet on the seat of a chair, Erin hugged the mug close to her chest and stared at a spot in the distance. Or maybe a spot in the past. "That day, Coop took me to Vera and Jason's. But he came and saw me... so many times over the next few days. He told me about how God loved me and had a plan for me. How my messy choices kept me away from Him. He listened when I told him about ruining my relationship with my mom and about having nowhere to go. That whole time I was so scared that I'd end up back on my own. Vera and Jason were great, but they weren't equipped to take me in long term. I didn't know how to get in touch with my mom... Then, a few weeks after Coop rescued me, a social worker came to talk to me. She asked a lot of questions. A lot. Then she asked me what I wanted. I begged, I mean tears and everything begged her to let me live with Coop."

Like a jolt of electricity, the information burned through Harley. She'd lived... here? The father he'd known would never have gone to a trap house and rescued someone. He would have yelled with righteous indignation from the pulpit about purging their fair community of heathens like Alec. Like Erin. But rescue?

"You said you knew who he was? Before that day?"

"Before my mom left, while I was still in school, he'd come talk to the students about staying safe, making good choices, staying away from drugs. He even explained options for getting clean if we were already using. Of course, he couldn't say anything about Jesus in school, but we all knew who he was. I remembered him telling us that we could call him, day or night, if we were in trouble and he'd be there. No matter what."

"That's not the man I knew."

Her eyes finally came up to meet his, full of compassion and understanding. "After I came here to live with him, he told me about you."

"Yeah? I can imagine how that conversation went. 'Whatever you do, don't be like my boy.'"

"No, Harley. He loved you! He told me how he'd messed up, so bad, and that he would have given anything to make things right with you."

"I highly doubt that."

"Coop never stopped loving you."

This was too much. Harley ran his hand down over his eyes and across his beard. He had so many questions, but they all congealed until he couldn't figure out what he wanted to know. He linked his fingers behind his neck and buried his face between his arms. His father could not have forgiven him. If he had, that would mean he hadn't needed to stay away. That he could have come home. No. "No. I don't believe you."

"This morning I was in your dad's room looking for a box he kept. A box full of envelopes from you. He used to take it out when he prayed for you. He had three or four that he opened and read over and over. I wanted to find it and show it to you. I wanted you to see how much he loved you."

The envelopes flashed in his mind. His self-imposed penance. "Dad... kept those?"

"Every single one."

There hadn't been much in the way of notes. The occasional scribble on a scrap of paper. What could he have said? Apologizing and begging for forgiveness in a letter felt... cheap. Like a cop-out. And he'd always thought there was plenty of time. He dropped his hands from his neck and met her eyes. "Did you find them?"

"No. But I know they're there somewhere." She paused and looked away before continuing. "Did you know he went looking for you?"

He could feel his mouth drop open. "He what?"

"When he got the first envelope. It was postmarked Cincinnati. He said he got on his bike and drove straight through to get there. Nineteen hours. He looked for you for days, but... Cincinnati is a big place, and—"

"And I wasn't even there anymore."

Erin nodded and set her mug behind her on the table. "After about a week he came home. That's when he started coming to the school and talking to the kids that hung around on The Green and down by the ball field."

"And you... How long did you live here?"

"Almost four years. Until I went away to trade school. I wasn't the only one. Cori stayed here for a while when her parents were going through an ugly divorce and she was caught in the middle. That's how we met. And others. Most for a night or two, maybe a week. I was the only one that... lived here. Vera helped out, too. Kind of a mom when we needed it." A smile tugged at her lips. "She's still mothering me."

The realization that Erin had lost Coop, too, struck Harley hard in the heart, pinching and squeezing until it hurt. He pushed off the counter and gathered her into his arms. He was sure he didn't know the stranger she was talking about, but he could see the pain etched on her face and he hated it. Wanted to erase it.

Muffled from where her face pressed against his shirt, Erin continued. "There's a verse in 2 Chronicles that says 'If My people, who are called by My name, humble themselves, and pray, and seek Me, and turn from their wicked ways; I will hear from heaven, and forgive their sins, and heal their land.' Your dad said he read that verse in a Gideons Bible in a ratty motel in Cincinnati, and that it was his wake-up call. He said he'd always thought it was up to him to straighten people out, but the reality was that he was supposed to humble himself and pray and seek God and turn from his own sinful ways. Then God could *use* him to heal this town."

"I wish I could have known the man you're describing," Harley said past the lump that had formed in his throat. He felt the wetness on his cheeks and didn't care.

Erin's arms tightened around him. "You're a lot like the Coop I knew," she whispered. An unfamiliar feeling spread through his chest at her words. Warm and buoyant. It felt a lot like pride. He'd never felt proud of being compared to his father. Maybe once upon a time he'd wanted to be just like his dad. Fun, adventurous, good. It had been so long ago he hadn't quite remembered what it felt like, that pride, that longing. He liked the feeling. A lot.

They stood in the kitchen for a long time. Quiet. Holding onto each other. The silence felt right. Never mind the fact that Harley didn't think he could have spoken even if he'd wanted to. After what seemed like forever, Erin pulled back and slid off the table.

"Come on," she said, taking his hand and tugging him toward the back of the house.

He followed, but his steps slowed as they reached his dad's room. "Other than the minute I stood in the doorway this morning, I haven't been in this room since my mom passed away. Sixteen years." He took a tentative step through the door and looked around. Erin slipped an arm around his waist and held on tight.

His first thought was that he needed to run. His skin crawled with it. But he needed to stay, too. And that was because of Erin. She stood next to him, watching him and waiting. If she hadn't been there he would have already been headed out of town.

Stepping fully into the room, he eased away from her arms and ran his fingers over the footboard on the bed. The blankets lay pushed back as if his father had just gotten up that morning. He'd been right, Cori's cloth bag did look like his mother's crazy quilt. And yes, it was still on the bed. He looked away and his eyes caught on the study area in the corner. Walking over, he rubbed the toe of his boot in one of the worn spots on the floor in front of his dad's easy chair. The carpet was almost gone. "Dad must have spent a lot of time in this chair."

"That he did. How did you know?" Her voice was quiet.

"He wore the carpet away where his feet sat."

Erin walked around the bed to where Harley stood and looked down. "I don't think that's what those are from," she murmured. Harley raised an eyebrow and Erin stepped toward the chair, but instead of sitting, she dropped to her knees, fitting them into the threadbare spots.

"Do you honestly think dad wore out the carpet... praying?"

Erin pushed to her feet and slipped her hand into his. "Yes, I do. I'm sure of it."

Harley shook his head. "I don't remember my dad praying like that. I remember loud, booming prayers from the pulpit and the blessing recited before meals. I don't think I ever once saw him on his knees."

"He told me what he was like before you left. He said that when Jules passed away, he lost sight of a lot of things. Until you were gone he had no idea what grace and mercy were. He changed, Harley. He said he'd always believed *in* God, but that he hadn't accepted His compassion until he came face-to-face with the lengths a father is willing to go to forgive his child." The words were soft and tender and, oh, how he wanted to believe them.

"Dad wore the carpet out... on his knees." he swallowed hard and rubbed a hand over his face. This was too much.

"He prayed all the time. Here on his knees, while he worked on his motorcycle, at the kitchen table. We would pray together on the porch after dinner, or tucked up to the stove in the living room."

Harley looked at the chair again trying to wrap his head around this man he hadn't even known. So much had been lost when his mother passed away. The fact that his father had found his way out of the grief was both fantastic and frustrating. Fantastic for his old man, frustrating that he had yet to get there himself. Maybe he never would.

Before he could comment, his gaze landed on a couple of photos on the side table. They leaned against the base of the lamp, tucked next to his dad's Bible and curled with time. Nothing fancy, just snapshots of a grinning young woman. Harley snatched them off the table, his stomach plummeting and his mouth going dry.

"Harley?"

"I need air." He rounded the bed and didn't wait for Erin, just took the shortest route to the backyard and dropped onto the new steps. Struggling to breathe, he stared at the photographs still clutched in his hand. They were both of the same girl, her smile brilliant, her eyes dancing with joy and just a smidge of mischief, just the way he remembered them. The first picture was her in a navy blue cap and gown, the field-house at the

University of Maine in the background. The second showed the girl in her wedding gown, turned away from her groom to grin at the camera. She looked so happy. So *not* ruined. Even in the fresh air, Harley was having a hard time drawing a breath.

Erin followed him, and he felt her hand on his arm as she eased down onto the freshly painted boards. Felt her lay her head on his shoulder and slip her fingers into his. He stared past the photos at his work boots without seeing either. Erin was quiet and he appreciated that.

"Do you know her?" he asked, handing over the photos.

"Not personally. She was someone your dad helped before he rescued me. I think her name is Julie."

"Julianne." Harley took the photos back and smoothed them out on his knee. "When I left town ten years ago I didn't leave alone. I took my girlfriend with me. At first, we thought it would be a great adventure. So stupid. After a few months of living out of crappy motel rooms and struggling to find work, she wanted to come home. There was no way I was coming back here. We fought."

Harley stood and walked a few steps away from Erin. Her comforting hand in his was so undeserved. He crossed his arms and stared blankly into the darkened yard, his breath ragged puffs in the cold air. Finally, he continued. "She told me she thought she was pregnant. I was so mad and so scared. I took what money we had and the bike and I just left. Drove away and didn't look back. Until about a month later, when I couldn't even look at myself in the mirror anymore."

"Oh, Harley—"

"No," he snarled. "Don't be that way!"

"What—?"

"Don't be all tender and caring and… and… you! Did you not hear what I said?" He rounded on her. "Did you not hear me just say I left my pregnant girlfriend, penniless, in a grubby motel?"

Erin stood and came over to where he stood. She smiled up at him and a little of the fight drained away. "What I heard you say was that you were a very scared seventeen-year-old boy who didn't know what to do."

He made an exasperated sound and tried to step away, but she reached out and took his hand.

"Harley, Julianne was your dad's first rescue. He found her in Cincinnati, brought her back. He helped her get her GED and get into college."

Sucking in a lung full of air, Harley tried to stop his world from spinning. All these years he'd feared... "I went back. I went back and looked for her. I was frantic, but she was long gone. I always assumed the worst. That she'd died or that she and my kid were living on the streets."

"She wasn't pregnant."

Harley's heart nearly stopped. For ten years he'd told himself he didn't get a do-over. No happily ever after, no white picket fence, no two kids and a dog. There was no second chance for a man who abandoned his first chance the way he had. And some of that still clung. "It doesn't matter. I left. I've hated myself for so long." His voice hitched in a most unmanly way, but Erin didn't seem to care. She wrapped her arms around his neck and clung to him. After a few minutes, she stepped back and slid one of the snapshots from where he had them gripped in his hand.

"I can't make you forgive yourself, but I can tell you that Julianne has forgiven you. Look at this picture. She's married. She's happy. She's living a life that isn't any of the things you feared. It's time you forgave yourself."

He took the photo back from Erin's fingers and stared at it in the dim light from the back door. Julianne was fine. She was more than fine, she was happy. So much of what he hated about himself centered on those first few months on the road. Stealing his father's bike, leaving town with Julianne, running away, abandoning her. It had driven the rest of his life. Punishing himself had become his way of life. He wasn't sure he could stop, but he could at least be open to the possibility. Squeezing her hand tighter in his, he looked down to where their fingers were joined. "Can we start over? All of it? Right from the first time I laid eyes on you here in the backyard?"

She grinned at him before leaning in, her face tipped up to look him in the eye. "I'd like that."

Harley pulled away and stuck out his hand. "Hi. I'm Charleston Beck. Cooper Beck was my dad. It's nice to meet you."

She took his hand and clasped it in a firm grip. "Erin Wallace. Cooper Beck introduced me to Jesus and I loved him very much." Her voice hitched and she stopped talking for a second. "Nice to meet you."

Harley tucked a wayward strand of hair behind her ear. "Do we have to start... everything... over, or can I still kiss you?"

She pressed her cheek into the palm of his hand. "I was kind of hoping you would."

The fingertips that had slid behind her ear now ran down the smooth column of her neck, tracing her collarbone where it peeked out of her shirt collar. He watched as her pulse quickened under his touch and he grinned as he brought his lips down on hers.

"I went to the library this morning and did some digging," Erin said, fishing a folded piece of paper from her pocket. They'd moved back inside when their fingers had started to numb from the cold. Fresh cups of coffee and long conversations about his dad had warmed Harley from the inside out. "Well, Mrs. Wolcott did, but look what we found."

He took the paper from her, but with her smiling face tilted up, he couldn't resist leaning down to brush his lips across hers. She tasted of too-sweet coffee and the happy sound she sighed made him grin. Burying his face in her hair, he brushed a kiss along the side of her neck but then pulled back. If he wasn't careful he could get lost in kissing her. Erin was respectable and pure and he sure as heck wasn't going to ask for more than he ought. Instead, he skimmed the printout.

"Whoa."

"Yeah. Mrs. Wolcott said she once overheard Novak and Lyle arguing outside the library. That's how she knew to search for Arnie instead of Skylar. She said Lyle'd called him that."

"If the information in this article got out, it would finish him at that church. Aren't they all about peace and harmony? I can't imagine it would go over well to have a leader who'd been arrested for…" Harley paused and looked back at the printout. "Conspiracy to commit aggravated assault against a police officer."

"And the use of arson in the execution of a hate crime," Erin added, pointing at the bottom of the page.

"How is this guy not in jail?" Harley asked in disbelief.

"It says he made bail. I can't imagine that's all it took! He changed his first name and then just moved to Summer Harbor without anyone being the wiser?"

"On the other hand, who would suspect the leader of a peaceful religious organization in Maine was a violent arsonist?" Harley tapped the paper. "If Lyle knew this, why didn't he go to the police?"

"If he knew who killed Jason, why didn't he go to the police?"

"Good point."

"I do think that moves Sky— I mean Arnie Novak to the top of the list when it comes to who had a serious problem with Lyle Jay."

The way she scrunched her nose when she was thinking was adorable. "You've got your Nancy Drew face on again," he teased.

Erin laughed. "I thought it was my… what was it? Starsky and Hutch… face."

"I'm Starsky, and you're… way too beautiful to be Hutch."

She blushed and took a sip of coffee. "I was just thinking that Lyle seems to have had more than a few enemies."

"Enough that it's getting less and less likely his crash was a freak accident. "

"Maybe we need to be looking at this from a cop's point of

view," Erin suggested.

Harley stretched his long legs and let the chair tip back until it bumped the wall. "Motive, means, and opportunity?"

"Exactly."

"In that case, who had motive to get Lyle out of the way?" he asked

Sitting up straight, Erin began counting off on her fingers. "Top of the list. Skylar Novak."

"Overheard fighting with Lyle on more than one occasion. Lyle knew who he was and most likely what he'd done."

Erin counted on another finger. "Edwin Hurst."

"Motive? He wanted to buy Finch and Jay's, but Lyle wouldn't sell. With Lyle out of the way, he's got a better chance of buying it. Maybe. He didn't seem to think so, but maybe he's just blowing smoke."

"But murder?"

"It does seem drastic."

"Alec Cohen."

Harley's voice got quiet. "Do you think he's capable of—"

"Yes."

Anger began to simmer along his veins again, but this time he held it in check. He wasn't going back there. "It's obvious that all three disliked Lyle."

"But enough to kill him? I mean, I didn't care for the man either but murder? That's a stretch, isn't it?"

"Anyone else?" Harley asked.

"I don't want to say it." Finally, she met his eyes. "Vera. But it isn't her, so let's move on. Did they have opportunity?"

"That wouldn't have been hard. Lyle's bike was pretty hard to miss and he rode it everywhere. Someone could have done something to it while it was parked on the street, in his dooryard, or even at the shop if they were sneaky."

"Means?"

"It isn't rocket science to make a bike crash. I think any of them could have figured out how to sabotage the motorcycle. The tricky part is, how did the police miss it? I wish I could get a look at it," he said, hearing the frustration in his voice. "See if I can find anything amiss. It'd be a lot easier to narrow down who might have done something if we knew *what* was done. Or even *if.*"

"Where is it?"

Harley shrugged. "Chief Briggs said they took dad's bike to Finch and Jay's after the accident and kept it under lock and key until the guy from the state was done. Maybe they did the same thing with Lyle's?"

"I feel like we're missing something."

"Or we're grasping at straws." A silence settled over them, both lost in thought. Harley took a sip of coffee and sighed. "I don't need to see it, but I kind of wish you'd found that box this morning."

The sadness that crossed Erin's face bit at him and he wished he hadn't said anything. It didn't matter. He was, slowly, starting to see that he'd been wrong about his dad for a long time. He didn't need a box of who-knows-what to show him that. Opening his mouth to say so, he was surprised when Erin's eyes grew big and she jumped up. "I didn't find the box, but I did find something weird. Hold on." She walked to the back of the house and returned holding a battered composition book.

"What's that?"

"I have no idea." She flipped it open revealing long columns of dates, times, and locations that filled the pages. In the margins were pairs of letters and the occasional note. "I found it in Coop's room this morning. It was tucked into a box full of old clothes. I don't recognize it. I never saw him writing in it, but... there are pages and pages like this and it's Coop's handwriting."

Harley took it from her and flipped through to the end. "These entries are from the week before he died." He ran his finger down the column of dates, stopping about halfway. "What do you suppose *LJ* and *RL* mean?"

"I don't know, but look back here." She flipped to an

earlier entry. "These dates are just before he came for me. Look. *AC*. Here and here. Then on the day he rescued me, *EW*. I think EW is me. It never shows up again after that date."

"And AC?"

"Alec Cohen?"

"If AC is Alec, and EW is you... Could LJ be Lyle?" Harley asked.

"Maybe. I don't know any other LJs in town, although that doesn't mean anything."

Harley continues flipping through the pages, stopping near the end and staring at the page. "Erin?" He spun the page around to face her. "Was this the day Jason died?"

Her fingers fluttered to her lips and she nodded.

Borrowed Jason's truck

Did they think it was me?

Scrawled in the margin, as if Coop had returned to the page and added them later on, were the words:

Yes, Lord; you know that I love you.

Yes, Lord; you know that I love you.

Lord; you know everything. You know that I love you.

I will (still and always) follow you

"What does 'Did they think it was me?' mean?" Erin asked, her voice not much more than a whisper.

"I have no idea." Harley stared at the page, feelings he couldn't quite identify warring in his chest. "Listen. I think we need to pay a visit to Chief Briggs. Ask him if this book means anything to him. Tell him about Skylar Novak. Share our suspicions about Lyle. See what he has to say."

"What are we going to say? 'Some people sort of didn't like the guy'? We have nothing."

"We have the book."

"Which could be nothing."

Frustration simmered, but she was right. What did they have other than a notebook that didn't make sense? "Alright, so we wait on talking to the police."

"I need to go home," Erin managed to get out before stifling a yawn. "I'm exhausted and I *have* to work on your porch tomorrow or Keaton's going to fire me."

The legs of Harley's chair snapped back to the linoleum as he stood. "I think we're both exhausted and will have much clearer heads tomorrow." He reached out and offered her a hand up, pulling her to him when she stood. He knew they should go, but he couldn't resist taking her face in his hands and kissing her one more time. "Come on. I'll walk you home."

The following morning had dawned damp and dreary. A heavy sky hung low over the harbor. Rain would occasionally pour from one of the wind-whipped clouds, drenching everything in its path. Harley wasn't a bit surprised to find the house dark and Erin's truck nowhere to be seen when he arrived. The sleepless night had driven him mad. His overwhelmed mind kept him tossing and turning until he couldn't stand it another minute. A couple of hours with his gloves and bag hadn't been enough to quiet his jumbled thoughts and so he'd decided to walk through the drizzle to his dad's house and try working on the bike to clear his head.

That hadn't worked either and he'd ended up standing at the window staring at nothing. Hours later he was startled to hear the door open behind him and he wondered how long he'd been lost in thought. The downpour earlier had been blown out to sea and a tentative bit of sunlight was breaking through the clouds here and there making the slicked scenery glisten.

"Hey," Erin said shyly.

"Hey." He grinned. "I was glad to find you *weren't* on my roof this morning."

"Ha! No. Keaton put me on an indoor job, but I got done early. Is everything alright? When I came in you looked to be a million miles away."

"Yeah, just... last night was a lot to take in." He stepped across the space, feeling on edge and craving the feel of her lips on his. After brushing them with a kiss he pulled her gently into his arms, smiling when her arms tightened around him. "When you walked in, I was thinking about this blasted thing with Lyle and his accident. I just wish I could get eyes on Lyle's bike, you know? See if I can put my finger on what happened."

"Why don't you?"

"Why don't I… what?"

"Go look at Lyle's bike." She pulled back far enough to meet his eyes and smile up at him. "I'll drive."

"OK, Hutch, let's go."

The garage bay doors at Finch and Jay's were closed to the chilly, rain-drenched afternoon air, but it was busier inside than he expected. All four bays had bikes in them and the mechanics were all hard at work. Harley's boots thumped against the cement and one of the mechanics waved.

"Be right with you." He finished tightening a nut and pulled a rag from his back pocket, wiping his hands as he made his way over to them. "What can I do for you?"

"I was hoping to speak to Dox. Is he in?"

"Sorry, Mr. Finch isn't in today."

He tried to smooth the frustration out of his voice. "I was hoping to take a look at Lyle Jay's Knucklehead. Is it here?"

The mechanic shifted his feet and looked anywhere but Harley's eyes. "Yeah, it's here, but I don't think I'm supposed to let anybody see it. The guy from the State Police was here and all, but then Mr. Finch locked it back up. Until the Chief says otherwise," the man jerked his head toward a closed door in the back of the garage, "that's where it stays."

"I understand," Harley ground out. Alright, so he wasn't as successful with keeping the frustration out of his voice that time. Deep breath. "Could you have Dox get in touch when he gets back?"

"Sure, sure." The man scooped a pencil and an ancient-looking memo pad off the cluttered counter. "What was your name again?"

"Harley Beck. He'll know how to get a hold of me."

The mechanic scribbled on the pad and, ripping the top sheet off, affixed it to the wall with a pushpin. "There you go."

"Thank you," Erin said as they turned to leave.

"That was a waste of time," Harley grumbled once they were outside.

"Maybe. But now we know exactly where Lyle's bike is. Besides, that wasn't the only thing we wanted clarification on. What about Skylar Novak? Do you think he'd admit what they were arguing about now that we know his real name?"

"Only one way to find out," Harley said. Erin grinned and climbed into the truck.

Skyler Novak couldn't contain his look of surprise when Harley and Erin approached the church. Teetering atop a tall step-ladder, he appeared to be fixing the gutter above the front door. Scurrying down, he licked his lips and with nervous movements tried to find a place for his hands. Eventually settling on crossing his thin arms over his chest, his feet picked up the edgy motion. "Mr. Beck. What can I do for you today?"

"Mr. Novak, I have some more questions I was hoping you could help me with," Harley began in his very best friendly-neighbor voice.

Irritation wafted off the man, but he got it under control and affixed a serene look on his face. "Yes, my son?"

Harley crossed his arms and forced his voice to stay neutral. "We believe we know what you and Lyle Jay were arguing about the day before he died."

For once, Skylar Novak didn't resemble a sepia-tone photograph. A scarlet flush climbed up his neck and frosted his ears. It mottled his cheeks and seeped into his brow line. "I don't think I like your tone. Now, if you'll excuse me—" He turned and began walking away with prim steps, leaving the ladder where it rested against the building.

"Arnie," Erin called, her voice pitched low so only he would hear.

Novak stopped and spun toward them. The face that had, moments before, been stained red with indignation, now blanched to a sallow cream color. "How...?" He licked his lips again and his gaze darted around. He stepped closer and lowered his voice. "I don't know what you think you—"

"We—" Erin started to argue, but Harley caught her hand and squeezed. Best not to show their hand just yet. She nodded before continuing. "We've been asking around, someone heard Lyle call you Arnie," Erin said, her voice quiet and comforting. Harley bit the inside of his cheek to keep a straight face. He wondered if Arnie Novak would be able to resist that tone any better than he could.

The man's shoulders slumped in what looked like relief and his tone turned indifferent. "I very much doubt I'll be any help. As I told you the other day, it was all said in confidence. All I can say is that he found out. I don't know how, but he did. The vile man offered to keep quiet... for a price."

"He was blackmailing you, too?"

"There were others? That doesn't surprise me. I'm really not sure why I let him keep blackmailing me. It isn't like a name change is all that big a deal."

No, it wasn't. Something was off. The man should be afraid that they knew more, but he seemed aloof, indifferent. As if he thought he was untouchable.

"He didn't have anything more on you than the name change?" Harley asked.

"No, of course not. I'm a simple holy man tending his congregation." Harley could read the lie on the man's lips even before Arnie changed the subject. "And while I disliked the man, other people in this town had much more substantial reasons to despise Lyle Jay than I did."

"Such as?"

"It's not like I'm going to give you a list," Skylar said with a stamp of his foot. Then he seemed to reconsider and the arrogant lift of his chin returned. "Or maybe I will. One you might want to be looking at is Vera Whittley. Apparently, she had a... particular distaste for the man."

Harley felt Erin stiffen and suck in a sharp breath. "Vera?"

she asked in a voice that hitched ever so slightly.

"Oh, yeah. Hated the man." There was a flicker of something in the cleric's eyes that Harley couldn't quite identify. It looked... smug. Or evil. But was gone so fast that he wondered if he'd imagined it.

"Do you know why?" Harley asked.

Novak forced an uninterested tone and picked at a bit of dirt on his sleeve. "I don't know. Something to do with her husband, or your father."

"My father?"

"Oh, yes." The glimmer Harley'd seen earlier flickered again and was joined by something almost malicious. "The way I heard it Vera was right in love with your father." As if catching himself, the man's face turned pious once again. "Like I said. I won't be much help. Now, if there's anything my congregation or I can do...Please let us know," he said before rushing into the church and slamming the door.

Harley wanted to kick the ladder in frustration but restrained himself. That hadn't gotten them quite where he'd hoped or expected.

"It couldn't have been Vera," Erin whispered. "Could it?"

"Grief does crazy things to people. Makes them do crazy things sometimes." A sharp pang hit Harley's chest and he suddenly couldn't breathe. Grief makes people do crazy things sometimes. Crazy things like trying to control every aspect of your son's life? Like stealing a motorcycle and running away? Like preaching against the horrors this world offers to the point of compulsion? Like punishing oneself for years rather than seeking forgiveness?

Harley pressed the heel of his hand into his chest. Could all the things that drove a wedge between him and his father have been the result of their grief over losing Jules Beck? The back of Harley's throat burned when he tried to inhale.

"Are you OK?" Erin asked.

"Yeah, why?" Harley tried to put on a nonchalant face and pretend that nothing was wrong.

They climbed into her truck and he sat in silence looking out the passenger side window all the way back to the house. He could feel Erin sneaking glances at him as she drove, but she didn't push and he didn't offer an explanation. What could he say when he didn't even know what was going on in his own head? When they reached the curb, Erin reached out and caught his hand, squeezing it. He tightened his fingers around hers but didn't trust his voice. She seemed to understand.

"I'll see you tomorrow?" she asked.

He nodded and hopped down from the cab, waiting on the sidewalk until she'd driven away. Once inside the garage, he leaned against the closed door and gasped for air. He always thought better, processed better, when he was busy. He needed to be busy. Or he needed to run. He cast a longing look at the Norton, but shook the thought away. No more running.

With that thought foremost in his mind, Harley pushed the garage door open and walked his Norton out into the driveway. But only to give him space to work on the XL-1000. His mind still reeled, but working on his dad's bike began to soothe his spirit.

What could he remember from before his mother passed? Or before she got sick? Memories he hadn't let himself entertain for decades slowly overtook his mind. His father reading to him and his mother beside the fire in the living room, curled on the couch with blankets and hot chocolate. Hours spent in the garage working on the bikes. Cold, moonless autumn nights on the porch watching the stars. Picnics on the beach. Church. Laughter. Love.

Then it started to disappear. Little by little, stripped away until nothing remained except grief.

Coming to grips with the truth was going to take a lot more than a few hours in the garage but over the rest of the evening, the clink of tools against metal and the satisfaction of making whole what once was broken calmed him. If his father could find a way out, maybe there was a tiny flicker of hope for him after all.

❦

Whatever had Harley tied in knots the day before, he still wasn't sharing. Erin poked her head in the garage door Thursday morning, but it was obvious that he still needed to be alone with his thoughts. She understood. The porch roof awaited, her place to think and process.

Late in the afternoon, she was finishing the last shingle and the last verse of a hymn when Harley let out a roar of pain, followed by a blue word that made Erin cringe. She dashed down the ladder and toward the garage, throwing the door open just as Harley reached for a rag hanging on a nail inside. Blood was dripping from his hand and his lips were forming another curse when he realized she was standing there, eyes huge. He snapped his mouth closed and pressed the rag to his hand.

"What happened?" she asked, stepping forward to look at the wound.

"I must have caught my hand on the belt." He nodded toward the shredded tire from the Norton. "I grabbed it to put with the garbage and…" He pulled the rag away, revealing a smooth gash across the heel of his hand.

"A shredded tire did that?" Erin's stomach churned looking at the laceration and how close it was to his wrist. She swallowed hard. "I've got a first aid kit in the truck. Let's get that taken care of properly."

Harley was sitting on the edge of the porch holding the rag to his hand when Erin returned, first-aid kit in hand. She placed it next to him and carefully removed the piece of cloth, now sticky with blood. "That probably wasn't the cleanest thing to grab. Is motor oil bad for open wounds?" he asked.

Erin snickered. "Probably. This might sting. Sorry." She poured some hydrogen peroxide on the cut and grimaced when Harley sucked in a breath.

Once she was done cleaning it she took a closer look. "Do

you want to go get stitches?"

"Stitches?" He pulled his hand away from her and looked at it, confused. "A broken belt shouldn't... No, just slap some butterflies on there. It'll be fine."

As soon as she'd bandaged his hand he pushed off the porch and paced toward the garage with purposeful strides. Erin followed. When he reached the tire, he squatted down and started to carefully turn it, examining every square inch. The curse that had been on the tip of his tongue earlier slipped out. "Someone did this on purpose."

"What!?"

Harley pointed to a piece of metal embedded in the rubber, and a sick feeling settled in her core. "Is that... a razor blade?"

"Pressed into the tread on the tire, it will work its way deeper and deeper until it pops the tire."

"That's awful!" Erin gasped. "Why would—? Who—?" She could feel panic rising in her chest.

He must have seen it on her face because he wrapped an arm around her shoulders. "Hey. We were fine, and I could be wrong. I mean, it's possible I picked it up off the road at some point."

Erin nodded, but the bitter taste of fear still lingered. What would have happened if he'd been doing eighty on the interstate instead of thirty-five on a back road? She shuddered at the thought.

Standing, he pulled her up to stand with him, taking her in his arms. "Thanks for the bandaids. Sorry about the cussing. I'm working on that."

"I know." She slipped her arms around his waist and snuggled into his embrace. "I should head out so I can shower before choir practice. But... if you need me to skip it and stay... If you need me, I can be here."

"Nah. It's all good. Go to choir practice." Harley smiled. "If you leave the truck at your place I'll walk you home when you're done."

"That sounds nice." She stood on tip-toe and kissed his

cheek but didn't step away. "Are you sure you're OK? I feel like I shouldn't leave."

"Yeah. It's all good." He called her name as she was heading for the door, and she stopped and turned. "Let's not say anything about the razor blade until we figure out what's going on, alright?"

She nodded and felt an icy shiver slide down her spine. Had someone honestly tried to kill them? Only...not *them* because there's no way anyone would have known that she'd be on the bike. Had someone tried to kill *Harley*?

An hour later she was still turning that horrible thought over in her mind when she arrived at the church. She'd gone home and showered, stewing over the discovery Harley had made until she was a bundle of nerves.

Sawyer was leaning against the railing outside the church doors, waiting for her. "Hey, kid."

She took a deep breath. Time to focus! "Alright, mister, time to prove you're not all bluster."

The older man laughed and held the door open for her. "Oh, this is going to be fun."

A knock startled Harley and he straightened from where he'd been bent over the bike to find Edwin Hurst peering in the open garage door. He frowned at the man. "Hurst."

"Harley."

"What can I do for you?"

Edwin pasted on what Harley suspected was his deal-making smile. It probably worked for most people, but to Harley, it looked annoyingly fake.

"I was just stopping by to see if you'd thought about reconsidering my offer?"

Harley's grip on the wrench he was holding tightened until his knuckles started to ache. "No."

"No, you haven't thought about it?"

If his hold got any tighter, he would either bend the steel or break a bone. He relaxed his hand and set the wrench down on the workbench. "No, I'm not interested in your offer."

Edwin's smile stayed in place, but it looked more forced than ever. "Now Harley, we both know you can't keep the place. The taxes alone will sink you."

Harley looked away, hating the fact that Edwin was right. Unless something changed, he wouldn't be able to keep going with double mortgage payments, taxes, and late taxes, not to mention the repairs that needed to be done. He wanted to pick the wrench up and throw it, but this was probably a time to be more tactful than that. Harley almost laughed at himself. Him? Tactful? Yeah, right. He wished Erin was there to share her calm. "Why do you want it so badly?"

"I'm just trying to help you out. That's all." The change in Edwin's demeanor was so slight that Harley almost missed it. A tightening of his face around the artificial smile, a brightening of his tone. Harley wasn't convinced. "Listen. Think about it, OK? The money I'm willing to give you for the place would make a nice inheritance from your father. Better than the debt he left you. And the shares in the real estate development would mean you'd have a continual income. It's a win, no matter how you look at it." The realtor put out his hand. "All I'm asking is that you think about it some more."

He'd thought his friend Noah had been exaggerating the past spring when he said what a weasel the man was. Now he didn't doubt it for a minute. Harley took Edwin's manicured fingers in a brutal grip, not bothering to brush his hand on his jeans first. He had trouble biting back a smile as Edwin winced at the tight hold. The man pulled back and then looked down in disgust at the smudges of grease Harley had left behind. Harley bit the inside of his cheek to keep from laughing. That right there was what he thought of the man's offer. He turned back toward the bike, hiding the smug smile, and went back to working on the gas line. When the man didn't leave, Harley sighed and stood again, getting comfortable leaning against the workbench. He wanted to talk? They'd talk.

Edwin had turned to the bike, a touch of admiration in his eye. "This was your dad's."

Nodding, Harley straightened away from the bench and ran a hand over the gas tank he'd just reinstalled. "How well did you know my father?"

"I knew Cooper well enough." Edwin drew his black brows together in a frown and tapped his lips with one fingertip as if thinking hard about how much to share. "Such a shame."

Harley wondered if Hurst was saying it was a shame that his dad had passed away, or if he was referring to his failed business dealings. "Do you remember seeing him or talking to him right before he passed away?"

Edwin thought again before answering. It felt like he was measuring his words. Weighing them. For truth? Or was he picking and choosing truth? Harley was prepared to take whatever the man said with a grain of salt.

"Yes, as a matter of fact, I did see him. The day before he passed away if I remember correctly. May I ask why?"

Harley rested a hip on the bike. "I probably should have done this a long time ago, but I've started trying to piece together the last few weeks before the accident. All I've gotten so far is that he might have spoken to you."

"It's a small town," Edwin said. "I can't be the only person he saw before he died." The man's olive skin darkened over his cheeks leading Harley to wonder what he was hiding. Anger. Or fear.

"What did you talk about?"

Edwin narrowed his eyes. "The house, of course. I was so close to talking him into selling—"

"I thought you said you *had* talked him into selling."

"Semantics."

Yeah, right. "So you talked about the house…?"

"You have no idea how frustrating it's been to watch the property sit here, unoccupied, for three years."

Harley's hands started to fist at his sides, but he forced them to relax. Reaching up to run his hand down his face, he realized that the bone-crushing weariness he'd felt for... well... forever wasn't there. Huh. Instead of the tired gesture that had become part of him over the years, he pushed his hand through his hair and changed the subject. "We took your advice and spoke to Alec Cohen about his fight with Lyle."

"That so? Get anywhere?"

"You were right that they didn't get along. Not sure if he hated the man enough to kill him, though."

"Skylar Novak, Alec Cohen, Vera Whitley—"

"You," Harley added with a pointed look.

Edwin bristled. "Watch it."

"Just keeping it real," Harley let out a humorless chuckle as he sank back down on his haunches and fit the thin, black fuel line into place.

"Anyway... That list is interesting."

"How so?"

"It's just that those folks all had some pretty strong feelings where your father was concerned as well."

Harley's hands stilled on the bike. And then began to shake. What? He blinked, trying to wrap his head around Edwin's words. "Explain," he said through gritted teeth.

"Oh, it's just that your father liked to stick his nose into a whole lot of things that weren't any of his business. It made enemies, that's all. Much like you and that goody-two-shoes girlfriend of yours."

"Novak, Vera, Cohen... you?"

"Not me, but yeah, the rest."

Harley was having a hard time getting his brain to engage. Did someone do... something... to his father's motorcycle? The thought made his stomach sour. "Novak I get. My dad wouldn't have been able to stand the guy. But Cohen? And Vera?"

"Alec Cohen was not shy about spouting off that he detested your father. Not sure why. Vera... Well, Vera barely let her husband's body cool before she was chasing after the good Reverend Beck. I heard he let her down gently, but she wouldn't accept it."

At first, the idea someone had sabotaged his father's bike seemed ludicrous. Who would do that? But it was taking root. Growing. There were too many similarities between Lyle's accident and his dad's to ignore. Harley stared beyond the XL-1000 without seeing. It took a few beats to realize Hurst was back to talking about Lyle.

"Do you honestly think someone... vandalized Lyle's motorcycle?" Edwin asked.

Blinking the garage back into focus, Harley shrugged. He wasn't keen on letting the guy know he'd razed him with one small seed of an idea. "I don't know." He cleared his throat. "If I could get a look at Lyle's bike I might be able to figure that out, but it's locked up tight at Finch and Jay's."

"I doubt it's locked up *that* tight. I mean... if I can get a look at it..."

"You saw Lyle's bike?" Harley said in surprise.

"Yeah, well, I wanted to buy it from the guy back when he first built it, but he wouldn't sell."

"Sounds like a recurring theme for you," Harley muttered.

"Very funny. Anyway, I wanted to see how bad the damage was. I thought maybe after the smoke settled I could talk Dox into fixing it up and selling it to me."

"Not likely, Hurst," Dox Finch said with disdain from the open doorway of the garage.

Both men turned to where Dox Finch stood, one shoulder propped against the door frame. He wasn't looking as beat down as the last time Harley'd seen him. That was good. He still looked wrung out though. His jeans hung a little too loose on his hips, his leather motorcycle jacket open over a wrinkled t-shirt.

Edwin crossed his arms and watched the older man for a moment. "I didn't expect to run into you this evening," the realtor said. "Saves me a trip over to your shop though. I surely hope you've reconsidered selling the shop."

"Not tonight, Hurst," Dox said with an annoyed shrug of his shoulders.

The rise and fall of Edwin's chest picked up speed and sweat beaded on his upper lip. "You can't be serious!"

"Why do you want it so bad anyway?" the older man asked, narrowing his eyes at the realtor.

Harley watched as the other man carefully pulled himself together and gave a careless shrug before sauntering out the open door past Dox. "Think about it Harley," he called over his shoulder.

"Edwin trying to get you to sell, too?"

Harley grunted. "Among other things."

"Yeah. This wasn't the first time he's pushed me, and I doubt it will be the last." He shook his head and scooped up a large box from outside the door. "One of my guys said you stopped by earlier and I thought it was fate since these came in today."

Harley raised a brow and peeked into the box. His heart nearly skipped a beat when he realized it held the handlebars, forks, tire, and rim he needed for the XL-1000. They looked brand new, all gleaming metal and black paint. They were magnificent! But— "Dox, man, I told you I couldn't afford them."

"I know. But you need them for the rebuild and... Think of it as my gift to your old man. He was a good friend for a long time." The older man's voice got thick and he took a deep breath.

"I don't even know what to say." Harley took the pieces from Dox and laid them on the workbench with reverent care. "Thank you."

It was more than parts to a bike. It represented years of friendship.

Dox ran his hand over the saddle and across the gas tank of the XL-1000 as he walked around it. "I haven't seen your dad's bike... In a while. Not since—" The older man's voice hitched.

The emotion was not lost on Harley. Even after all this time.

"I'm almost done with the rebuild. I thought it would take a lot longer, but... I've been pretty focused. These are all I have left." A satisfied grin spread across his face. "I wonder if I can get the old girl on the road tomorrow?"

Maybe he'd take it up and show Clyde.

The idea Edwin had planted moments before tickled at the back of his mind. Was it possible someone had a hand in his father's accident, too? Harley swallowed. "You said you weren't the one who worked on Dad's bike, but do you remember seeing him the week before he died?"

If Dox was surprised, it didn't show on his face. He smiled a sad smile and looked up. "Yeah, sure. We saw each other here and there. I think he came in to order some parts that week. He always kept stuff on hand here in the garage so he could work on the bike. With winter coming he wanted to start on a project. New instrument cluster I think. Or rewiring it. I can't remember."

"That's actually been a huge help." Harley opened the bottom drawer of the workbench and pulled out the new speedometer, setting it next to the box. "Do you remember if he was... I don't know. Worried? Or if something was bothering him?"

"What's this all about Harley?"

Swallowing hard, he met the older man's eyes. "Honestly? I don't even know. Erin and I have been looking into who might have had reason to mess with Lyle's bike..."

"That getting you anywhere?"

"Maybe? We went and talked to Alec. I'm not convinced he had anything to do with it, but he pointed us in another direction. Did you know that Lyle was blackmailing people?"

Dox's eyebrows shot toward his hairline. "He what now?"

"We've talked to two people who both claim Lyle was blackmailing them. If there are two there might be more. Anyway, someone mentioned that the same people who had reasons to hate Lyle might have also..." He almost couldn't say the words aloud. "Well, might have had issues with Dad, too."

The older man stood for a moment in stunned silence before placing his hand on Harley's shoulder and squeezing it tight. "Do you honestly think someone sabotaged both their motorcycles?"

With a growl, Harley stepped away, smacking his hand down on the workbench with a bit more force than necessary. "I don't know, OK?! I don't know who could have... or would have done something to their bikes. I don't know why they crashed when they were both excellent drivers. I don't know... Anything! I want there to be a reason." He could feel his emotions boiling and he somehow dragged them back to a simmer. "I can't invent a reason where there isn't one, but every time I turn around these days someone has an opinion about who hated Lyle. I just... I don't know!"

Dox didn't appear at all fazed by Harley's outburst. He leaned against the wall by the bike with his hands in his pockets. "Sometimes gut feeling is spot on and sometimes it's way off base. Listen, the guy from the state police is done. Come by the shop tomorrow and I'll show you Lyle's bike. Maybe if you see that there wasn't a thing wrong with it you can put this behind you. Maybe you can put both crashes behind you."

Harley dragged his hand down his face. "Fine."

"That's my boy." Dox squeezed his shoulder again before thumping him on the back and heading toward the door. Turning back, he nodded at the bike. "Your dad would be some proud of you getting that all fixed up nice like that. Some proud."

Harley stood for a long time looking at his dad's bike after Dox left. Was the man right? Would his father be proud of him? It wasn't something he'd cared about in the past, but now? Now he let Dox's words settle and seep into him.

It wasn't just restoring the motorcycle though. The realization dawned on Harley that there was more in his life that he hoped would make his father proud. Things he'd never thought about before but could see were a result of the man's influence. Like his work ethic. He'd never been let go from a job because he slacked off, and that was a direct result of watching his father work tirelessly. At his job, at his hobby, and, before his mother passed away, at his family. His sense of right and wrong had been born listening to the man, both in the pulpit and on the back porch. The hunger for justice that was now pushing him to find a reason for Lyle's accident, and possibly his father's, could be traced back to passionate sermons and earnest discussions with his mother over dinner. He hoped he'd done his best on the bike. But more than that, he hoped he'd do well in life, too. That he might end well.

Pushing off the workbench, Harley wheeled the toolbox to the front of the motorcycle and started installing the new handlebars and forks. The thing was so close to being ready to ride again! If he could put in the time…

A look at the time told him Erin would be done at the church soon. Looked like he might be putting in a long night, but it would be worth it to get the final touches on the bike. Stepping out the garage door, Harley was startled to find Mark Puckett crouched beside his Norton in the driveway.

"Mr. Puckett?"

"Charlie!" The big man's voice boomed as he pushed himself to his feet. "I was walking down to the church to meet Frannie and walk her home and I saw this beauty sitting here. Couldn't resist a little ogling. You sure have done a fine job keeping it up over the years."

"Thank you, sir."

"I remember when your father first purchased it. Used to come over here and hang out in his garage with him while he tinkered on it. You were just a little tyke." The older man patted the seat. "Good memories. And I see you're working on the XL-1000, too?"

"Yes, sir. Almost finished." Harley disengaged the kickstand and started pushing the Norton into the garage.

"Oh, let me give you a hand there," Mark said as he grabbed

ahold of the opposite handlebar.

Once the second bike was inside, Mark walked over and stood admiring the other bike. The approval on his face made Harley grin. It was always nice to have another mechanic praise your work. Maybe that's what his dad would have looked like, standing there with a clear look of appreciation on his face. He hoped so.

"I'm glad you decided to go with all authentic parts. Your dad would have wanted that."

"I know. It was important to me to keep it the way he kept it. I'm going to try to finish it up tonight. Maybe even ride it tomorrow."

Mark clapped Harley on the back. "He'd be proud."

Harley choked up and couldn't do anything but nod his head.

"Well, my girl's probably waiting for me by now," Mark boomed.

"Hold up and I'll walk with you. Erin..." Harley felt the back of his neck warm when the older man gave him a knowing look.

Pulling the garage door down, he listened to it bump on the cement floor as they walked down the driveway. The air was brisk and quiet in the twilight. Mark talked about the upcoming World Series and the score from last week's football game as they made their way to the church. Harley only half listened. He was so close to finishing the motorcycle that his palms itched to start it. He could remember hearing it purr to life when his dad would kickstart it. A low grumble that throbbed in your bones. It was a beautiful sound. He hoped it would sound like that the first time he fired it up. Were sounds like smells when it came to memories? Would the sound bring back the easygoing days of his childhood?

When they rounded the corner of The Green, Harley could see the two ladies just coming out of the church doors, their laughter floating on the breeze.

"There's my girl," Mark called.

Both women looked in their direction and both their faces lit up. He was growing to like the lightness in his chest when he saw Erin, and the pleasure her smile could bring. And don't get him started on all the crazy things he felt when her hand slipped into his.

"Hey." Well, that was inadequate!

"Hey yourself," she replied. Her smile deepened and filled her eyes and he knew he was a goner.

The older couple had started walking back in the direction they'd just come. "Nice to see you, Mr. Puckett," Harley called.

Mark looked over his shoulder at Harley. "Good to see you, too, my boy! You keep up the good work!"

"Yes, sir."

As they walked toward Erin's apartment Harley draped his arm over her shoulders and drew lazy circles on her sleeve with his fingertips. It was quiet, the streetlights just beginning to blink on as the sky darkened.

They'd turned onto Main Street and were about halfway to Erin's apartment when she cleared her throat.

He looked down when she didn't continue. "What's up?"

Erin took a long time to answer. "My mother called a few days ago."

Harley's fingers stilled on her arm, but he willed himself to show no other reaction.

"She wants me to come down to Cape Cod." Erin started fidgeting with the edge of her shirt with nervous fingers. She probably wished he'd say... something.

He wanted to beg her not to go. But...

They reached the stairs to her place and he stopped, turning her to face him. "I would give anything— everything to make things right with Dad." He rested his forehead on hers and sucked in a breath that shook before continuing. "Go, make things right with your mom. Don't look back and wish you had."

She let out a sad laugh and sagged onto a step. "Now you sound like your dad. He told me over and over, if I was ever given the opportunity to make amends, take it! We tried once. He helped me write a letter, but I never heard anything from her." Her shoulders slumped.

"Honey." He gentled his voice, filling it with all the tenderness he felt. "Go do what you need to do."

"I don't want to leave." It was a whisper that he barely heard.

Taking her face tenderly in his hands, he held her gaze for a long moment. Then the truth of what he was about to say sunk in and he brushed his lips against hers before continuing. "Take as long as you need." Even if that meant forever, it would be worth it. But, oh how his heart ached at the thought. "I'll still be here when you come back."

Please come back.

CHAPTER FIFTEEN

E rin knew she was dreaming, but even knowing the truth, wasn't enough to calm her racing heart. Something was wrong. Inexplicably, terrifyingly wrong. In her dream, an all-consuming darkness growled and churned like the sea after a storm. Fear coursed through her. Palpable. She reached out, trying to find something real. Her hands came up empty. The growling became deafening and she shot straight up in bed, panting. The panic attack continued to sink its claws in though. Anxiety slithered along her nerves making her chest hurt. It was still dark out and the silence of pre-dawn was almost as complete as the overwhelming noise of her dream had been.

With her heart still pounding to the point it hurt, Erin threw the covers back and scrambled to pull on the jeans she'd discarded on the floor the night before. Catching her toe on the cursed box under her bed she went down hard on her knees. With a cry of both pain and frustration, she hauled herself back onto her feet and bolted across the floor. Something was wrong, whether real or imagined, and she had to figure out what, or she'd go crazy.

Harley.

Her mind screamed it as she fumbled with her work boots. He wouldn't even be up yet, but she had to see him. Had to see with her own eyes that he was fine. She stumbled down the stairs and climbed into her truck, barely looking as she hit the gas and shot out onto the street.

Thank You, God, she breathed as she raced toward the Acadian Adventures shop on empty streets. *I don't want to hit anyone, but I can't slow down. Please let Harley be OK. Please!*

Without even taking the time to turn off the truck or close her door, Erin bounded up the steps and pounded on the door to the apartment above the shop. When no one answered she banged louder, slapping her palm against the glass.

"Harley!"

A light flicked on at the back of the apartment and a very sleepy, very rumpled young man trudged to the door. His hair stood out in every direction and he wore only a pair of plaid pajama bottoms.

"What?" he asked over a yawn when he opened the door.

"Is Harley here?"

"Yeah." He nodded toward the other side of the apartment. "Last door."

She took off without giving the man a second look and knocked on the door he'd indicated. Nothing. When her second and third knocks were also met with silence, she pushed the door open.

Empty.

The fear she was feeling was baseless. She knew that. It had just been a dream.

A creepy, vivid dream, but still just a dream.

And yet it didn't matter.

Terror drove her from the apartment and back to her truck. Within minutes she was at Coop's, throwing the truck into park and racing from it again. The house was dark and silent.

She cupped her hands against the window in the garage door. In the gray light of daybreak, she could just make out Harley's Norton Commando, sitting where he'd left it.

But Coop's bike was gone.

Harley must have finished it and taken it out for a test drive. Had the growl of the machine's engine been what she heard in her dream? Had he driven by her apartment? Maybe hoping she was up to show off his hard work? If so, he could only be a few minutes ahead of her.

Erin tore back to her truck and was moving even before the

door was closed. Leaving Summer Harbor behind, she pushed the old truck to its limits with the pedal on the floorboards. The headlights did little in the dulling light and she had to concentrate to see the ribbon of pavement ahead of her. Winding her way along the shore, she prayed she was headed in the right direction.

As dawn revealed more of the road, Erin hit a straight stretch heading west into Gull's Cove and picked up speed until the pickup shook with it. Fog billowed across the roadway in the low places, but every second it seemed she could see a little farther ahead. Finally, the motorcycle came into view. It was traveling at nearly the same speed she was and Erin stood on the gas pedal, willing the truck to overtake it.

After long seconds dragged out in front of her, Erin gained enough ground to come up behind Harley. Pulling into the oncoming lane, she matched his speed, unsure what else to do. He risked a look to the side and their eyes met for a fraction of a second before they both snapped their eyes back to the road. He had a death grip on the handlebars and fear had hardened his face into a stony mask. When she looked over again, Harley had peeled his fingers off the left handlebar and was reaching for the bed of the truck. Erin got the idea and edged closer.

A flash of light ahead caught her attention and she braked just in time to pull in behind the motorcycle and avoid a head-on collision with an oncoming car. The car's horn blew long and loud as it flew past, but the sound almost didn't register. All Erin could see was the front wheel of the bike starting to wobble.

She gunned the engine and crawled out next to him again. Ahead, the road made a sharp turn to the left. Huge granite cliffs loomed ahead of them. A weather-beaten white cross lay toppled at the base of the cliffs, marking the place where Coop had died. If Harley didn't get off the bike now, he wasn't going to survive either. She could see on his face that he knew it, too. She drifted as close as she dared and watched as Harley looped his arm through the large metal wing where the side mirror was mounted.

As soon as he'd pulled his weight from the bike to the mirror, Erin pulled her foot from the gas pedal. She couldn't make the turn at this speed either.

Lord, please help him hold on!

Braking as hard as she dared, Erin watched in horror as the motorcycle flew ahead, catching on the shoulder and turning end for end into the cliffs ahead. She couldn't see Harley's arm from where she sat and had no idea if he still clung to the side of the truck. He hadn't been on the bike when it disintegrated, that was all she knew.

Coming to a complete stop, Erin sat in silence, staring straight ahead. Her hands didn't want to let go of the wheel and she couldn't bring herself to look in the rearview mirror. What if she saw Harley's mangled body in the road? She squeezed her eyes shut.

A thump on the side of the truck made her eyes fly open and she threw herself out the door. Rounding the back, she found Harley sitting on the ground. He was leaning against the running board and cradling his left arm against his chest, breathing so hard she worried he'd hyperventilate. Tears sprang to her eyes and washed down her cheeks as she dropped onto the gravel shoulder and threw her arms around his neck.

He let out a loud groan. "I think I dislocated my arm," he ground out through gritted teeth.

She couldn't stop touching him. His face, his other arm, the knee he had pulled up against his injured arm, his other leg.

"Is that it?" she asked with a sob. "Is anything else hurt?"

"Hey, hey," he said, cupping her face with the hand of his uninjured arm and rubbing the tears away with his thumb. "I'm alive. Thanks to you." She pressed her cheek into his palm, unable to form words and trying, desperately and unsuccessfully, to hold it together. "Speaking of which, how did you—?" He was interrupted by the sound of sirens.

The police cruiser braked hard behind the truck, spitting gravel into the air.

"Erin? Is that you?" A deep southern drawl preceded the tall African-American cop around the back of her truck.

She looked up but didn't move from Harley's side. "Hi, Wade."

"I got a call about a motorcycle and a truck playing chicken with a tourist. You wouldn't know anything about that now, would you?"

"*Not* chicken," Erin scoffed.

"What on earth happened?" the policeman asked, looking over the wreckage.

"That's what I'd like to know," Harley said, still speaking through gritted teeth.

"I'm Wade Smith," the man said to Harley as he squatted next to them. He put a hand on Erin's shoulder. "Are you hurt?"

She shook her head but didn't trust her voice.

"The ambulance should be right behind me. While we wait, why don't you start at the beginning and I'll give a look here?" Wade asked as he assessed Harley for injuries other than the obviously wrecked shoulder.

"I wasn't in the crash," Harley said, nodding to the pile of rubble the XL-1000 had been reduced to.

Wade let out a long whistle. "I would say that's a blessing and a half. I don't think we'd be having this conversation if you had been."

"There was something wrong with the brakes."

Wade stayed crouched down at eye level, but pulled a notepad from his pocket and rested it on his knee. "When did you first notice that?"

"Coming down the last hill before Gull's Cove. It's pretty flat before that, or the speed limit increases on the downhills, so I didn't notice. I started picking up speed, but when I tried to slow down nothing happened."

Wade wrote in his notebook and then looked at Erin. "And

you...?"

"I honestly don't know. I woke up scared that something had happened to Harley and tore out of town looking for him. When I caught up to him I could tell the bike was out of control. He grabbed the mirror and..." Fresh tears filled her eyes.

Harley looped his good arm around her neck and pulled her close, pressing his lips to her hair. "Shhh..."

Wade tapped Harley's boot with his pen. "Seems like Someone was looking out for you this morning." The policeman pushed to his feet and strode over to the remains of the motorcycle. He touched nothing but looked at it carefully.

Harley used his legs to push himself up the door of the truck until he was standing and then, clutching his arm against his chest, he walked over to join the policeman. Erin followed a few steps behind trying not to look at the motorcycle, or what was left of it. If she'd had nightmares after they laid the Norton down, seeing firsthand what could happen in a crash would add dramatic and terrifying details.

"Check the brake cable," Harley said. "I know I attached everything properly last night, but this morning it was like the brakes weren't even there."

Wade used his pen to lift the end of the cable.

"Cut."

Harley let a blue word escape under his breath.

"We've been thinking," Erin said as she turned to the policeman. "That someone may have done something similar to Lyle Jay's bike."

Wade narrowed his eyes. "The guy from the State Police didn't find anything. I can't see him missing something as obvious as a cut brake cable."

"What if," Harley began, a pensive look on his face. "What if someone covered their tracks?"

"That's a bit of a stretch, don't you think?"

"Maybe, but I know for a fact at least one person was in the room with the bike before the state guy showed up."

Wade straightened to his full height, a frown forming on his friendly face. "And who might that be?"

"Edwin Hurst," Harley replied.

"Edwin got into the garage where Lyle's bike's being stored?" Erin asked in a horrified voice.

"I will definitely be checking into that," Wade said, his scowl pulling his brows down.

"If Edwin could get in, I imagine anyone could have," Harley added

"Wade," Erin said. "You should know that this isn't the first incident Harley's had with someone vandalizing his bike."

The deputy's head snapped up. "You've had other issues?"

Harley pulled a face before blowing out a long breath. "We had a blowout the other night. Yesterday I found a razor blade in the tire."

Wade whistled and made a note. "Any idea who might have done that? Or this?" he asked, indicating the wreck with a jut of his chin.

Erin bit her lip and looked at the ground. "We've sort of been asking around about Lyle's crash. Maybe whoever tampered with his bike also tampered with Harley's."

The policeman scowled at them. "You think maybe that's something you should leave to the police? Or, at the very least, share what your suspicions are?"

"Sorry," Erin mumbled. "In all fairness, we didn't have proof of anything, so coming to you or Chief Briggs and saying 'hey, we think someone made Lyle's bike crash' seemed ridiculous."

Wade studied them for a few beats before relaxing his shoulders and sighing. "So what did you find out?"

"We think Edwin Hurst, Alec Cohen, and Skylar Novak all had motives," Erin replied. Harley cleared his throat and Erin sighed. "And Vera Whittley."

"Care to elaborate?"

"Edwin wanted to purchase Finch and Jay's, but Lyle wasn't interested. I know that seems like a minor thing, but the man seems desperate," Harley said.

"Lyle Jay was blackmailing Alec Cohen," Erin continued. "And while that seems more plausible than Edwin, Alec claims to have already gotten free of Lyle."

"And Novak?"

"Skylar Novak is actually *Arnie* Novak. We confronted him and he admitted that Lyle was blackmailing him, too," Harley answered. "And... you might want to check into him for... other things as well."

Wade raised an eyebrow and made a note in his book. "And Vera?"

"I don't think—" Erin began.

"She claimed that Lyle knew who killed her husband Jason three years ago," Harley interrupted. "But he refused to tell the police who it was."

"Would any of these four have had access to your bike?"

Harley pursed his lips and looked down at the ground. "I left the garage unlocked last night. It was late when I finished working on the bike and I forgot to lock up. Anyone could have gotten in. Then this morning I was in such a hurry to get the thing on the road there's no way I would have noticed the cut brake cable."

Wade studied his notes, flipping back through the few pages he'd filled. "Alrighty. I'm going to call the State Police and make sure that this bike doesn't go anywhere near Summer Harbor until they are done with it. I'm also going to have them take another look at Lyle's bike while they're at it." The loud whine of an approaching ambulance cut through the stillness. "Meanwhile, you need to go have that shoulder looked at."

What seemed like a week later, but Harley supposed was only a few hours, they walked out of the ER. Erin had run the gamut from scared to angry to relieved and was now in hover mode, fussing over him. He wasn't going to lie, he liked the mother-hen side of her.

"How long did the doc say I had to wear this stupid thing?" he asked, trying to adjust the strap on the sling holding his arm so it didn't rub on his neck.

"Two to eight weeks."

"Not happening," he said with a snort. "Two days. Maybe."

"I'm just glad it was only dislocated and nothing was torn." Erin fished her keys from her pocket. "Come on. I'm taking you home and ordering take-out from The Whale. I'm starving."

Harley's stomach growled and he grinned. "I could eat."

Getting into her truck presented a problem. Without the use of his left hand, he was reduced to levering himself awkwardly into the passenger's seat, and shimmying into place while trying not to move his shoulder. It took far too long and he was breathing hard by the time the door was closed. Pulling his seatbelt across his lap was another challenge altogether.

"Here, let me help," Erin said, leaning across the seat, but staying clear of his sling.

He let go of the buckle and slid his fingers around the back of her neck instead. She stilled and looked up at him. He ran his thumb along her jaw and down the side of her neck, following it with his eyes. She was so beautiful. "Thank you," he said. His voice was hoarse and he swallowed. "I'm alive because of you. Today—"

Her lips stopped him mid-sentence. When she pulled back her eyes were serious. "I didn't save you today, Harley. God used me to save you, but He did it, not me."

"You honestly believe that?" he asked in a quiet voice.

"I do."

He nodded and released her neck, letting wisps of her hair slide through his fingers. She buckled his belt and drove them to the kayak shop. He didn't want to lean on her going up the stairs, but the adrenaline from the morning was long gone and the pain pills the doc had prescribed were making his limbs feel like pool noodles.

"Oh, my goodness!" Lily Emerson exclaimed, hopping down from where she'd been perched on a stool at the kitchen counter. "Harley! What happened?"

"Man, what happened to you?" Noah's voice was rich with concern and he strode forward to help.

"Note to self, do not take the pain meds again," Harley tried to joke as he swayed on his feet.

No one laughed.

Lily was standing next to him looking very worried and Noah hadn't taken his hand off Harley's good shoulder.

"I'm fine. Really. I just dislocated my shoulder." Which was beginning to ache like a son of a gun.

Lily sucked in a breath. "What—?" Her voice pitched high with concern.

"When he grabbed the mirror on my truck this morning... while doing ninety."

"Excuse me?" Noah asked.

"Someone cut the brake cable on Dad's bike," Haley said as if that would explain everything. Lily and Noah just stared agape at him.

"And then Harley took it for a drive this morning. I managed to catch up to him in time, but the bike's..." Erin trailed off.

"Gone," Harley added. All that work, all that time, and he'd failed. Again.

"I'm so sorry, man," Noah said before shifting his focus to Erin and sticking out his hand. "Erin, friend of Cori's, right?"

"Yes. Nice to see you again."

"You were at Harley's birthday party the other night, right?" Lily tapped her lips with her index finger as she studied Erin. "I know you from somewhere else, though. Wait, it'll come to me." She paused for a second before her eyes lit up. "Church!."

"I thought I recognized you the other night, too," Erin said with a grin.

"Oh my goodness," Lily gushed as she slid back into her seat, pulling Erin along to the next stool as she talked. "Can you believe how absolutely adorable Pastor and Maggie's baby is?"

"I know!" Erin agreed. "She's the cutest little thing. I think she looks just like Maggie."

"That she does, but, without a question, she is daddy's girl."

"I don't think the man could be any prouder."

Lily's ability to put people at ease was spectacular. Harley was sure it came in handy running the bed and breakfast that she owned. He wanted to say something, but all his fuzzy brain could think of was how sweet Erin would look holding a little bundle of beautiful baby and it caused a lump in his throat that made speaking next to impossible. Her mama-bear mode was probably just as impressive as her mother-hen mode.

"And with those three older brothers, the poor girl won't be dating until she's forty!" Lily laughed. "So, what do you do, Erin?"

"I work for Finnley's," Erin said, glancing over Lily's shoulder and meeting Harley's eyes.

She was checking on him. He liked that.

Very much.

"Oh, I know Keaton. These guys work for him over the winter. Do you work in the store?"

"She's been working on Keaton's crews per-diem." Harley jumped in. He could hear the pride in his voice and he hoped Erin could hear it, too.

"Oh, my goodness! How did you decide on construction as a career? I mean, it must be tough."

"You'd know," Noah chimed in, smiling down at Lily. His voice tinged with pride. Turning toward Erin, he explained. "Lily used to work in the corporate world, so I'm guessing she's well versed in... how does that song go? 'A man's world'?"

A rueful smile tugged at the corner of Erin's lips. "That it is. What I would like to do is build furniture full-time. That's what I went to school for. The construction gig is just something I do to pay the bills. Not that I don't like doing it," she was quick to point out. "But eventually I want to have a storefront of my own and sell handmade furniture."

"Really?" Lily's voice held a bit of awe. Yeah, well, she wasn't the only one who was in awe of the lovely Ms. Wallace.

"Listen," Erin slid off her seat and moved to his side.

"Neither of us has eaten today. We're both starving. Our plan was to order some takeout from The Whale and then try to piece together what's going on. You two up for a real-life game of Clue?"

"I'm in," Lily said with a smile.

"Yeah, of course. Let me know what you guys want and I'll pop over to The Whale and place the order," Noah offered.

While the others debated what to order, Harley tried to get comfortable. He was still struggling to wrap his head around what had happened and the brain fog from the painkillers wasn't helping. He fidgeted with the sling again. His shoulder still ached, despite the meds, and the cut on his hand from the razor blade had reopened as well. He thought the doc was going to stitch it up, but he'd ended up with a brand new set of butterfly bandages and strict instructions to keep it clean and let it heal. He rolled his hand over and rubbed his thumb along the gauze on his palm. The cut brake cable, the razor blade. What on God's green earth was going on?

"Be right back," Noah said. He leaned down to kiss Lily before loping out the door and down the stairs.

"Are you sure you're OK?" Lily asked as soon as the man was out of sight.

"I'm sure. It could have been so much worse." Harley's whole body shuddered as the realization began to sink in of how very close to death he'd come today. It wasn't that he hadn't flirted with death before. He had. On more than one occasion. However, this was the one and only time he could remember caring. And he cared because he wasn't sure where he was headed when he died. That thought hit him like ice water to the face and he sucked in a sharp breath as his knees went weak. Erin shot him a concerned look but didn't ask if he was alright. Again. Thankfully. Because he wasn't. Yeah, his shoulder throbbed, but that was just pain. No, he knew with certainty that he was not OK in his soul and that scared him more than he was willing to admit to anyone.

Lily squeezed his hand. "I'm glad you weren't hurt too

badly."

Erin stepped around Lily and leaned over what looked like photographs on the counter. "Are these from your engagement?" she asked.

"Aren't they gorgeous? I still can't believe it. Noah planned it all out and it was perfect. I mean, he brought my sister up here from Boston without me knowing, and his folks from the mainland. The photographer..." Harley could almost see the hearts in her eyes.

"She did your engagement photos that same night?"

"Yes." Lily waved a hand at the scattered pictures. "She got these pictures of the moment he asked me to marry him, and then we went down to the beach and she took these," Lily said as she pulled a stack of more formal shots from the bottom of the pile and spread them out, running her fingertips over them. "She sent over the proofs today and we were just looking through them trying to pick one for the engagement announcement."

"They are stunning!"

"She is amazingly talented. I think we're going to have her do the wedding, too. I love them all, but I think I want this one for the announcement." Lily slid one out of the pile and handed it to Erin, who grinned and turned it toward Harley. Noah was holding Lily on the dance floor and the love on their faces was unmistakable.

"It's perfect," Erin said.

"There are so many good ones, though. It's hard to choose." Lily started spreading the photographs across the counter.

"Parker's going to send somebody over with our food when it's ready," Noah said, letting himself back into the apartment.

Erin raised a brow. "I didn't know The Hungry Whale delivered."

"They don't," Noah replied, flashing a grin. "It helps to be best friends with the owner. Now, Harley, man, if this is what you do on your days off, I'm going to stop letting you take them."

"Trust me, it wasn't planned. Man, I'm so sorry about the rest of the seas—"

Noah's hand shot up to stop him. "All I care about is that you're alive. Sorry about the bike."

"Do you honestly believe someone sabotaged your motorcycle?" Lily asked. Her eyes had gone wide and Noah wrapped his arms around her, pulling her tight against him.

"I guess you'd know a little bit about sabotage, wouldn't you?" Harley asked, sobering as he remembered the previous spring. He turned to Erin. "Lily here had quite the welcome when she came in June to first look at the inn. Let's see, a cut climbing rope, wasn't it?"

"And knifed tires," Noah added

"Don't forget the worst directions ever," Lily said with a shudder.

"That's awful," Erin said,

"It was pretty scary, but it all worked out in the end." Lily beamed up at Noah. Then she stepped away to get out plates, silverware, napkins, and cups. "So yes, I would know a bit about someone trying to get rid of me. But... Harley...? Why...?"

"I'm not certain."

"We think it might be connected to Lyle's crash," Erin said.

"We've been asking a lot of questions and we're wondering if we got too close to someone." Harley was about to go on when the door popped open and Sawyer strode in carrying a stack of takeout boxes.

"Hey all, Parker sent me over with these."

"Keaton isn't keeping you busy enough? You have to moonlight as a delivery boy?" Noah elbowed the man and they laughed. "Honey, remind me to give him a big tip."

Lily laughed and started handing out the take-out boxes. "Loaded nacho fries for Harley and Noah. Grilled lemon chicken and broccoli Alfredo for Erin. Broiled haddock and beet salad for me. And the burger must be yours," she said as she passed the last one to Sawyer.

"Sure is."

"Stay. Eat with us. We're playing Clue," Erin added with a wink at Harley.

"Clue?" Sawyer looked around, confused. His eyes landed on Harley's sling. "Dude! What on earth?"

"And that's where the game of Clue comes in," Erin said as she dished up her dinner.

"I'm going to say 'Colonel Mustard in the library with a candlestick'," Sawyer said before taking a huge bite of his burger.

"Good guess," Harley said. "But no."

"Where do we even start?" Erin asked, turning to face Harley.

"The beginning would be my vote," Noah chimed in.

"The beginning, huh?" Harley ran his hand down over his face and all Erin wanted to do was soothe away the stress. She reached over and squeezed his knee, coaxing a smile from him. "Right after Lyle Jay crashed his motorcycle, Erin pointed out that she found it hard to believe he couldn't control the bike on a straight stretch of road."

"You all know what he did for a living before he bought the shop, right?" Erin asked, but three sets of eyes just blinked back at her. "He was a motorcycle stunt driver."

"Oh my," Lily whispered.

"I did not know that." Noah's eyes had gotten large as he stared at Erin.

"How did we not know that?" Sawyer asked around a mouthful of fries.

Erin shrugged. "I remember Coop being pretty impressed. Anyway, I just couldn't shake the feeling that something wasn't adding up."

"Then that realtor—"

"Edwin Hurst?" Lily asked in disgust.

"That's the one," Harley continued. "He's trying to get me to sell the house. While we're discussing that— I'm not selling, by the way— Erin suggested that the man might have had something to do with Lyle's crash since he seemed more than a little desperate to get his hands on the motorcycle shop."

"What is his deal?" Lily asked. He was trying to buy the inn, too."

"We aren't sure. He's claiming it was just a friendly offer, but Dox said the guy was pushing them pretty hard to sell."

"There's... something... going on with that guy," Lily said. "I don't know what, but... something"

"Well, while he's claiming up and down he didn't have anything to do with Lyle's crash, he mentioned the cleric at that weird... I don't even want to call it a church—"

"Is that why you were asking about it the other day?" Noah asked.

"Yes. After I talked to you about the place, I went over to speak to the guy. He got real squirrelly when I mentioned Lyle and the accident."

"Did he tell you anything?"

"Not at the time. Just said Lyle was there for confession and that he couldn't tell me anything," Harley replied.

"Then, Sunday evening I was talking to my landlady, Vera Whittley," Erin continued. "She believed Lyle knew who killed her husband Jason three years ago, but that he refused to go to the police with the information."

There was a sudden intake of breath around the table and Sawyer started coughing on a crumb from his dinner.

"That's awful!" Lily exclaimed.

"You don't think Vera...?" Sawyer trailed off, a pained look on his face. "She couldn't have done anything to Lyle. Right?"

"We don't think so, it's just a piece of the puzzle," Harley said. "A few days later I was talking with Dox about something else and *that* conversation inadvertently led us to a mechanic up the road by the name of Alec Cohen."

"We went and talked to him, and get this, Lyle was

blackmailing him!" Erin added. "He *also* mentioned the cleric, Skylar Novak."

Noah let out a whistle and Lily looked suitably shocked.

"Don't forget laying the Norton down," Harley added quietly.

"Right! Shortly after we talked to Alec, Harley laid the Norton down because of a blown front tire."

"Ouch!" Lily said, then turned toward Harley. "You were on the motorcycle when it—?"

"We." Erin shuddered. "We were on the bike. And in case anyone's wondering, I don't need to do that again. Ever."

"It gets worse," Harley added. "Someone made it blow out on purpose."

"What?" Lily all but shouted.

"Found a razor blade in the tire," Harley added.

"Whoa," Sawyer said. "That's cold."

"Later that night we ran into Edwin again and he mentioned both Vera and Alec having problems with Lyle," Harley continued. "I planned to talk to Alec again, but I haven't made it there yet."

"Meanwhile, I did a little digging online and found out Skylar Novak's real name is *Arnie* Novak and, get this, he's out on bail, facing charges for a bunch of nasty crimes."

"We passed that information on to Deputy Smith this morning," Harley was quick to add.

"What does all that have to do with Lyle?" Noah asked.

"Turns out Lyle was blackmailing Novak, too," Erin continued.

"Let me get this straight," Lily said. "Edwin Hurst, who, by the way, I have dealt with and can attest to him being a viable suspect, this Cohen guy, the man who runs that weird... church, and your landlady all had motives to hurt Mr. Jay?" When Erin nodded Lily turned to Harley. "And did they all have access to your father's motorcycle?"

"I accidentally left the garage unlocked last night. Anyone could have gotten in."

"Anyone? So, not just those four?" Noah asked.

Erin felt like they were going round and round in circles. They needed a new clue, or to think of something they hadn't thought of before. This wasn't getting them anywhere! Frustrated, she started stacking plates and taking them to the sink, clearing debris into the trash, and wiping down the island. The three men continued rehashing the details, but she was worn out. They were no closer to figuring things out than they had been an hour ago.

Lily helped her tidy up and then walked over to the photographs that were still spread out on the end of the counter and began picking them up. As Erin walked past, Lily laid a gentle hand on her arm.

"Are you doing alright?"

Erin stopped and hugged her arms around herself. "Part of me wants to believe that this is all just happenstance, but if Harley's going to get hurt... I can't ignore it."

"We will do just about anything to protect the men we love, won't we?" Lily asked, looking over her shoulder at Noah.

"Oh, I don't think... I mean, I'm not... We're not..."

The face Lily pulled told Erin the woman didn't believe a word of it. "Girl, we've been in the same room all of what? An hour? And we can all see it. Maybe not love, yet, but there's something there. Don't let that go. It's special."

Looking over to where Harley was leaning on the counter, letting it hold him up, while the three guys discussed the demise of Coop's motorcycle, she could feel what Lily was talking about. Deep inside. She could love Harley.

Maybe she already did.

"You're right," she whispered.

"Mmmhmm." Lily patted her hand.

Sawyer pushed off the counter. "I wish I was more help, but of that whole list, I only know Vera, who doesn't have a violent bone in her body. Plus, I'm beat. I think I'm going to call it a night."

"Thanks for trying to help us sort it out," Erin said.

"Sure thing, kid."

"'Night," Harley said as the man nodded to the others and headed for the door.

"I think that's our cue, as well," Lily said.

"Especially since I'm down a man tomorrow," Noah added with a wink for Erin.

"Sorry, man." Erin could tell it pained Harley to be letting his friend down.

"Do not, under any circumstances, worry about it. You hear me?" Noah held Harley's gaze.

Lily gave Harley a tight hug, avoiding his injured arm. "I'm glad you're OK."

"Thanks." He returned the hug one-armed and Erin saw him try not to wince. His shoulder must be throbbing.

"Same here, man. Glad you're not dead." Noah gave him a long look before ushering Lily toward the door.

The sentiment had been meant to lighten the mood, but Erin heard the deep truth of his friend's words. The quiet of the empty apartment descended on them. Harley pushed himself off the stool he'd been leaning on and wobbled to one of the huge couches that made up the living room.

"I like this place," Erin said as she followed him.

"It's great."

"How many people live here?"

Harley lowered himself to the cushion but moved restlessly as he tried to make himself comfortable.

"You OK?" Erin asked. Seeing the man in pain hurt her heart.

"Yeah, just... everything aches. Everything." He closed his eyes and rested his head on the back of the couch. "Right now there are only three of us living here. Over the summer there were more. Next year Noah's planning on twelve to sixteen."

Erin's eyes grew huge. "Wow."

"He realized early on that offering housing to staff at a reasonable rate made it a whole lot easier to keep them employed. *And* returning year after year."

"Makes sense. I pay an arm and a leg for the one room I rent from Vera, and she's practically family."

"It's crazy. He'd already bought the building, so he turned the second floor here into one huge apartment. He lives on the third floor, but I don't know if he's going to stay up there once he and Lily get married."

"Why so many next year?"

"He's expanding the business, bringing on new people. He's going to offer rock climbing, biking, hiking... I don't even know all he's got in the works."

"That's impressive."

Harley lifted his good arm and nodded for her to join him on the couch. Trying to be careful not to jostle him, Erin curled up next to his side, resting her head on his shoulder, and closed her eyes. She was exhausted, but she couldn't think of any other place she'd rather be right that second.

"This is the best I've felt all day," Harley murmured, tightening his arm around her shoulders.

She agreed, and she longed for nothing to change. Ever. But change was inevitable, and she needed to tell him something. However, that longing kept her quiet. They were silent for a long time. As the hushed evening stretched, the exhaustion of their crazy day settled in. She wondered if Harley had fallen asleep, but every once in a while the fingers resting against her arm would trace a design. A long time later she finally lifted her head. Time to face the fact that change was inevitable.

"I've been thinking," she started. Oh, this was so much harder than she'd thought it would be! "Maybe it's time to go see my mom."

Harley was silent for a while before answering her. "I told you the other day that you should go. You should make amends with her if you can. A part of me wants to be selfish and ask you not to go or if it has to be now, but of course, it has to be now. Because once it's too late, it's too late." He rubbed his thumb down the outside of her arm and pulled her tighter to his side. "So, as much as I don't want you to go... I think it's a good idea."

"You're not upset at me leaving with everything that's going on?"

"Honey, of course not. Especially for something like that."

"I don't know when I'll be back."

"I know."

She wondered if he heard what she didn't say, too. That she didn't know *if* she'd be back. Or at least if she'd be back in any reasonable time frame. What if she could fix this rift she'd created with her mother years ago? What if she could mend the things she'd broken with her childish decisions? "What if something else happens while I'm gone?"

"If I promise to be extra careful will it keep you from worrying?"

"No."

"I didn't think so."

She laughed. "Just don't get hurt... again, OK?"

He pressed his lips to her temple. "I'll do my best," he whispered into her hair.

She snuggled back into his side. "I want to go the day after tomorrow before I lose my nerve. But... will you come to church with me Sunday morning before I leave?"

"Of course."

Sometime later Harley groaned, pulling her from sleep. They were still sitting on the couch, Erin curled up under his good arm. "What's wrong?" she asked, sleep slurring her voice.

"I thought I could make do without the pain meds, but the way my shoulder's screaming..." He tried to extricate himself from the couch but moaned again.

Erin sat up, yawning and stretching as she stood. Moving to the kitchen, she fished a glass out of the cupboard and filled it with water.

"You need sleep, " he said when he came to stand next to the sink. He knocked back the pills she handed him and set the glass in the sink. "Come on. Let's get you home."

Standing on tiptoe, Erin pressed a kiss on his cheek. "I can get myself home. You need sleep, too."

He cupped her neck with his good hand and rubbed his thumb over her cheek, jaw, and down her throat. "Man, I'm going to miss you," he said as he closed his eyes and rested his forehead on hers.

Yup, she could love this man.

CHAPTER SIXTEEN

T he second time stepping into the old church vestry didn't make Harley break out in a cold sweat like it had the first visit. Baby steps. He shook the greeter's hand and pulled at the collar of the dress shirt he'd found in the back of his closet. He might have worn it to a wedding. Once. Pulling at the collar again, he hoped it was covering his neck tattoo. Frannie Puckett caught his attention with a little wave and came over to hug him.

"It's so good to see you again, Char—Oh, gosh! What did you do?" She reached a tentative hand toward the sling but stopped short of touching it.

"Dislocated my shoulder. I'll be fine."

She patted his face instead. "Well, that's no fun," she said and then bustled off toward the front of the sanctuary, pulling sheet music from her oversized purse as she went. A warm hand slid into his and he turned to find Erin smiling up at him.

"Hey," she said.

"Mornin'."

"How's your shoulder?" She reached out and brushed a gentle touch on his arm where it hung in the sling.

"It'll be fine. Just sore."

"I got worried when I didn't see you all day yesterday. I stopped by, but Gage said you'd slept the whole day."

Harley gave her a sheepish smile. "Yeah. Between the pain and the pain meds, I was wiped. Sorry I missed you."

"No, don't worry about it. I'm glad you were able to rest. I used the time to pack and clean my apartment." Her face lost a little of its happy glow, but she shrugged it off. "I saved you a seat. And…" She looked up at him with a shy smile. "…I'm singing again this morning."

A smile spread across his face but before he could respond Frannie started playing the piano and people started hustling to their seats. He was happy to see that Erin had claimed two seats in the back row. Maybe someday he'd be comfortable moving a bit closer to the front, but the fact that she knew he wasn't there yet pleased him.

A pocket handkerchief appeared on the pew near his knee and his eyes snapped up to find Sawyer standing at the end of the pew. "You may want that," the man whispered before stepping back to let Erin out.

Harley arched a brow at his friend, but the older man had turned to follow Erin down the aisle. Pastor James introduced Erin and Sawyer and thanked them for blessing the congregation with special music that morning. Harley wasn't sure what the burly construction worker was up to, but if Erin was singing, it would be splendid.

Sawyer took Frannie's place at the piano and began to play. The familiar notes of *Just As I Am* filled the room, sweet and slow but gaining strength.

The guy was good.

Exceptionally good.

Erin stepped up to the pulpit and took the mic and holding Harley's gaze, raised it to her lips.

Just as I am, without one plea,

Harley already knew she believed he could come to God just as he was. She'd made that clear. The problem was, he wasn't sure she was right. But, oh, how he wished she was!

But that Thy blood was shed for me,
And that Thou bid'st me come to Thee,

He gulped in air as the words settled in his chest. He'd heard the hymn hundreds of times growing up, but had he just heard that line for the first time? Jesus' blood was shed for… Harley Beck? Pitiful, sinful, wretched, Harley Beck? And not only that, He was bidding that same pitiful, sinful, wretched man to come to Him? The longing in Harley's heart flamed to life in a breath-stealing fire as he continued to listen.

O Lamb of God, I come! I...
...need Thee, O I need Thee
Every hour I need Thee

There was a murmur through the congregation as Erin and Sawyer switched up the hymn, melding one classic into another as if that was how it'd been written. But then the words hit him and the moment the truth of them sank into his soul was like a jolt of electricity. That was what he'd been fighting.

The needing.

He'd fought the needing because he'd wanted to punish himself for all the wrong he'd done. He didn't need God punishing him, he had that sorted. But... he did need God. He needed God to heal his brokenness. That was something he'd been trying to figure out for years but couldn't. The punishment he dealt himself never seemed to be enough to redeem him. Tears blurred his vision, but his eyes never left Erin's.

O bless me now, my Savior, I come...
...just as I am, Thou wilt receive,

How many times over the past few weeks had he asked himself if it could be that easy? He wasn't sure, but he was asking it again. Could it be that simple? Come as you are and God will receive you? Please... please let it be true.

Wilt welcome, pardon, cleanse, relieve;

Oh, God, please! I don't deserve any of that. But... I know You can... if You want to. Please! Please pardon my sin, cleanse my horrid sinful soul, relieve me of the anger and unforgiveness I've carried for so many years. Please!

Because Thy promise I believe,

Harley's eyes finally left Erin's. Closing. Tears wetting his cheeks. *Yes, God! I believe! I believe Your promises!*

O Lamb of God, I come, I...
...surrender all, I surrender all;

All to Thee, my blessed Savior, I...
...come...
...Just as I am.

By the time the last notes faded away, Harley was crying and almost couldn't hold back a sob that rushed up his throat. He swallowed it down but didn't even try to stem the flow of tears.

I surrender all, Lord. I do. Please take me just as I am.

The handkerchief that had appeared near his knee earlier was damp by the time Sawyer returned to his seat. The man sat looking straight ahead and Harley was grateful that he didn't make a big deal of the mess Harley was. He picked up the worn-soft white square and dried his face again as he watched Erin move into her place in the choir.

By the time she rejoined him in the back row, Harley was hopeful that all that remained of the moment he'd had during her song were red eyes. He kept those facing the pulpit but pulled her close when she settled in next to him and rested her head on his shoulder.

"That was beautiful," he whispered. Erin smiled and snuggled into the crook of his arm, laying her Bible across their knees so he could read along, too.

Harley wanted to tell her that her song had spoken to him, changed him, drawn him to the Lord like a road that led home. The words clogged his lungs, though. She was leaving right after church, and he didn't want his newly rekindled faith to make her feel like she had to stay. He couldn't live with himself if he thought she'd traded reconciling with her mother for him. No, she needed to drive away and not look back until she was good and ready.

If at all.

That thought hurt.

He'd held everyone at arm's length for so long, never getting close or depending on anyone. He'd made an exception with Noah, and now... Erin had wheedled her way under his skin in a matter of days and he had fallen for her. Fast and hard. But she didn't need to know that. She needed to leave and he would make it as easy as possible.

Piano music drifted toward the rafters and the congregation rose to sing a final hymn. Harley stood, his good hand in his pocket, and listened to Erin sing along. Tried to imprint her voice on his memory. When the song ended, she gathered her Bible and sweater.

"I'd like to say goodbye to a few people before I... leave." Her voice hitched a little and she turned away quickly.

Harley stood at the back and watched her pull the pastor's wife in for a tight embrace, and the pastor shook her hand and patted her shoulder. She got hugs from Frannie and Mark, too. Even Sawyer pulled her in for a bear-hug.

Cori had skipped up behind Erin and waited until Sawyer let go before all but launching herself into her friend's arms. "I can't believe you're leaving! Again!" Cori wailed.

Erin's eyes filled, but she blinked the tears away. "I'll be back. I promise."

Cori sniffed dramatically. "Fine. Go."

Erin pulled the waif-like woman in for another tight hug. "I love you, Friend."

"I sort of like you, too, I guess," Cori mumbled in a dejected tone.

Erin laughed and pulled one of Cori's long messy braids, coaxing a smile. After Cori flitted off to talk to someone else, Erin returned to where Harley waited.

"OK." Her voice was thick, but she was holding it together. "I'm ready to go."

They walked to her apartment side by side. Harley wanted to reach for her hand, but if he did he knew he wouldn't be able to let go. He'd hold on for dear life and that would make this all so much harder than it already was. All the worrying that he'd hurt her, and here he was, the one with the broken heart.

He helped her load her things into the back of her truck. It wasn't much. A few beat-up boxes and a battered suitcase. "Are you leaving the rest of your things?" he asked, trying to tame the hope in his voice.

"This… is it. Just in case I'm gone longer than a few days I packed everything up. Force of habit."

Her answer pained him, but he didn't let it show. She was at least considering the idea of not coming back, and he couldn't blame her. Given one more chance to make peace with his father, he'd pack his meager belongings onto his bike and high-tail it out of town, too.

She shoved at a beat-up old cardboard box that wasn't going where she wanted it to. "I nearly left this one under the bed. I can't even remember what's in it." She reached to pull it free of the truck bed. "If I haven't needed it in three years I can probably chuck it, can't I?"

Harley put his hand on it to stop her. "Save it for another day. You need to get on the road. It's a long way to Cape Cod."

She heaved a sigh that stabbed at his heart and slammed the tailgate closed. Turning toward him, she pulled something out of her pocket and held it out to him.

"I made you something," she said, not meeting his eyes, a blush warming her cheeks. He held out his hand and she placed a small purple object in his palm. "It's a keychain."

A chunk of purple sea glass with gold leaf along one rough edge hung on a gold ring suspended from the keychain. It was stunning, but not delicate or feminine, despite the color.

"It's the sea glass you found on the beach on Blueberry Island." The pink on her cheeks deepened and he wanted so much to pull her into his arms, kiss her until she forgot she wanted to leave, and then, just for good measure, beg her to stay forever.

He did none of those things.

"It's lovely. Thank you." So inadequate, but he was struggling with words right now. Pulling his keys from his pocket, the mussel shell he'd found at Lookout Point came, too, and he held it up. A snail had drilled a perfect hole in the end and it gave him an idea. "I found this on the cliff the night we were at Lookout Point." He slipped the shell onto her creation and the glass nestled perfectly in the cup of the shell. "Every time I use my keys I'll remember that night," he murmured as he threaded the chain onto the ring holding the penlight. "I promise I will never take it off."

Erin smiled, but it faded quickly and she skirted around him, walking to the side of the truck. She stopped and stood by the door, biting her lip. He longed to ask her to stay. Or to run away with her. But those weren't the right thing to do. The right thing was to make it easy for her to go.

"Call the shop when you get there, OK? Let me know you arrived safe and sound," he said as he opened her door and all but shoved her inside.

"Harl—"

He closed the door, cutting her off. He couldn't take it. Couldn't bring himself to hear her say goodbye.

No, not goodbye. Because he couldn't stand it if this was goodbye. This was just 'see you later'. It had to be.

She rolled down the window and gave him a look that said she was wise to him. "Be careful. Please."

He met her eyes for a second before nodding and thumping the hood with the palm of his hand. "You better get going," he said, schooling his voice to stay steady.

She pressed her lips into a thin line and started the truck. "I'll be back... when I can." He nodded and stepped back, watching as his heart pulled away and drove out of town, leaving a wound he wasn't entirely sure would heal.

The melancholy that had settled onto Harley's shoulders as he watched Erin drive away began to suffocate him. He needed a distraction. He started walking without having a destination in mind but wasn't surprised when he found himself in front of his dad's house.

Fishing his keys from his pocket, he unlocked the door and stepped inside, listening to the silence. Erin had filled the place with something bright and cheerful. He could smell the coffee she'd made the last time she was there and the hemlock, spruce, and fresh paint from the porch. If he listened hard enough he imagined he could hear her singing.

The afternoon sun cast the kitchen and living room in a warm glow that was in direct contrast to his mood. A few steps brought him to a stop where the kitchen linoleum met the worn carpet. Two and a half years and he hadn't been able to look into the room. Even with Erin and all he'd been able to face with her by his side, the living room, his mother's domain, hadn't been on the list. Homesickness wrapped his chest in an iron grip. He took a deep breath of the familiar scents. Murphy's Oil Soap and old books. With one tentative step, he moved out of the hall and fully into the room.

Her piano still stood against the far wall. Dusty now, and... He tapped a key and cringed. Yup, out of tune. Her favorite hymnal sat open on the music shelf. Leaning closer, he chuckled. Of course, it was open to *Just As I Am.* He straightened away and surveyed the rest of the room. With a pang, he realized her chair was gone, replaced with a comfortable-looking sectional that faced the small wood stove in the corner. The bookcases he remembered lining the walls were still there, although it looked like the titles had changed since he was a kid.

Sinking onto the arm of the sectional, he waited for the big emotions to come. Anger. Regret. Grief. Guilt. Even loneliness. But instead, something akin to hope flickered to life inside him and he remembered the words Erin had sung that morning. Standing, he picked up the hymnal from the piano and scanned the page until he found the line.

Just as I am, Thou wilt receive, Wilt welcome, pardon, cleanse, relieve;

There appeared to be something written in the margin of the page, but the slanting rays of the sun weren't enough to read it. Harley flipped on the light clipped to the music shelf and held the book under it. Along the edge of the page, his mother had written *Psalm 30:5.* He rubbed his thumb across it before returning the songbook to its place.

Psalm 30:5? Where had he seen his dad's Bible? Harley strode to the room at the end of the hall but paused before pushing open the door. Other familiar scents greeted him there. His father's aftershave. The dull must of old pages. The slight tang of an ancient citrus air freshener. Stepping farther into the room, he tried to breathe, but it was hard with his chest tight with emotion.

Finding the Bible on the table next to his father's easy chair, Harley lowered himself to the timeworn seat while he thumbed through the book looking for Psalms. It took him longer to find it than he wanted to admit.

His anger lasts for a moment, but His favor lasts for a lifetime. Sorrow may tarry for a night, but joy comes in the morning.

Welcome. Pardon. Cleanse. Relieve. That sounded an awful lot like 'favor that lasts a lifetime'.

Harley settled back in the chair and flipped through the tattered pages. The binding sagged in his hand and the pages slid open to a page in the fifteenth chapter of Luke that was more frayed than the others. The ink in one section had been rubbed until it almost faded from the page. Squinting, he could just make out the verses.

And he left there and came to his father. But while he was still a good ways off, his father saw him and was filled with mercy, and ran and took him in his arms and kissed him. And the son said, 'Father, I have sinned against God and against you. I am not worthy to be called your son'. But the father said to his servants, 'Bring the best clothes, and put them on him, and put a ring on his finger, and shoes on his feet. And kill the fattened calf, and let us eat it and celebrate. For my son was dead, but is alive again; he was lost, but now is found.'

Shadows began to darken the room as Harley read the passage a second and a third time. Then he read it again. And again. As he slid his thumb along the edge of the page, he noticed something penciled into the margin. Flipping the light on, he leaned closer and sucked in a shaky breath. Scrawled in his father's brusk script were the words *Dear God, please bring Charleston home.*

Resting the Bible on his ankle where it crossed his knee, Harley put his hand over his eyes. Had his father honestly prayed that he'd come home? After the way he'd acted? After the way he'd left? After stealing the bike? Had Erin been right all along? Several minutes later he opened damp eyes and read the words again, running his fingers along the once-gilded edges of the page. His thumb bumped against something and Harley turned the book up to discover a ribbon bookmark a little farther into the text. He slid the ribbon up, opening to the sixth chapter of Ephesians, and again found a passage worn from repeated handling. This one much shorter, but no less affecting.

Fathers, do not incite your children to anger, but bring them up in the discipline and instruction of the Lord.

Again his father had written in the margin. This time Harley's eyes burned with hot tears.

God, forgive me! Please restore my relationship with Charleston so that I may beg his forgiveness, too.

The grief and anger and remorse from the past ten years flowed through him, erupting in a savage yell that echoed in the small room.

"Oh God..."

He rested both feet on the floor, closed the worn book, and hung his head in shame.

"I don't deserve any forgiveness, God." His voice was loud in the silent room. "Not from You, not from Dad. But... I'm beginning to think that's the point. I don't deserve it, but You're still willing to give it. Please... Receive me. Pardon me. Cleanse me. Take me and make me what You want. I don't want to be angry anymore. I want to be the man Dad always hoped I'd be. I'm so—"

The tears that came now choked off his words and wrecked him, but they also brought a cleansing peace he hadn't expected. With the last rays of the sun fading, Harley drew in a ragged breath and opened the Bible again. He turned the pages slowly, reading his father's notes and the scriptures he'd highlighted over the years. Minutes dragged into hours as he feasted on his father's words.

A truth settled over him and he grinned. He was also feasting on his Father's Word.

As evening sank into night, he reached the end of the New Testament. As he closed the book he noticed the edge of a piece of paper peeking out from where it was tucked between the last page and the back cover. Sliding it out, Harley unfolded it and began to read, but soon had to bite off the blue word that wanted to escape his lips.

Erin hadn't even made it out of Summer Harbor before she'd had to pull over. She couldn't see the road through the tears blurring her vision and burning her throat. After several minutes of sobbing into her hands, Erin had wiped her face with the sleeve of her flannel shirt and given herself a little pep talk. She wasn't leaving for good. She'd be back, maybe even soon. She had no way of knowing if she could fix the things she'd broken, but she was doing the right thing. She would drive to Cape Cod, beg her mother's forgiveness and they would figure out where life went from there. Besides, Harley hadn't seemed that broken up about her leaving. Maybe she'd read more into their meager relationship than there was. He was handsome and worldly. He probably had girls lined up. Ones he'd romanced on his bike and ones waiting for a ride. After all, girls liked the bad-boy persona.

Even as she slammed the truck into drive and peeled onto the road, Erin knew she was being ridiculous. Lying to herself. It felt like the only way to make herself leave, though. Because if she told herself the truth she'd have to say that he hadn't even looked at another girl since he'd met her. And that he'd romanced *her* on his bike, that *she* was the one who liked the bad-boy persona. Well, if she told herself the truth she wouldn't be able to force the truck to keep heading south. So instead she lied to herself the whole way off the island.

The whole way to Bangor.

The whole way down the interstate.

Right up until she couldn't anymore.

Pulling off at a rest stop somewhere in Massachusetts, Erin jumped out of the cab of the truck and sucked in deep gulps of cool air trying to head off the crying jag she felt coming. She'd never make it to her mother's at the rate she was going.

An elderly couple eyed her from their vehicle and she managed a smile she didn't feel before turning back toward the truck and laying her head on her folded arms across the hood.

Lord, please...

No more words came and she squeezed her eyes shut trying to form her plea into something eloquent.

My Spirit will help you in your weakness. When you do not know what to pray for as you should, My Spirit intercedes for you with groanings too deep for words.

Comfort flowed around her, reaching in to take hold of her heart. She breathed it in and held it to her ragged soul. The Holy Spirit would fight for her, she only needed to be still and let Him. She went into the restroom and splashed cold water on her face. The peace was tenuous but growing stronger, and she squared her shoulders. She could trust God to work this whole situation out for His good. Meeting Harley, searching for answers to Lyle's crash, falling in love—

She looked herself in the eye in the mottled mirror above the sink and let the thought settle. It was time to admit she already loved the man. His tough exterior, his broken parts, his humor, and his grief. The realization brought a smile to her lips but also a sadness. She'd left. Just driven away, and she had things she needed to do. She couldn't just turn around and run back. But, oh, how she wanted to.

Please, Lord, keep him safe and... just... keep him until I can get back. Someone messed with his bike, twice, don't let it happen again. Don't let him get hurt again.

She climbed back into her truck and merged into traffic. It was dark and traffic was getting thicker as she ticked off the miles toward her exit. Her cheeks stayed wet as she drove. It wasn't just Harley she was leaving. When she'd been born again she'd also gained a new family. Cooper. Vera and Jason. Later, Sawyer. Mark and Frannie. Pastor James and Maggie. Now, Lily and Noah. Cape Cod, if she stayed, meant starting over. Everything. And the loss hurt deep in her soul. It would be a long time before running into folks from church, like Mark and Frannie at the Lookout Point, would be a common occurrence. She dashed at her cheeks with the back of her hand.

"Time to suck it up, buttercup!"

A horn blew behind her and Erin realized she had slowed down to well below the posted speed limit. Something had started flitting into the back of her mind. Pieces to the puzzle, disconnected and muddled, floated just out of her grasp. If she could just...

The horn blew again as Erin wrenched the steering wheel to the right and floored it down the off-ramp. Two of the pieces finally fell into place. She had to get a hold of Harley. He wasn't safe and he didn't even know who to watch out for.

She pulled into a gas station and used an old decrepit payphone. Holding it gingerly in two fingers she wished she could have disinfected it. The number she had for Harley's apartment rang and rang with no answer. She tried Sawyer and at least got voicemail. She left a quick cryptic message and tried the apartment again. Unable to reach anyone, Erin got back on the interstate, this time headed north. She tried calling multiple times at multiple gas stations and convenience stores along the route. No answer.

Most of the streetlights had clicked off by the time Erin rolled back into Summer Harbor in the middle of the night. Fog shrouded the streets and the town was quiet. She bit her lip, trying to decide where to start looking for Harley. There was a good chance he was at the apartment above the shop, sound asleep. Should she wake him? She rubbed her eyes. Between packing up her things and cleaning the apartment and worrying about Harley she hadn't slept in close to thirty-six hours and the sleep deprivation was messing with her head. She turned down the street where Coop's house sat and was surprised to see lights on inside.

The truck coughed to a stop and Erin bolted for the kitchen door.

"Harley!" she called as she burst inside.

"Erin?"

His long strides brought him down the hall to the kitchen. In an instant, he was crushing her to his chest with his one good arm. "What are you doing back here?"

Stepping into his embrace was like coming home. Why did she ever think she could leave? Wrapping her arms around his neck, she pulled him tight, burying her face against his warm neck. "I think I know who messed with Lyle's bike. And yours."

Harley set her away from his chest so he could look her in the eye. "What are you talking about?"

"I think it was Mark."

"Mr. Puckett?!"

"I know it sounds crazy, but... Remember when we went to their house for dinner? Frannie was telling us about Lyle and how he pretty much stole the shop out from under them, but Mark was trying to change the subject the whole time. Then, Mark was at Lookout point right before you blew that tire, *and* he was here while you were working on your dad's bike. He had motive, means, and opportunity!"

"I don't know. It seems like a long time to wait to do something out of revenge. I mean, that must have been thirty years ago."

"You have to admit that it makes more sense than Alec."

"Or Edwin Hurst."

"Or Vera."

"If we had some kind of proof that someone had done

something to Lyle's bike like someone did to mine... A signed death threat would make things so much easier right about now."

"We should at least go talk to Wade," she said. "Probably should have talked to him a long time ago."

Harley tucked a stray lock of hair behind her ear and ran his thumb along her jaw. His eyes held hers. "I missed you."

"I was only gone for twelve hours," Erin said, her eyelashes fluttering closed. The truth was, she'd missed him, too. A lot. Leaning into his hand she sighed. "I want to fix things with my mom. I do. I know that the whole mess when I was a teenager is one hundred percent on me, but... I don't think I can move into her world. It just feels... wrong."

Harley got a strange look in his eyes and pulled Erin close. Wrapping his good arm around her to hold her tight to his chest, he touched his lips to her hair. He was quiet for a long time. Eventually, he let go and drew a few sheets of folded paper from his back pocket. He wouldn't meet her eyes when he handed them to her. A frown had darkened his face and her heart started to hammer in her chest. Sinking into a chair, she smoothed out the papers on the table and tried to make sense of what she was reading. Turning the pages faster and faster, her lungs grew tight.

"I..." She looked up to search his face and found it grim. "I don't understand."

Harley hunkered down in front of her, balancing on the balls of his feet, and rubbed a slow circle on her knee. Just like he had after she lost it seeing Coop's bike in the garage. He met her eyes, finally, his lips tight. "It looks like my dad tried to work it out with your mom to have you move back home, but..."

"She didn't want me." It shouldn't hurt this much. After all these years it shouldn't make her heart feel like it was being ripped in two. She turned back to the first page and tried to read, but her eyes blurred, and she had to gulp back a sob.

"Hey, hey," he soothed. "That's not all it says. Look." He

turned a few pages. "Dad fought for you. He went to court, multiple times. He eventually got legal guardianship of you." His voice grew husky. "He chose you, honey. He loved you."

She pressed her hand to her mouth in a vain attempt to hold in the emotions bubbling from her. "All this time I thought *I* was the one who broke our relationship. That if *I'd* done more, or been better, or tried harder, she would have loved me."

"I shouldn't have shown you those," he said, reaching for the papers.

"No," she said, her voice vehement. "I needed to know this. I can't believe he never said anything. We talked about... everything."

"I can understand why he didn't."

She read through the court documents a second time, the shock of what they said dulling as she saw how hard Coop had fought for her. First, he'd fought to reconcile her with her mother, and then he'd fought to keep her. No one had ever fought for her. Not ever. Until Coop.

"The social worker makes a lot more sense now." At his raised eyebrow she continued. "This woman from the state came and asked me tons of questions. Things like 'do you want to continue living with Cooper Beck' and 'do you ever feel scared or threatened by him'. I thought she was crazy. I wanted to stay with him and he would never, ever have done anything to hurt me."

Reaching up, Harley scooped the papers from the table, refolded them, and eased them into his back pocket as he stood. Reaching out, he took her hand and tugged her up out of her chair. "Come on. I want to show you something."

He led the way back to his dad's room and picked up the Bible, turning it to show her the notes he'd found the previous afternoon.

"Oh, Harley..."

"You may not have found that box you were looking for, but if I'd needed anything else to prove he'd forgiven me... This did it."

Erin sank into Coop's chair, tucking her legs up under her, and Harley sat on the edge of his dad's bed, facing her. "I realized yesterday that I'd been running, scared and angry, for too long. And that what I needed was for Jesus to take me, just as I was, and fix me from the inside out. You showed me that. Or He showed me that through you. Either way, while you were singing yesterday I... How did you put it the other day? I 'gave Him all my junk and left it at His feet'."

She knew her eyes were glistening and she didn't trust her voice, but the smile that spread across her face must have said it all because Harley grinned back, a bright new light shining out from within.

"Come on," Harley said hours later. They'd been talking about his dad and God and forgiveness and repentance, and while he hated to stop, it was time to end this nonsense about Lyle's accident. "Let's hit the coffee shop and then go talk to Wade."

"I didn't even realize it wasn't night anymore," Erin said, smothering a yawn.

He grinned as she slipped her fingers against his palm. Even exhausted, she was lovely. "Depends on who you ask I guess."

Despite the early hour, the shop was busy, and they tucked in at the end of the counter while they waited for their order to be filled.

"Hey, man, no sling?" Sawyer asked, sliding onto the stool next to Harley.

"Nah." Harley grasped his friend's hand in a firm shake. "Couldn't stand the thing."

I thought you'd ditched us for Cape Cod," the older man added, squeezing Erin's shoulder. Before she had a chance to respond, the barista, already looking harried at six in the morning, handed over their coffees.

Sawyer took a tentative sip, but smacked his lips and set the cup down. "Hot!"

"Y'all saving these seats for us?" Noah asked as he and Lily slid into the last two empty stools.

"We're headed to Brynlyn's studio to order our engagement announcements," Lily said to Erin as she sat down. "Early mornings call for extra strong coffee." She was pulling the folder of photos from her bag as she spoke and started leafing through the proofs.

"May I?" Erin scooped up a stack of prints. "The light in these is unbelievable. How did she even do that?"

"I don't know, but I love them all! It was so hard to pick just a few."

Erin pulled her eyebrows together in an adorable little frown when she was concentrating and Harley had to force himself not to grin like an idiot. He was a goner and he didn't care who knew it.

"Oh, gosh," Erin suddenly exclaimed. "Lyle's in these pictures. See? Here, and here." She pulled six photos out of the stack and lined them up.

Everyone leaned closer to look over Erin's shoulder. The photos were all of Noah and Lily on the dance floor, but behind them and to the side sat Lyle Jay. The photographer had caught him eating, paying his bill, standing to leave, and shrugging into his jacket. Lily let out a quiet whistle.

"Hmmm?" Noah looked at her.

"It's nothing." She leaned in. "Just... that's a six thousand dollar motorcycle jacket."

"What?" Erin picked up the picture of Lyle thrusting his arm into the sleeve.

"It's Versace."

"Trust her on this," Noah said with a smirk.

"I do kind of know fashion a little."

Erin met Harley's gaze. "Didn't Dox say the business was struggling? Maybe going under? How could Lyle afford a six thousand dollar motorcycle jacket?" she asked.

"Maybe he had it for a while?" Harley suggested.

"No, that's from this year's collection," Lily said.

"All that work he had Keaton doing on his house would have cost him a pretty penny," Sawyer added. "Even now at the end of the season we're swamped and he'd have been paying top dollar to get the work done before winter. Besides the fact that the house itself easily cost him three million dollars."

It was Noah's turn to let out a whistle. "As a business owner here in town I can attest to the fact that I'm not bringing in anywhere near enough to be buying a three million dollar house, or even a six thousand dollar jacket."

"Sounds like maybe our man Lyle had a side business going," Sawyer said.

Everyone was quiet for a long moment as the barista returned with Noah and Lily's coffees. As soon as the woman was out of earshot, Erin cut her voice low. "We know Lyle was blackmailing two people. Could he have been blackmailing more?"

Sawyer crossed his huge arms over his chest and nodded toward the photos. "I'd say that's a distinct possibility."

"Would blackmail be enough to cover a thirteen thousand dollar a month mortgage though?" When the others gaped at her Lily shrugged. "It's sort of my thing. Fashion, real estate, hotels... I'm your girl!"

"If that's the case, there's no way Lyle was hitting up Alec Cohen or Arnie Novak for that much a month. Even if he had more people, I think that amount is a stretch." Harley said.

"Don't forget," Erin chimed in, "Alec wasn't paying him anything, just working for free."

"Right."

"So he had to have some other form of income," Sawyer said. "Was he rich from his days as a stunt driver?"

"I doubt it," Erin said. "I mean that was, what? Thirty years ago? Has he lived in that house since then?"

"Nah," Harley said. "When I was a kid he lived in a tiny place beside the shop."

"So, did he come from money? Inherit the house? Make a killing in the stock market?"

"Not that I ever heard," said Sawyer. "As far as I know he just owned the motorcycle shop. And he had to sell half of it to Dox over twenty-five years ago when times got lean, so that makes me think the money thing's newer."

"And he only bought *half* the business," Harley added. "He swindled the other half out from under its owner,"

Erin nodded. "Mark and Frannie were telling us about that."

"Mark Puckett?" Sawyer asked.

"Yes," Harley answered. Sawyer let out a long whistle and looked at him. Harley raised a brow.

"Nothing to do with this, but there was some history between Mark and your dad." Sawyer looked long and hard at Erin before continuing. "When Pastor Beck started to shift his focus to the youth in our community, some folks at church weren't too happy. Stupid, but that's how some people are. It's all about appearances. Anyway, in the beginning, Mark was one of them. Started eyeballing the pulpit. Even petitioned the deacon board to remove Pastor Beck and install him as pastor. Moved into town to be close to the church and everything."

"I don't remember that," Erin whispered.

"It was early on, maybe even before your time. Eventually, most folks came around or moved on. But at the time—" Sawyer sucked air through his teeth and shook his head. "It was messy. When Pastor Beck passed away, Mark stepped in as interim. I think he planned on being the next pastor."

"What happened?" Lily asked.

"Way I heard it, one of the deacons knew Pastor James was looking for a church. They met with Mark and smoothed it all over, but..."

Harley and Erin exchanged a stunned look.

Lily took the photo from Erin and looked at it for a moment. "Let's assume Lyle *was* up to no good, and that he kept proof of it. Where would he keep it?"

"The shop?" Noah suggested.

"Nah, too many people there to find it," Harley answered.

"His house," Erin and Sawyer said in unison.

Sawyer took another gulp of coffee and then push himself off his stool. "And I've got a key." As four sets of eyes stared and a couple of mouths hung open, he shrugged. "What? I'll let you guys in, but I'm not doing anything illegal. You run it by Wade first and get his permission."

"I'm on it," Noah said as he leaned over the counter, motioning for the barista to hand him the phone.

"And... why do you have a key?" Lily asked.

"I was working on Lyle's place when he died. Keaton put me on another job while things got sorted out, but technically I'm still on that job."

"What, exactly, are we looking for?" Harley turned to Erin. "I was... sort of... kidding about the signed death threat," he whispered, drawing a tired giggle from her. She was beat. She needed a nap or she was going to fall over.

"Remember the last day I worked on it with you?" she said to Sawyer. "I wandered into the wrong room looking at the view out the window. Lyle flipped out that I'd seen his safe. If he was hiding something, that's where it would be."

"He'll meet us there," Noah said when he rejoined the group. "Let's go solve the craziest game of Clue ever."

It took three vehicles and twenty minutes to get everyone from the coffee shop to Lyle's five-thousand-square-foot mansion in Gull's Cove. Wade was waiting for them when they arrived, leaning against his cruiser with his ankles crossed.

"OK, listen," he said once they were all there. "This is... a gray area. Because Sawyer has a key and the homeowner's permission to be inside, I have no reason to stop him from going in. And if he takes you all with him, well, still not breaking the law. Also, because the homeowner is deceased, I don't... technically... need a warrant. That being said, this is not how these things are supposed to go down. So if I say enough, I mean it."

Everyone nodded and Sawyer pulled the key from his

pocket, unlocked the door, and stepped aside. Erin hurried past him and led the way up the stairs to the suite she'd wandered into while working on the house weeks before.

"This place is gorgeous," Lily whispered as she followed Erin down the hall.

"Right? I guess for thirteen thousand a month it had better be."

They entered the bedroom and Erin pointed to the painting that neatly covered the wall safe.

Wade swung the canvas to the side. "I don't suppose anyone knows the code to open it?" he asked, staring at the keypad.

After a few moments of silence, Erin looked at Harley. "His most prized possession was his motorcycle. What year was it?"

"1939," all four men said in unison.

Erin stepped forward, but Wade stopped her. Pulling a pair of rubber gloves from his pocket, he punched in the code and chuckled when the lock disengaged.

"That should not have worked." He opened the door and they all leaned forward.

"Is that...?" Lily asked.

Wade whistled. "I believe it is."

"Something tells me you weren't wrong about that side business," Noah said to Sawyer.

CHAPTER SEVENTEEN

Wade stood back with his hands on his hips. "Y'all seein' this, too, right?"

Harley stared at the open safe trying to make sense of what sat in the open door. He wasn't sure what he'd been expecting, but a long row of nearly empty bags of various colored pills, and a stack of white bricks that looked to be made of some kind of powder sure wasn't it.

Plus cash. Stacks and stacks of cash.

"Is that drugs?" Lily asked in a hushed whisper.

"I do believe so," Wade replied. With his hands still encased in rubber gloves, he carefully slid a book Harley hadn't even noticed out from the safe and flipped it open. It was filled with columns of numbers and dates similar to the one Erin had found. He was about to point it out when the policeman turned to the group. "And I think this is the point where I say 'enough' and we all clear out."

No one complained.

Outside, with the sun burning off the morning fog and the air heavy with the smell of the sea, Harley leaned against the bed of Erin's pickup and watched the toe of his boot dig into the crushed shells on the driveway. That ledger had to be part of this, but why had his father been keeping a notebook similar to that of a drug dealer? His first inclination to tell Wade about it had faded as the implications mounted. Had his dad been involved somehow? Had he known what was going on? Had he helped? That thought made Harley's blood run cold.

Noah stood nearby, his fingers laced behind his neck. Sawyer leaned on the truck, too, his arms and ankles crossed, staring at the house. Lily and Erin stood to the side watching Wade talking on the radio.

After what seemed like forever, Noah finally spoke. "Is 'Lyle Jay in the mansion with drugs' an appropriate Clue solution?"

Harley snorted a laugh.

"What I don't get is what the drugs have to do with him crashing his bike. With or without help," Lily said.

"If anything, they make this whole thing *more* complicated," Erin added.

"If Lyle was killed over drugs, wouldn't the person have taken them?" asked Sawyer. "And the cash?"

"And if he was making bank on the drugs, why bother blackmailing people?" Harley chimed in.

Wade joined their group, a roll of crime scene tape in his hand. "You folks are free to go," he said, nodding at Sawyer, Noah, and Lily. "I'm going to string this up and then, Harley, I was wondering if you would come and take a look at Lyle's bike with me? I want to make sure we didn't miss something and I'm thinking you've got a good eye."

Harley nodded and the deputy walked back to Lyle's front door. He didn't know what the man hoped they'd find. What would the ramifications be if they did find something? Noah stepped forward, pulling Harley from his thoughts, and took his hand in a firm shake before pulling him in for a part hug part chest bump before draping his arm over Lily's shoulders and heading for his Jeep.

"See ya 'round," Sawyer said with a salute to Harley. He then pointed at Erin. "See you at work."

"Alrighty," Wade said as he rejoined them. "You up to checking out that bike?"

"Sure thing." Ready or not, Harley wasn't giving up the opportunity to get a look at the machine.

"Is it just me, or does it feel like we're farther away from figuring out what happened than we were before?" Erin asked once they'd climbed in the truck and were following the police cruiser toward Finch and Jay's.

"Seems like," Harley said with a sigh. What had begun as a search for someone who hated Lyle Jay enough to kill him had turned into something far more complicated.

They pulled into the lot behind Wade and followed him into the garage. One of the mechanics nodded at the policeman as they strode through the space, but didn't pay much attention to them. Wade pulled a set of keys from his pocket and unlocked the door at the back of the shop, throwing the lights on as he walked in.

The once-beautiful Knucklehead lay in a crumpled heap in the middle of the bay. One butter-yellow fender was crumpled, the tire ripped free of the rim. The headlight and handlebars lay mangled beyond use. The custom azure paint job on the gas tank had been clawed off by the pavement, and little remained of the front forks.

Harley puffed out a sigh and squatted down next to the wreckage. It had been a thing of beauty when it was whole. A collector's dream. He ran his hand along the bent front fender and over the scant remains of one fork.

"This is where the brake cable on mine was cut," he said, pointing it out to the policeman. "This one's intact."

"So it wasn't tampered with?"

Harley smoothed his good hand over his beard before reaching out and fingered the thin red cable again. If the brakes weren't the issue, what else could have caused the classic to crash? He looked over the motor, rear wheel assembly, gas line, and throttle. Now that he was in the garage with the wreckage it seemed stupid to think he could have seen something the guy from the state police missed. Maybe all of this nonsense was just bad luck and coincidences after all.

"What are you thinking?" Erin asked from where she leaned on the door frame. He glanced over his shoulder and realized she was using the doorframe to keep herself upright. She looked ragged and wrung out and a pang of guilt hit him. As much as they wanted to sort this thing out, she needed sleep more.

"I'm not quite sure." Harley pushed to his feet and studied the bike for another minute before turning to Wade. "Let me mull it over?"

"Of course." The deputy followed them out the door and locked it behind them.

They were passing the motorcycle the mechanic had been putting up on the lift earlier when Harley stopped and turned to get a better look at it.

"Easy on the eyes, this one," the mechanic said.

That she was. A mint condition 1972 Triumph X-75 Hurricane in classic vermillion. The black leather seat looked brand new, and the polished chrome triple exhaust shone. But something else had caught Harley's eye. Something beyond the rare bike. He reached out and fingered the bright red cable running along one of the front forks.

"That there's not strictly authentic," the mechanic said, nodding toward the brake cable. "But it's the only brand we keep in stock. If the owner wants black we're going to have to order it in."

"You say this is all you stock in the shop?" Harley asked.

"Yeah. They're not a common brand, but Mr. Jay, may he rest in peace, swore by them. Most of the time customers don't care. This is such a classic though, I'm thinking the owner might want the authentic look."

"And Lyle's Knucklehead...?" Harley let his voice trail off.

The other man laughed. "Oh, no! There was nothing on that bike that wasn't one-hundred percent original."

Wade was already fumbling with his keys when Harley turned back toward the rear of the garage. In moments the cop had the door open again and he and Harley bent over the wreckage. Just as Harley remembered, a red brake cable was attached to the front brakes of the bike. He followed it up to where it should have attached to the handlebars, but it dangled loose.

"Where are the rest of the pieces?" Harley asked. "Stuff that wasn't attached after the crash?"

Wade looked around. "I thought it came here, but..." Stepping to the side he detached the radio from his shoulder and began speaking to someone on the other end. While the deputy was trying to locate the missing bits of the motorcycle, Erin sidled up to Harley.

"What does that mean?"

"I think it means that after it came here, someone snuck in and switched the old, cut, brake cable with one off the shelf."

Erin was quiet as she stared at the bike, eyes wide with shock. Then, while Wade was still engrossed in his conversation with dispatch concerning the missing debris, she turned those huge eyes Harley's way. "We need to go to your dad's house. Now!" she said as she grabbed Harley's hand and pulled him toward the door without so much as a goodbye wave to the frustrated cop.

As she drove, Erin could see Harley out of the corner of her eye. She had a hunch, one she hoped was wrong. Prayed was wrong. She couldn't bring herself to say it out loud and instead gripped the wheel, pretending that she didn't see the questions on his face.

At the house, Erin headed straight for the garage and waited while he unlocked it. Scooping up the old, busted handlebars Harley had removed from his dad's bike she ran her fingers along the one red brake cable.

"This looked out of place the other day," she said. "Now I know why."

Harley held it for a long second before letting go and hurrying to the back of the garage where he started rummaging around in the workbench. He came back with a gray and black box in his hand. He popped the box open and pulled out a brand new black brake cable with chrome ends. He handed the cable to Erin and reached for the cardboard box on the floor, dumping the contents onto the cement. It only took a minute for him to find what he was looking for. When he stood back up he looked like he was going to be physically ill. Opening his fist, he held another chrome end, this one cut from its cable. His hands were shaking as he reached for the red cable, still attached to the handlebars with both ends intact.

It took a few beats of her heart for the enormity of what she was seeing to sink in.

"Someone replaced the brake cable after the accident. Just like Lyle's. This…" He gestured at the crumpled metal in Erin's hands, "wasn't an accident. How did I not see this before?"

Erin felt as though something reached out and crushed her chest, forcing all the air from her lungs. "I'd hoped I was wrong."

Harley ran a hand through his hair as he paced away from her. "The other day Edwin said it was strange that our list of suspects for Lyle's crash all had reasons to hurt Dad, too."

"What?" Erin asked, her sleep-deprived brain struggling to keep up.

"Edwin said that Alec and the Novak guy hated Dad and that Vera had been in love with Coop for years before she married Jason, and then became obsessed with him after Jason passed away, but Dad wasn't interested."

For the first time since this whole thing started, Erin could picture Vera as the villain. Please no! "Sawyer added Mark to that list. Plus Edwin himself."

"I think it's time to go talk to Chief Briggs."

Erin tried to nod but was interrupted by a yawn.

Harley's lips turned up in a smile. "Let me rephrase. I think it's time *I* went to see Chief Briggs. You're asleep on your feet."

She meant to protest, but when she opened her mouth another huge yawn took over and she swayed on her feet. "I'd like to tell you you're wrong, but…"

"I'm not."

Reluctant to let any part of the mystery be solved without her, Erin hesitated. So what that she hadn't slept in over two days? She was fine.

Then the room began to tilt.

No.

No, she wasn't fine.

"Listen, go take a nap on the couch." Harley ran his knuckles down her cheek and nodded toward the house. "I won't be gone long."

He hated to leave Erin behind, but she was exhausted. Besides, he hadn't yet decided what he wanted to do where the ledger was concerned. Rolling it, he tucked it in his back pocket and headed out on foot.

God, I'm not too good at asking for help. From anyone, least of all You. But if You wouldn't mind giving me a little wisdom here, I'd appreciate it.

Should he hand it over to the police, even if it ended up implicating his dad in something nefarious? Or maybe he should burn it and hope no one other than Erin ever knew about it? No, that one left a bad taste in his mouth. If only he knew what all the columns of numbers and letters and dates meant! And why Lyle had a similar one in a safe full of drugs. Shoving his hands in his pockets, Harley let out a sigh and squeezed his eyes shut.

Please.

You know that for those who love Me all things work together for good. The plans in the mind of a man are many, but it is My purpose that will stand. Trust Me with all your heart, not your own understanding. Haven't I told you to be strong and courageous, not frightened or dismayed? After this, you will know the truth, and the truth will set you free.

Peace settled over him as he opened his eyes and saw the police station directly in front of him. A few minutes later he was being ushered into the Chief's office. Jim Briggs straightened in his chair. "Well now, what can I do for you this afternoon young man?"

Harley laid Coop's ledger down on the table and the older man picked it up, thumbing through it.

"We found that at Dad's. It didn't mean anything until this morning when Wade found a similar one in the safe at Lyle's. I still don't know what it means, if anything, but I wanted the police to have it. I also have reason to believe someone cut the brake cable on Lyle's bike. And mine." Harley's voice lowered with emotion. "And Dad's."

The older man's eyebrows shot up, and he tapped his pen on the desk calendar for a second before pushing to his feet. He stepped around Harley to the door and stuck his head out. "Thelma, would you get Wade in here?"

"Sure thing, Chief." Thelma slid the little dog she was holding onto the floor and picked up the phone.

"I don't know much of anything about motorcycles or mechanical what-not," Chief Briggs was saying as he pulled his head back into his office. "That's why we had a guy from the state come to look at your dad's bike, and Lyle's. Maybe my deputy will know more. As for that book..." He tapped it where it sat on his desk. "I don't know what to make of that either." There was a long pause while he flipped through it again, running his fingers along the columns. Eventually, he raised solemn eyes to meet Harley's. "I liked your dad, Harley. We always saw eye-to-eye on things. I hope you know I wouldn't have let his accident go if there'd been any hint of a reason to think foul play was involved."

"I know, sir."

After a rap of knuckles against the door, Wade stepped into the room. "What can I do for ya, Chief?" he asked in a voice mellowed by his southern drawl. "Oh, hey Harley. Everything alright? You and Erin took off while I was still on the radio."

"Harley here may have found some evidence in an old case." The Chief pulled a folder from his filing cabinet and slid it across to his desk, Wade raised a questioning brow at Harley before picking it up and thumbing through the few pages.

The moment he made the connection between the victim's name and Harley's was obvious and his eyes snapped up. "Was this—" He paused and gentled his voice. "Was this your father?"

"Yeah."

"Please accept my condolences," the policeman said in a sincere tone before going back to the file. "It looks like we had a guy from the state police come look at his bike, too, but nothing was found to be suspicious? So we ruled it an accident."

Chief Briggs nodded. "That about sums it up."

Wade turned back to Harley. "But now you say you've found some new evidence?"

"To be honest, we don't know what we found." Harley scooped the notebook up and handed it to the policeman, waiting while he thumbed through it.

"Similar to the ledger we found this morning. Any idea what these letters mean?" He pointed at the margin.

"Erin thought maybe they were initials," Harley replied.

"That's not the only thing," the chief interjected. "Tell him about the brake cable."

"On Lyle's bike?" Wade asked. "I was there when we discovered that."

"No. On my dad's. Same as Lyle's."

Wade's eyes widened. "So you think the two are related?"

"Lyle, an experienced driver, crashes. My dad, also an excellent driver, does the same. My bike. All in the same location. Plus the number of people who had serious problems with Lyle, and the tire on my Norton... This notebook and the ledger from the safe. It's starting to feel like it's got to be more than random unconnected incidents."

"Do you mind if I come and take a look at your bike?" the deputy asked.

Harley breathed a sigh of relief. They were at least willing to listen.

Opening the door to the garage a few minutes later, Harley

pointed out the red cable on the mangled handlebar and the razor blade sticking out of the tire from his Commando. The policeman pulled a flashlight off his utility belt to get a closer look. Standing, he ran the back of his knuckles along his jaw as he thought. "Anyone else have access to this garage?"

"No. Except for the other night when I forgot to lock up."

"You park the Norton in the driveway a lot? Out on the street?"

Harley shrugged. "Most of the time it's parked in the alley behind the kayak shop."

Wade made some notes on the pad he'd pulled from his pocket. He rubbed his chin again and looked over the garage. "I'm guessing you have a theory about how this is all connected?"

"Erin and I haven't fit all the pieces together, but we were starting to think Mark Puckett looks good for it all."

"Mark Puckett? Deacon at the Summer Harbor Community Church? That Mark Puckett?"

"Hear me out. He's the only one we can see with motive, means, *and* opportunity. He wanted Dad out of the way because he wanted the pastorate. We were at the Pucketts' for dinner a few weeks ago. Frannie was telling us how Lyle swindled the motorcycle shop out from under her father, and out from under Mark and Frannie in the process. At the time, I know we mentioned that we didn't think Lyle's accident was... well, an accident. When we started asking around about who might have had something to do with Lyle's crash, maybe he decided he needed to stop us. Mark stopped by while I was working on Dad's bike," Harley added. "He knew I was almost done and knew I would be taking it out for a test drive. He also had access to the Norton the evening we blew the tire."

"So he knew you were snooping around?"

Harley nodded and Wade looked over his notes again. "You have some good points, but I don't think it's enough to pursue. However," he added when Harley moved to argue. "I am willing to go speak to Mr. Puckett."

"That's all I was hoping for," Harley said with a sigh of relief.

After Wade left, Harley let himself into the house as quietly as possible. As he'd hoped, Erin was sound asleep on the sectional in the living room. He thought for a second about waking her, but she didn't need to tag along with him on the errand he was going to run. Instead, he tiptoed out the back door and rolled his Norton into the street so he didn't wake her. He'd be back long before she stirred, anyway.

CHAPTER EIGHTEEN

Harley pulled the invoice from his pocket and handed it to Alec Cohen. They'd shown it to Dox days before, but the thing had been all but forgotten as they searched for answers to Lyle's crash. With the discovery that morning of sabotage to his dad's bike, the piece of paper had been thrust back into his mind and he needed answers.

"I'm not sure I understand," the other man said as he looked at it, then back at Harley.

"It's from Finch and Jay's. For work done on Cooper Beck's motorcycle a few days before he died. Dox said that's your code, that you did the work."

Alec looked at the bill again. Did his hand shake? Harley crossed his arms over his chest, making sure his biceps bulged. He drew his brows together in a threatening glare. If the creep's hands hadn't been shaking before, they ought to be now.

Alec swallowed. "Yes, I fixed a few bad electrical connections for him. He used to do that stuff himself, but he said his eyes were getting tired. Why?"

"It appears that someone tampered with the bike," Harley replied. "You worked on it, so…"

"You don't think I—" Alec's voice had risen and he darted a glance at the other end of the garage. Another mechanic was working on a chopped bike with huge handlebars and Alec nodded toward the office door behind the counter.

Once in the room with the door closed, Alec sagged onto the rickety stool tucked behind a desk piled with order books, invoices, and long-empty coffee cups. He puffed out a sigh before setting the invoice down on the desk with great care and pulling his eyes up to meet Harley's. "I did the work, but I didn't see anything on the motorcycle that concerned me. And I certainly didn't *do* anything to it to make it crash if that's what you're insinuating."

Frustration that had been building for days seeped into Harley's voice. "And I'm just supposed to take your word for that?" he asked through gritted teeth.

"I wouldn't—" All of a sudden Alec seemed to realize his voice was raised. He took a deep breath and lowered it. "I wouldn't have done anything to hurt Pastor Beck."

Harley snorted in disbelief. "Erin said you hated him. That she even heard you threaten him!"

"That was before."

"Before what?"

Alec stared long and hard at Harley before fishing around in the pocket of his jeans. "It isn't something I like to flash around," he said as he pulled out a handful of change, laid one of the coins on top of the slip, and slid both across the desk.

Harley still stood with his arms crossed watching the mechanic. Waiting. When the man said nothing more, he reached out and picked up the coin, looking at it carefully.

A three years sober chip from Narcotics Anonymous.

It was shiny gold and looked brand-new. He rubbed his thumb over it before setting it back down on the desk in front of Alec.

"Explain."

The man sighed and ran a hand through his already messy hair. Shame weighed his shoulders down until they slumped. "There are a few folks in town who know about this," he said, tapping the coin. "But precious few."

He ran his hand over his eyes and down his face in a gesture that Harley recognized all too well. Soul weary. A pang of something that might have been empathy pinched Harley's conscience, but he pushed it aside. He didn't want to relate to the man, but he had to admit that he saw a lot of himself in the tough persona and the devil-may-care attitude. Relaxing his stance slightly, he waited for the other man to continue. Right now he needed answers. He'd deal with feelings later.

"A couple of months before Pastor Beck died, I OD'd." Alec turned away to stare out the window. "Somebody must have called 911. When I woke up in the hospital, he was there, waiting. Praying." He turned back to meet Harley's gaze and a strong emotion shimmered in his eyes. "He'd been there the whole time. No one else came. Not even my parents. Just him. He tried to convince me that I needed to do something about my problem. I wasn't having any of it and got high again the next day. But... he kept after me. Eventually, he suggested AA here in Summer Harbor. It's not very anonymous when everyone in town knows who you are, though, so I refused.

"A few days later he tracked me down and told me he'd found a meeting on the mainland. Even offered to go with me. I wanted to get clean, but... I was so scared. I got completely plastered the night before we were supposed to go and somehow ended up at Pastor Beck's house. He got me sobered up and the next day he borrowed someone's truck and drove me to my first NA meeting. All the way to Bangor. That was over three years ago. I haven't touched the stuff since."

Alec's voice got thick and he tapped the coin. "I got this last week. Without Pastor Beck... I'd be dead. I know it." He paused and met Harley's gaze. "When he passed away, I was on the mainland going to an NA meeting. I swear to you, I did not have anything to do with it."

"He..." Harley began, his voice quiet. "...rescued you?"

"I still can't believe he never gave up."

"There was a time, not too long ago, that I wouldn't have believed you. But... I'm beginning to think that the Pastor Beck who died three years ago wasn't the same man I called 'Dad' ten years ago."

Surprise flashed on Alec's face. "Wait. Pastor Beck was your father?" When Harley nodded, the man stepped forward with his hand outstretched. "I owe your dad... everything. That wiring? He paid the shop, then paid me under the table 'cause he knew Lyle wasn't.'"

It felt strange to be shaking Alec's hand, and stranger still to feel a sort of rapport with him. Not to mention the pride he felt in thinking of the impact his father'd had. Maybe that was the strangest feeling of them all. Then again, what hadn't felt strange over the past month?

Alec let go of Harley's hand and reached out to scoop up the chip. He flipped it into the air with his thumb and caught it, turning it over in his hand. "I've been going to NA for three years, but I'm only on step eight. Guess I'm slow. I haven't gotten up the nerve to tackle step nine."

"Which is?" Harley asked.

"Making amends to the people I've harmed. I finished step eight a while ago, 'make a list of all people I've harmed, and be willing to make amends'. Erin's at the top of that list." He scrubbed the toe of his work boot on the cement floor. "She tell you about us?"

"She did."

"And you didn't throttle me? I'm impressed. I'd have deserved it if you had. I need to tell her how sorry I am. For everything. I'm so glad Pastor Beck got her out that day. So glad that I didn't have the opportunity to drag her in any further."

"I think she'd like to hear that."

"I'll tell her the next time I see her. I promise."

"I don't suppose you know of any reason someone might've wanted my dad out of the picture, do you?" Harley asked, hoping for a new lead he could chase down.

Alec met Harley's eyes. "Pastor Beck helped a lot of people, and doing that made him some enemies."

"Anyone in particular?"

"Well, at the time I would have said Rocco Lowell was at the top of the list."

"The mobster?"

"That's the one. Maybe he was the whole list. I know he was the one funneling drugs into Summer Harbor, and Pastor Beck was working mighty hard to put the man out of business. One junkie at a time."

"So you're saying Rocco Lowell might have vandalized my dad's motorcycle three years ago?"

"Not Rocco himself. He never got his hands all that dirty. But he had lackeys to take care of things. Honestly, I was surprised when he didn't send someone after me when I decided to get out. Then again, he got arrested right after, so he probably had other things on his mind."

"You wouldn't happen to know who did his dirty work, do you?"

"Sorry." Alec shook his head. "That was always well above my pay grade. However, rumor had it that Rocco had a kid coming up in the organization. Nasty guy. Maybe he wanted to prove himself to Daddy?"

"Any idea who that might be?"

Alec shrugged. "Can't remember his name. Or maybe I never knew it. Too far down the food chain."

Harley nodded and stuck his hand out. "I'm glad you got out."

Alec met Harley's eyes straight on. "If you're right and someone did have something to do with your father's crash, I swear I'd help you if I could." Just as Harley was stepping through the office door Alec continued. "Lyle on the other hand… If someone helped him out of this world, I think maybe it'd be best to just let it go. They did the world a favor."

The sunlight shifting between the branches of the willow and through the living room window fell across Erin's face, waking her. Stretching, she slid her feet to the floor and stood. She'd only been asleep for a few hours, but it was just what she'd needed. Her lips curved up. It'd been years since she'd fallen asleep on Coop's couch. It felt… right. A look at the clock confirmed that Harley had been gone a lot longer than she thought he'd be. Not to worry! She grinned as she slipped on her shoes. She'd go meet him at the police station. Maybe they could grab dinner at The Whale, or take a stroll on the beach.

The old truck sputtered and gurgled as it tried to turn over, finally catching after several tries. The police station looked quiet. She pulled to a stop and cut the engine, hoping it would start again. Inside wasn't any more lively than outside and Erin was surprised she couldn't hear Harley's deep voice in the stillness.

"Can I help you?" asked a slight, older woman whose nameplate read 'Thelma'.

"I was looking for Harley Beck? I thought he'd be here."

"Oh, that boy left ages ago. Went to his father's place with Deputy Smith to look at something. Maybe you can catch him there?"

An uneasy feeling began to gnaw at the pit of Erin's stomach. She thanked Thelma and stepped back outside just as Wade pulled up to the curb.

"Afternoon, Erin," he said as he slid from the driver's seat.

She dredged up a smile. "Hi, Wade. I'm looking for Harley. Thelma said you two went to Coop's place?"

Wade glanced at his watch. "Yeah, but that was... well over an hour ago. I've been following up on Harley's hunch about Mark Puckett."

"And?" she asked when he didn't elaborate.

"I know you two seem to think the man's good for cutting the cables on Lyle's bike, and Harley's—"

"And Coop's."

"And Coop's. But I'm not buying it. I just had a chat with Mark and I don't get any kind of a vibe from him that he even knew about the cables being sabotaged. He's either an outstanding actor, or he didn't have anything to do with it."

Erin had started to worry her bottom lip with her teeth. Had they been wrong? Had they missed something? She replayed conversations with Edwin, Skylar, and Alec in her mind, but couldn't put her finger on anything.

"I do have some more information concerning that notebook y'all found though." The policeman pulled his notepad from his pocket and flipped through a few pages. "I compared it to the one we found at Lyle's this morning and the columns line up pretty close. Not the same, but enough that I think Mr. Beck was keeping tabs on Lyle. And Lyle... Well, best I can tell he was running drugs for Rocco Lowell back before Mr. Beck passed away. Haven't any idea who he's been running them for since then, but if the ledger's accurate, he's kept up a pretty good business these past three years."

"You don't think—" Her voice squeaked and she cleared her throat. "You don't think Coop had anything to do with drugs, do you?"

"Nah." Wade smiled at her. "There were some phone numbers in the front of the book. I called them. Turns out when Mr. Beck passed away he was working with an FBI agent gathering evidence against Lowell."

"And that didn't look suspicious to anyone?" Erin could feel anger sizzling in her veins.

Wade held up his hands. "I've known for all of fifteen minutes. Cut me some slack."

"Sorry."

"According to the guy at the FBI they didn't know the name of their 'anonymous informant'. Now, if you'll excuse me, I need to go talk to the Chief."

Erin balled her hands into fists and planted them on her hips, but stepped aside so he could pass. She mulled this new information over while she coaxed the truck to start again. In the light of day, thinking Mark Puckett capable of murdering Cooper Beck and Lyle Jay, and attempting to murder Harley and herself, seemed far-fetched. If Coop had been keeping an eye on Lyle and was gathering evidence against him and his mobster boss, someone connected to drug trafficking in Summer Harbor would be a much more likely suspect for their murders than a deacon of the church.

Tapping her fingers on the steering wheel, Erin tried to

decide what to do next. She drove back down the street where Coop's house sat, hoping to see Harley's bike in the driveway, but the house and garage were still dark and there was no sign of the motorcycle. Next, she headed to the kayak shop, but found the apartment locked up.

"Hey, Gemma," she said, sticking her head in the shop. "Have you seen Harley?"

"He hasn't been here in days on account of his shoulder."

"OK, thanks," Erin mumbled as she headed back to her truck. She sat in the cab for a few minutes. Where would Harley have gone? She wiped her hands on her jeans where they had started to slick with nervous sweat. Think! Had he gotten the same information she had from Wade? Would he have tried to chase down a lead without waking her from her nap? And if so... who? Their only other suspects were Edwin Hurst, Vera Whittley, Skylar Novak, and... Alec Cohen, who had admitted to selling drugs for Rocco Lowell.

Slamming her hand against the wheel, Erin threw the truck into gear and rushed onto the street. It didn't take her long to pull up in front of the garage where Alec now worked. She scanned the lot for Harley's Norton. Was that it? One the right color and shape stood near one of the open garage bays, but Erin wasn't sure. She jumped from the truck and marched to the open door, stopping to squint at the bike.

"She's a beaut, ain't she?" asked a wizened old mechanic wiping his hands on a rag. "I'm afraid she ain't for sale if that's what you're thinking. It came in last week for some bodywork."

Not Harley's bike after all. She straightened away from the motorcycle. "I'm looking for Alec Cohen."

"Alec's makin' a coffee run. Ought to be back any minute. You want to wait or I should tell him you stopped by?"

"Has anyone else stopped in looking for him?"

"A gentleman on a fine-looking bike was here earlier." The man narrowed his eyes at her. "Say, is Alec in some kind of trouble?"

Before she could answer, not that she knew what to say anyway, a big pickup with the name of the shop emblazoned on the door rolled into the yard. Sure enough, Alec hopped out carrying a cardboard tray of huge coffees.

"Alec!"

He stopped short. "Erin?"

"Have you seen Harley this morning?" she asked, taking a tentative step toward him.

"Yeah. He was here about half an hour ago." He looked wary, like he didn't know quite what to make of her being there.

"Any idea where he was headed?"

"No, but I did remember something after he left. When you see him, could you tell him the kid's name was Arnaldo Lowell?"

"Ummm...what?"

"We were talking about Rocco Lowell and I told him the guy had a kid tryin' to move up in Daddy's organization. But I couldn't remember his name."

Warning bells started going off in her brain. "Thanks," she called as she ran for her truck.

"Erin, wait up." Alec set the coffees on the hood of his truck and jogged after her. "Listen, I was messed up back then. Not an excuse. There is no excuse. I'm awful, awful sorry about... everything. I wish I could go back, have a do-over."

Erin let out a shaky breath. "I don't understand."

"Like I was tellin' your boyfriend this morning, Pastor Beck didn't give up on me after he came and took you. Got me the help I needed. I just wanted to say how sorry I was and, while I don't deserve it, I'm hoping someday you might forgive me."

Something hot welled up in Erin's chest and pressed on the back of her eyes. The better part of a decade's worth of fear and remorse and unforgiveness drained away with the apology, and Erin could see that the quiet timid man who stood before her now wasn't the same one she'd known. Stepping around the door she'd been using as a shield, she reached out to squeeze his arm. "Of course I forgive you. I'm glad Coop never gave up on you. God never gave up on you either."

"I know that, now." The smile he gave her was shy and boyish. "Thanks."

Emotions choked her and all she could do was nod, before jumping into the truck. She'd deal with her big feelings later. Right now she had to focus. She refused to panic. Harley was a grown man who could take care of himself. Except... visions of him hurtling down the road and clutching the mirror on her truck flashed through her mind.

Lord. Where is he? What am I missing?

Erin drove back through town, slowing near every motorcycle, hoping to find Harley's. Not at Coop's. Not at the kayak shop. Not parked in the street near the police station or the coffee shop. There weren't that many places left to look.

"Finally!" she said to no one in particular when she saw it. She smiled, triumphant that she'd found him and wondering what the man was up to. She fully intended to give him a piece of her mind just as soon as she saw him! No fair playing Starsky, but leaving Hutch asleep on the couch. Cutting the engine, she cringed as the truck coughed and died with a finality that would make the most skilled mechanic wince.

The inside of the building was dark and cool, and the door bumping closed sounded loud in the stillness.

"Hello? Harley?" she called, but her voice just echoed back to her. She glanced out the door again to be sure that she wasn't wrong about the Norton. No, there were the scratches from their tumble the other night. It was Harley's. She slipped farther inside, even though she felt like she was trespassing. "Harley?" she called again

The stillness was starting to give her the creeps.

Time to go.

Now.

As she hurried toward the door something shimmered on the floor, caught by a small beam of sunlight. Erin stopped and reached down to pick it up. Harley's keychain. The one she'd made for him using the shiny mussel shell from Lookout Point and the piece of sea glass from Blueberry Island. There's no way he would have left it behind, unless...

Erin burst back through the door and ran to the truck. Even before she tried turning it over though, she knew it was a lost cause. The engine barely ground out one sickly grumble before fading to nothing more than a mechanical whir and a ticking sound. She rested her head on the wheel.

What now, God?

Think!

Slowly she raised her head and stared at the motorcycle. No. No way. There was no way in this world she was getting back on a bike. Ever.

The mussel shell dug into her hand.

That wasn't true. She would for Harley.

And she had a feeling they'd been wrong all along.

Dead wrong.

CHAPTER NINETEEN

"**Y**ou don't need to do this," Harley said, trying to ignore the barrel of the gun biting into the flesh covering ribs.

"Shut up! You don't have any idea what I *need*."

Harley pressed his lips together over teeth he was grinding so hard they ached. The key chain was the only clue he could think of leaving to let Erin know where they were headed. Now he wished he hadn't dropped it at all. He knew her well enough to know that if she figured it out she'd come to his rescue. And if she came to his rescue she was going to get herself killed. His stomach soured. No, he shouldn't have left it.

There had to be a solution.

A way to get away from the gun that didn't involve meeting his maker today. It dawned on him that the thought didn't scare him like it had the other day and he smiled. At least he was ready if that was how the morning ended.

"Why'd you do it?" he asked, slowing his steps over the uneven path. If he could keep the man talking maybe he could come up with a way to get control of the gun. Or, at the very least, find a way to escape. A long shot. But maybe...

The crashing waves below the cliffs at Lookout Point were as rough as he'd ever seen them. Evidence of a storm brewing off-shore. They thundered against the sheer rock face, boiling and churning as they rushed steadily in and out. The wind that accompanied the storm whipped at his t-shirt and raised gooseflesh on his arms, but he knew it was nothing compared to the cold of the water far below them. It wouldn't matter though. The cold wouldn't have time to take him because his body would be smashed to pieces on the rocks long before hypothermia set in. That was all assuming he was pushed over the edge and not shot.

Wow.

So many different ways to die today.

He shuddered at the thought and tried not to panic.

"Why? Because he'd done things he shouldn't have done. The man was a wretched excuse for a human being," the man snarled.

"So... you cut the brake cable on his motorcycle and then covered it up?"

"It wasn't that hard. It'd been done before."

"You'd done it before?" The sour taste of fear coated his mouth as realization dawned. "To Dad's bike?"

The man stopped but didn't respond right away. "Not me."

Like a punch to the gut, the breath he'd been holding whooshed out only to be sucked back in when he heard Erin coming just before she burst out of the woods.

"Stop!" she screamed, her voice carrying over the roaring wind and crashing surf.

Every muscle in Harley's body tensed in preparation for the bullet he assumed was going to rip into him at any moment. The gun pressed hard against a rib and he wanted to call out. Perhaps in pain. Perhaps just wanting Erin to run.

In surprise, Dox Finch swung Harley around by his bad arm. The movement produced a very unmanly whimper. Blinking away the flash of pain, Harley met Erin's eyes and pleaded with her to run.

"Well now, sugar, isn't this convenient," the older man said over Harley's shoulder as he raised the gun, making sure Erin could see it. "Here I thought I was going to have to get rid of you two separately."

Erin raised her hands and held Harley's gaze. He hoped she could read his mind.

Run.

Don't hesitate. Don't slow down. Just... run.

But she must not have understood. Or she ignored what she saw.

Dox waved the gun in Erin's direction and motioned her toward the side of the cliff. "Get over there or I'll put a bullet in your boyfriend here."

"Why, Dox?" she asked. With her hands still raised, Erin began picking her way toward the side of the cliff.

"Why, why, why! All you two want to do is ask why! You realize that you've brought all this on yourselves with your snooping and your questions, right?" He turned inch by inch to keep Harley between himself and Erin. The gun ground into Harley's ribs. "I never planned to kill anyone else. Shame I have to get rid of you busybodies."

Harley watched Erin's face blanch as she stumbled on a crack in the granite. Instinct had him reaching for her.

Dox yanked back on the sore shoulder. "No, no, no, lover boy. Stay put."

The gun barrel scraped across flesh, leaving the sting of abraded skin in its wake. Man, it hurt! But he didn't react. Instead, he watched Erin stop at the edge of the cliff just a few feet away. Close enough for him to touch if he could just reach out.

"You killed Lyle," Erin said, more statement than question.

The gun eased up a little bit and Harley drew in a shallow breath. "When I saw the brake cable on the handlebars of Coop's bike I knew Lyle'd switched it out after the crash. I knew it was one of ours and I knew Coop would never have used it. Too much of a purist. I confronted Lyle and he... He just laughed at me. Cooper Beck was my friend." The older man's voice hitched.

"What—?" Erin gasped.

"Lyle killed Dad?"

"But... why?"

"Lyle said Coop had been gathering evidence against Rocco Lowell for the FBI. The man found out and had Lyle take him out."

Harley couldn't help the intake of breath this time. Tears burned the back of his eyes and he searched Erin's face hoping for... What, he didn't know. Anger? Pain? Misery loves company, right? They could be miserable together... for a few more minutes. Her eyes were wet and tears ran down her cheeks, but she didn't move her hands from where they were raised.

"Why would Lyle tell you that?" Harley asked, trying to keep the man talking. "You could have just gone to the police."

There was a long pause before Dox answered. "Lyle... knew things."

"About you?"

Dox crowded them both closer to the cliff but stopped just shy of the edge. "Guess it doesn't much matter if y'all know since you won't be telling anyone." The gun pressed painfully into Harley's rib again. "Lyle had evidence that I'd hit Jason Whittley."

Erin gasped and both hands that she'd been holding up clamped over her mouth, her eyes huge in her pale face.

"*You* killed Jason?" Harley asked.

"I didn't even know I'd hit him. It was foggy and I might have had one too many down at the pub. When I woke up the next morning and found out he'd been killed... I didn't know it was me until I got to the shop and Lyle had my truck in there fixing the front-end. Said he'd seen the damage and knew what I'd done. I panicked, but Lyle said he'd take care of it. I just had to keep my mouth shut. Three years of pretending you hadn't taken a man's life... changes you.

"After I confronted Lyle that night I was so angry. I left the garage and his Knucklehead was just sitting there. It felt like a gift. I cut the front brake and loosened the back one while he was busy stripping every penny we had from the shop safe. I thought no one would ever be the wiser, same as with Coop's. I didn't know what to do when you two stopped by with your suspicions. I'd been so careful. Even followed him out of town and took back the money he'd stolen after he crashed."

"The razor blade in the tire? That was you?" Erin asked, anger lending strength to her voice and carrying it over the gusting wind.

"It isn't like I want to kill you two, but at this point, it's you or me. I was banking on you guys going a whole lot faster when that tire blew."

Harley saw Erin tremble and her hands shook a little as she glanced over the edge of the cliff, but she gathered herself together and looked Dox in the eye. "And Harley's bike?" she asked.

"When the flat tire didn't take you two out like I thought it would, I had to do something. I'd ordered the new parts for you long before Lyle was even gone. The night I brought them over I just waited until you weren't around and slipped back into the garage. I was hoping you'd be together again. Imagine my surprise when you survived. How did you survive, anyway?"

"Erin's incredible, that's how," Harley said, winking at Erin. A small smile touched her lips despite their predicament.

"Enough talking," Dox grunted, shoving the gun into Harley's back and nudging him toward Erin.

Knowing this was the end, Harley stepped forward and took her face in his hands. Not even hesitating, he leaned in and pressed his lips to hers. The kiss was far too brief and even he had tears in his eyes when he pulled back. "I love you," he whispered.

Her eyes met his, full of wonder and hope. "I love you, too."

"Touching. Really. But it's time to say goodbye, sugar." Dox reached around Harley with the hand not holding the gun and gave Erin a tremendous push.

Her arms windmilled and the scream that left her lips ripped at Harley's heart. Without thinking, he reached for her, but just as his fingertips brushed hers he felt the gun at his back again. Only this time there was enough force behind it to send him hurtling over the cliff as well.

There was a moment after her feet had left the edge of the cliff, where Erin was airborne. Light as a feather caught in the wind. Maybe it was her imagination, but for half a heartbeat she soared above the crashing waves as if suspended on the gust billowing up the cliff. The instant her body began to fall, however, terror ignited every cell of her being and she scrabbled with her hands, nails, feet, anything to try and find something. Latch onto something. Cling to something.

Oh, God! Help!

The sharp needles of a pitch pine scraped along her legs, slowing her fall. Frantic, she clawed at the weather-beaten shrub growing from a crack in the granite. At the last possible instant, her fingertips curled around a gnarled branch and she clung, suspended over the crashing surf.

Erin had only a fraction of a second to drag in a shuddering breath before her hands were knocked loose by Harley's body landing squarely on top of the tree. She tried to tighten her grip, but the sharp needles pricked her hands and she felt them slipping free. In a last attempt to gain a finger hold on something, Erin let go with her right hand and reached out, searching for something solid. She met with the soft warmth of Harley's outstretched hand and dug in with everything she had. Harley wouldn't let her fall.

Just as quickly as she'd started to fall she came to an abrupt stop. Harley howled in pain and she almost let go.

Almost.

Dangling from Harley's arm, she turned to the side and tried to find a footing, clawing with her feet at the slick rock. Twisting and turning, she tried to find anything to help her gain her footing.

"Erin, stop." Harley ground the words out through gritted teeth, but they didn't register until he said them a second time, louder and laced with anguish.

She stilled, suspended above the surf, and met his eyes. His lips were pulled back in a grimace and pain had his eyes nearly closed as he breathed hard through his nose. She looked down along his shoulder and had to bite her lip to keep from crying out when she saw the grotesque angle his shoulder and arm made. He'd grabbed her with his left hand and the recently dislocated shoulder was quite obviously dislocated again. His other hand was caught in the branches of the pitch pine that had stopped their fall. He was clinging to it for all he was worth, but the agony of holding her was making him pant.

"I think I can—"

"Don't. Move," he said through gritted teeth.

She stilled her body as best she could, hanging like a pendulum, and met his eyes. He held her gaze for a long moment before his eyes slid closed on a groan. How did he think this was going to end? He couldn't pull her up. She couldn't find anything to grab onto. If she even tried to turn and look at the cliff she would pull herself free of his grip. She couldn't watch. Couldn't bear seeing him fight the pain of holding her.

Couldn't watch him let go.

Closing her eyes she prayed. *God, we need Your help! Please!*

Something bumped her shoulder and her eyes flew open. Being very careful not to move anything but her head, Erin turned and almost wept when she saw a rope dangling from the top of the cliff.

"Harley!"

His eyes were still closed and she knew he hadn't seen the rope. With great effort, he blinked and she watched them widen in surprise when he saw the rope.

"I'm going to grab it with my free hand," she said. He grimaced but nodded. As hard as she tried not to move her body, she still heard him whimper a blue word through his teeth.

"One of you got a hold of that thing?" someone called from the top of the cliff. Erin tried to see who was on the other end of the rope, but the blessed shrub was blocking her view.

"Almost!" she yelled back. Then she lowered her voice and

spoke to Harley. "I've got it. I'm going to let go."

He set his mouth in a grim line and nodded. She closed her eyes, unable to watch the pain she was about to cause, and let go. The rope tightened painfully around her arm where she'd twisted it, but it held and she swung away from the rock face before drifting back into it, slamming her shoulder. The rope started moving up and she clung to it until she reached the lip of the granite. Scrambling over the edge, she fell in front of Wade Smith's shiny black police shoes.

"There ya are," he said in the slow southern drawl that made everything that came out of his mouth sound calm.

"Harley," she said between gasps of air. "Dislocated... his arm... again."

Wade yanked the rope up and tied a large loop at one end before shimmying to the edge of the cliff and calling down to Harley. "Hey, man, I'm going to lower a loop. I need you to get it around your chest so I can haul you up." The policeman turned back to Erin. "I'm going to need your help getting him up."

It took long, agonizing minutes to secure the rope and even longer for the two of them to work Harley's large frame up and over the cliff. Erin hadn't realized she was holding her breath until the man she loved crawled one-armed over the last bit of rock and a sob erupted from her chest. She scrambled to where he lay gulping in air and dropped onto his chest, hysterical sobs threatening to consume her.

"Hey, hey. Shhhh," he soothed, brushing her hair aside with one hand.

"I've got an ambulance on the way," Wade said from where he stood nearby, coiling the rope up on his shoulder and elbow.

Erin sat up and looked at the cop. Just beyond where he stood sat Dox Finch, handcuffed to a small pine tree. "How..."

"Well, after you and I spoke I decided I wanted to talk to Harley again, too. I didn't have any more luck finding him than you did, but when I saw you take off on his motorcycle like a bat out of... well, you know where, I followed you. Managed to get within earshot just in time to hear this man confess to everything. Sorry it took me a minute to get the rope down to ya. Had to get Dox here in cuffs and get back to the cruiser." He dropped the coiled rope on the ground beside them and walked over to where Dox was sitting, shoulders slumped. "Maddox Finch, you are under arrest..."

Harley gripped Erin's arm and held her gaze. "You drove my bike?"

"I'm sorry. Please don't be mad! The truck wouldn't start and I—"

He stopped her mid-sentence by pulling her down for a kiss. He slid his hand up her arm to the back of her neck, tangling his fingers in her hair. When he finally loosened his grip and she pulled away a fraction of an inch, he was grinning.

"I love that you rode my bike. That you overcame your fear of motorcycles for me."

"I would do anything for you." Erin curled into the crook of Harley's good arm and closed her eyes. "But maybe not riding the motorcycle *ever again*."

Harley sat on the tailgate of Erin's truck, his arm back in its sling and a scowl on his face. "I know the doc said no heavy lifting, but I think I could have handled a couple of damp boxes."

The storm brewing off the coast had made landfall before the paramedics even arrived to look at Harley and Erin. Gusting winds and torrential rain had driven them off the top of the cliff, and by the time they'd all gotten back to Summer Harbor, everyone was soaked to the skin.

It wasn't until late in the afternoon, as they were leaving the ER, again, that Erin had remembered her truck. Sitting in the dooryard at Finch and Jay's, all her worldly possessions in the bed. Soaked

Now, Erin leaned against Harley's good shoulder. "Thanks for the help, Sawyer."

"No worries, kid," the older man said as he came back for another box. "I think you need a new starter. Took me a minute, but I got the old girl going."

As Sawyer headed up the stairs with one of the soggy cardboard boxes in his arms, Erin came around to stand between Harley's knees. Careful not to touch his injured shoulder, she took his face in her hands and held his gaze for a long time. "Are you OK?"

"Somehow I think recovering from a second dislocated shoulder is going to take longer than the first."

"That's not what I meant."

"I know." He closed his eyes and brought his forehead down to rest on hers, a troubled sigh escaping his lips. "I feel like if I'd found the brake cable sooner..."

"Finding it sooner wouldn't have brought Coop back."

"I might not have been able to bring Dad back, but I could have been looking for his killer this whole time." Harley's reply was ragged. Emotions roughening his voice. "All the if only's I've barely been able to keep at bay, are now all I can think about. If only I'd been here. If only I'd never left. If only I'd come home sooner. If only I'd told someone where I was. If only I'd kept in touch with... anyone."

Anger, frustration, pain, and regret from the last ten years rolled off him and Erin closed her eyes, holding him, offering silent support.

Harley sucked in a deep breath and she felt his shoulders relax. Cupping her cheek with one hand he looked her in the eye. "How about you? Are you OK?"

"Yeah. I'm still pretty numb. It's going to take a while for my brain to wrap around it all."

"I'm sorry your plan to go to your mom's didn't work out. You could still go, you know. The drama here's over. You could head out first thing in the morning."

"No." Erin looked away but leaned into his palm. "I called her while Sawyer was getting the truck. She told me not to bother. I'd already missed the luncheon she'd wanted me to attend, so... She said there was no point."

"Oh, honey." He pressed his lips to her temple.

Closing her eyes, she drank in his comfort. It was going to take a while to move away from blaming herself for this toxic thing with her mother, but she knew it would all work out someday. "I turned it over to God a long time ago. He'll work it out in His time."

"That He will," Harley whispered before pressing a kiss to her lips.

The creak of the stairs announced Sawyer's return and Erin straightened away from Harley enough to smile at her friend. "Thanks again. Those boxes were heavy enough dry. Wet? I knew there was no way I could haul them back up to the apartment."

"If it keeps you around, I'm happy to help," he replied with a wink, reaching for the last box. He was sliding it toward the tailgate when one side gave out, spilling its contents across the bed of the truck. "Oh, gosh, Erin I'm sorry." He hopped into the bed and started trying to return the papers to the disintegrating cardboard.

"Sawyer, wait. That box is all junk. Just paperwork from high school and odds and ends from my room. I think I'll just chuck it."

"You're sure? I can cram it back in here," he said, lifting the now-empty box in the air.

"No, I'll take care of it." He didn't answer but was looking inside the box. "Sawyer, I said I'd take care of it."

"This box feels... too heavy."

"What?" Harley asked, turning to see where Sawyer was squatting in the bed of the truck.

"This box..." The older man shook it upside-down. Nothing fell out, but the sound of something moving around inside it was unmistakable. He set the box next to Harley on the tailgate and hopped to the ground. They all peered into it, but there wasn't anything left at the bottom.

Sawyer flipped the box over and pulled out his pocket knife, using it to slit the packing tape on the bottom of the box.

"Oh, my..." Erin breathed.

Harley's eyes had gone wide as he stared at the contents hidden in a false bottom.

"Why do you have pictures of Rocco Lowell and Skylar Novak?" Sawyer asked, reaching for a stack of photographs.

"Not me," Erin whispered.

Harley reached for a stack of photographs, too. "How did you end up with them?"

Erin stared blankly at the box. She'd been toting it around since she left Summer Harbor three years ago. "Coop must have hidden them in my things when I left for school. He must have known—" Her voice halted with emotion. "He must have known something was going to happen and hid these as best he could."

Under the photos were notebooks like the one she'd found in the closet days before. Sawyer pulled one out and started flipping through it. "Um, guys? I think you might want to call the FBI." He flipped the book around for them to see. Detailed notes in Coop's distinctive scrawl. Who was dealing and who was supplying, when and where sales took place, dates and times when Rocco Lowell had been in town, conversations Coop had overheard. Page after page of information.

A little dazed, Erin reached into the box and pulled out a sheaf of papers. More evidence the man had collected?

"I get that he was gathering information for the FBI on Rocco, but what's up with Skylar Novak?" asked Sawyer. "How does he play into all of this?"

Flipping back through the first stack of pictures he'd pulled from the box, Harley handed one to the other man. "They look pretty chummy in this one. Maybe Coop thought Novak was on Rocco's payroll?"

"Arnaldo," Erin whispered.

"What?" both men asked in unison.

"This morning, when I was looking for you, I went to see Alec—"

"You faced a lot this morning," Harley said, pride and awe in his voice.

Erin felt her cheeks warm. "Anyway, Alec said to tell you 'the kid's name was Arnaldo'."

"What kid?" Sawyer asked with a look of confusion on his face.

"Alec Cohen told me that Rocco had a kid, but he couldn't remember the guy's name."

"Hold on." She flipped back to the beginning of the stack of papers she'd been looking through and pulled out a photocopy of a birth certificate. "Arnaldo Novak Lowell. His mother's name is Skylar Novak."

Sawyer carefully set the photographs he was holding back in the box. "I'm going to steal a line from Wade. 'I think that this is the point in the evening when I say 'enough' and we all clear out'. I'm going to find a dry box to put these in and then one of us is taking them to Wade."

CHAPTER TWENTY

Harley had thought that this part of the story would have turned out a little different. A long time ago he'd given up hoping for a happily ever after, but at this point, he'd half expected there to be some kind of hail Mary pass at the end of the fourth quarter that would let him keep his dad's house and rebuild his dad's bike and get the girl. Even though it wasn't turning out how he'd thought it would, he still had hope that God would work it all out.

Hope was new.

"I've got another stack of boxes. You want me to work on the living room or your father's bedroom?" Noah asked.

Harley reached for half the boxes. "I'll work on Dad's room, you go help your girl."

Noah nodded and headed toward the sound of Lily humming. She was boxing up the hymnals from the bookcase next to his mom's piano. Beyond the living room, he could hear Gemma and Cori in the kitchen laughing as they washed and boxed his parents' wedding china. He was happy to give Gemma a day's work now that the shop was pretty much closed, and of course, Cori already knew the kid and had been talking her ear off since they'd arrived an hour ago.

Friends.

Having friends was something he hadn't even noticed was happening in the years he'd been back home. And it was home. Even if he didn't get to keep the house, Summer Harbor was home.

The word didn't scare him anymore. Instead, there was a rush of warmth and rightness when he thought of it.

Taking his stack of cardboard, Harley walked to the end of the hall and stood in the open doorway to his father's bedroom. He wasn't surprised when Erin slipped in next to him and put her arm around his waist.

So he'd gotten the girl.

It was the rest of it he was still waiting for God to work out.

"It's all going to work out," she murmured.

He pressed a kiss to the top of her head. "I know."

"Do you want help? Or is this a room you need to tackle on your own?"

Smiling down at her cute upturned face, Harley stole another kiss before nudging her into the room. "I will always want you by my side."

Wow, that sounded so corny.

He didn't care. It got a grin out of her and when she was happy, he was happy.

Stepping fully into the room, she came up short. "Whoa."

"Yeah. I asked Pastor James if he wanted any of Dad's study books and commentaries. He cleaned out most of the shelves."

"Great! I think Coop would have liked that. A lot."

"Me too."

"Hey, man," Sawyer said as he sauntered in behind them. "I brought my pickup and a trailer. What do you want me to start hauling out?"

Harley's chest swelled at the help his friends were lending. It had been a week since he'd dislocated his shoulder the *second* time and the doc said he still had weeks before he'd be able to use his arm again. Harley bumped a stack of boxes with the toe of his boot. "It'd be great if you could take these."

Sawyer nodded. "Are these bookcases going, too?"

"No, those are built-in," Harley replied.

"Well, this isn't," Sawyer said, pushing one of the supports on the bottom of the bookcase loose. Every few feet there was a plank of wood about a foot across and eight inches high. Extra support under the heavy shelves of books. They looked like something his dad had jury-rigged to keep the bottom shelves from sagging, but one of them looked different than the rest and that's the one Sawyer was now pulling free.

A gasp from Erin had Harley's head snapping around. "That's Coop's box" she whispered

Harley squatted down next to the bookcase and wriggled the box the rest of the way out. It was very much like the ones Erin still made in Jason's workshop. Dovetailed corners, silken finish.

There was a soft rap on the door and Noah stuck his head in. "Chief Briggs is here to see you."

Tucking the box under his arm, Harley followed his friend down the hall. When he got to the kitchen he found the policeman standing, hat in hand inside the kitchen door.

"Afternoon, Harley. I was wondering if I might have a word."

Harley nodded toward a chair at the table. He waited for the policeman to sit down before joining him, sliding the wooden box to the side. "What can I do for you, Chief?"

The older man blew out a long breath and set his hat on the table. "Well, first off I wanted to let you know where we're at on some things. Maddox Finch has been charged with murder and attempted murder. He pled guilty, so the trial won't be all long and drawn out. I imagine he'll get quite a few years, all things considered."

"And all the evidence Dad collected?"

"That's a heck of a thing. Turns out that the FBI was struggling to put their case together against Lowell. They've got one guy in witness protection who's set to testify, but without other evidence, they weren't all that hopeful. However, with what you all found they feel they've got a pretty good chance of finally making some charges stick to the man."

"And his son?" Erin asked from where she was making coffee.

"Skylar Novak, A. K. A. Arnie Novak, A. K. A. Arnaldo Lowell. Caught that little weasel trying to hightail it out of town with every last penny the church had packed into the trunk of his car along with a couple million dollars worth of drugs. Guy was still claiming we couldn't touch him while we're taking him into custody. Idiot. Once the FBI stepped in though, he turned state's evidence pretty darn quick to get out of the charges against him. Singin' like a bird as they say."

"So, he was Lowell's son?" Harley asked.

"Oh, not *just* his son. Turns out he took over a good portion of Daddy's business after Rocco was arrested. Kept a low profile there at that church, but the whole time was funneling drugs into Summer Harbor. Used the confessional at the church for drug/money drops. No one knew it was him, even Lyle didn't know Novak was the one taking over Rocco's business. Rocco'd been using the confessional at the church long before Arnie showed up. The man kept real quiet. Even paid Lyle the blackmail money so he wouldn't get suspicious."

The policeman turned to Erin. "He also confessed to killing Jason Whittley."

Erin gasped "What? Why?" Harley pulled her down onto his lap, rubbing a hand up her back.

"He says it wasn't Whittley Rocco ordered killed." He turned back to Harley. "It was Coop."

The shuddering breath Erin pulled in wrecked Harley. If only he could wipe all this away. He pressed a kiss to her temple. "Because of what Dad was doing? Collecting the evidence?"

"Exactly. Seems that Coop borrowed Jason's truck to drive some kid to the mainland. Jason was walking home from Coop's place after dropping the truck off when he was hit. Similar build, similar dress, dark, leaving Coop's house. Novak mistook Jason for Coop and ran him down."

"It wasn't Dox?" Erin asked.

"No, it wasn't. Lyle made Dox think he was guilty when in reality it was Arnie Lowell. You ask me, they shouldn't have cut him any deal at all. Just use the evidence Coop collected and let Arnaldo rot in jail." The cop looked down at his hat where it sat on the table and fiddled nervously with the brim. "That's not all I came to say though. I grew up in this town when my dad was the chief of police. Back then it was just a quiet little tourist stop populated by lobstermen and inn owners." He wiped a hand across his eyes. "All I've ever wanted was to keep it like that. Keeping the peace became a religion to me. Your father saw it. I think a lot of people are seeing it. Maybe I'm the only one who couldn't."

Erin moved to the cupboard and pulled out three mismatched mugs that hadn't been packed yet. She filled them with coffee and took a seat next to Harley.

Chief Briggs nodded his thanks and reached for the sugar bowl. "It isn't that I purposely overlooked things, I just..." He trailed off and looked around the kitchen as if searching for the right words. "My father had this case thirty-five years ago. They found this guy dead in the park. I'd just started here as a deputy. My dad was sure it was murder. He combed the town looking for witnesses, and interviewed locals and tourists alike. It became an obsession. At one point he even arrested a kid who'd hitch-hiked into town." He let the story hover as he sipped his coffee. "Anyway, to make a long story short, it turned out the guy was high and fell off the bandstand. Hit his head on a rock. But by the time the medical examiner had figured that out my dad had become so obsessed that he wouldn't accept the truth. It ruined his reputation. I guess ever since then I look harder for a simple solution than I do for the truth.

"To be honest with you, Harley, I don't think I'm very good at this job. Don't get me wrong, I love being a cop, but it's a lot different than it was forty years ago. I've watched friends from the academy flounder as crime runs rampant and many of them never make it to retirement. The last decade that's all I've wanted, just to make it to retirement."

Erin reached out and patted the old man's hand. He smiled a little before continuing. "All that's to say that this case, and that murder last spring, opened my eyes to the fact that it's time to move on. I've submitted my letter to the town and recommended Wade as my replacement. The missus and I are flying down to Florida next week to look at places. I didn't want to leave without... well... saying I was sorry for how things were dealt with three years ago. I never imagined... Still can't wrap my head around someone murdering Pastor Beck."

The man stood and extended his hand to Harley who still sat somewhat slacked-jawed. "You take care now son. Stay out of trouble, you hear?" Then he nodded to Erin before pressing his hat back into place and letting himself out.

A low whistle from the living room told him the others hadn't missed the conversation.

As everyone gathered in the kitchen again and Erin pulled out more mugs. While they sipped their coffee and chatted, mostly about the police chief's visit, Harley pulled the wooden box they'd found back in front of him. Opening the top, he stared long and hard at the careful collection of envelopes, not even noticing when Erin shooed the others from the room. Every single one he'd ever sent home, neat and in order. He slid the first one out and with shaking fingers opened it. His entire universe narrowed to the slip of memo paper from a seedy motel on the outskirts of Cincinnati.

He remembered writing it.

I'm fine was scrawled across it. He wished he'd written something more.

I love you, Dad.

I miss you.

I'm so sorry.

Can I please come home?

Tears stung his eyes. Any of those would have been an improvement over the two inadequate syllables.

And been closer to the truth.

Because he hadn't been fine.

The old guilt tried to raise its ugly head, but Harley tamped it down. He was forgiven. By God. By his father. By Erin. And even by himself. That guilt was gone.

He was about to replace the scrap of paper when he noticed something else inside the envelope. Opening it all the way he gasped. Inside were five crisp one-hundred-dollar bills. His self-imposed penance. One of the many ways he'd found to punish himself after the disaster with Julianne. He'd worked construction for a couple of months, rented a room in a cheap hotel that took cash and didn't ask for ID, and sent home all but what he thought he needed to get to the next state.

Pulling out the next envelope he found the same thing. And the next, and the next. Harley sat with the box in front of him. The enormity of it had sucked most coherent thought from his mind. He sensed more than heard Erin come back into the room.

"What was Dad thinking?" he asked, snapping the lid closed in frustration. "Why didn't he use the money?"

He reached out and flipped the lid open again. The envelopes were still there. Tucked one after another like a road map of seven years of his life. After a lengthy pause, he pointed to the first one. "Ohio, about two months after I left. St. Louis, Nashville, Atlanta. West to Denver, then Minneapolis. Across the plains to Montana, south as far as Tucson. Stops along the Pacific Coast Highway. A year to get from Missoula to Florida. And a last, convoluted route through Texas, the mid-west, and along the east coast until..."

"The blacktop led you home."

Harley nodded, unable to speak around the lump in his throat. He slid one envelope out from about halfway through the box. It was more worn than the rest and he fingered it, turning it over in his hands. Postmarked from a town in Arizona two days before Christmas the year he'd turned twenty. As far as he could remember it was the only one he'd written more than a couple of words in. Most contained no note at all. He slipped the paper free of the envelope and read the words he'd penned almost seven years ago.

I'm fine and the Commando's still running great. Merry Christmas, Dad

He slipped the single sheet of paper back in alongside fifteen Benjamins. That Christmas he'd been homesick. Desperately homesick. Not that he would admit that to his father, but he had longed, with all his being, to turn the bike north.

"He used to read that one over and over," Erin whispered.

"I usually only had a few hundred bucks to send him, but I'd been working construction that summer and fall. It paid well and I felt a little more flush." He pulled the bills out. "I would have given ten times this to come home that Christmas." She turned in her seat and took his hand in her warm one. He turned his palm up to lace his fingers with hers and stared at their joined hands for a beat. He liked how her fingers filled in the spaces between his, like the dovetailed corners of her boxes. He still didn't feel like he deserved her. "Instead of coming home, I spent Christmas driving west looking for the next place to stop."

Kissing her knuckles where their hands joined before he turned back to the box, he started removing the envelopes one at a time, slipping the money free and setting it aside. His friends returned to quietly sit with him. Silent support he felt deep in his heart. Setting the last few bills on the stack, Harley ran both hands down his face and laughed in disbelief.

"I sent my dad a little less than forty-two-thousand dollars. That's enough to get current on the mortgage, settle up all the taxes, and still have a bit left for repairs."

Sawyer reached over and clamped a hand on Harley's good shoulder. "You want me to unload those boxes, don't you?"

"Yeah, I kind of do." Harley chuckled and began replacing the envelopes in the box when he noticed a few sheets of paper folded in the bottom of the box. Lifting them out, he unfolded them and thumbed through the pages.

"What is it?" Erin asked, leaning against his side.

"Looks like the paperwork from Edwin Hurst that he insisted Dad was going to sign."

"Did he? Sign it, I mean."

Harley flipped to the end. "No."

They both leaned over where he'd laid the last two pages side by side on the table. One was the contract from the realtor, unsigned and with sections highlighted. The other was a map of Summer Harbor with about ten properties outlined in red. Hurst's own house, Coop's place, a couple residential properties in the same general area, the Butterfly Cove Inn now owned by Lily Emerson, a restaurant, a vacant lot, two more houses, and Finch and Jay's. Looking at them on the map it was easy to see that they formed an arc that stretched from the tops of the cliffs overlooking the pebble beach all the way to where the national park started at the edge of Harrier Lake.

A glance up at Erin's face told him she was just as confused as he was. She narrowed her eyes at the page and leaned closer before pointing to the corner of the map. In faint pencil, as though it had been erased, Coop had scrawled 'What are you up to?'

"What...?"

"I have no idea." Harley stared at the pages for a few more seconds before refolding them and placing them back in the bottom of the box under the envelopes. "A mystery for another day I suppose."

Erin snort-laughed as she reached for the coffee mugs on the table. "I am so done with mysteries right now," she said, taking the mugs to the sink to be washed.

It took his friends a lot less time to bring everything back into the house than it had taken them to box it up. By mid-morning, he and Erin were the only ones still at his dad's place.

"I want to run this money to the bank and then... There's somewhere I'd like to take you," he said.

"As long as it doesn't involve motorcycles, murderers, blackmail, or falling off cliffs, I'm in," Erin said before standing on tiptoe to press her lips to his.

Erin wasn't sure where they were headed, but they'd left Summer Harbor hours before and were driving up US Route 1 in her truck. She hoped they could avoid getting stranded.

The scenery was beautiful. Rural fishing villages, blueberry barrens, and the little coves and inlets of the coast had long ago given way to forests and potato fields, and even a dusting of snow from the storm that had blown through the week before.

"Next right," Harley said from beside her.

She knew he'd been itching to drive, but he was being good about not stressing his shoulder until it had healed. She pulled into the parking lot of an old-fashioned general store and turned off the truck.

"Harley, my boy!" called an old man from the front door when they climbed out. "You didn't ride that beauty you usually do, but you've got yourself a beautiful chauffeur instead!" The man winked at Erin and held the door open for them. She liked him immediately.

"Clyde, I'd like you to meet Erin."

The man wiggled his bushy eyebrows. "Nice to meet you, my dear."

Erin chuckled and held out her hand. "Nice to meet you, too."

They pulled stools up to the counter and Clyde grabbed three root beers from the cooler. Harley told her about meeting the old man and about all the good advice he'd imparted. They told Clyde about the mystery they'd helped solve, about almost dying more than once, about finding the money to keep the house, and about crashing Coop's Harley-Davidson. The man looked like it caused him physical pain when they admitted the bike was beyond repair.

"I might be able to salvage something off it, but... It's going to need far more than I can afford to put into it." Harley hung his head. "I have to say, admitting that I tried and failed doesn't sit well."

"Sounds to me like you did exactly what you set out to do. The rest was out of your hands."

"You're right, he is wise," Erin said with a wink for the older man and a tender smile for Harley.

"Clyde, the real reason we came... Well, I wanted to tell you something. I took your advice."

"Now, sonny, I hand out advice like it's candy. You're going to have to be a lot more specific than that."

"All of it. I took all your advice. Got right with Erin, got right with myself. Made peace with my dad. All of it. Most importantly, I got right with God."

Clyde teared up as he came around the counter and pulled Harley in for a tight hug. Erin knew the feeling. No matter what else had happened, that one thing was the happy ending she'd hoped for.

They sat and talked for quite a while, and the sun was low on the western horizon by the time they stood to say goodbye.

"Now you hang on just a second, sonny." Clyde led the way outside and around to the back of the store. A dilapidated shed clung to the side of the building by sheer will. He hobbled over to the door and wrestled it open, peering into the dark space.

"Just checkin' for 'coons." Clyde said over his shoulder. He must have been satisfied that there were none because he reached in and pulled the chain on an ancient porcelain light fixture, casting the space in a dim yellow glow. A bulky shape toward the back of the shed caught Erin's eye and she watched as Clyde reached over and pulled the dusty tarp free.

Grinning from ear to ear, the older man stepped back out the door. There, chrome glowing in the fading light, sat a pristine Harley Davidson motorcycle.

"Is that...?" Harley breathed.

"An XL-1000, all original, mint condition."

"Oh my..." Harley ran the fingers of his good hand behind his neck as he took a step forward. "Clyde, this is—"

"Yours."

"What!? No. No way. I can't afford to buy it from you."

"Well, that's good, 'cause I ain't sellin' it. I'm giving it to you."

Harley sucked in a breath. "I can't accept it."

"Well, now you're just hurtin' my feelings," Clyde said in a sullen voice that was belied by the twinkle in his eyes. "Listen. I don't have any kids. I got no one to leave it to. I can't ride it.

I don't need to sell it. I'd enjoy seeing you ride it. I'd enjoy that a whole heck of a lot more than I enjoy keeping it back here under a tarp."

"I don't know what to say."

"You say, 'thank you, Clyde, I'll take real good care of her and I'll swing by on a regular basis for you to take a look-see'."

Harley chuckled. "Thank you, Clyde, I'll take real good care of her and I'll swing by on a regular basis for you to take a look-see."

"Now, was that so hard?" he asked with a wink for Erin.

A motor rumbled to a stop in front of the store and the old man hobbled off to take care of the customer. Harley stood staring at the bike. Erin slid her arms around his waist, closing her eyes when he pressed a kiss to the top of her head.

It was odd how things worked out sometimes.

You know that for those who love Me, for those who are called according to My purpose, all things work together for good.

All things?

All things.

THE END

DEAR READER

Thank you for reading my second book, Where the Blacktop Leads Home. I fell in love with Harley while writing my first book, but I knew he was a complicated man and his story was going to be hard to tell. Was it ever! All the twists and turns he took gave me a run for my money. I'm so glad he met Erin and finally let the blacktop lead him home.

The characters that I create as I'm writing feel very real and I can't wait to get to know them better. Who will be next? Will we find out what it's going to take to make Parker stop working 80+ hour weeks? Will Sawyer allow someone to get close, even though he feels he's past his prime? What about Lily's sister, Olivia? Will she continue to flirt her way through life, or will she find someone worth settling down with? I can't wait to explore these stories and so many more in the coming years! I hope you'll join me on each and every adventure. God bless!

ACKNOWLEDGEMENTS

I thank my God upon every remembrance of you,
PHILIPPIANS 1:3

As always, I would like to begin by thanking God for His direction and wisdom as I wrote this book. There were many times when I wondered where the story was going. In the end, I can see the message so clearly that He wanted shared. He loves you and He longs for you to come home to Him.

After writing my first book during the crazy that was 2020, I wasn't sure I could do it again. My husband, Ken, was my rock. He managed to keep me moving forward, gave me time and space to write, and encourage me keep writing when I wanted to give up. I love you, sweetheart!

To my children, Caleb, Lincoln, Bethlehem, Ellissa, Lydia, Yosef, and Fiona, thank you for letting me have the time to write, for putting up with some long days and distracted moments, and for still thinking it's pretty cool that your mommy wrote a book. And To 'my oldest', Jared, you continue to inspire this series and I look forward to incorporating your stories and knowledge of "Summer Harbor" into many more books. You guys are amazing and I love you more than words can say.

Alan Smith, a simple 'thank you' doesn't comes anywhere close to expressing my gratitude for your help with this book. I could not have written a lot of it without your patience and willingness to answer even the dumbest motorcycle questions. You're the best!

I also want to thank Jean-Baptiste Cyr for taking the time to walk me through police procedures, laws, and what would be plausible where Wade and Chief Briggs were concerned. I learned a lot and and really appreciate you pointing me in the right direction.

Thomas, thank you for proving that I had written part of chapter ten perfectly.

Aunt Dawn and Uncle Jim, thank you for endless hours at your dining room table to write and edit!

A huge thanks to my biggest fans, my parents. Having you read my first draft was a serious boost to my ego! I knew it stunk, but your excitement over the story gave me the motivation to keep going and to make it better.

Tiffany and Beret, thank you both so much for being my beta readers and giving me the feedback I needed to make the book better. You are dear friends and I thank God for!

A special thank you to my copy-editor, Rose. I am so very grateful for your ability to see my mistakes when I cannot. Your excitement and encouragement mean the world to me. You are a gift!

ABOUT THE AUTHOR

Jenny Worster

Jenny was born and raised in rural Maine where she still lives with her husband and their seven children. She was a teacher before becoming a stay-at-home mom. Writing has always been something she loved to dabble in, but it wasn't until 2020 and being stuck at home for days on end that she decided to finish a book (her  debut novel, Where the Sea Lavender Grows). In addition to writing, Jenny runs a non-profit with her husband which works in Ethiopia.